# Chain a Lamb Chop to the Bed

# Chain a Lamb Chop to the Bed

An Ellie Bernstein/Lt. Peter Miller Mystery

## Denise Dietz

**Five Star • Waterville, Maine**

First Edition
First Printing: November 2005

Published in 2005 in conjunction with Tekno Books and Ed Gorman.

Set in 11 pt. Plantin.

Printed in the United States on permanent paper.

**Library of Congress Cataloging-in-Publication Data**

Aalborg, Denise Dietz.
    Chain a lamb chop to the bed : an Ellie Bernstein/Lt. Peter Miller mystery / by Denise Dietz.—1st ed.
        p. cm.
    ISBN 1-59414-422-2 (hc : alk. paper)
    1. Women detectives—Colorado—Aspen—Fiction. 2. Police—Colorado—Aspen—Fiction.
    3. Painters—Crimes against—Fiction. 4. Overweight women—Fiction. 5. Aspen (Colo.)—Fiction. 6. Dude ranches—Fiction. I. Title.
    PS3554.I368C47 2005
        813'.54—dc22                                     2005024283

## Dedication

For Susan Goldstein, who sent me Judith Viorst's *Alexander and the Terrible, Horrible, No Good, Very Bad Day* when I was having a terrible, horrible, no good, very bad day.

# Acknowledgments

A huge thanks to Doug P. Lyle, MD, who patiently answered my questions about drugs.

An appreciative thanks to Lynn Whitacre, who has always been there for me, even when I spelled her name wrong.

An extra-special thanks to Erin Mullarkey. As Thomas Moore would say: "And blest for ever is she who relied, Upon Erin's honour and Erin's pride."

A fervent thanks to Pat Wallace, who edited *Eye of Newt*, as well as "Lamb Chop."

A humble thanks to my husband and soul mate, the multi-talented Gordon Aalborg, author and sculptor, who—somehow—manages to remain sane while I'm in the throes of intense creativity.

And last but certainly not least, thank you Jean Neidich. If Jean hadn't founded Weight Watchers, I wouldn't have lost 55 (and a half!) pounds and written the "diet club" mystery series.

"Eating is self-punishment; punish the food instead. Strangle a loaf of Italian bread. Throw Darts at a Cheesecake. Chain a lamb chop to the bed. Beat up a cookie."

—Gilda Radner

# One

Not quite camouflaged by tree trunks, the carnivorous mammal gazed at the beautiful nude woman who reclined in an antique bathtub.

The woman wasn't frightened. Maybe she hadn't noticed the shaggy black mane and tufted tail. Or the amber eyes that glittered lustfully. Maybe she had, for her lips, slightly parted, seemed to say: "Are you thirsty, sweetie? Are you hungry, sweetie? Are you by any chance a vegetarian, sweetie?"

Desert sun shed its lemon-colored light over roller-coaster dunes and a small oasis of palm trees with blue-tinged fronds. The woman's red flowing hair met silvery sand. Her left arm lay alongside the bathtub's rim, her hand curled into a subtle summons, like a child waving bye-bye backwards. The tub's water flirtatiously splashed against her breasts.

Although he hadn't actually moved, the carnivorous mammal's tawny body appeared to have sidled closer. And although he didn't actually lick his chops, he looked rapacious, voracious, hungry as a—

" 'Tiger, tiger burning bright, in the forests of the night.' "

"It's a lion, Peter." Ellie Bernstein drew her gaze away from the painting that enhanced the art gallery's off-white wall. "And the lion is prowling through the deserts of the

9

day, not the forests of the night."

"I suppose you can do better," her significant other said, his voice filled with mock indignation. "Mick and Sandra swear you have more quotes than a chocolate-chip cookie has chips."

Before she morphed into a diet club leader, Ellie had worked part-time at the library. There, she'd memorized obscure poems, epigrams, and aphorisms. Her son, Mick, and his girlfriend, Sandra, lived in Boulder, Colorado, and they were right. She did have more quotes than a chocolate-chip cookie has chips, even though she hadn't wolfed down cookies, chocolate-chip or otherwise, in a long time. Well, to be perfectly honest, she sometimes succumbed to Girl Scout cookies. Chocolate mint. Who wouldn't?

"Come on, do better," Peter challenged.

" 'I like little pussy, her coat is so warm,' " Ellie recited. " 'And if I don't hurt her, she'll do me no harm.' Jane Taylor, English poet, died around eighteen twenty-fi . . ." She swallowed the rest of her words at the sound of Peter's laughter. "Stop it! Everybody's looking at us."

"I like a little pussy," he gasped.

"Little, not 'a' little. Do stop chortling, Peter. Act your age."

"Since when does laughter have an age limit?"

"It doesn't, unless it's lecherous."

"Low blow, lady. Lecherous implies old men who suffer from gout. My laugh was raunchy."

"Suggestive."

"Risqué."

"You always have to have the last word, don't you?"

"Yup."

She stepped back a few paces. "Speaking of suggestive, that's one of the most sensuous paintings I've ever seen.

You can almost reach out and touch its heat."

"How much does it cost, Norrie?"

That brought a smile to her face. Most people called her Ellie. Only Peter called her Norrie, short for Eleanor. Because, he said, she ig-*nored* his advice.

"The price tag reads NFS, not for sale," she said. "It's from the artist's own collection and that appetizingly vulnerable woman is his wife Heather."

"Okay, I'll buy you a painting that's FS."

"Peter, how sweet." Ellie tightened her belt, dividing the petals of several red poppies. The poppies made a spectacular splash across the front of her white dress, size twelve. "Garrett Halliday paintings start at around five thousand dollars."

"You've got to be kidding. For five grand we could attend a starving artists sale and I could buy you a hundred paintings, a hundred frames, and dinner at Uncle Vinnie's Gourmet Italian Restaurant."

Ellie watched him glance around the gallery, noting (as she had) that people wore everything from evening gowns and tuxedos to air-conditioned-at-the-knees jeans, topped by bustiers and trendy T-shirts. One patron, who had wandered in from the 1970s, sported sculpted sideburns, bellbottoms, and The Grateful Dead.

In point of fact, she already owned a Garrett Halliday painting . . . *Pussy Willow*. She had posed for it, along with her cat, Jackie Robinson. Well, to be perfectly honest, Garrett had used a photograph. Ordering a cat to sit still would be like asking it for a urine sample. Her painting graced one wall of the gallery, on loan for this exhibit. Had her perceptive detective noticed that the woman in the antique tub and the woman in *Pussy Willow* bore a striking resemblance to each other? There was a good reason for that, but it could wait until later. Peter had said that, after the show, they'd attend an improvisational jazz session at the Dew Drop Inn. She loved jazz. He preferred country-western, the more western the better, and wasn't that a perfect way to describe their relationship?

Across the room, not far from her painting, stood a heavy man and a skinny woman. From a distance, the woman looked like Olive Oyl, with a platinum rather than black neck-bun and small, high-heeled slippers that Cinderella had most likely offered for sale on eBay. As Ellie idly watched, the man held a lighter's flame beneath the tip of a fat cigar. A chorus of "pee-yew!" and "put it out!" greeted his first puff. Someone came running with an ash-tray and—

"For five grand I could even buy you a starving artist," Peter said, making an about-face, turning away from the lion-bathtub painting.

"What would I do with a starving artist?"

"Introduce him to your diet club members. Before and after. He could be the after."

Ellie slanted an amused glance at the tall man who stood beside her, at his thick dark hair and silver-streaked mustache. His blue-gray eyes sparkled with tender mischief. His nose, once broken then reset incorrectly, angled toward the left of a mouth that enjoyed kissing.

Those same lips that could caress her into a kaleidoscope of oblivion could assume a frowning line of professionalism while announcing: "You have the right to remain silent." A detective with the homicide division of the Colorado Springs Police Department, Peter helped—or hindered—when she played part-time sleuth.

Her mental dictionary kicked in. *Sleuth.* Short for sleuthhound. *Nosy.* Short for nosy parker; chiefly British.

Her handsome sleuthhound, whom she loved illogically, madly, passionately, often called her a nosy parker. Born and raised in Colorado, Peter wasn't the least bit British, but sometimes he sounded a tad anachronistic, as if he'd spent a former life as one of Sherlock's sidekicks. Conversely, when Peter got hot under the collar, he sounded all-American cop.

She looked up into his face, rising above a blue denim collar and a Mickey Mouse tie. "It doesn't work that way, honey," she said. "If I introduced a starving artist to my diet club members, they'd fatten him up in three shakes of a lamb's tail. How many times have I told you that a person doesn't lose weight by starving? A good, healthy, balanced food program—"

"Okay, okay, no starving artist. Maybe, instead, we can find a small raunchy Halliday and put it on lay-away."

"I think the best we can do is find Garrett Halliday. Here he comes now."

Ellie finger-combed her shoulder-length hair. Although she hadn't seen Garrett in five years, she considered him a close friend. He called her ex-husband "Tony Baloney" and her son "Bernstein Bear" and her mother, whom he'd met once, "Dragon Lady." Ellie had been his "little red-feathered cygnet," an obvious misnomer since she hadn't been exactly little, a plump rooster was the only bird she'd even remotely resembled, and her blush of youth had been the blush of Estée Lauder.

And yet tonight she felt she deserved the nickname "young swan." To be even more precise, she felt like the swan in *The Ugly Duckling*.

As she licked her index finger and ran it underneath her eyes, eliminating any trace of smudged mascara, she remembered how Garrett had always flirted shamelessly, his innuendoes sincere, while his soul mate Heather, secure in her own sensuality, had looked on with an indulgent smile.

*Pride goeth before a fall,* Ellie's mother liked to say. But all the same, Ellie couldn't stop grinning. Because the last time she'd seen Garrett Halliday, she'd weighed an additional fifty-five pounds.

Garrett looked delicious. He could have been simmering on top of a stove. Rastafarian dreadlocks enhanced his café au lait face. Parsley-flaked eyes crinkled at the corners. A beet-red shirt had been tucked into cocoa-colored cords, and he exuded the same sexy excitement as a dynamic singing star; country-western; ache-y-break-y. Bottom line: Garrett Halliday looked like a man who could first ache, then break, hearts.

Following in the artist's wake was a short, voluptuous woman. Her spike-heeled sandals defied gravity. Her hair, the same color as the desert painting's sand, sported a Dutch cut, not unlike the Buster Brown boy who lived in shoes. Haircut aside, anyone with the IQ of a Q-tip could see that she was most definitely not a boy, nor for that matter, a child. A low-cut black dress emphasized incredible cleavage, then fell in pleated swirls to the top of her thighs. When she accelerated, her undies were visible. Ellie had seen her undies before. No, not undies. Panties. If one skated on thin ice, one wore panties. Toting a half-empty champagne bottle and a half-full crystal goblet, she looked like an advertisement for a friends-don't-let-friends-drive-drunk campaign.

Peter gave a muted whistle. "Is that Halliday's wife?"

"Of course not," Ellie said. "His wife's in the bathtub."

"What?"

"Does she look like the woman in Garrett's painting?"

"Oh. Right."

14

"She's his mother," Ellie said.

"No kidding. Then I'd like to have a few sips of whatever youth potion she's been taking. Halliday has to be in his forties while his mother can't be more than thirty."

"She's actually his stepmother, Adrianna Halliday. Once upon a time she was Adrianna Bouchet, the Canadian figure skating champion, and she'd raise a few eyebrows with her abbreviated undies . . . I mean panties . . . hello, Garrett."

As Ellie stared into the artist's classic-featured face, a childhood rhyme came to mind and her fingers flexed. *Here is the church, here is the steeple.* She considered herself medium height. Garrett was as tall as a steeple.

"Ellie?" His gaze touched upon her body. "Ellie, you look lovely. I must capture your hair with my paintbrush."

"You've already captured my hair. And my heart." As she easily feigned the light, flirty tone she'd always used with Garrett, she glanced at Peter. Who looked bemused.

No, not bemused. A-mused.

"My little red-feathered cygnet," Garrett said, and to Ellie his voice sounded like the chocolate frosting on a devil's food cake, "where are your succulent Rubenesque curves?"

"I gave up succulent Reuben sandwiches for three ounces of melted, low-sodium cheese."

"I adore your new angles," he said, "especially those shadows beneath your breasts and between your legs. When are you going to pose for me again?"

"Any time. Twist my arm."

"A pleasure."

Lifting and rotating her arm, he nibbled a kiss on her wrist-pulse.

Ellie glanced at Peter again. She tried to remember if

he'd ever seen her play the coquette—and came up empty. Later, if necessary, she'd explain that Garrett had been the only man in her overweight past to turn her inside out and decipher what lay beneath her "Rubenesque curves."

"That's a nice twist, Garrett," she said, bringing her attention back to his ticklish wrist-nibble. "Do you want me to pose here and now?"

He shook his head. "We must find ourselves a secluded studio, my lamb. I'll paint you clothed in nothing more than a cluster of purple grapes. The grapes will enhance your auburn hair and turquoise eyes. Then I'll eat them, one by one."

"My eyes?"

"No. The grapes. But I'd love to lick your eyes shut."

Oh, God, this time she couldn't read Peter's expression. Would he understand that Garrett was teasing, what Heather used to call stirring? Before Ellie could conjure up an explanation, Garrett said, "Where's Tony Baloney? And how's that adorable son of yours? Michael. My Bernstein Bear."

"Tony and I are divorced," Ellie replied. "He's in California, selling real estate. I think he caused the latest earthquake, a scare tactic so he could list more houses. Michael's not exactly a Bernstein Bear anymore. He calls himself Mick, after Jagger, and he's formed his own band, Rocky Mountain High. He attends the University of Colorado, English Lit major. He's also taking creative writing courses. Like mother, like son, I guess. I've been working on a mystery novel I started eons ago. It's not easy, writing books. But every time I think about giving up, I remember what Heather used to say. 'If you drop a dream, it breaks.' "

Apparently, Garrett had only caught the first five words

of her monologue. Arching an eyebrow, he said, "You're divorced?"

"My mother says I'm recycled." She turned to her recycling center. "Peter, this is Garrett Halliday. Garrett, Peter Miller."

While the two men shook hands, Garrett's companion refilled her goblet, shook the champagne bottle, then shook it again. With a petulant moue, she placed the bottle against the wall. Returning to Garrett, she poked his ribs with a sharp elbow. At first he brushed her off. Then, as if dredging up a corpse, he said, "Ellie Bernstein, Peter Miller, may I present Adrianna Bouchet Halliday?"

Social graces intact, Garrett's mobile mouth twisted into an expression Ellie couldn't decipher. So she smiled a greeting and said, "I watched you win the Canadian Nationals on TV, Madame Halliday. You skated to Leonard Bernstein's 'Oh, Happy We' from *Candide* and you were wonderful."

"*Merci beaucoup.*" Sidling closer to Peter, Adrianna lifted her right wrist to his lips. "Your *mustache*, it is so soft, monsieur. Are you an *artiste?*"

"Only in his choice of neckties," Ellie said. "Monsieur Miller is *un gardien de la paix.*"

Adrianna abruptly lowered her arm and returned her right hand to the stem of her goblet. "*Parlez-vous français,* Madame Bernstein?"

"A little. I visited Paris once, a graduation gift from my wealthy grandmother. *Ou sont les WC's, s'il vous plaît?*"

"Where's the toilet? Oh, you tease."

Adrianna's smile didn't reach her cornflower-blue eyes, and Ellie wondered why.

"We've been admiring this painting," Peter said, his first words since Garrett and Adrianna's cyclonic appearance,

17

even though Ellie knew he was cataloging impressions then guiding a mental computer mouse toward the "Save" icon inside his head.

Garrett chuckled. "Thanks, Miller. My bathing woman and lion cliché is from an earlier collection. I've changed my style. I'd sell the damn thing except it's Adrianna's favorite."

"*Oui.* I love Monsieur *Leon.*" Adrianna cocked her head. "Are you perhaps a sister to Garrett's wife, Madame Bernstein?"

"Only in spirit. I'm older than Heather, but we used to tell everyone we were separated at birth." Focusing on the canvas, Ellie said, "The colors are vivid, Garrett, the mood sensual. Holy cow, the title's misspelled. D-e-s-s-e-r-t. *Desert Song* would only have one 's.' "

"But dee-sert has two."

"Of course." Ellie smiled. "The lion wants the lady for dessert."

"I thought about you when I painted it." Garrett winked at Peter. "When I was a struggling artist, my wife and I dined on piece de resistance de peanut butter. Ellie would invite us over for dinner at the drop of a hat, especially holidays, only she called them 'hallidays.' She'd baste a turkey, char-broil a steak, roast a leg of lamb, and she always whipped up sugary desserts that melted in your mouth."

"Speaking of sugar and spice and everything nice," Ellie said, "where's Heather?"

"She's not into braving crowds." Momentarily, Garrett's face betrayed a deep anguish. Then—*click*—as if somebody had slid a transparency into a slide projector, his demeanor changed to one of annoyance. "Ouch," he said. "Adrianna, stop poking my ribs. What the bloody hell do you want now?"

She turned her goblet upside-down. "Empty."

This time, Garrett's laughter sounded strained. "Since Heather couldn't attend," he said, "Adrianna's playing hostess. She's definitely into public affairs, aren't you, my pet?"

"So are you, Garrett. Please, my glass, it is empty."

"You've had enough."

"*Merde!*" Pouting prettily, she turned her face toward Peter. "You will bring me more champagne, Monsieur Policeman, *oui?*"

Before Peter could respond, Garrett said, "Forget it, Miller. She's already consumed more bubbles than an irreverent kid who's forced to gargle Ivory mouthwash. Ellie, let's get together soon and do art. Now, if you'll excuse me, I'll find the chauffeur and have him drive my *mother* back to the hotel."

Adrianna's eyes narrowed. She tossed her silver-blond hair. The sudden motion apparently triggered dizziness. Staggering backward, she sagged against the woman-lion-bathtub painting.

"Careful darlin', that big ole cat's gonna chew you up and spit you out," Garrett drawled. "Adrianna? Baby, are you okay?"

"*Merde,*" she said weakly.

Her goblet fell, shattering against the gallery floor. Adrianna followed the goblet's descent, and the only thing Ellie could think of was: *Pride goeth before a fall.*

Then she thought: *Poison! Adrianna's been poisoned!*

But Adrianna hadn't stopped breathing. In fact, the petite blonde exhaled wine fumes.

*She's rag-doll-drunk,* Ellie thought. *Dead, if you'll excuse the expression, drunk.*

Peter instinctively stepped toward Adrianna, but Garrett

19

had already scooped her up into his arms, and Ellie could have sworn his lick-your-chops expression duplicated his painted lion's. Rapacious. Voracious. Hungry.

# Two

Ellie felt like Scarlett O'Hara.

Scarlett at the bazaar.

The scene where Scarlett's feet dance, hidden by a booth's valance.

Seated rather than standing, elbows on cocktail napkins, chin cradled in her hands, Ellie's feet danced. She didn't have Scarlett's minuscule waist, nor did she possess a Southern accent, but her beau drove her nuts (in a good way) with his Clark Gable grin.

"I'm hungry," she said, her voice pure Coloradoan. "Those gallery hors d'oeuvres were *not* on my Weight Winners menu. I couldn't even pretend the egg rolls were protein."

Lowering her arms, she leaned back in her chair and glanced around. The Dew Drop Inn was dimly lit and bursting at the seams. Clad in black shorts and yellow halter tops, cocktail waitresses swarmed like giant bumblebees. The Dew Drop's owner, Charley Aaronson, was checking the ID of a young man who looked only slightly older than his shoe size. The aroma of popcorn, lime juice, pineapple and coconut overpowered the stench of sweat. Mounted above the bar was a mute TV, where Denver Nuggets and Houston Rockets traded dribbles.

A jazz combo dominated a small, raised stage. The vocalist, a bleached blonde with earth-stained roots, held a microphone to her lips. She looked as if she wanted to suck its amplified tip. In a breathy voice, she gasped, "Fee-vah all thru-hoo the na-hite."

"If I can snare a server, I'll order us something to eat," Peter said, then winced.

Ellie knew why he winced. He sat so close to the Baby Boomer behind him, he could probably smell the man's Old Spice deodorant.

*She* could smell it. One of her dubious assets was a great sense of smell. She could identify perfumes by name, too, probably because tendrils of scent used to emanate from her ex-husband's clothing. The scents were almost always verified by the credit card receipts stuffed inside his pockets. White button-down shirt, White Shoulders perfume, white (sometimes yellow) receipt.

Old Spice's companion, who looked vaguely familiar, had drenched herself with Opium perfume. Ellie didn't particularly care for Opium, so she reached into a wooden salad bowl, captured a handful of popcorn, and held it under her nose like a potpourri sachet.

Maneuvering his chair closer to the table, Peter tried to talk above the blare of mouth organ, polyphonic sax, keyboard, and a melancholy licorice stick.

"Dessert song," he said. "So you do have a thing for starving artists."

"Define thing." She pelted him with the popcorn. "Five years ago my marriage was tumbling downhill faster than Jack and Jill, but I never considered having a 'thing' with Garrett. Assuming I had the chutzpah to cheat on Tony, Garrett only had eyes for his wife. You saw the lion painting. Heather's beautiful."

"Just like my Norrie. The nude in the bathtub was a turn-on, but I prefer your grape-highlighted hair."

"Everything tonight seems to be a turn-on, Peter. You're holding back a secret, and I know what it is."

"You do?"

"Sure. You've just solved an unsolvable crime and received a grateful bonus check from an anonymous donor. More than enough to buy me a Garrett Halliday painting, an ornate frame, and a scrumptious dinner at Uncle Vinnie's Gourmet Italian Restaurant."

"Give me a break, Norrie. Since when have I worked on a case you didn't know about?"

"True. Was Adrianna a turn-on?"

"Hardly. I don't respond well to women who say *merde*," he said, grinning his Clark Gable grin.

*Touché,* she thought. Peter knew she'd gone to Catholic schools where the nuns didn't allow cussing. Her ex-husband didn't like to "swear in front of girls," and God forbid she should cuss in front of Tony. She had once hit her thumb with a hammer and screamed, "Heck, ohheck, ohheckdarn!" When she and Peter first met, during the diet club murders, her most profane expletive had been "holy cow." Bullshit had been as foreign as . . . well, bull shit. Until Miller-osmosis kicked in.

Clutching the mike with one hand, the jazz singer made a fingered fan with her other hand. "Oooh, ahhh, everybody's got the fee-vah," she sang, fanning her face with her fingers.

"Now I know how come you own a Garrett Halliday painting," Peter said. "When you told me Halliday's price tag, I wondered."

"Before they moved to Aspen, Garrett and Heather lived in Colorado Springs. Heather worked as a teller at my bank. The first time we saw each other we did a mutual double take. We look alike, except way back then I weighed a tad more . . ." She paused, thinking sixty pounds was a tad more than a tad more.

"Tony found Garrett a nice rental at a price he could afford," she continued. "Garrett and Heather often joined us for dinner and the painting was a gift. Heather and I *swore* we'd keep in touch." She shook her head ruefully. "As for Garrett, he always gives good flirt. No, that's unfair. He really, truly likes women—tall, short, fat, thin—and women sense that, so he attracts them like a magnet. Physical attributes and hair color aside, the women in his paintings remind me of Audrey Hepburn. Men wanted to sleep with her and women wanted to *be* her. Am I making any sense?"

"Yes, Audrey."

Behind Peter, the Boomers were arguing over *The Devil's Advocate*. Who played the wife? Ashley Judd or Charlize Theron? Old Spice pumped his fist. Opium Lady stood up, swiveled, and stomped toward the Dew Drop restrooms.

"I can't imagine why Heather didn't come to the gallery opening," Ellie said. "Garrett's 'not into braving crowds' was a crock. Crowds have never bothered Heather. She's a people-person."

"It's been a while since you've seen her, Norrie. Maybe she's changed."

"Maybe." She heard the doubt in her voice.

"More wine, sweetheart?"

"No, thanks. I don't want to end up like Adrianna, falling down drunk. She's one sick lady."

"Yup. Everybody's got the fee-vah. Where's Garrett's father? Why wasn't he at the gallery?"

"How do you know he wasn't?"

"Adrianna's a 'trophy wife.' He'd want her by his side, on a tight rein."

Again, Ellie admired Peter's capacity to catalogue

mental impressions. "John Halliday died last year," she said. "It was in all the papers. Reporters loved to write about him. They always compared him to Howard Hughes because Halliday was supposedly eccentric and his first wife, Garrett's mother, was an actress. She appeared with Dorothy Dandridge in that Carmen movie." Ellie crushed a piece of popcorn between her thumb and first finger. "Adrianna's a 'merry widow,' although she didn't seem all that merry tonight."

"Aha."

"Is that 'aha' an insinuation, Peter? Adrianna may look great in undies. She may even have an aging Lolita, *femme-naïf* appeal. But Garrett and Heather are very much in love, or at least they were the last time I saw them. Stop playing sleazy detective. Soon you'll light an unfiltered cigarette and call me a dame."

"A dame, my crossword puzzle addict, is an aristocrat. Speaking of French-Canadian bluebloods, do you know why Adrianna quit skating?"

"Some say she clubbed a rival over the head, taking her out of contention. It happened in a dark corridor, the skater was hit from behind, and she, the skater, never saw the perp. The skater's brains were scrambled. She recovered, but the crime remains unsolved. Adrianna subsequently fell on the ice and permanently injured her knee. Karma, I guess. A few months later she posed for *Playboy* and met John Halliday. What time is it, honey?"

He squinted at his watch. "Ten-fifteen."

"Melody should be here soon. She was so busy directing everything at the gallery, we just waved hello."

"Now there's an artist I can afford. When is the gallery going to spotlight her work?"

"This September. Right now Melody's happy managing

25

the gallery, and she's responsible for landing Garrett. He usually exhibits locally, in Aspen. Holy cow, Peter. That's the second time you've grinned at the word 'Aspen.' "

"You're such a fine detective, Norrie."

"Why are you grinning like that?"

"Like what?"

"My cat. Have you swallowed the proverbial canary?"

"Are you absolutely certain you don't want any more wine?"

"What's up, Lieutenant?"

"Me. We have vacation reservations. Seven days, one stress-free week, at a ranch near Snowmass, right next door to Aspen. We leave the day after tomorrow."

"Holy cow, Peter, a horse ranch?"

"Very good, Norrie. Most people would have said hippopotamus ranch."

"But I can't leave Colorado Springs."

"Why not?"

"Weight Winners. I have my weekly lectures and—"

"Find someone to cover for you."

"Jackie Robinson won't stay at a kennel."

"We'll take him with us. The ranch allows pets."

"I'd love to see Garrett again. And Heather. How long have you had this planned? Why didn't you tell me earlier? Last week, for instance? Or last night?"

"Last night we were busy."

"Since when do we 'busy' in silence?"

"True. You like to wheedle when my defenses are down." He glanced down at his lap. "My defenses are up. Or will be, as soon as we leave this madhouse."

"I've got nothing to wheedle about," she said, ignoring his spicy hint. "The last few C.S.P.D. crimes have been *Murder, She Wrote* reruns, eminently solvable."

"Let's go home and put some Dixie Chicks on the stereo. Or," he bribed, "Peggy Lee."

"Soon." Ellie fiddled with the stem of her wineglass. "Garrett looked like Leo."

"The kid in that *Titanic* movie?"

"No. Leo the MGM lion. Monsieur *Leon*. The lion in the bathtub painting. Garrett was practically licking his chops when he carried Adrianna from the room."

Peter Groucho'd his eyebrows. "Let me carry you from the room, Norrie. I want to pay homage to those lovely shadows beneath your breasts."

"We can't. I promised Melody we'd meet her here."

"Okay. But when we're on vacation there won't be any distractions, just sex and sunsets."

"A ranch," Ellie said. "I don't know anything about horses. I have Mick's tattered copy of *The Black Stallion* and I've watched the Kentucky Derby on TV. And Mr. Ed . . . a horse is a horse, of course . . . holy cow! I've never skied in my life, if you don't count my Robert Redford fantasies."

"Ah, *Downhill Racer*," Peter said, ignoring her fantasy confession.

"Too bad you have to go uphill before you come downhill."

"It's off-season, Norrie. The slopes close in May. Aspen licks its winter wounds and gets ready for summer. The ranch will be tourist-free, practically deserted. The wranglers, kitchen staff, and miscellaneous personnel get a month off, leaving behind a skeleton crew."

"How do you know? Have you been there before?"

"Once. Four years ago. My sister, her husband, and their three kids visit every year at this time. Here comes Melody, although I swear you'd need X-ray vision to spot anyone in this crowd."

As she approached the table, Melody Dorack's brown eyes danced with excitement. Scissors-licked curls bounced on her shoulders like curlicues of shaved wood. A Weight Winners graduate, she wore a short green dress that revealed her newly discovered assets. A yellow scarf was knotted at her neck pulse. From the chin down she looked like an R-rated Girl Scout.

"Where's your other half?" Rising, Peter tried to free a chair, inch by inch. He bumped Old Spice and shrugged away the man's glare.

Opium Lady was, presumably, still sequestered inside the restroom— Ellie thwacked her forehead with the heel of her hand. No wonder Opium Lady looked so familiar. She had unraveled her platinum bun and changed into designer jeans and what looked like a cashmere sweater, but she still bore a resemblance to Olive Oyl. And Old Spice was the man who'd lit up the fat stogie at the gallery. Later, Ellie had caught a glimpse of him handing out business cards. Most people trashed them.

"Gordon's at home with a nasty virus," Melody said. "Everyone else gets sick in the winter but my husband prefers to wait for warmer weather."

Her voice was the antithesis of her name; high and scratchy, like fingernails across a chalkboard. The screechy timbre, due to a teenage tragedy, had resulted in what Melody called her Deep Throat Scar.

"How's everything at the gallery?" Ellie asked.

"Hectic. And terrific. People made the trek from all over. Castle Rock. Denver. Boulder. We just about sold out."

"Why wasn't Heather there?"

"Heather?"

"Heather Halliday."

"I knew who you meant, Ellie, but Heather hasn't been seen very much since the fire."

"What fire?"

"Three years ago Garrett's studio caught on fire. Before anyone could stop her, Heather ran inside, through the flames, to save Garrett's paintings. She was badly burned."

"Oh my God! I didn't know. How badly?"

"She's had a bunch of skin grafts, but the right side of her face is disfigured. She rarely appears in public, and when she does she wears a heavy veil to hide her scars." Offhandedly, Melody fingered the scarf at her neckline.

"I didn't know," Ellie repeated. "No one told me." She blinked back tears. "Talk about opening mouth, inserting foot. I asked about Heather. At the gallery. I asked why she wasn't there. No wonder Garrett looked so . . . so . . ."

"Unhappy?"

"More than unhappy. Anguished. Wait a minute. Garrett's lion painting. All his paintings. Heather's face is—"

"Unflawed. Garrett paints her over and over the way she used to look. It's so sad, especially since Heather supported him through the lean years and could now stand by his side and share his success."

Melody yawned, gave Ellie a sheepish smile, then said, "To put it bluntly, Heather's *responsible* for his success."

"What do you mean?"

"Seven, maybe eight months after the fire, *People* magazine did a big write up, with photos. They focused on how Garrett continued painting Heather despite her 'disfigurement.' They called Garrett and Heather 'the romance of the century.' Folks ate it up, especially women. CNN turned it into one of their *People* profile segments and soon the demand for Garrett's 'Heather paintings' exceeded the supply. Even better, his print and postcard reproductions sold like hot cakes, and they continue to sell well today. But despite his undeniably blatant narcissism, I think he was uncomfortable with the article and TV exposure because he emphatically refuses to exhibit outside of Colorado. And I know for a fact that he's been courted by some of the finest, most lucrative galleries in London, Paris, and New York."

"Are you saying that if Garrett didn't paint his wife, he wouldn't be so popular?" Peter asked, cutting to the chase. "Or successful?"

"That's exactly what I'm saying. Garrett's a phenomenal artist, but Heather is his . . . attention-grabber. Or, as they say in the musical *Gypsy*, his 'gimmick.' "

"I can't wait to have a nice long visit with her, poor lamb." Ellie felt tears threaten again.

"Ellie, it's been three years since the fire," Melody said softly. "Heather helped me with the exhibit. She's a tad reclusive, but fine. You don't have to drive all the way to Asp—"

"Peter made reservations at a dude ranch."

"The ranch isn't far from Aspen," he clarified.

"We're leaving the day after tomorrow, assuming I can find someone to cover my Weight Winners classes," Ellie said. She took a deep breath and let it out slowly. "I'm going to *kill* Garrett. He should have called me, told me about Heather."

"I'll cover your classes," Melody said. "I'll even give an art lesson, have people draw themselves the way they want to look. Would you like to take a poll on how many 'stick figures' I get?"

Peter nudged Melody, then placed his finger against his lips. "This is a secret," he said around the finger, "but Eddie Arcaro over there was just telling me how much she wants to ride a black stallion in the Kentucky Derby."

Ellie shook her head. "When my son was barely out of diapers, I read *The Black Stallion* to him, and I know that Eddie Arcaro was a famous jockey who rode horses in the Kentucky Derby, but the closest I've ever come to a derby was when Tony entered Mick in a soap box derby. Mick won but was disqualified. Tony built the damn car, or go-cart, or whatever the heck it's called, and added some sort of driving mechanism. It's supposed to be gravity propulsion only, and I've never ridden anything except a carousel horse . . ." She paused for breath, aware that she was jabbering. Oh, God, poor Heather, so beautiful, so secure in her beauty she'd never spent one red cent on cosmetics. Not even mascara!

Meeting Peter's gaze, Ellie saw that his blue-gray eyes were warm with compassion. Then he patted Melody's shoulder and said, "Let me order you a drink, honey."

"Thanks, but I have to play nurse." She winked. "Wasn't it Mary Poppins who sang something about sugar helping the medicine go down?"

Old Spice pivoted in his chair and stared at Melody. "Hi there," he said.

"Hello," she said, her voice uncertain.

"Me and the wife met you at the gallery."

"I'm sorry, but I've forgotten your name."

"Lassiter, first name Owen," he said, as though indexing himself in a telephone directory. "Me and the wife bought the redhead on Santa's lap."

"Yes. I remember now. You chose a terrific painting, Mr. Lassiter."

"The wife picked it out. She said it was a good investment."

Melody nodded. "*Christmas Carol* is from an earlier pe-

31

riod. We had three première-period paintings on exhibit and—"

"I thought that only happens when the artist goes belly-up."

"Excuse me?"

"I thought the price only goes up when the artist drops dead." Lassiter glanced toward the restrooms. "The wife musta fell in."

*A good investment, my foot,* thought Ellie. The eroticism in *Christmas Carol* was more subtle than Garrett's up-to-date paintings, but if you had a sleazy imagination, Santa could be sampling the flame-haired "Carol."

Rising, Lassiter began to plow his way to the bar. He bumped into one of the bumblebee cocktail waitresses. He seemed to chastise her. Even from a distance, Ellie could see the girl's face turn red. Then he appeared to apologize. Pressing some money against her palm, he gestured toward the restrooms. The waitress shook her head. He fumbled in his pocket and pulled out more money. The waitress nodded.

"Gosh, you guys, I should have introduced you," Melody said.

"Introduced us? Oh. Lassiter." Ellie's nose twitched at the lingering scent of Old Spice and beer-belches. "Don't apologize, Melody. I can't stomach a man who calls his wife 'the Wife.' "

"Me, either. Phone me when you get back from Aspen, Ellie, and we'll make arrangements to return your painting. I think it's one of Garrett's best, along with *Dessert Song* and *Christmas Carol*. His recent works are brilliant but more eclectic. And if you ever need money badly, early Hallidays are worth a fortune. We had several offers, even though *Pussy Willow* was clearly marked NFS." She winked again.

"Bye, Peter. Have fun jockeying 'Eddie Arcaro.' "

As she headed for the exit, Peter sat down. "Why did you lend Melody your painting?"

"Garrett wanted it displayed and Melody scanned it onto the brochure, along with a more up-to-date painting. We used my maiden name, for identification purposes, to keep anyone from tracking me down. Except for Wylie Jamestone, Garrett Halliday is Colorado's most popular native-son-artist, especially when it comes to serious collectors. But I didn't know, until now, that Heather had played a major role in Garrett's extraordinary success."

Peter flicked an imaginary Groucho-cigar. "What's the magic word, Norrie?"

"Sugar?"

"Nope. Wrong. Ride. It's time for some riding lessons. We'll start with the tub. Then the bed. Okay?"

"Okay," she said, reaching for some popcorn. "I wonder if Garrett meant anything by that remark."

"What remark?"

"Garrett said Adrianna was into public affairs. She said he was, too."

"They were talking about the art exhibit."

"Were they? Melody thinks Garrett's narcissism is a put on, a pretense, but I don't agree. Earl Wilson once said, 'Marriages are like diets. They can be ruined by a little dish on the side.' "

"I wouldn't call Adrianna a little dish."

Capturing her arm, nuzzling her palm, Peter ate the popcorn. Then he licked, searching for leftover salt. She tried to ignore the warm sensations that coursed through her body, centering in the shadows between her legs. "What would you call her, honey?"

"French cuisine. I prefer spicy American ribs, not to

mention breasts, thighs, and . . . what's that juicy heart-shaped thing on the butt of a chicken?"

"My mother calls it the part that goes over the fence last. Maybe I imagined the emphasis Garrett placed on his public affairs remark."

"You're the one who defended Halliday when I aha-ed."

"I know, but that was before Melody told me about Heather. If Heather's a lost lamb, Adrianna's a lamb chop."

"What does *that* mean?"

"Haven't you ever ordered lamb chops at a restaurant, Peter? They cost a fortune, they're small and tender, and you gobble them up in less than no time."

"Adrianna's no lamb chop, Norrie. She's too indigestible."

"Then why did Garrett Halliday look like his damn lion?"

A scream drowned out whatever explanation Peter might have offered.

Owen Lassiter's cocktail waitress emerged from the restroom. Waving her arms, she looked like a bee warding off humans.

Peter jumped to his feet, then swore a blue streak when he tripped over the chair Lassiter had abandoned.

All conversation stopped dead. Even the TV basketball players quit dribbling, as if God had blown a whistle and shouted "Foul!"

Standing in the corner, melting into shadows, an art gallery patron stared at the lion-woman-bathtub painting.

NFS. Not For Sale.

Could *Dessert Song* be destroyed?

Impossible. There were too many people bustling about. Stolen?

Out of the question. Garrett and the manager who looked like a poodle had left the gallery, but a couple of Security R Us Neanderthals were posted at the exits. In any case, the conformation of the bathing woman, while detailed, showed her left profile.

Chewing two sticks of gum with teeth that looked as if they were grinding coffee beans, the art patron walked toward another exhibit, also labeled NFS. Titled *Pussy Willow*, the auburn-haired woman who dominated the canvas caressed a black cat whose eyes resembled the silky aments of a pussy willow.

Just like *Dessert Song*, the woman-cat painting was from an earlier period, when Heather Halliday's face had been whole, beautiful, unflawed, when each brush stroke counted, when every color was uncontaminated, as if Garrett Halliday had borrowed waxed rainbows from a box of crayons.

Six other Halliday paintings had escaped the funeral pyre.

The art patron—delayed by road construction—had reached the gallery late, only to find that *Christmas Carol* had been sold to a lady who looked like Popeye's girlfriend.

*Polly Wants a Quaker* lived in Garrett Halliday's Aspen gallery, where the chi-chi catalogue valued her at ten thousand dollars, a high price for a "ho," even if she did come with a horse and buggy straight out of *Friendly Persuasion*. The movie's honky goose graced the canvas, too. And while you'd be able to share more than one night with "Polly," the art patron couldn't scrape up the ten grand. In any case, the art patron needed . . . what was the word? Something hard to pronounce. Oh, yeah, anonymity.

Assuming it was authentic, a pre-fire painting belonged to a man named Rudolph Kessler.

And three paintings were in the art patron's private collection; three redheads shackled to the wall. Despite exquisite torture and multiple knife wounds, they had, somehow, survived.

One fine day they'd die.

# Three

Church bells chimed "You'll Never Walk Alone."

Which was strange, thought Rudolph Kessler, because he could have sworn it was Friday. Still, it was hard to judge without his electric clock. Time measured days and vice versa. Inside his spotless kitchen, a black-and-white spotted cow circled the clock's numbers, second by second, moo-tick, tick-moo, a time to be born and a time to die and the friggin' clock didn't work.

Church bells mean Sunday, so it must be Sunday.

On Sundays, after church, Gracie liked to watch those TV movie guys. She always wrote down their thumb-picks, even though the Kesslers saw maybe one movie a year.

Hey! (*Hey-is-for-horses*, his mind muttered.) Why wasn't Gracie collecting her ink pen and writing down thumb-picks?

Hangfire! Those weren't church bells. No siree-bob. The lady next door was playing her friggin Gospel records.

Draining the last driblet of beer from his Budweiser can, Rudy began to stack it on top of the other empties. He paused to belch and waited for Gracie to tell him to cover his mouth with his hand. When she didn't, he reached high above his head. "Ain't no mountain hiiiigh enough," he sang, "to keep me away from you, Grace."

The newest can teetered, settled briefly, wobbled, and he watched the whole hollow-can-skyscraper crumple and

37

scatter across the wooden floor.

"Doggone, there goes my Empire State Building." Folding his fingers into the shape of a gun, he chanted, "Rat-a-tat-tat, rat-a-tat-tat, they shot and killed Faye-friggin-Wray. Yes siree-bob, King Kong still lives. I'll be a monkey's uncle. You hear that, Gracie? You're married to a monkey's uncle. That makes you a monkey's aunt."

Silence.

"Don't wanna be no monkey's aunt, Gracie? Hey!" (*Hey-is-for-horses.*) "Remember when we flew to New York City and climbed to the top of the Empire State Building? Remember how I sang ain't no *building* high enough to keep me away from you, Grace? Remember how we play-acted Cary Grant and Deborah Car-with-a-K and you kissed me and everybody clapped?"

Silence.

"Empire State Building *fall*ing down, my fair Gracie."

Silence.

"It ain't my fault," Rudy whined. "It's the friggin Bud. Coors stack better. But I ran out of Coors yesterday. Or was it the day before?"

Maneuvering through the debris, he cane-tapped his way to the john.

Gracie's bathrobe still hung from the door hook. Gracie's shower cap still decorated the tub's faucet. Gracie's toothbrush still waved its bristles from the plastic water glass. Dog*gone!*

He stared at the tub. The wall above needed more grout. Gracie loved that word, grout. She said it looked like it sounded. "My Gracie lies over the ocean," he sang. "My Gracie lies over the sea. My Gracie lies over the ocean. Oh, bring back my Gracie to me."

Inside his head, the last line echoed: *Oh, bring back my Gracie to me.*

After doing his bidness, he caught his reflection in the mirror above the sink. A week's worth of ashy stubble clung to his chin and his neck had wattled like a turkey's. Thin strands of oyster-colored hair looked like Gracie had stitched Mamie Eisenhower bangs across his forehead with her sewing machine. His eyes were red and puffy and he smelled like baby's spit-up.

He shook his head, trying to clear away the fog he'd been living in for the past week. He couldn't remember any-thing—except the drinking. And the singing. He sang when he drank too much, so he could never pull the wool over Gracie's eyes, no siree-bob. He'd start singing, like Frank Sinatra lived inside his head, and she'd say, "Had yourself a little snort, eh Rudy?"

"Had myself more snorts than you can shake a stick at, Gracie," he yelled, "and it's all your fault!"

His cane turned into a hockey stick as, heading for the kitchen, he swatted beer-can-pucks, aiming them at a framed needlepoint of Paris, France.

"I see London, I see France, I see Gracie's underpants."

A can bounced off the Eiffel Tower. Rudy clawed his hand into the shape of a microphone. "Kessler scores a goal and wins the Olympics," he announced. "Impics, impics, impics," he pretend-echoed. What was it his Little League team used to say before they ate pizza? "Two, four, six, eight," he chanted, "who do we appreciate? Canada, Canada, yaaaay!"

He knew he was rambling like a friggin rose. Gracie called it blathering. If the TV worked, he'd turn it on. A TV ate blather. And burped it back at you. Not like an echo. More like alphabet soup.

As he limped through an archway, the cows greeted him. From potholders. From Gracie's teapot. From dishtowels. From salt and pepper shakers. Even the friggin' wallpaper—cows!

Hangfire! Elsie was standing in her usual place on the windowsill, in between the purple cow and Ferdinand the Bull, but Elsie had a dead plant growing out of the hole in her back. When was the last time Gracie watered Elsie?

On the wall, the clock's cow had died at six-thirty. If you squinted, the cord that dangled to the outlet looked like a skinny stream of black blood and the spotless kitchen wasn't spotless anymore.

Dirty dishes greased every counter and KFC buckets dominated Gracie's hand-painted-with-smiling-daisies garbage pail. The pail was open. Its cover, at an angle, looked like a flying saucer from one of them old black-and-white alien gatecrasher movies, where you knew they used a trash can cover for their spaceship-in-the-sky but you didn't care because, somehow, a trash can cover looked scarier than a real spaceship. Usually Gracie's pail was closed. "Careful, Rudy, don't let Oscar the Grouch out," she'd say after *she'd* had a few snorts. They didn't have any kids or grandkids, but sometimes Gracie watched that TV show *Sesame Street*. She said she liked Elmo, who sounded like her high school science teacher.

Rudy opened the icebox. He waited for the little light to go on, then remembered. *They* had turned off the electricity. *She* hadn't paid the bill.

A can of Bud and a carton of orange juice kept each other company on the first shelf, next to Gracie's homemade pickles. The pickles looked like green fingers. With warts. The ice box, minus its ice, also cooled—or would have cooled—a half loaf of blue bread and a plastic burp-top bowl, missing its burp-top, covered with aluminum foil. His next door neighbors had given him the bowl, so he'd have to wash and return it. But, for now, he was afraid to smell the food inside. He might—what was Gracie's favorite expression? Oh, yeah. Toss his cookies.

Grabbing the beer, Rudy kicked the ice box door shut on the acidic odor of putrefying orange juice.

"Yowch," he cried. "Hurt my foot and no one cares."

Mournfully, he shuffled toward the living room phone. *They* hadn't turned it off yet. His fingers tap-danced the grocery store's number. "Howdy-Doody," he said (Gracie always laughed when he said hello like that). Then he ordered a couple cases of Coors and a dozen Van Camp's Pork and Beans. Beans would keep him regular and he didn't need consti-friggin'-pation right now.

"Who's this?" asked the boy on the other end of the line.

"It's Rudolph Kess—"

"Rudolph the red-nosed reindeer?"

*Friggin' snot-nosed kid!* "It's Rudolph Kessler, you punk. I got an account."

"We ain't allowed to deliver no more stuff till you pay what's owed on your account, Mr. Reindeer."

"Sez who?"

"Sez my boss."

"Then I'll just take my bidness someplace else." Slamming down the receiver, leaving his warm beer on the telephone table, Rudy limped toward his armchair. "It ain't fair, it ain't my fault," he whined, sinking into the chair and resting his sore foot atop a hassock.

*They* said Gracie had died in a car crash when he knew very well she'd skipped town with Keith Kosmowski, who sold insurance. At fifty-three, ten years younger than Rudy, Gracie answered Keith Kosmowski's phones. But *she* hadn't bought insurance, so *they* had taken Rudy's last cent for the coffin and funeral.

Standing on shaky legs, Rudy retrieved Gracie's lace hanky from his trouser pocket. He sniffed the hanky, which smelled like Gracie. He shoved the hanky back into his pocket, changed his mind, and shoved it down his undershirt, close to his heart. Then he looked around the living room.

It was a nice room when it was clean and beer cans didn't carpet the floor. The color TV was very nice—when the electricity worked. During football season he and Gracie watched the Denver Broncos. "Dee-fence," she'd yell. "Dee-fence, you effin' donkeys!" Last Christmas he'd bought one of them tape machines. Gracie sure loved that machine. She'd tape *Wheel of Fortune*, then replay it and shout out all the answers ahead of time.

Staring at the pictures on his wall, he envisioned Gracie screaming, "Buy a vowel, you idiot, buy a E."

Lots of pictures decorated the walls. Gracie sure loved them three little kittens who'd lost their friggin' mittens, but his favorite picture showed a pretty lady sitting at her dressing table in front of a mirror. First you saw her back, then her face and part of her body. The reflection stopped above her bazookas, which was a friggin' shame. One more inch and you could see her bazookas. But it was fun to look at and think about and you could decide for yourself how big her bazookas were. Basketball big, if you wanted. Gracie said the picture was worth lots of money, three thousand maybe, even with the lady's bazookas hid.

Yes siree-bob. Nice house. Nice TV. Nice car.

He had bought a used Cadillac, but *they* said it was all smashed up on Interstate 25, between Colorado Springs and Security, when he knew for a fact that it had disappeared with Gracie and her friggin' boss, Keith Kos-mow—

Someone knocked on the front door.

"Who's there?" Glaring at the door, Rudy wondered if his neighbors toted yet another burp-bowl casserole.

"Mr. Kessler? I called yesterday." The voice, squelched, came through the keyhole and mail slot. "I'm here about the ad in the newspaper, Mr. Kessler. The painting you've got for sale."

*Oh, doggone,* Rudy thought, as he remembered placing one of them classified ads to sell that there picture of the lady in the mirror. Gracie said it was worth lots of money. Gracie said the initials in the corner, G-friggin'-H, belonged to someone famous.

Actress Goldie Hawn was the only famous G-friggin'-H Rudy knew, not counting the guy with the suntan—George Hamilton. Gracie had bought one of them George Foreman grills, only it was made by Hamilton Beach, so she called it George Hamilton. "I'm gonna cook weenies on George Hamilton," she'd say.

The girl who wrote down the ad let him use GH as one word but said he couldn't use friggin'. So the ad read "FOR SALE picture of lady in mirror by GH." The classified girl said Rudy's phone number made it a ten word special and the paper was running the special for three weeks, cheap, did he want that? He said okey dokey.

Now, he opened the door. "Come in," he said. "I'm Rudolph Kessler. Sorry the house is such a mess. My wife's gone for a spell. Hey! Hey-is-for-horses, that's what Gracie always says. Sit down; take a load off. Can I get you a beer?" Too late, he remembered he didn't have any more.

But the visitor was walking toward the picture. "It looks authentic, Mr. Kessler."

Rudy watched the visitor ogle the pretty lady's face, then stare, up-close, at the G-friggin'-H.

"Yes, it's genuine." The visitor spoke in a church-whisper. "*Alice's Wonder Land* . . . from an earlier period. Three thousand, right?"

"Three thousand?"

"For the painting, Mr. Kessler."

"Call me Rudy."

"I suppose you prefer cash, Rudy."

"Cash?"

The visitor smiled. "I stopped at the bank and withdrew—"

"Five. I want five thousand."

"I didn't bring that much cash. Will you accept a personal check?"

"You'd pay five thousand smackeroos for one picture?"

"Yes."

"Well . . . okey dokey, then."

*I don't wanna sell,* he thought. *Now that Gracie's gone, I won't have anyone to look at.*

Five thousand smackeroos! He could pay off his grocery bill and tell that snot-nosed kid to deliver enough Bud and Coors to last the spring and summer. He could put flowers on Gracie's grave and get the electricity fixed so he could tell her the answers to *Wheel* and she'd know he didn't really believe she'd run off with Keith Kosmowski.

"I've changed my mind," he said. "I want ten thousand."

"What? Look, Mr. Kess—"

"It ain't for sale." Trembling, he leaned on his cane.

"Now just a minute. I drove a long way to get here and when I called—"

"I got other pictures. Here's one of kittens. Ain't they

cute? I'll let you have it for ten bucks."

"I want *this* painting, Mr. Kessler."

"No! She's mine. You can have that there mountain free for your trouble."

Rudy limped over to a framed scenic print, hung above a curved highboy whose drawers held fancy polished dinnerware, steak knives, photo albums, marble fruit, and linens. The substantial chest sported a mirror with a scalloped wood frame. He thought he saw Gracie. Her reflection smiled at him. She didn't want him to sell the pretty lady. It was okey-dokey.

He felt his cane grabbed from his hand. "Hey . . ."

The first blow landed on his right shoulder.

"Yowch," he yelped. "Hey, stop that!"

Another blow. Harder.

"Hey!" (*Hey is for horses!*)

The next blow hit his back, but it was his ribs that seemed to cave in. Losing his breath and balance all at once, Rudy grabbed at anything. Six legs wobbled: Rudy's and the highboy's. Rudy's legs crumpled first. Then the highboy toppled, pinning him to the floor, showering him with silverware and napkins from the drawers. A marble apple grazed his temple. A marble grape invaded his eye.

*Dee-fence,* he thought.

But he couldn't fight back, not with Gracie's highboy stealing all his breath. He felt himself do his bidness in his pants, just like a baby.

Clutching Kessler's cane in one hand, the art patron watched the highboy's mirror shatter. Its silver-backed glass looks so pretty, like glittery flakes of snow scraped from a Christmas card. Until the shards cut Kessler's face.

Still furious, out of control, the art patron jumped on top of the antique highboy and danced a wild, stomping jig.

Rudy gave one last weak "Hey." Then, with his dying breath, he said, "Gracie . . . I let the Grouch out."

"You stupid bastard!" the art patron shouted.

Someone kicked at the front door.

Someone said, "Mr. Reindeer, you okay? Mr. Reindeer, it's me, Jerry from the grocery. My boss said I should deliver your order since you lost your wife so sudden and all, but you gotta sign the receipt. I'm sorry I made fun of you on the phone. Jeez, Mr. Rein . . . Kessler, open the door. This stuff's heavy."

The art patron jumped down from the highboy and grabbed at *Alice's Wonder Land*.

Instead of wire-and-hook, Kessler had nailed the frame to a wall stud.

Scooping up a steak knife, the art patron tried to cut out the canvas, starting at the top left-hand corner. But the artist had used tough sailcloth, rather than linen or hemp, and the knife was serrated, its marginal teeth too dull.

The doorbell's concordant chimes chorused Jerry's random knuckle-knocks.

In a frenzy, the art patron snagged a napkin, slashed at the painting with the knife, then wiped all prints from the cane and the painting's frame.

Lips locked in a grim grin, not unlike a salmon that spawns and dies, the art patron wiped the knife's handle and placed it in Rudy's lifeless hand.

# Four

Jerry looked like a rabbit trapped in headlights. His nose twitched and even though it was warm outside, the temperature well above normal, he wore a fur-lined cap with dangling earflaps.

"I heard someone say 'stupid bastard,' " he told Lieutenant Peter Miller, "but it coulda been Mr. Rein . . . Mr. Kessler. I seen him talkin' to hisself."

"When did you see that?" Peter asked.

"Before the funeral. I delivered some beer. And his dead wife."

"You delivered his dead wife?"

"No, sir. He was talkin' to hisself *and* his dead wife. He said he saw her underpants."

"Kessler's wife died three weeks ago," clarified Will McCoy, Peter's partner.

"You heard someone say 'stupid bastard,' " Peter prompted.

"Yessir." Jerry's Adam's apple bobbed. "But them drapes was drawn so I didn't see nobody. Mr. Rein . . . uh, Mr. Kessler was layin' there like that when I opened the door. I put my fingers on his neck like they do on TV, but I couldn't feel nothin'. His eyes were open, starin' at that there picture. It was creepy. He called and placed a grocery order, over the phone, ya know? I was luggin' a couple cases of Bud and beans and I couldn't see over the top, swear to

God. Guess he'll never pay up on his grocery bill now."

*God'll never pay up?* Peter surreptitiously chewed a couple of Tums. At the same time, he wondered how he could keep details of this inexplicable crime a secret from Norrie. He had to admit she was a pretty fair detective, but he knew that killers didn't always play fair. With a sinking feeling in his Szechuan-inflamed gut, he realized his hope was hopeless. He and Norrie planned to leave tomorrow morning at seven a.m. but she rarely, if ever, missed the local ten p.m. newscast and, already, the alphabet vans had parked across the street: KKTV, KOAA-TV, even Denver's KMGH—how the hell had *they* arrived so quickly?

The coroner had pronounced the victim dead (no kidding, thought Peter) and Will McCoy was taking notes. Peter sneaked a peek at his partner's conglomeration of chicken scratches and hieroglyphics. When typed onto an official form, McCoy's thumbnail sketches often read like free verse, which never failed to amaze and impress Peter.

Jerry paled and sank to the floor near Peter's feet. Drumming a beer can with a pencil, he sang, "All of the other reindeer used to laugh and call him names."

"Will, take care of the kid," Peter said. "I think he's about to puke."

"Aw, Pete, leave him alone. He sounds like Gene—"

"Autry?"

"No. Krupa."

"Roo-doff with your nose so bright—"

"Get him out of here!" Peter yelled.

As McCoy bent to one knee and secured Jerry's armpits, a man and woman entered Kessler's kitchen through the back door. Peter took an angry breath and opened his mouth to yell "Stop!" But before he could, the man and woman walked into the living room.

Peter shooed them back into the kitchen, where they told him they were listening to Elvis sing "You'll Never Walk Alone" and "His Hand in Mine" and "Clean Up Your Own Backyard" and they didn't see anyone come or go except that there boy who was singing Christmas carols in May for Christ's sake. They lived next door and they minded their own bidness, but they thought the cops should know that Rudy had been acting real schizo lately. Gone ape, you might say. Rudy swore his wife Grace had run off with Keith Kosmowski, and Keith still here in his State Farm office with a wife and five kids.

Peter asked the neighbors why Kessler might have destroyed the painting.

Well, Grace bragged how her picture cost more than that artsy-fartsy stuff on *Wheel*'s wheel, they said, and Rudy thought she'd run off with Keith Kosmowski, so he could have ruined it for revenge. Strange how Rudy only cut up half the lady's face. Wasn't that a pisser? Rudy Kessler, sure to Jeeesus, wasn't playing with a full deck.

Rudy had a Tupperware bowl that belonged to them, they said, and they'd like it back, please, if the cops didn't need it to test someone's what'cha'macallit.

"DNA?" Peter asked, his head commiserating with his digestive tract.

"Yeah, that's the stuff," said the man who lived next door.

The lady in the painting looked like Ellie Bernstein, said the woman who lived next door. You couldn't tell real good since the lady's face was all cut up like one of them whores in that creepy Jack the Ripper movie, but the woman who lived next door had seen the painting lots. She'd even joined Ellie's diet club, except she didn't lose much 'cause her hubby made her quit. The man who lived next door muttered something about how he didn't want his wife to look like a toothpick and besides it cost good money to join that club.

*As opposed to bad money?* Peter summoned a uniform to herd the nosy neighbors home. Then he took a closer look at the slashed painting.

The lady's face did resemble Norrie's, her one remaining eye blue-green, her hair that special shade of red; Irish Setter rather than Orphan Annie red. And despite the serrated knife-cuts, Peter could make out the painting's arrogant signature: G-period-H-period.

# Five

Merry as a cricket, Ellie sang. Even to her own ears, her voice sounded like the reiteration of trills from the magpies that dotted an azure sky. The magpies soared, despite any perceptible breeze. Seen through the car's window, they brought to mind shiny black-and-white-feathered kites.

"Have you ever considered singing lessons?" Peter's right hand caressed the steering wheel while his left arm dangled outside the window.

No wonder his left forearm and hand were so bronzed, Ellie thought. "Low blow," she said. "I've been told I sound like Perry—"

"White?"

"Who? Oh, Clark Kent's boss. No, Peter, Como," she fibbed, aware that, on the best of days, her voice sounded like a ventriloquist's hand puppet. "Perry Como sang about a wheel spinning round, round, round. Remember?"

"I think that was before my time."

"You rat. Sometimes you can be very—"

"Funny?"

"No. Frustrating."

"Me? Frustrating? Didn't you spend last night obsessing over Rudolph Kessler?"

Ignoring the rhetorical question, Ellie adjusted her seatbelt, then crossed her left leg over her right leg. Peter's Plymouth Scamp had developed a severe case of senility, in-

tensified by incurable bronchitis, so he'd borrowed his partner's classic 1987 Cabriolet convertible and it hummed
down the highway, its tires spinning round, round, round.
Leaving the ragtop up, Peter had opened the front windows. The air was scented with pine needles and she could
see clusters of pink, low-growing, weedy plants that looked
like bridal headgear for groundhogs.

Nice. She'd have to remember that image for her mystery novel, assuming she ever got back to writing the damn
thing.

She sniffed and said, "You know what, honey? If seasons
had their own smells, spring would smell like bleached
sheets hanging from a clothesline."

"What about summer?"

"Fresh-squeezed lemons and sprigs of mint. Autumn
would be burning leaves and football pads."

"How do you know what football pads smell like?" he
asked. "High school?"

"No. I wasn't popular enough to hug a jock. Chess was
more my style. I dated a guy named Walker Seidman.
Walker was very esoteric, very . . . visceral. We played
chess. Walker liked my hair. He said it reminded him of
fresh-spilled blood. My ex was the quintessential football
jock. He once said his pads smelled like Gucci shoes. I used
that in my mystery novel. 'Tony's pads smelled like Gucci
shoes.' By the way, I've modified the plot. When I first
started writing *Deadly Playoffs*, the perp was Tony's wife
and the case was solved by a local TV sports commentator.
Now the perp is a Denver Broncos cheerleader and the case
is solved by a snoopy domestic goddess."

"I like your commentator better. He makes more sense."

"She makes more sense."

"She. Of course."

"Football players have adorable butts. When I answer those *Cosmo* orgasm questionnaires, I always choose a man's butt over a handsome face, or even a great personality. Garrett Halliday has an adorable butt, but you'd give him a run for his money."

"I'd rather have Halliday's money than his butt." Peter navigated a sharp turn. "Orgasm questionnaires?"

"That was before we met," Ellie said, her cheeks hot.

"What does winter smell like?"

"Ice cubes soaked with club soda. Honey vanilla ice cream. Celery stalks dipped in buttermilk dressing."

"Aha. I knew we'd get to food sooner or later. All I had to do was snoop. Are you hungry, sweetheart?"

"I wasn't until now. Do you know the definition of 'snoop'?"

"I didn't until I met you."

"Snoop means 'to eat on the sly.' "

"Have you been slyly eating?"

"No."

"Okay. We'll stop for lunch. After we eat, I'll find a liquor store and buy you a six-pack of your favorite wine cooler. I want you to chug it down, all six bottles."

She blinked, surprised. Peter drank an occasional Scotch or beer, and she sipped an occasional glass of wine. Long gone were the days when she chugged White Russians in order to blunt Tony's verbal abuse.

"I want you sedated for our trek across Independence Pass," Peter said. "Aren't you scared of heights?"

"Yes. But I'm not scared of mountains. You'll be driving, so I'll simply relax and admire the scenery."

Peter toed the clutch pedal. Glancing down at the tense muscles in his denim-clad leg, Ellie felt like purring.

On the back seat, Jackie Robinson didn't purr. He had

fought the effects of the vet's tranquilizer, leaping about the luggage, issuing continuous meows from his furry Persian throat, sounding like the Dew Drop's jazz vocalist. Then he had curled up on the back seat, in between a couple of suitcases. Asleep, he looked like a black funeral wreath.

Ellie retrieved a pack of sugarless gum from her purse and offered Peter a stick. He shook his head. "Can't drive and chew at the same time?" She waited for a snappy comeback. "Peter?"

"Sorry. My mind was wandering."

"Serafina Lassiter?"

"Who the hell is Serafina Lassiter?"

"The Olive Oyl woman." When Peter still looked perplexed, Ellie said, "The woman inside the Dew Drop restroom."

"Why would I be thinking of her? She started to pass out, clunked her chin against a sink, bit her tongue, and bled all over the place."

"That's her story."

"What's yours?"

"Her husband put something in her drink. She threw up. Then she staggered to the sink and—"

"Norrie, you've got a wonderful imagination. Annoying, but wonderful. Why would Lassiter put something in his wife's cocktail?"

"I don't know. Call it a gut feeling."

"Based on the fact that you didn't like Lassiter."

"Did you?"

"No. But I don't believe he tried to poison his wife."

"He paid the cocktail waitress to check on his wife . . . to find her dead body."

"He paid the waitress because he couldn't go into the ladies room himself."

"Okay, you're probably right. So, if you weren't thinking about Serafina Lassiter, were you thinking about Rudolph Kessler?"

"Not even close. I was pondering where to stop the car, unsnap your shirt, and strip off your jeans," he teased. "Until I realized your boots would be a deterrent."

She watched him try to simulate a leer, but the sun was in his eyes and the best he could come up with was Groucho's twitchy brows and Harpo's mischievous smile, as if Clark Gable had lobotomized into the Marx Brothers. Looking down at her squeaky-clean, blue-leather-and-suede cowboy boots, she arched one of her own auburn eyebrows. "You don't like my boots?"

"All they need is a set of spurs that jingle-jangle. They're so new they smell like—"

"Football pads," she said with a grin. "Your old sneakers are pungent. We can use one as a pacifier for Jackie Robinson when he wakes up. I wonder why he slashed half her face?"

"Who? Jackie Robinson?"

"Wait a sec. Which side of the face was slashed?"

"What are you talking about?"

"You know very well what I'm talking about. Rudolph Kessler's painting. The one you thought looked like me. Which side of the face was slashed?"

"The left side. Why?"

"According to Melody, Heather scarred the right side of her face."

"What does that have to do with—"

"The mirror."

"What? I don't think you can chew gum and talk at the same—"

"The mirror would have a reflection. Left would be

55

right. You said the painting was *Alice's Wonder Land*, the one with the mirror."

"I said too much last night. I started to un-stress with dreams of my first vacation in years. Then you told me you weren't wearing panties."

"I wasn't."

"Then you evolved into Sherlock Holmes."

"He didn't wear panties, either."

Peter downshifted. "You don't play fair."

"And *you* play naïve so people will feel secure and let stuff slip."

"Confession is good for the soul."

"But bad for the reputation."

"Do you want me to pull off the road and ravage your reputation?"

"With my luck we'd probably land in a patch of poison ivy. As soon as we arrive at the ranch, we'll initiate the bed."

"I doubt it." Peter winced as another bug spattered against the windshield. "Beth will be scanning the horizon."

"I can't wait to meet her. Does she look like you?"

"She shaved off her mustache a long time ago."

"I meant her hair and eyes."

"Yes, she has hair and eyes."

"Color, Peter. What color are *my* eyes?"

"The color of harebells."

"You just made that up."

"No, I didn't. If you search carefully along the side of the road, you might find them. A blue, bell-shaped flower with dark green stems."

"Nice, Peter. Thank you."

"You're welcome. Beth's eyes are blue and her hair's brown."

"How old are the kids?"

"Jonina's fifteen. Ryan's ten and Stevie's eight."

"Don't they have school?"

"The boys' school let out last week. Jonina will miss a few days, but she's so bright it doesn't matter. She's in honors everything and she's already aced her classes."

Ellie heard the pride in his voice. "Jonina," she said. "What a pretty name."

"She's named for her father, Jonah."

"You don't like your brother-in-law?"

"I didn't say that."

"You didn't have to."

"Jonah's a very successful defense attorney. A goodly percentage of his clients are freed on technicalities and his favorite word is 'feasible.' 'Isn't it *feasible* the defendant slept with the victim and left the apartment before she was killed?' 'Isn't it *feasible* the duffel bag contained something other than a dead body?' He keeps needling until a witness says, 'Sure, I guess so,' or the judge grimly shuts him down. By then, of course, it's too late. Jonah will use it in his closing argument. 'Did you hear the prosecution's expert witness says it's entirely possible he made a mistake? Reasonable doubt, ladies and gentlemen.' Jonah has the most phenomenal courtroom charisma I've ever seen. Juries love him. Cops don't. Are you ready for our pit stop? There's a nice restaurant, just off the next exit."

"Okay." She rolled up her window. "I wonder why Rudolph Kessler slashed the painting before he was killed?"

"He couldn't slash it *after* he was killed."

Peter parked the car. Locking the doors, he left a slice of window open for Jackie Robinson, who was still dead to the world.

# Six

After she and Peter had avidly consumed buffalo burgers, home fries, and garden salads with poppy-seed dressing, Peter fed the VW from a gas pump.

Once they were on the road again, Ellie tried again. "Why do you suppose Rudolph Kessler slashed his own painting?"

Peter wove one hand through his thick hair, a stall tactic. Finally he said, "Kessler went nuts after his wife's smash-up. You should have seen his house, a mess. And his wife could have resembled the woman in the painting."

"Did she?"

"No. Recent snapshots and neighbor-descriptions revealed that she had short grayish hair with a fringe across her forehead. But once upon a time she could have looked like—"

"You're not telling me something."

"Ellie, stop it. We're on vacation."

"Now I know you're holding back. You're calling me Ellie, which means you're angry. Soon you'll cuss."

He mumbled some colorful expletives under his breath. "You will not get involved in this case," he finally said. "Neither will I."

"I'm already involved. The killer slashed a painting that looked like *me*, Peter. If that doesn't make me involved, I don't know what does. Involved and—"

"Scared?"

"No. Curious. I like to solve puzzles quickly, otherwise the missing answers nag at me. Until I met you, I'd stay up until the wee hours of the morning so I could finish Sunday's *New York Times* crossword puzzle on Sunday."

"Monday, if it's the 'wee hours of the morning,' and I sincerely doubt the killer knew the woman in the painting looked like you."

"How can you be so sure?"

"I can't. But I'm sure of one thing. We will not play detective, sleazy or otherwise, while we're on vacation. Is that clear?"

"Very. Why do you think Kessler's death wasn't an accident?"

"My lips are sealed. If you try and wheedle like you did last night, I'll lose control of the car. Forget Kessler and tell me what's new with your son."

"How do you know something's new?"

"You're not the only sleuth in this relationship. You called to say goodbye, gave him the ranch's number, grinned like a mom, and wished him luck."

"It's supposed to be a secret, but I don't withhold information from *you*, Peter. Mick plans to buy Sandra an engagement ring, even though he says you'd need a magnifying glass to see the diamond. His song 'Unglued' is starting to really pick up steam and he's just written a new song. Sandra recorded it and this time they used lots of backup. Horns, strings, the whole nine yards. Was Rudolph Kessler's antique highboy heavy enough to kill him?"

"Yes."

"Did the neighbors see anyone lurking?"

"No."

"DNA?"

"Doubtful. Unless he or she drooled into a neighbor's refrigerated casserole."

"Fingerprints?"

"Look, Norrie, harebell flowers, the ones that match the color of your eyes."

"Aha. Whose fingerprints were on the murder weapon?"

"The murder weapon was a piece of furniture. Any prints belonged to Kessler and, I'd imagine, his deceased wife. Not to mention Jerry, the food delivery kid, who touched everything, including the highboy, before he puked all over the crime scene. The knife, which killed the painting not Kessler, was in Kessler's hand. The autopsy will tell how much alcohol Kessler had in his system, but the rooms were littered with beer cans and he had a lame leg, so he probably staggered against every object in the house, which would account for the welts—"

"What welts?"

"Kessler had bruises on his shoulders. They looked like cane welts. But the bruises could have been caused by something else, for instance his bamboo drapes."

"The drapes were dismantled?"

"No."

Ellie couldn't control her reaction. Her mouth opened and a rude sound emerged, not unlike a whale spouting spray. "Tell me about the fingerprints," she said, dismantling Peter's bamboo-drapes-theory.

"There were no prints. If you ask one more question, I'll stop the car and you can bloody well hike back to Colorado Springs."

"Don't be silly. How would you explain my disappearance to your sister and my cat? There were no fingerprints," she said, thinking out loud, "so the killer wiped something clean that should have had Kessler's prints on it. Right?"

"His cane." Maneuvering onto a dirt road, Peter turned the car's engine off. "There were no prints on Kessler's cane. According to all the neighbors, he could barely move without it."

"So the cane caused his welts."

"Yes, the cane caused his welts. But the cane didn't kill him."

"Sure it did, if he was trying to get away from the cane and stumbled against the highboy."

"Please, Ellie, I'm on vacation. Read my lips. It's not my case."

"Okay, let's reconstruct the scene. Messy house, heavy highboy, Kessler's cane. You said the knife was in Kessler's hand. Where was his cane?"

"I warned you. Get out of my car."

"It's not your car, it's Will McCoy's car, and without me it will be much more difficult to arrange a Garrett Halliday interview."

"What makes you think I plan to interview Halliday?"

"Come on, Peter. Even if it's not your case, the C.S.P.D. would want you to tie up any loose ends."

"Loose ends? Ellie, I love you, but you seem to think police work is like one of those bridge hands they print in the newspaper, on the same page as the astrology column. Make the correct bid, lead with the correct card, execute a tricky finesse, and everything else falls into place."

"You play bridge?"

He nodded, a curt, angry nod. "I don't need your artist friend. Kessler's wife was organized, kept receipts. I think she had one for a stateroom on Noah's ark."

"Very funny. Did Garrett write her a receipt?"

"Yes. But Kessler bought the painting at Spring Spree, long before Halliday became rich and famous. Kessler paid

fifty dollars, which turned out to be a phenomenal investment."

"Not if it caused his death. Did he know how valuable
the painting was?"

"Probably. A neighbor said Kessler's wife said it was
worth more than that 'artsy-fartsy stuff on *Wheel*'s wheel.' "

"*Wheel*'s wheel?"

"That TV quiz show. Wheel of something. Wealth."

"*Fortune*, Peter. Tony was such an addict, we'd eat
supper in front of the TV. He hated it when I guessed the
puzzle after three or four letters, so I learned to keep my
mouth shut. Then Tony stopped coming home for meals
and I swore I'd never play dummy again, except when I play
bridge."

"And you've kept your vow. Don't forget, I've seen you
play *Jeopardy!* You really should try out for the show."

"Nonsense. I'd never be able to press that buzzer gizmo
fast enough. Maybe Kessler tried to sell the painting. He
opened his door to a stranger, who then stole . . . why
didn't the killer steal the painting?"

"Kessler nailed its frame to a wall stud."

"Why didn't the killer cut the canvas out of the frame?"

"It looked as if he wanted to, but the canvas was heavy
sailcloth, the knife a serrated steak knife, and the grocery
delivery kid was practically kicking the door down. I think
the killer ran out of time."

"May I assume you're checking classified ads and
Kessler's phone records?"

"I'm not checking anything. I'm on vacation. Stop
snooping, Ellie, and stop puckering. I'm mad. I want to stay
mad."

"Of course you do." Leaning sideways, still puckering,
she kissed his mustache, then traced his lips with her

tongue. Her hands roamed as she said, "Do you know how many years it's been since I made out in a car?"

"I'm fairly certain it was before Perry Como."

"Low blow, Lieutenant. I love western shirts. You don't have to fiddle with buttons. Snaps are so much quicker."

"Get your hands away from there. Watch out for the steering wheel. Put your hands back."

"You told me to take them away."

"Since when do you listen to anything I say? Seriously, if you ask one more Kessler-question, I'll drive to the top of Independence Pass, toss you over the precipice, and watch you fall head over heels—"

"In love. What are you doing with *your* hands?"

"Unsnapping."

# Seven

Ellie clutched the car's door handle so hard her knuckles whitened. "Falling," she sang, "*fall*ing in love."

The black and white magpies trilled with laughter and flapped their wings—a flying ovation.

Screw the magpies. If she didn't sing, she'd throw up. Or throw down.

Down had taken on a new meaning. According to Peter, they were only halfway across Independence Pass. Already, her stomach felt like a roller coaster. The kind of roller coaster that goes loop-the-loop. The kind that inches up, then, without warning, descends at a breathless pace. The kind where the carny guy doesn't believe you when you shout you're about to fall out. Or pass out. Or drop dead. Or drop down. Or throw up.

Peter and the carny guy were kindred spirits.

She fingered the talisman that swung from her neck. Yesterday she had abandoned her half-packed suitcase to visit an apothecary shop, run by a bona fide witch. The shop's proprietor, Sydney St. Charles, had recommended two amulets. Ellie didn't care for the first amulet's illustration, a flaming eye. Its invocation, however, would have kept her Safe From All Harm. The second talisman, For Warmth and Well-Being, depicted the head of a fox against a flame-spiked background. The other side of the disk stated: *Now these together run red; Man, fire, fox, sun, blood.*

She loved the fox.

Her witch-visit had been an impulse, generated by visions of fierce stallions with fierce, cloven hooves. But at this very moment, crossing Independence Pass, she was glad she had bought the well-being charm, even though the safe-from-all-harm charm might have been a tad more practical.

"Independence Pass opened last week," Peter said, shifting into second gear. "They close it for the winter, you know."

"I don't know." She fondled her fox necklace, dangling from a black shoelace. "I've never been to Aspen. A pass means to transfer a football to your teammate. Doesn't it also mean to come to an end?"

"What's your point?"

"This isn't a pass. It's a goat trail. I feel like Heidi. Heidi with breasts. Look at that sign. 'Narrow Road.' What road?"

"Relax. I gave you fair warning. We should have sedated you with wine."

"I'm not afraid of dying, Peter. I'm scared of falling."

"The altitude's only twelve thousand or so feet. Open your eyes. The scenery's beautiful."

"When I open my eyes I feel dizzy."

"Okay. Keep them closed."

"When they're closed I feel dizzy."

"Make up your mind."

"I can't." Because her mind was roller-coastering along with her stomach. If she opened her eyes, she saw sun-blurred, miniature pine trees, their distant branches beckoning. If she squeezed her eyes shut, she saw her body impaled on those same spike-infested treetops.

"Peter," she said, "I have to pee."

"There's no bathroom before the summit and I can't pull over to the side of the road."

"What side of the road? It's a sheer drop." Ellie squinted through her thick lashes. "You're right, the scenery's beautiful. And the air smells like iced coffee."

"You said spring smelled like bleached sheets."

"It's not spring anymore. Look at that leftover snow. Maybe it will cushion my fall," she said, her breath catching in her throat. "Oh, God, are those really bikers riding toward us? Do they have a death wish?"

"Do you? Stop clutching the door handle."

"Keep your eyes on the road! I have to clutch something. You're driving and Jackie Robinson's asleep. This is God's punishment for breaking my diet, eating a buffalo, not to mention greasy fries."

"I won't mention the fries if you won't."

"I'm belching buffalo, Peter."

"I told you, there's no restroom. If you have to whoops, lean your head out the window."

"Lean? No way. I'd be sucked out." She raised her eyes heavenward, saw the car's ragtop, and felt a hiccup rise in her throat. "God, *hic,* are you there? Oh, God, *hic,* now he's patting my shoulder. Not you, God, Peter. Dammit, Peter, keep your hands on the, *hic,* steering wheel and your eyes on the, *hic,* road!"

"You've got hiccups, Norrie."

"No, *hic,* kidding. I get hiccups when I'm scared, or did you, *hic,* forget?"

"I don't believe this. You've faced vicious killers and you're scared of a drive through the mountains?"

"We're not driving through. We're teetering on the, *hic,* edge."

Teetering was an understatement. Ellie could smell

empty air. True, she'd faced vicious killers during the diet club murders and the M*A*S*H murders, but they were nothing compared to this hell, this purgatory of endless, bottomless space, topped by a ribbon-thin line of tarred highway.

Correction. The vast expanse below wasn't bottomless, not even close.

Close, hah! The bottom was far, far away, even though a fall might swiftly shorten the gap. Fliers wore parachutes and boaters wore life jackets, but she didn't have any protection, not even a bungee cord.

"I should have packed a bungee cord," Peter said, reading her mind and patting her shoulder.

"Keep your hands on the steering wheel! I'll be good, *hic*, I promise. I won't interfere in your, *hic*, homicide cases. I'll take my vitamins and double up on calcium, *hic*, and I'll eat that awful bran cereal. Roughage, *hic*. I'll eat spinach every day until I look like, *hic*, Popeye. Popeye with, *hic*, breasts. Are we on the other side of the pass? Are we finally at the bottom?"

"Yup. Welcome to Aspen, Norrie."

She took a deep, hiccup-free breath and said, "Welcome to Aspen, goats and monkeys."

# Eight

No longer frightened, Ellie's felt her hiccups evaporate and her desire to urinate slack off.

"Goats and monkeys?" Peter quirked an eyebrow.

"I'm paraphrasing Shakespeare. He was writing about Cyprus, but after Independence Pass, goats and monkeys seem apropos. Oh, honey, Aspen's beautiful. The sky's so blue and the grass is so green."

"Mountain run-off. Aspen turns green when the rest of Colorado is just beginning to sprout."

"I wish I could sprout wings and take in the whole view, all at once. It was a wonderful idea, vacationing here. I'm going to forget all about Rudolph Kessler, even though there were no prints on his cane and . . . what are you doing?"

"Making a U-turn. Would you like to drive across the pass again?"

"No. Wait. Please. I'll be good. Aspen's so lovely. When I die, I want my ashes scattered over Aspen."

"I thought you wanted your ashes scattered during a Broncos game so the Broncos will be *fired* up and score touchdowns." A Raiders fan, Peter chuckled at his own pun.

As he drove toward Snowmass, she lapsed into silence. Holy cow, they'd have to cross the pass again in order to get home. Maybe she'd take Peter up on his offer to sedate her with wine. Maybe she'd share Jackie Robinson's tranquilizers.

*I won't think about the drive home. I'll just enjoy myself, goof off, have a great time. And I won't worry about broncos, the four-legged species that can't fit into shoulder pads or jockstraps. After all, a horse is a horse, of course—*

"Peter?"

"Yes?"

"How long have you been riding? I once saw equestrian trophies on a shelf in your office."

"When my sister and I were little, we lived on a ranch. Beth rides like the wind. You should see her take jumps."

"Jumps? Oh, God, here we go again. I can visualize myself falling."

"Me, too. Falling in love."

"I thought you already fell," she said with mock indignation.

"I did, the first time we met. You were eating an apple."

"*You* were eating an apple."

"A Granny Smith. You pestered me with questions."

"You pestered *me*."

"Questions, questions, all the time questions." He sighed. "But love is blind."

"And deaf."

"What did you say?"

"I said I love you, Lieutenant darling. You're such a smartass and you have trophies so you must 'ride good.' "

"You should know, sweetheart," he said, very Bogart, Humphrey to Lauren.

"I'm going to fall off," she said, very un-Bacall.

"Trust me. I'll help you back on." Peter drove through an entrance, beneath a rustic wooden sign lettered LONESOME PI ES. "Welcome to Lonesome Pines,

Norrie, even though one 'N' seems to be missing. It's about a mile to the main ranch house and guest cottages."

"Where's Gene Autry with his guitar? I'll bet the stars at night are big and bright."

"Are you making fun of the name Lonesome Pines? What about your friend Charley's Dew Drop Inn?"

"Sorry. I'm a city gal, Peter. I can change a tire, but I never learned how to nail a horseshoe. The closest I came was that Longfellow poem, you know, the one about the village smithy. Holy cow, is that your sister? On top of a horse?"

"Yup."

Ellie watched a tall woman slide her belly along the saddle until her boot-clad feet touched the ground. Then she ran toward the car.

Peter braked, turned the ignition key, and was out the door before the engine's Volksy wheeze had died down.

"You smell like horse," he said, giving his sister a bone-crushing hug.

"You smell onion-y." She turned her face toward Ellie. "How can you kiss a man who nibbles onions like peanuts?"

Peter's sister's voice was low, husky. Her horse seemed to be listening, its ears flickering, and the words *horse whisperer* flashed through Ellie's mind. So did the words *man listener*. While Peter's sister wasn't blatantly sexy, her voice was.

"I'm Elizabeth," she continued, lighting a cigarette, "Beth to my friends. Please call me Beth. May I call you Ellie?"

"Of course." Ellie dismounted, so to speak, from the car. "Or you can call me Norrie. Your brother coined the nickname. He says I ignore his advice."

Beth laughed and said, "I like this one, Pete."

*This one?*

"Beth, do you mind if Norrie and I check in? We have a sedated cat and . . ." Pausing, Peter looked at Ellie and winked. "My girl here wants to listen to Gene Autry records." He glanced over his shoulder. "Before I forget, the 'N' is missing from the Lonesome Pines sign. For a moment there, I thought we'd be staying at Lonesome Pies."

If Peter's hand-through-hair was a stall tactic, his sister's smoking achieved the same purpose. She took several deep drags on her cigarette, blowing smoke out through her nose and mouth. Finally she said, "Somebody's been stealing letters, Pete. So far, we've had to replace the 'I' and the 'P' and one 'E.' " She stared at the red convertible. "Is that new?"

"It's not mine. I borrowed it from my partner."

"What a pretty car. Introduce me to your partner."

"He's married, Beth."

"So am I." She shrugged. "By the way, Mike Urvant has settled in South Dakota. Permanently. Duke Dombroski's in charge now. Remember him?"

"Big grizzly bear of a man? John Wayne fetish?"

She nodded. "Duke's up at the main house, waiting to show you and Norrie around. He's made some major changes. I'm talking indoor swimming pool, sauna, new barn. His work's paid dividends. Except for off-season, this place is booked months in advance. Oh, I'd better warn you. We've got one 'unauthorized' guest. She's from your neck of the woods. Martina Brustein, the romance author. She writes under the name Marty Blue."

"I've read her. I mean, I've read her romantic suspense novels." Ellie felt her cheeks bake. "She's somewhat raunchy, but if you skim over the sex scenes you'll find a

71

nice mystery. Not that I ever skimmed. Why is she unauthorized?"

"Technically, Lonesome Pines closes down in May so the staff can make repairs. Martina's using the ranch as a retreat, to write her next book. We rarely, if ever, see her, not even at meals. She prefers to eat alone, inside her cottage, but I'm fairly certain she'll come out of hiding next Friday when Duke throws his annual barbecue. No one can think, much less write, during that ruckus."

Peter groaned. "I forgot about the barbecue. Maybe Norrie and I can catch a quiet war movie in Asp—"

"No way, Mr. Antisocial! That's not fair to 'your girl.' The ranch will be loaded with superstars." Beth crushed her cigarette beneath a boot heel, then crooked her arm through Ellie's. "Richard Gere, for one. You'll probably rub shoulders with Adrianna Bouchet, the infamous Canadian figure skater. And Garrett Halliday, Aspen's Andy Warhol."

" 'In the future everyone will be famous for fifteen minutes,' " Ellie quoted.

"Warhol didn't know Garrett Halliday when he said that." Beth folded a stick of green gum and shoved it into her mouth. She chewed avidly, just before she said, "Garrett's been quoted more times than Paris, Britney, and the Donald put together. Aspenites worship the water he walks on. I mean, the snow he skis on."

"You sound awfully sarcastic," Peter said.

"Do I, Pete?" Beth looked as if she craved another cigarette. She chewed her gum faster. "If you want my opinion," she said, "Garrett's mouth is going to get him in big trouble someday."

"Forget mouths." Peter slid onto the front seat of the convertible. "Norrie prefers tight butts."

"Tight butts?"

"I've known Garrett Halliday for years, Beth. I think your brother might be jealous, although I've told him that Heather has captured Garrett's heart completely." When there was no response, Ellie said, "Aren't they still in love?"

"It's been ages since anyone's seen Heather. Except for Garrett's paintings, she doesn't exist."

"Oh, she exists. According to my friend Melody, Heather helped plan Garrett's Colorado Springs art exhibit."

"Hop in, Norrie," Peter said. "See you later, Beth."

While Peter navigated curves, Ellie admired the landscape, dotted with distant livestock, mostly horses. She remembered family excursions when she and her brother, Tab, had stared out the back of their mom's station wagon, playing count-the-cows. One moo-moo, two moo-moos, three moo-moos—

"Holy cow, Peter, there goes your sister."

"She's headed toward the barn. I wish she'd slow down."

"Why? She seems to enjoy riding."

"Beth enjoys everything," he said. "Riding, reading, gardening, gourmet cooking, you name it."

"She sounds perfect."

"No. She's not perfect. For example, years ago she had an affair with Mike Urvant, the man who owns this place. He was a rodeo star, a big buckaroo with big bucks."

"Why didn't she marry him?"

"She was already married."

"Oh."

"Don't get me wrong. Beth wanted to divorce Jonah and marry Mike, but Mike didn't want to get 'branded.' He gave her the old heave-ho. Beth was miserable. And furious. My sister has one mean temper."

Peter's eyes gleamed with memories. "Beth broke a plastic ukulele over my head because I said she was too little to play my guitar. Then there was the time she took all the boards out of my bunk bed. I slept on top and—"

"What happened?"

"I sprained my wrist."

"No, I mean what happened to Beth and Mike?"

"Beth reconciled with Jonah. They moved from Boulder to Denver, where she became the perfect wife and mother."

"And Mike?"

"He met with a freak rodeo accident, screwed up his back, and built this ranch. Karma, Norrie, just like your friend Adrianna."

"She's not my friend. Wait a sec. You play the guitar?"

"Yup. Brace yourself, sweetheart, we're here."

Before she could decipher his enigmatic "brace yourself," Peter had parked and dismounted from the car. Ellie dismounted, too. Then Peter palmed her elbow and led her toward the manager's office.

A middle-aged man leaned against a porch post. Ellie would be willing to bet that he had once been attractive but had let himself go to seed. His belt buckle dented his gut, which hung, like a suspended basketball, above his belt. Beneath his eyes were miniature saddlebags. His beard tried, unsuccessfully, to hide a double chin, and his fingers looked like bratwurst sausages.

She cursed her sensitive nose. He smelled as if he bathed every Saturday night, whether he needed it or not. Thank God today was Saturday.

"So you're Pete's little lady," he said. "Welcome to Lonesome Pines, Mrs. Miller."

"Ms. Bernstein."

"You and Pete ain't hitched?"

74

"No." Had she possessed hackles, Ellie would have felt them rise.

"Well, shoot," Duke Dombroski said. "I can tie the knot, little lady. All Pete hasta do is rope ya. Then I can brand ya."

Grinning from ear to ear, he nudged *Pete* with an elbow.

Had she been a porcupine, Ellie would have released her sharp, erectile bristles.

# Nine

Without lifting a finger, Duke Dombroski shifted a toothpick from one side of his mouth to the other. "I'm a minister," he said. "On the side."

*And I solve murders,* Ellie thought, *on the side.*

"I'm in the food business," she said, borrowing her mother's phraseology. Her mother couldn't come to terms with Ellie's diet club affiliation. Lecturing for Weight Winners was too inglorious, too plebeian. Also, a dieter would have to allow for, and/or admit to, imperfections.

On the other hand, "amateur sleuth" was okay, a genteel diversion. So was "mystery author." Mom adored Mary Higgins Clark, whom she'd met at a book signing. "A real lady," Mom had said, "and slender. You could learn a thing or two from her, Ellie."

Would Mom regard Rudolph Kessler's antique highboy as a genteel killer? Sure she would. And the slashed canvas would be categorized as an elite crime.

That train of thought derailed when Ellie heard the trills from her black and white magpies, which had followed her all the way from Colorado Springs. Bringing her attention back to the ranch manager, she watched him take off his cowboy hat and scratch his flattened Grey Poupon hair. His body emitted a sound. Flatulence? Muted wind chimes?

To her surprise, he fished a cell phone from his jeans pocket. It was like watching Gary Cooper reach for a cel-

lular phone during a pivotal scene in *High Noon*, except Dombroski outweighed Cooper by a hundred pounds and no matter how much weight Ellie lost, she'd never be mistaken for Grace Kelly.

She recalled a couple of lines from Longfellow's poem. " 'The smith, a mighty man is he,' " she muttered, watching Dombroski walk a few paces away. " 'With large and sinewy hands. And the muscles of his brawny arms. Are strong as iron bands.' "

Peter nodded and grinned, apparently relieved that she hadn't responded to the ranch manager's machismo attitude with anything more acerbic than Longfellow, who wasn't acerbic at all.

From beneath lowered lashes, Ellie studied Duke Dombroski. Peter had said something about a John Wayne fetish, but Dombroski didn't look anything like his hero. His beard had the consistency of a Brillo pad. He sported a defensive linesman's neck and Santa's jelly-belly. Bowed legs ended in boots that smelled like fertilizer.

Making an about-face, he returned the phone to his pocket. "That was Mike Urvant," he told Peter. "Remember him?"

"Yup."

Peter's brusque reply sounded okay, but Ellie saw him tense.

"Mike's on the road, headed toward Denver," Dombroski said, walking forward. "He might drop by for a spell, but he might not. Mike's what'cha'macallit . . . notional."

Peter nodded. "Where was he calling from?"

Dombroski shrugged. "I didn't ask." The hand that had scratched his hair now scratched under one armpit. "Do you and your little lady want to see the new barn and pool?"

"No." Peter shook his head, as if to clear away cobwebs.

"No, thanks. I want to get Ms. Bernstein settled in first."

"Oh, for goodness sake," Ellie almost hissed. "Kill the Ms. Bernstein. You too, Mr. Dombroski. Call me Ellie. Or Norrie, if you prefer."

"Call me Duke, Miss Norrie. I've given you a cottage near the main house and dining hall. Don't make no sense hikin' a far piece for grub." He focused on Peter again. "Reckoned you two was married good and proper, Pete, so there's only one bed."

"No problem. I'll sleep on the floor."

*In your dreams,* Ellie thought.

"I've been dying to ride," Peter said, and this time his voice sounded earnest.

Duke flung a glance over his shoulder, as if the barn was inside the house rather than behind it. "Stable's brand-spankin' new, Pete, slicked up ya might say."

"Do you still have Blackie?"

"Yep. But he's old and ornery. Mike wants him retired before we get sued by some tight-assed spinster who don't know a horse's tail from his mane, 'scuse the cuss Miss Norrie. We have Blackie's son, Satan."

*Satan?* Ellie felt her face blanch. *Oh, God.*

"Satan ain't saddle-broke," Duke continued. "Wranglers won't touch him with a ten foot pole. Don't want you tryin' neither, Pete, and that's an order. Mike's got a bronc buster in mind."

Duke's toothpick surfed his lips. "We got Blackie's daughter, too. She's a pint-sized filly, smart and dainty-gaited, but don't let that fool ya. She's wild natured, just like her pa. We named her Lucy, short for Lucifer. Can't call no gal Lucifer, though it sometimes fits, if ya get my gist." An elbow-nudge followed. Then, just in case Peter didn't get the gist or the nudge, Duke said, "You know, *hot.*

I'll have Kit Halliday saddle up Lucy for your little lady, whensoever y'all get booted and spurred."

At least Duke kept calling her little, Ellie thought. A few years ago he might have called her Pete's roly-poly lady.

Holy cow. Spurred? Was that cowboy-speak or did Duke mean it?

"Better not saddle up Lucy," Peter said. "Norrie's a beginner."

"She don't ride?"

"I've taught her the fundamentals."

Right, Ellie thought. The tub. The bed. The tub again. Peter didn't rib-nudge so Duke didn't catch the innuendo.

"Kit Halliday," she said, shading her eyes from the setting sun. "Is he Garrett Halliday's, um, kin?"

"*She's* his niece. Lives with him and his brother, her father, in Aspen. Best ridin' instructor there ever was, even if she *is* a damn petticoat, beggin' your pardon for the cuss Miss Norrie. Kit's got a knack for healin' sick horses, which saves on vet bills. Mike doubled her salary and gave her a cottage, though she don't need the money or the cottage, stayin' with her uncle and all. Shucks, she's even got one of them swanky downtown lofts in Colorada Springs. She shares the place with . . ." He scratched his head again. "Some gal . . . funny name . . . Moony, that's it, same as Loretta Lynn's hubby. Lucky for Mike and me Kit don't go there much. Too bad we'll lose her when she gets hitched."

As Duke paused for breath, Ellie said, "She's engaged?"

"Nope. But I reckon she will be soon. She's a young filly, dainty-gaited and wild-natured like Lucy, and she's sure to hook up with one of her uncle's fancy dudes."

*Fancy dudes?* Ellie stifled a snort inside a cough. No way would Heather allow any lady killers hanging round. Heather wasn't a prude. Fair-minded in her sympathies, tastes, and interests, she was catholic. But she was also Catholic. Like Ellie, Heather had endured a rigorous religious upbringing. Unlike Ellie, Heather had never strayed very far from Church precepts.

"Mike bought a new Maytag, Pete," Duke said, "so Miss Norrie can warsh her unmentionables and your skivvies. And there's one of them newfangled steam-irons in your suit."

Ellie hadn't heard a suite called a suit since her Uncle Fred emigrated from Hungary and worked the swing shift at a Holiday Inn. Every year Uncle Fred would come for Thanksgiving dinner. Looking more like a maitre d' than a desk clerk, he'd chuck Ellie under the chin and comment approvingly on the pounds she had gained. To Uncle Fred, weight equaled prosperity. Until he married a skinny Denver debutante. He stopped coming for Thanksgiving dinner and Ellie missed the goulash he contributed. Thanksgiving just wasn't Thanksgiving without Hungarian goulash.

"Supper's served at six-thirty sharp," Duke added. "See ya then." Tipping his hat brim, he navigated the porch and walked inside the house, the screen door whining behind him.

Peter strolled toward the car. Facing him, Ellie walked backwards, her stomach churning. Only this time the vinegary agent was indignation rather than indigestion.

"There's a hint of smoke coming out of your ears," he said, "and your harebell eyes are mere slits."

"Chauvinistic buzzard!"

"Aw, c'mon, you're overreacting."

"Am I? Do you know what the great John Wayne himself once said about liberated women? 'They have a right to work whenever they want to as long as they have dinner

80

ready when you get there.' By the way, where did Duke get the impression we were hitched?" She watched Peter shrug his broad shoulders, looking even broader in his snappy cowboy shirt. "You made the reservations, Lieutenant. Didn't you use both our names?"

"No. We're sharing a cottage. What's the damn difference?"

"We're sharing a *suit,* and the damn difference is that for years I was Mrs. Anton Bernstein, Tony's wife. I wasn't Ellie. Or Eleanor Maiden Name Bernstein. Back then, people rarely hyphenated their last names, not that Tony would have hyphenated." She heaved an exasperated sigh. "Why can't you understand? I've grown up, declared my independence, and now I want to be me."

"You are you. Why can't you be Eleanor Maiden Name Miller and still be you? I wouldn't mind being hyphenated."

"It doesn't work that way, Peter. If we were married, you'd trot off to your precinct every day—"

"A horse trots."

"Okay, *drive* to your precinct while I vegged at home, reading mysteries, solving crossword puzzles, defrosting lamb chops, Maytagging skivvies, and gaining weight."

"Don't compare me to your ex-husband."

"Who should I compare you to? Duke Dombroski? John Wayne? And please don't freeze your jaw like that."

"This vacation is off to a great start. Would you like to carry the luggage, Ms. Independent, while I retrieve your cat and defrost my chops?"

"Fine." Grabbing two suitcases and a laptop computer, she staggered down the path, kicked open the cottage door with one foot, entered, and glanced around.

Although the outside was Abe-Lincoln-log-cabin, the inside looked bright and . . . *charming* was the first word that came to mind. Yellow dotted Swiss covered a couple of windows. Near the fireplace, wood had been neatly stacked. Polished steer horns hung above the mantel. A plush cinnamon-colored couch and matching chair dominated a multi-hued looped rug, while a TV and VCR sat on top of a triple-tiered bookcase. A teacart sported an automatic coffee maker and microwave. The east wall proudly displayed a cuckoo clock and a framed portrait of John Wayne, painted on black velvet.

Walking into the bedroom, Ellie gasped with delight. A calico-cushioned rocker paid tribute to a scrap of cowhide. More dotted Swiss, lavender this time, curtained a huge picture window. The light fixture was an old wagon wheel, its bulbs encased in glass candle holders. A cherry-wood dresser smelled like furniture oil, and the queen-size bed possessed a divine-looking mattress. Dropping her suitcases, placing her laptop computer and cell phone on top of a bedside table, Ellie admired an angel with spread wings, carved into the bed's headboard.

Across from the bed, directly above an old-fashioned, stork-embossed water bowl and pitcher, hung a Garrett Halliday painting, the initials G.H. eclipsing one corner. The painting depicted a flame-haired woman clad in a sheer negligee. She stood, one leg raised, her trim ankle resting on the edge of a table. It had to be Heather—Heather washing her toes. In the painting, next to a white water pitcher, a vase held an abundance of raffish, buoyant flowers and herbs. The blossoms were depicted with minimal brush strokes, yet Ellie could almost swear she smelled flowers. And herbs.

A small, engraved plaque underneath the painting gave its title: *Thyme for Rosemary's Lavation.*

"Like it?" Peter asked. He had taken off his sneakers before entering the cottage and his arms were filled with a droopy Jackie Robinson.

"Yes. Oh, yes. That crusty old Duke couldn't have decorated these rooms."

"Nope. My sister did."

"I should have guessed. That's why we have carte blanche during off season."

"Yup." Stepping closer, Peter scrutinized the painting. "Yesterday, when I called Beth, she said she bought two Garrett Halliday paintings from Kit Halliday, both at reasonable prices." He stared at the extravagant initials as if he'd never seen them before and Ellie could have sworn she saw a small crease form between his eyes. "I'm not sure what constitutes 'reasonable,' " he added with a lop-sided grin.

"Aha! You called Beth. What happened to 'it's not my case'?"

"It's not. My phone call to Beth was my last 'official' phone call. As soon as I stepped outside the precinct door, our vacation started." He placed the cat on the cushioned rocker. "Take off those boots, Norrie, then your jeans."

"Now? It's only an hour until supper. Don't you want me to Maytag your skivvies?"

"I'll 'warsh' them tomorrow. I'll even Maytag your unmentionables." Cradling Ellie's face with his palms, he tongue-tickled the roof of her mouth.

"Your sister's right," she said, retreating from his lips and tongue. "You do taste onion-y. I didn't notice it before, when my butt was wedged between bucket seats and you were whispering sweet Willie Nelsons in my ear. I really must shower, honey. Damn, my zipper's stuck. Please help me with my zipper."

He placed his hands behind his back. "Are you my little lady?"

"That's blackmail, Peter. Never mind. I'll be anything you want me to be, if you unzip my jeans. I smell like Duke's boots."

"Let's shower together. I'll wear my 'skivvies' so you won't be tempted to break your token vow of chastity."

"After dinner I'll break, and that's a promise."

"You don't have to break, sweetheart. Just bend a little."

# Ten

The dining hall was rustic—pine wood floors, walls, side-boards, tables and chairs. A beaver would OD, thought Ellie. There were many planked tables, but the small group only used two; one for the adults and one for the children. The latter was enhanced, or safeguarded, by a red and white checkered oilcloth that smelled like . . . oilcloth. Sour milk. Sauerkraut. A hint of ammonium hydroxide. And something even stronger; something that most likely included the instructions: "Flush eyes with water. Call a physician if irritation persists."

Ellie sat between Duke and Peter, across from Beth. Duke had bathed, thank goodness. She pictured him in the tub, his thick fingers wrapped around a long-handled scrub brush, a rubber ducky blockaded by his belly. She'd have to use that image in her mystery novel, assuming she ever got back to writing the damn thing.

Wearing a flowered skirt and a white T-shirt, both circled by a turquoise-studded belt, Beth didn't look like the woman who'd met her brother's convertible. Her milk chocolate hair, damp from a shower, cascaded down her back in clusters of thick, carefully combed tangles. Her blue eyes were enhanced by black kohl, smudged just right, and her luxurious lashes were to die for.

Next to Beth sat Marion Dombroski, Duke's twenty-something son. Marion was around five-ten, his body lean, his muscles ropy rather than sinewy. Beneath dark, angel-winged brows, his eyes were the same shade as his long, coffee bean colored hair. He had an aristocratic nose with small, neat nostrils. His cupid-bow mouth could have been effeminate. Instead, it was sensual and softened his other features. Ellie knew that "Marion" was John Wayne's given name, but she wondered why Marion Dombroski had never opted for a nickname.

Peter studied an empty chair and place setting next to Marion. Then he focused on Beth. "Okay, sis, the kids are all accounted for, but where's Jonah?"

"I would guess he's giving an impassioned summation to a jury."

"On a Saturday night?"

"Oh, right, it's Saturday. In that case, he's probably asleep in front of the TV, watching the Colorado Rockies get their butts kicked."

"There's that sarcasm again. What's going on?"

"Not now, Pete. Good grief, Jonina, stop scowling and sit down."

Ellie slanted a glance toward Peter's niece. Her body had been stuffed into a pair of too-tight designer jeans, the pregnant pockets embroidered with Pooh, Tigger, and a mournful Eeyore.

*Jonina should have worn a skirt like her mother's or jeans that fit,* Ellie thought, experiencing a pang of empathy. Throughout her childhood she had tried to stuff her body into clothes that were trendy rather than flattering. Jonina's budding breasts were beautifully sculpted, but even underneath a denim shirt, her pink elasticized halter emphasized every ounce of additional pudge.

"Why can't I sit next to Uncle Pete?" she whined, finger-combing her bangs away from her forehead. "I don't want

86

to eat at the children's table."

"You're still a child, kiddo," Beth said.

"I am not. Ryan and Stevie finger-paint with their food. They're disgusting."

"Hush, Jonina." Beth's first finger punctuated the air.

"Marion agrees with me, don't you Marion?" Jonina directed her appeal toward the only adult who was even remotely close to her age. When he just shrugged, she said, "I could use that empty chair and sit across from Uncle Pete. Please? Pretty please? With sugar on top?"

"That chair's for Kit Halliday," said Duke. "Maybe she hightailed it over to her uncle's house. Just the same, we'd better wait and see. Kit knew you'd blow in today, Pete, but I told her you got yourself bait-fed and hooked, thinkin' you and Miss Norrie was hitched, so she might be feelin' distressed. Here comes the food. Don't it smell good?"

Despite the ranch manager's John Wayne-ish chitchat, Ellie—who had never been called bait in her life—blushed. At the same time, she wondered why a hooked Peter might distress a young, dainty-gaited, wild-natured Kit Halliday.

Shifting her gaze away from Duke, Ellie watched a plump woman set out heaping platters of mashed potatoes, lima beans, buttered corn, steaming biscuits, and fried chicken. A mental calculator clicked calories until it short-circuited.

Up until now she had always been able to find "legal" food at any dinner table, even restaurants. A dude ranch meant hearty fare, she wasn't that naïve, but if tonight's spread was customary, sticking to her Weight Winners program would be virtually impossible.

Just like her brother, Beth metabolized by chewing.

So, apparently, did Marion.

Ellie said, "Do you have any salad in the kitchen, Mr. Dombroski? Lettuce? Tomatoes? Carrots? How about apples? Horses eat carrots and apples, don't they?"

"Call me Duke. You one of them veggie-tarians, Miss Norrie?"

"No . . . I . . . fried chicken isn't really on my die . . . um, food program. I'm sorry to be such a picky eater."

Jonina, now seated, tossed her brown, sun-streaked ponytail. "If Norrie doesn't have to eat, neither do I."

"I told you to hush," Beth said. "And it's Ms. Bernstein, not Norrie."

"Norrie's okay, Beth." Ellie stabbed a chicken breast with her fork, stripped the skin, and nibbled Crisco-saturated white meat.

"Tomorrow we'll drive to Aspen for dinner," Peter whispered. "Seafood, omelets, anything your heart desires."

"Thanks, honey, you're sweet," she whispered back, "but I stashed some 'legal' snacks inside my suitcase, just in case."

From the corner of her eye, she saw Jonina shovel food into her mouth, her fork rising and falling rhythmically, her cheeks expanding like a chipmunk's, her face pink-patched from the effort of trying to swallow without chewing.

*A Weight Winners candidate,* Ellie thought. *No. I'm on vacation. Jonina's weight problem is none of my business. I'm not some born again loser.*

"Disney's showing a special on Celine Dion," Ryan said. Tall for ten, he had his mother's blue eyes and his Uncle Peter's midnight hair. "Do you got cable, Mr. Duke?"

"Have, not got," Beth said, her voice weary.

"No, son," Duke replied. "There's too much cussin' on cable. Anyone who wants to hear swear words can rent themselves a movie at the video store. Others can borrow a movie from the office. We got John Wayne, Shirley Temple, Roy Rogers and the like. If movies ain't your cup of tea, we got checkers, cards, arcade games, and—"

"Me and Stevie played games all day. Let's go home, Mom."

"Stevie and *I*, Ryan, and it's very rude to interrupt. Say you're sorry to Mr. Dombroski."

"SorryMisterDombroski," the boy recited, his apology one word.

"Now," said Beth, "eat your supper."

"I don't like it."

"You haven't even tasted it. You like Kentucky Fried Chicken, don't you? Tonight we're eating Colorado Fried Chicken. Look at your sister. She's already helped herself to seconds."

Ellie stifled a groan. Before leaving Lonesome Pines, she'd have a talk with Beth. At age fifteen, Jonina was impressionable and she sought kudos from her mom. Surely Beth could channel praise for Jonina's appetite into praise for sports or creative endeavors or physical attributes. The girl's golden-brown hair was lovely and she had her uncle's soft, blue-gray eyes and—damn! Ellie had known Peter's family less than one hour and already she was kibitzing.

Marion ate quickly, his gaze straying toward Kit Halliday's empty chair. Nobody talked about the riding instructor's absence, but Ellie, for one, noted Marion's range of expressions—feigned indifference, anger, despair. Then, without saying a word, he left the room.

Beth pushed her food around her plate while Peter watched.

Stevie, a freckle-faced, sandy-haired sprite, spilled his glass of milk. White liquid hopscotched the oilcloth and splashed onto Jonina's shirt. She jumped up, overturning her chair.

"Stevie did that on purpose!" she screamed. "And Ryan only said he wanted to watch Celine Dion because I said it first. He doesn't even know who she is."

"Yes, I do. She sang the Titanic song. She also sang 'bout Beauty and Robby Benson."

"Beast. The Beast, not Robby Benson."

"You think you're so smart, fatso. Robby Benson played the Beast."

"It's a cartoon, Ryan. Real people aren't in cartoons."

"What about Roger Rabbit? He's in a cartoon with real people."

"The penguins in that Mary Pockets movie danced with real people," Stevie said.

"Poppins." Ryan scowled. "How many times have I told you it's Poppins, not Pockets?"

"I wanted to stay home and Daddy said I could," Jonina cried, stung by her brothers' accuracy. "I hate you, Mom." Abruptly, she raced from the room.

Beth followed, her exit punctuated by the strident ring of a wall telephone.

"I'll take the boys for a walk after supper, give my sister a chance to deal with Jonina," Peter huffed into Ellie's ear. "Is that okay with you?"

"Of course. You don't have to entertain me every single minute."

"Phone's for Pete's little lady," said the plump woman who had served their fattening feast. "It's Mr. Halliday."

"Never reckoned you'd hook up with one of them veggie-tarians, Pete," said Duke, his teeth crowned with mashed potatoes. "Miss Norrie's pretty and all," he added, as if Ellie had already left the table, "but couldn't ya rope yourself a gal that eats red meat?"

"She roped me," Peter replied.

If Ellie had been a skunk, she would have ejected a pungent secretion.

# Eleven

A cuckoo clock cuckooed ten times. Peter waited until the last 'oo' died out before he said, "What did Halliday want?"

Ellie sat next to Peter on the couch, in front of the fireplace. He drank beer, she sipped Diet Pepsi. They had just finished watching a very young Roy Rogers purge the bad guys and woo a very young Dale Evans. Before that, Deanna Durbin had sung her way into Robert Stack's heart. Stack looked like a young Elliot Ness, assuming Ness had decided to flaunt lipstick and eye makeup.

Since the nighttime temperature dipped below forty degrees, the toasty fire was functional as well as beautiful. Peter had turned off the VCR, the TV, and all lights except for one lamp, and the dancing flames generated a series of coven-like shadows.

John Wayne stared, uncharacteristically passive.

Jackie Robinson prowled, sniffing for scents of familiarity. Ignoring his water and food bowls, he found one of Peter's sneakers and happily buried his furry Persian face amid the laces.

"I called Heather Halliday before leaving the Springs," Ellie said, "and left a message on her answering machine. I didn't know the name of the ranch, but apparently Kit Halliday told Garrett we'd be staying here. He suggested dinner tomorrow night, at his house. He said to bring my 'little gentleman' along. That's my feeble attempt at a joke, Peter. Smile."

"Sorry." He stretched his bare feet toward the fire. "I'm worried about Beth. When I returned Ryan and Stevie to her cottage, she wouldn't talk about Jonah. She said she had a headache and was gulping down pills. That's not her style. My sister has always been so healthy, except for the usual childhood diseases and, um, cramps from her, um . . ."

"Period, Peter. The pills could have been aspirin, for her headache."

"No, Norrie. I couldn't read the label but it was definitely a prescription."

"Maybe this time I can snoop with your permission, woman to woman, find out what's bothering—"

"No. Please. Beth would kill me if she knew I'd talked about her with a stranger."

"I'm not a stranger. Well, I guess I am, to Beth."

"No, you're not. I want you to be close to my family." His heavy sigh seemed to whisk across the fireplace and stir the flames. "After Mike Urvant's rodeo accident, my sister had a brief breakdown."

"Define brief."

"A couple of days. I held her hand and urged her to talk about it. She wouldn't, and still won't."

Leaning sideways, Ellie kissed his mustache. "Was it only this morning we left Colorado Springs?"

"I meant to give you a romantic interlude, but I think I've landed you smack-dab in the middle of a family crisis. I don't know what'll happen if Mike Urvant decides to pay the ranch a visit. Maybe nothing. Beth is 'notional' too."

"Please don't worry about me, Peter. I've forgiven your rope remark and I can't wait to see Heather. Tomorrow night it'll be my turn. No more chauvinistic bonding."

"Is that what I was doing?"

"*Yep,*" she mimicked, nudging his ribs with an elbow.

He finally laughed. "That tickles."

"It won't tickle if you make another dopey rope re-mark."

"No more ropes, you have my word, but I'll still talk about getting hitched."

She decided it might be prudent to change the subject. "Guess what, Peter? I crossed Independence Pass and survived. And I met my first horse, except I forgot to ask Beth its name. Probably Beelzebub."

"Close. Brownie."

"Oh, thank God. I love brownies. With ice cream on top."

Stretching his arms toward the ceiling, working out kinks, Peter said, "I just realized that you and Independence Pass have a lot in common."

"Why? Because I'm independent? Because I court danger?"

He shook his head. "The pass wasn't named for those cliff-hanging roads. It's situated near the town of Independence, now a ghost town, which was founded on July Fourth."

"Then why do we have a lot in common?"

"Your curves." He fanned his face with his fingers, burlesquing the Dew Drop chanteuse. "You give me fe-vah. Let's climb into bed and . . . why are you staring at the fire with that fretful expression?"

"Jonina. Did you see her gobbling down her food?"

"So what? She's a growing kid."

"If you say it's baby fat, I'll strangle you. That's what everyone always told me. Jonina should be growing taller, not wider. Beth even complimented her for taking seconds."

"Sorry, but I agree with my sister. Praise Jonina's appetite, encourage her to eat, and she won't become bulimic."

"She might anyway. Peer pressure. Where are you going?"

"Bathroom. *Beer* pressure. That was my feeble attempt at a joke. Smile."

She did. But when he returned she was glaring at the fire again.

"What's wrong now?" he asked.

"Rudolph Kessler. I keep wondering why someone tried to destroy Garrett's painting."

*Maybe it's a warning,* she thought, *and I'm the target.*

But why? The perps from the diet club murders and M*A*S*H murders were safely incarcerated, they didn't have vengeful friends, and anyway, she hadn't sleuthed much lately.

"It doesn't make sense," she said. "There must be Halliday paintings all over Colorado. Even I own one. Why go after that particular canvas? Why kill Rudolph Kessler?"

"The real question is, why are you so obsessed with Kessler's murder? If we were in Colorado Springs, you'd snoop and wheedle and drive me crazy. But we're on vacation."

"Would it make any difference if I told you I was being spied on at the art gallery? I thought it was my imagination until I learned that someone had slashed my face."

"Someone slashed a painting, not your face, and you yourself said everybody was looking at us. Remember? I made that pussy crack and—"

"It happened later, after Garrett and Adrianna exited the gallery, when we toured the whole room. Especially when we stood in front of me holding Jackie Robinson. Garrett's painting of me, I mean. *Pussy Willow*."

"Okay, let's assume you're right. Did you get a good look at the person who spied on you?"

"No. That's why I thought it was my imagination."

"Did it ever occur to you that he or she was comparing you to the redhead in the painting?"

"Yes. That's my point. He or she planned to kill me, and there I was, at the gallery."

"Listen to yourself, Ellie. Planned to kill you?" Peter tugged at the snaps on his shirt. "I'm going to bed. You can sit here and chew your cud."

"Thanks a lot, *Mister* Pete. I'm not some damn fool cow."

"You're not a detective, either, even if you like to think you are."

"I can't turn off my brain like you'd thumb a light switch."

"Please thumb the light switch before you hit the bed."

Ellie heard the bedroom door slam.

Surrounded by black velvet, John Wayne smirked.

After tossing more wood into the fireplace, she sat and pondered the new flames. Kessler's neighbors hadn't seen anyone lurking, but they might have noticed a strange car. American? Foreign? What color? Colorado plates?

The lamp's light bulb seemed to hover above her head like a light bulb in a cartoon, denoting revelation. Except nothing relevant was "revelated."

Wait a sec. In *Alice's Wonder Land*, Garrett's exquisitely rendered mirror reflection stopped above the breasts, negating sixty excess pounds that could have belonged to Ellie. So maybe the killer didn't know Ellie from a hole in the wall. Maybe he wanted to slash Heather's face. Maybe he had a thing against redheads. Maybe he didn't like Maureen O'Hara movies.

Damn! Peter was right. Ellie wasn't a bona fide detective. She didn't have a Mike Hammer office. She didn't have a Spenser secretary or a Bolitar cohort. She didn't have a private investigator's license, she couldn't defend herself against thugs with her fists, and she didn't have one indisputable clue. Rudolph Kessler's death was a jigsaw puzzle with most of the pieces trashed. Maybe Garrett had a missing piece. Maybe he could solve the puzzle.

Maybe the perp was a burglar who'd been interrupted. It could be as simple as that. Then why slash the painting? Was the motive an "if I can't have it, no one else can" impulse? After all, the frame had been nailed to the wall.

Assuming the perp was an ordinary, run-of-the-mill thief, would he have known the painting's worth? Had the newspapers publicized Garrett's prices? Ellie couldn't remember, but it would be easy to check. All she need do was call Melody, who had issued press releases to the *Gazette*, the *Denver Post*, the *Aspen Daily News*, and just about every other Colorado newspaper. But even if the papers had touted prices, how would an art thief link a recently widowed senior citizen to a Garrett Halliday painting?

Suppose Rudolph Kessler knew the painting's value and put it up for sale? Suppose he advertised in the paper? Suppose someone phoned Kessler and they agreed on a price? Suppose the perp entered the house, grabbed Kessler's cane, and—

"Norrie, I'm sorry." Peter, minus his clothes, stood framed by the doorway. Behind him, the bedroom's wagon-wheel lights shone faintly, regulated by a dimmer switch. "Can I help you with your boots?"

Speechless, her gaze riveted on his body, she nodded.

Straddling her left leg, he stripped off her boot and sock. Then he straddled her right leg. The right boot was tighter.

She had to push against his butt. That provocative motion reminded her of *Thyme for Rosemary's Lavation*, the Halliday painting inside the bedroom, especially when Peter carried her to the mattress, scooped up a washcloth, and began cleansing her feet with warm water from the old-fashioned water bowl.

"This little piggy ate lamb chops," he said, climbing on top of the bed.

"Roast beef, not lamb chops," she murmured, the warm water generating a sensual tickle, the shadows between her thighs responding. "And you shouldn't say piggy to a diet club leader."

"Sorry, ma'am." His voice betrayed his amusement. He washed the piggy who went to market, the piggy who stayed home, and the piggy who cried *oui-oui-oui*.

Eyes half-shut, Ellie focused on Garrett's boudoir painting. His lion-woman-bathtub painting teased while this one pulsated with eroticism. Heather seemed to imply that love was the gift of oneself.

No. Sex was the gift of oneself.

Aroused, Ellie gave with enthusiasm.


Moving quickly, crouching low, looking like the Hunchback of Lonesome Pines, the art patron entered the barn and scrutinized the horses.

Brownie.

Buttermilk.

Merrylegs.

Scout.

Pegasus.

Blackie.

Lucy.

Satan.

*Tonight . . . Pegasus.*

Atop the chestnut mare, riding bareback, the art patron exited the barn.

The art patron's thoughts echoed the cadence of Peg's canter.

*Maybe a ride.*

*Will clear my head.*

*I didn't mean to kill.*

*The hey-is-for-horses man.*

*But he made me lose.*

*My goddamn temper.*

*Please, God, don't let me.*

*Lose it again.*

The Lonesome Pines sign was tempting . . .

And easily reached if one stood on top of a horse's back . . .

Like a circus bareback rider.

Soon the sign read LONESOME.

Peter heard the clip-clop of a horse's hooves and wondered if Beth rode away her frustrations.

She'd done it before.

She always rode too fast and insisted on jumping high fences, as if speed and extreme height would help her escape the bridges she'd burned. Especially a bridge named Mike Urvant.

Mike Svengali Urvant, who liked to call Peter's sister "Beth-be-nimble."

*Beth be nimble, Beth be quick, Beth jumped over the candlestick.*

Beth, the perfect wife and mother, president of the PTA, soloist in the church choir, organizer of charity auctions and bake sales. Beth, who had once watched a movie being shot near Denver, who had gazed adoringly at Victor Madison and caught the famous horror film director's eye. Hired as a bit player, she told Peter that making movies was dull as ditch-water. "You sit on your fanny," she said, "until they announce your scene. Which they shoot over and over until you want to scream. When they weren't filming my scenes I played stud poker," she added with a cat-smile. "By the end of the shoot I'd won seven hundred dollars."

In her wallet Beth carried a SAG card and a press card, along with her credit cards, library card, and 25%-off-any-book-in-the-store card. She could program a computer *and* a VCR. One quick glance at a car's engine and she could diagnose the problem. When she didn't have time to work out at the gym, she sweated over her own exercise equipment. She could give a sick horse a shot, braid its mane in Bo Derek cornrows, and she rode like the wind.

Her only armor-chink, her Achilles' heel, was the opposite sex. A man could be three saddlebags short of a camel if he was strong enough, or he could look like Fred Mertz if smart enough. The two attributes, strength and intelligence, rarely came in one ideal package. Not even her husband could measure up. Beth's defiant urge to search and test and touch and taste until she found perfection was as addictive as her cigarettes. She had begun smoking at age sixteen and her search for the perfect man, the perfect bed partner, had begun shortly thereafter.

Beth was also an expert at self-flagellation.

Which meant what? That tonight's mood was due to a recent affair? With whom? Damn, did that really matter? And how would Mike Urvant factor into the equation, if/when he visited Lonesome Pines?

The hoof beats sounded louder. Heading, Peter assumed, toward the barn. So what? This was a ranch. People rode. And ate.

*Ride-eat, eat-ride.*

Intriguing similitude, he thought with a smile, burying his face against Norrie's belly button.

"More," she murmured.

"You bet, sweetheart. I promised you sex and sunsets, didn't I?"

They might as well make the most of tonight, he mused. Ride-eat, eat-ride. Tomorrow Norrie would experience her first horseback-riding lesson, and he had a feeling that by tomorrow night she'd be too sore to ride anything.

Except, maybe, the rocking chair.

# Twelve

Martina Navratilova Brustein glanced at the featherbrained cuckoo clock, just before she hauled herself from the couch and walked over to the door.

"He's late, Becky," she said. "How shall we punish him?"

The long-haired, mostly-black calico didn't answer, nor did Martina expect an answer. With those big silky ears, her cat was a terrific listener and Martina often read her manuscripts out loud. Fortunately, Lonesome Pines allowed pets. Ever since the death of her mate, Tom, Becky craved Martina's presence. The cat was devoted and very affectionate—for a cat—but she seemed to loathe the guest who stood outside the cottage.

As Martina crossed her arms over her breasts, she heard her tummy growl. On top of an antique table, a white china plate held the remnants of her supper. From day one she had insisted they serve her salad: Caesar, Waldorf, chef, anything but noodle. Tonight they had concocted a chicken salad—limp lettuce and overripe tomatoes and skinless chicken that smelled suspiciously like fried chicken, even though she had nicely demanded broiled chicken. Lord, what she wouldn't give for thick, juicy pork chops, coated with breadcrumbs, and mashed, no, scalloped potatoes. Chocolate cheesecake. Brown Betty. A sliver, just one teensy sliver, of Key Lime pie.

Her tummy growls diminished, replaced by the sound of knuckles rapping at the door. *Don't weaken,* she thought. *He made you wait. Now he can wait.*

He needed to be disciplined, like a naughty puppy. Someone had once told her that it took forty-two repetitions before a dog would obey one command. And if the dog goofed on number forty, you'd have to start all over again.

"Martina, let me in," he pleaded.

"Or you'll huff and puff and blow the house down?" Not a bad analogy, she thought, comparing him to the big bad wolf. On second thought, she'd better clarify the connotation. She didn't want him comparing her to one of the three little pigs.

"I have a care package for my grannie," she said in a high-pitched voice, thinking she sounded more like Fran Drescher than Fran Drescher. "And I sincerely hope you won't eat me."

Silence.

Was he walking away? She opened the door and felt the cold night air wash over her, breeding goosebumps. He stood just outside the door, his hands in his pockets, a stupid grin on his face.

"Get inside," she said, "and tell me why you're late. It had better be good. I won't accept a flat tire, a dead body, or the dog ate my homework."

"How about a glitch at the gallery? An argument never resolved."

"Artist angst," she said. "Yawn."

"Regrettably, my dear, the problem has *got* to be ironed out."

"Yawn."

Indignant, he said, "Why do Garrett Halliday paintings

have less significance than Martina Brustein books?"

"Because they're *my* books. I don't give a hoot about your paintings. Maybe I'd give a hoot if G.H. painted *me*. In fact, I'd be more than happy to pose. Why don't I pose like that slutty redhead in *Titanic*? I've even got an emerald necklace in my bank vault."

She expected him to stare scornfully at her body, perhaps raise an obligatory eyebrow, but he merely shed his jacket and tossed it toward the couch. "When we first met," he said, "you didn't even know who I was."

"Big deal. I'm not into art. If you told me Picasso's pseudonym was Nora Roberts, he might pique my interest." She pointed to a black horse, painted on black velvet. Its front hooves thrashed a blue sky. "As far as I'm concerned, that's art."

"So are book covers. Please don't forget that I painted a cover for one of your bodice rippers."

"Please don't call *Dream Dancer* a bodice ripper. That pithy turn of phrase went out with pet rocks. Heroes don't rip bodices in a Marty Blue romance. They don't have to. My ladies unclothe at the drop of a hat."

With a laugh, he took off his hat and dropped it. Becky's whiskers quivered as she clawed the hatband's cocky feather.

"There goes your hat," said Martina, watching the feather disintegrate.

"I have other hats."

She slanted a glance at the clock. "I wish Becky could reach that stupid cuckoo."

He stood duck-footed, his legs apart. "Come here, Marty Blue," he said, unzipping his fly, "or I'll rip your bodice."

As if intimidated, her hands coyly covered her breasts,

sheathed by a brand new negligee. Normally she wore muumuus, day and night. Muumuus hid her gratuitous flab; an occupational hazard. Seated at her computer, popping M&Ms and Peppermint Pattys as if they were vitamin pills and communion wafers, her weight and blood pressure had climbed so high that her doctor had issued a warning. Quit smoking and lose weight or she might not make it to her next book's deadline.

She quit smoking, bleached her teeth, and gained twelve pounds.

Her editor suggested a fat farm. Aware that Martina loved horses, a fellow author recommended Lonesome Pines. Martina could drive to the ranch, rather than fly— she hated flying—and horseback riding was good exercise. Best of all, she'd have her own guest cottage where she could write to her heart's content, undisturbed. When she heard they allowed cats, it clinched the deal.

Lonesome Pines closed down for the month of May, but Martina and her checkbook had solved that little impediment. Luckily, the ranch kept its staff on board, including a cook who, obviously, had never watched Emeril.

Despite all the lovely horses, Martina found ranch life dull. Yawn, yawn, yawn. Her pages piled up, but she wrote crap, cliché after cliché after cliché. Her Muse had apparently been a Greek goddess named Marlboro, and she seriously considered taking up smoking again.

Hungry and depressed, she had driven to Aspen and wandered into an art gallery. The man who escorted her through the gallery could have played the hero in her erotic romances. She knew she didn't have a come-hither face and form, so she tried to impress him with her fame and fortune. She bought a G.H. painting, *Polly Wants a Quaker*. Ten grand down the drain, she thought, as she signed the credit card slip with a flourish and shoved her Marty Blue signature under his nose. She told him she had appeared on Oprah. He said that, several years ago, he had painted the "clinch scene" on one of her book covers. Small world, she said.

He said her author photo didn't do her justice and she looked younger than thirty-five—in truth, she was about to turn forty. He took her out for cocktails and dinner. She rarely drank because she couldn't hold her liquor. He held her head. Then he drove her back to Lonesome Pines, helped her inside her cottage, kissed her on the forehead, and sped away. The next afternoon she called a cab, which cost a bloody fortune, but she needed to retrieve her car, parked behind his gallery.

To her surprise, he was waiting for her. He said they'd start from scratch, cocktails and dinner. She said she loved the word cocktail, especially the first syllable. He said he preferred the last syllable. They never made dinner, but this time it wasn't because she drank too many cocktails. The next morning she dumped three hundred crappy pages and started her book all over again.

He was as addictive as chocolate, and she knew that her writing had taken a turn for the better. Her laptop practically hummed. She lost seventeen pounds and feared losing *him*. Then she discovered that he was addicted to her, too. He craved her brand of sex, the kinkier the better. She began to harbor feelings of what her romance heroines might call "eternal togetherness."

She masked those feelings, having realized early on that he valued what her romance heroes might call her "confound independence." As long as she controlled the relationship, he'd stick, and if that meant denying him every once in a while, so be it. She had no clue what she'd do when her R and R ended. Sell her house and move to Aspen?

They always met furtively. He didn't sport a wedding band but she'd never asked him about a wife. She had once followed him home from the gallery, her heart in her throat. He lived in a big house on top of a steep hill. She didn't dare get any closer than the bottom of the hill.

To be perfectly honest, she didn't want to know if he was married. She might inadvertently mention it, open a can of worms. She hated worms—naked, soft-bodied, slimy maggots! God should have employed a worm rather than a snake to disrupt Eve's idyllic garden.

Martina felt like Eve—*before* the serpent had crashed God's party. Life was good. And now, a bonus! Yesterday had brought a diet club leader to the ranch. And not just any diet club. Weight Winners. With franchises all over the world. *And* a skinny actress-spokesperson who wore beautiful, skinny clothes. Martina had actually thought about joining Weight Winners, but could never leave her computer long enough to attend an introductory meet—

"Let's get this show on the road, my dear. I haven't got all night."

He sounded like an impressionist doing Ed Sullivan; let's get this *shoe* on the road. "I've got all night," she snapped. "And then some."

He was basketball-player-tall. Since she was barely five-two, he hunkered down until they were face-to-face. She placed her hands on his shoulders for balance, leaned forward, and nipped his neck.

"Ouch," he said, rising. "You little vampire!"

"No, darling, I'm your little Lady," she said with the same inflection she might have used to audition for Hugh Hefner: *I'm your bunny, Slut.* "Tell the truth," she purred.

"What would you do without me?"

"Get some sleep."

She had punished him enough. Moreover, her body was sending pulsating signals to her brain. Riding was a unique form of masturbation, especially if one rode bareback, but she always felt unfulfilled. Even when she climaxed she considered it a prologue.

"Time enough for sleep when you're dead." Encircling his waist, she pressed her face against his shirt. As he wove his fingers through her short dark hair, she smelled perfume. Stepping back, she said, "I smell perfume."

"And I smell horse."

"I've been riding. Who have you been riding?"

"That, my dear, is none of your business."

"It's my business if you slept with another woman before you came here. It's my business if another woman made you late." She disguised her hurt feelings with unfeigned anger. "I don't like leftovers, darling."

"What you smell is second hand scent, not unlike second hand smoke. I really must hire a fumigator."

"Doesn't a fumigator get rid of pests?"

"Exactly." He stared into her eyes. "I didn't sleep with anyone, Martina, I swear."

He sounded sincere. She decided to believe him. She knew that if he ever left her she'd never make the bestseller lists again.

"Do you want to play Lady and Marquis de Sade," he said, "or should we call it a night? I'm exhausted."

"I'm not. And you, *my dear*, don't know what exhaustion is."

Glancing at the cuckoo clock, he shrugged. She saw the wicked look in his eyes. Goody. She wanted to write a new chapter and needed inspiration.

"Let's play Lady and Marquis later," she said. "Right now we'll play 'The Banana Boat Song.' Shall I tally your banana?"

He nodded. She knelt. His fly was still open. She opened her mouth.

And said, "By the way, darling, are you married?"

# Thirteen

Marion Dombroski stared bleary-eyed at the bottle of vodka. He reckoned it was only a matter of time before he peed his pants. The stables didn't have a toilet and he was much too nauseated to descend the loft ladder, stagger outside, and take a whiz behind the barn.

His desire to pee battled his desire to puke. Both battled his desire to cry.

But he wouldn't cry. Crying was for sissies. His mother had called him little Lord Fauntleroy before he was even old enough to know what it meant. She had also called him crybaby, and he knew what that meant. Darkness. The smell of sweat and boots and sheepskin and mothballs. The dismissive click of a key in a lock.

He heard Pegasus whinny. Poor Peg. She had been all lathered up and he should have rubbed her down. *Too late now, Marion!*

What a stupid name, Marion. A girl's name. True, it was John Wayne's Christian name, but nobody called the gritty Duke a sissy, not to his face they didn't.

Marion had once seen a movie, *Battlecry*. In the movie, a soldier named Marion died a hero's death. Before he died, the other soldiers made fun of his name. Mary, they called him. Sister Mary.

Wayne had called Marion "Bud"—after the John Travolta character in *Urban Cowboy*, not the beer—and for a while it stuck. Then Wayne fell off a horse and broke his neck and Bud was Marion again.

Funny how he could remember Wayne's face but not his mother's face. His mother had quit the ranch fifteen years ago, after Wayne's funeral. Marion had been seven and he begged her to take him with her. She said he looked too much like his brother and he'd remind her of Wayne and her heart would break all over again. Marion cried until his nose snotted. His mother told him to "act like a man" or she'd lock him in the closet. Clutching a handful of skirt, he had implored her not to leave him. She untangled his hand and said she'd write to him every day and send for him soon. The first year he got a birthday card—a month late, on what would have been Wayne's thirteenth birthday. The second year, nothing.

To this day he could remember, even *feel* the texture of his mother's skirt, but he couldn't conjure up her face. People said she was very pretty, with red hair. She didn't look anything like her brother Mike, people said.

Marion blamed Uncle Mike for Wayne's broken neck.

Uncle Mike had bought Lonesome Pines and hired his sister's jailbird husband, Marion's father, who way back then had looked like George Clooney in *Oh Brother, Where Art Thou?*

Unlike Clooney, the evidence against Virgil "Duke" Dombroski had been circumstantial. A syringe in his refrigerator (planted, Duke said) and his prints at the crime scene (along with dozens of other prints) and an eyewitness too stoned to remember his own name but not too stoned to pick Dombroski out of a lineup (with a little help from the cops). Duke's alibi, however, was shaky (his wife was a lousy liar) and he couldn't explain away the scratches on his face (from the nameless bitch he'd been with instead of his wife) and his P.D. sucked. So he accepted a plea bargain. At his first parole hearing, he relentlessly proclaimed his innocence. At his second, he said he was guilty, after all, and very, very sorry. He said a day didn't go by when he didn't pray for absolution.

He lied through his teeth, of course, but a repentant murderer, it seemed, was more trustworthy than an innocent murderer, at least in the minds of the parole board. Furthermore, Dombroski had a job waiting for him on the outside.

So, if Mike Urvant hadn't hired Duke Dombroski, straight out of prison, Wayne would still be alive and Marion would still be Bud.

He blamed Garrett Halliday, too. Even though Garrett and his father weren't on speaking terms, John Halliday had paid to board his son's horse at Lonesome Pines. That horse, Garrett's damn horse, had refused to take a jump and—

Pegasus whinnied again. So did Satan. Had someone entered the barn?

Marion said, "Kit?" Then, louder, "Kit?"

"No. It's me." The voice sounded young. And frightened.

"Jonina?" Battling his queasy stomach, winning the battle but not the war, Marion crawled to the edge of the loft. "What the hell are you doing here?"

She looked up. "My mom's mad at me and I couldn't sleep, so I thought I'd pet the horses, talk to them, you know."

"And *you* know you're not allowed to visit the barn unsupervised."

"That rule's for kids."

"That rule's for anyone under eighteen."

"I can pass for eighteen. I've bought cigarettes."

Though it hurt, he laughed.

"Don't laugh at me!" She stamped her foot. "I'm smarter than eighteen, too. My dad says my body hasn't caught up to my mind yet. Someday I'm gonna be a lawyer, Dom, and the youngest Supreme Court Jus—"

"Dom?"

"Don't take this the wrong way," she said, tossing her mane of golden-brown hair, "but you don't look like a Marion. And it's a weird name for a boy, un-cool, so I've decided to call you Dom."

"Where did Dom come from?"

"Well, duh! Dombroski."

Why hadn't *he* ever thought of that? Why hadn't *Wayne* ever thought of that? Dom. He liked it. "Do you want to come up here and talk?"

"Sure," she said. "Thanks." Then, "Usually you won't give me the time of day."

"It's night." He watched her clumsily navigate the ladder. He really should help her, but in his present state he'd probably fall from the loft.

"It'll be day soon," she said. "Before I left my cabin I heard that stupid cuckoo clock chirp three times."

"Cuckoos don't chirp, they cuckoo. Oh my God! Three? Three a.m.?"

"No, three *p.m.* We're having an eclipse."

Her voice oozed sarcasm and, momentarily, she sounded like her mother. Clutching the last rung of the ladder, she said, "What's the matter? Did you have a hot date or something?"

"Yeah. Only she never showed." He grasped Jonina's wrist and tugged hard, until she sprawled next to him.

"Ouch," she said, sitting on her heels and rubbing her

wrist. "Don't bruise the merchandise. Who never showed? No, don't tell me. Kit Halliday. Right?"

He thought about lying, giving her some other girl's name, but she was too smart, just like she said. And not bad looking, when you came right down to it. Beautiful hair and eyes. Someday she'd be a knockout.

What the hell was she wearing? Diffused moonlight from the loft's window revealed pink flannel pajamas with repetitive, black horse imprints. Across her breasts, the top read: NIGHT MARES.

He was still sprawled on his stomach. He managed to push himself up with his palms and not puke. Sitting cross-legged, he said, "I was supposed to meet Kit at Angel's Ravine. I'm sure she had a good reason—"

"Yeah. His name's Pete Miller."

"She's with Pete?"

"Don't be stupid. My Uncle Pete's with Norrie."

"Then where's Kit?"

Jonina shrugged. "How should I know? Oh, I get it. When Kit didn't show, you came here and got wasted." Glancing around, she spied the vodka bottle. "Can I have some?"

"No way. You're just a kid."

"I'm not a kid and I can prove it." She reached for her pajama buttons.

Should he call her bluff? "I don't care if you take off your top, Jonina, but I don't mess around with virgins so you might as well leave it on."

"Who said I'm a virgin? And who said I wanted to mess around with you?" Face red, she tugged at the buttons, then simply lifted the top up over her head. She pulled her arms free from the sleeves and tossed the shirt toward the vodka bottle. "There," she said. "That's better. It's hot up here."

It was, in fact, cold, and he couldn't stop staring at her

breasts. Although they weren't fully developed, they showed promise.

In fact, the night suddenly looked promising. If she told the truth, if she wasn't a virgin—

No! God, no! Had he lost his mind? Aside from the fact that she was only fifteen, messing around with the guests was a firing offense. And for him, much worse.

"What's that?" she asked. She sounded startled rather than frightened. Marion followed her gaze, but before he could respond she said, "Oh my gosh, it's a cat!"

"*My* cat," he amended. "Stanley Hastings."

"What a funny name."

"This guy, Parnell Hall, wrote a bunch of books about a down on his luck P.I." Marion glanced at the gray tabby, whose fluorescent eyes shone like lime-yellow Day-Glo. "Stanley Hastings gets into all kinds of trouble and he's not very brave, but . . . do you know what a P.I. is?"

"Of course. My dad's a lawyer."

"Right." Marion thunked his head with the heel of his hand, then wished he hadn't. "Stanley Hastings was starving to death when I found him. No one thought he'd live. They were wrong, obviously. Sometimes, Jonina, it's crucial to prove people wrong."

Bare bosom disregarded, at least temporarily, she snapped her fingers. "Here, kitty, kitty. Here, Stanley Hastings."

"He won't come to you," Marion said. "He won't come to anybody. I call him a feral housecat. He lets me feed him, but he won't let me hold him."

"Where's the gratification in loving something that won't love you back?"

Ignoring her astute question, he said, "What did you want to talk about?"

"Huh?"

Her arms were all goose-pimply. He could see that she desperately wanted to cover her breasts, but it was as if someone had double-dared her to jump from the barn's roof and fly. He knew that unless someone gave her an out, she'd never weasel out. She was ballsy as well as bright. She'd fly or die trying.

"Before," he said, "when you first walked into the barn, you told me you wanted to pet the horses and talk."

"My mom and dad are getting a divorce," she said, and burst into tears.

Tears he could handle. Tears made her look like a kid again. Hugging her legs, hiding her breasts, she wept against her pink flannel clad knees.

He took off his jacket, wrapped it around her, then shifted her into his lap. Momentarily, he panicked, certain her weight against his belly would release the floodgates, so to speak. But, thank God, his urgent need to pee had slacked off.

She cuddled against him and said, "It's all my fault."

"What's your fault?"

"The divorce. They're getting a divorce because of me."

"Oh, I doubt that. Kids always think—"

"I'm not a kid! And I really don't want to talk about it."

"Okay."

"You see, my mom's very popular. Everyone loves her. She was engaged twice before she married my dad. I've never even had a real date."

"And that's why they're getting a divorce?"

"No. Yes. I don't want to talk about it."

"Okay," he said, trying to keep the smile out of his voice.

"Mom says boys would like me better if I didn't act so brainy. Daddy says to leave me alone. Mom says Daddy spoils me rotten. They fight about it all the time. My bed-

116

room's next to theirs and sometimes I can hear them, you know, at night. Just before we came here, they had a *big* fight. I couldn't hear everything they said, but . . ." A sob inched up her throat. "I heard enough to know that they *had* to get married. Do you understand?"

"Sure. Your mom got knocked up so she married your father. Big deal."

"Then Daddy asked Mom if I was Mike Urvant's child."

Marion felt his eyes widen and his mouth gape open. "Mike Urvant? My Uncle Mike?"

"Yeah, your Uncle Mike. My mom met him at a rodeo, just before she met my dad, and a few years later she saw him again and I guess they had an affair and when it was over my dad took her back. I think Mike called and said he might visit the ranch and my dad found out and said we weren't going and my mom said yes, we were, we had to, and that's when he asked if I was Mike's child."

"And your mom said?"

"My heart was pounding so loud in my ears, I couldn't hear what she said, but Daddy stormed out of the house. The next day he came back and packed some stuff. I said I didn't want to go to the ranch and asked him if I could stay with him and he said yes, but I could tell he didn't really mean it. Daddy left and Mom gave me one of those it's-all-your-fault looks. She said Daddy would be busy finding a new place to live and she needed me to help her with the boys because she's pregnant again. Oh, I shouldn't have told you that. It's supposed to be a secret."

"I promise I won't say a word, Jonina, but none of this mess is *your* fault. Even if you're my uncle's child, which I seriously doubt, it's not your fault. How could it be? You didn't have anything to do with your mother getting knocked up. And if your dad spoils you, it's because you're easy to spoil. You're a good kid."

"I'm not a kid," she said, her words muffled against his T-shirt. "But I'm glad I told you about the divorce and . . . and everything. I feel much, much better."

Despite her declaration, she began to cry again.

Her tears were contagious. Marion found himself crying, silently, along with her. Because Kit hadn't shown up, hadn't even bothered to pick up a phone and break their date. Because he loved Kit and she treated him like crap. Because his father had lied about killing someone. Because his mother had lied, too. Because he couldn't remember his mother's face. Because he checked the mail every day, hoping there'd be a letter from her. Because, even after fifteen years, he was still waiting for her to send for him.

# Fourteen

Lelia Hamilton had been on her knees for hours, especially if one counted the hours she spent cleaning bathrooms.

That was her job, tidying the Lonesome Pines cottages. Making the beds. Mopping the floors. Washing the windows. Vacuuming the rugs. Dusting and winding the cuckoo clocks. Scrubbing the toilets. That was her job and she was damn good at it.

Movies, however, were her passion. Except she liked old movie stars better than new movie stars. Susan Hayworth. Loretta Young. Ingrid Bergman. Gene Tierney. And, especially, Jennifer Jones—whom she somewhat resembled.

Marion Dombroski had once asked her why she preferred movie stars from an earlier era and she had said, "Because today's stars are so teensy, no bigger than my hand. They all fit inside my TV. Years ago, when there was no TV, movie stars were larger than life."

"If you turn off the TV and go to the movies," he had said, "the actors are larger than life."

And she had replied, "Who can afford to go to the movies?"

She had been tempted to add, "Years ago you could tell the good guys from the bad guys. Years ago the bad guys invariably got their comeuppance. Or they died. Today they come back in sequels."

Her cuckoo clock was broken, or maybe Mama had forgotten to wind it before she went to bed. Forgotten, hah! Lelia didn't own a watch. And if she was late for a meal, or an appointment, Mama would say, "Guess you ain't as smart as you think you are."

That was Mama's response to everything, from a busted toilet to a broken fingernail. *Guess you ain't as smart as you think you are.*

Marion Dombroski said Mama resented Lelia's "smart genes."

As soon as she had a sizable nest egg, Lelia would move out of the cottage she and Mama shared. Until then, she'd have to be more vigilant.

Mama kowtowed to Kit Halliday. Lelia knew why, and Kit knew why, even though, for the most part, Kit was dumb as a box of rocks. No "smart genes" in that pretty head, unless you considered evil scheming a subsidiary of one's intellect. When Mama fawned over Kit, it reminded Lelia of Agnes Moorhead in *Jane Eyre*. Except Mama was shorter. And fatter. And Hispanic.

With a sigh, she glanced at the cuckoo clock again. It had stopped at 10:17 p.m. That meant it was well after midnight, coming up on dawn. She should have gone to bed hours ago, and she would have, except she knew that as soon as she closed her eyes THE DREAM would come— first vague, then explicit—and when she woke her mouth would be dry and her jaw would be sore from grinding her teeth and she'd be soaked with perspiration that smelled like cold, dead ashes.

She would have dreamed THE DREAM tonight because tonight she'd seen HIM. Here. At the ranch. At Angel's Ravine.

He had been walking—thinking, he said. He had stroked her face, then removed the pins from her hair so that it fell, unbound and wild, below her waist. As he cupped her breasts, he said, "I forgot how young and beautiful you are," and she wanted nothing more than to shed her clothes and sink to the ground.

Instead, she shook her head, negating a request he hadn't made.

Surprising her, he dropped his hands to his sides and said, "I want to paint your portrait. I need to paint your portrait. Please say yes."

She said, "No. Never."

He said, "Why not?"

She said, "You paint a woman's soul."

He said, "I wish that were true."

"I have hate in my heart," she said. "You cannot paint someone who has hate in her heart."

"So young," he said, "to have hate in your heart. I'm sorry, Lelia. If I could replace what was stolen from you, I would."

"It was stolen from you, too," she said with a flash of anger. "And I can see by your eyes that you are not sincere. Liar!"

He had turned on his heel and walked away, and the hate in her heart, newly ignited, had festered for hours.

Which was why she was on her knees, praying.

"Holy Mary, Mother of God . . ."

As she began to whisper the Rosary, she felt a familiar peace settle upon her.

"Pray for us sinners, now and at the hour of our death . . ."

She imagined light coming through the roof, forming a puddle around her knees. Having watched *Bernadette* more times than she could count, Lelia could recite every Jennifer Jones line. She even tried to lisp like Jennifer. But she had to admit that, in real life, Jennifer's Lady never spoke—at least not out loud.

Maybe because Lelia wasn't Catholic. Bernadette was, of course, Catholic. It probably helped to be Catholic.

"Eye for eye, tooth for tooth, hand for hand, foot for foot," she murmured, fingering her smooth wooden beads.

She had tried to confess to a priest once.

"He that diggeth a pit shall fall into it," she intoned, closing her eyes and savoring the texture of the beads. "Lord have mercy on us."

The priest was very young.

"Whatever a man soweth, that shall he also reap. Christ have mercy on us." She didn't know if she was praying right. Probably not, but it felt right. "Eye for eye, tooth for . . . oh, wait, I already said that."

Facing the young priest, she had chickened out. Muttered something about a Catholic fiancé and conversion, then fled.

She'd rather tell Jennifer's Lady, anyway. They had long conversations, Lelia and Jennifer's Lady, although Lelia had to admit that she played both parts.

Sometimes she felt like that girl in *The Exorcist*; Linda Blair . . . or was it Eileen Dietz? Lelia had read somewhere that Eileen Dietz played the bad parts.

If she hadn't chickened out, Lelia would have told the young priest that there were times when she felt possessed.

Jennifer's Lady said that Lelia should get on with her life, that she should clean the cottages and sculpt her angels. And pray, of course. But tonight—*this morning*—her prayers weren't working. The lulling peace had vanished like a puff of little-engine-that-could smoke.

Jennifer's Lady had also suggested that, if all else failed, Lelia should confront her demons.

# Fifteen

Beth Feldman, whose SAG card read Elizabeth Miller, finished pruning her pubic hair. Trashing her disposable razor, she entered the bedroom and sprawled naked across the bed. Then she got up and paced back and forth, even though the room was too much small for pacing, especially with her long legs.

Why the bloody hell weren't the pills working?

She had swallowed a couple of prescription sleeping pills, "borrowed" from Kit Halliday. Usually Beth logged Z's with habitual ease, but her senseless fight with Jonah had touched off a series of sleepless nights.

He had asked her if Jonina was Mike's child. Her answer had been stupid, immature, a sticks-and-stones retort— "That's for me to know and you to find out."

Jonah's question had been rude, insulting, but not unreasonable, and it could have been resolved with a simple one-word, two-letter response. If she wanted to extrapolate, she could have said that between Mike and Jonah she had suffered one of the most painful periods of her life.

When she first met Mike Urvant, he smoked unfiltered Camels. She had been a kid, a month shy of eighteen, and she wanted so badly to emulate him. But she couldn't cope with Camels so she went back to her bland, filtered cigarettes.

The story of her life.

Mike had been thirty and she had thought him oh-so-worldly-wise. On her eighteenth birthday, he handed her a cupcake. As she blew out the candle on top and made a wish, he checked into a motel. She had won ribbons. He had won money. He tossed the money on the bed and they wallowed in it, reveled in it. Surprised she wasn't a virgin, he became bolder; in retrospect, more arrogant.

Years later, when she saw *The Fantasticks*, she recognized herself as the girl who viewed the world through rose-colored glasses; the girl who wanted to do everything "just once before I'm old."

Totally enamored, thinking herself worldly wise too, she didn't realize that her whole existence revolved around Mike—rodeo star, sensualist, master manipulator. She wallowed (and reveled) in the envy of her peers, and if Mike had asked her to lick his boots, she would have stuck out her tongue.

Then he left for Europe—the European rodeo circuit. He gave her a fond pat on her fanny and said he'd give her a call when he returned to the U.S. of A.

*So long*, she sang, silently. *It's been good to know you.* She couldn't have sung out loud, even if she'd wanted to, since tears clogged her throat.

She had already dumped a couple of fiancés, one of whom threatened suicide, so why had she lost Mike? Clearly, at eighteen, she was all washed up.

Self-esteem hovering between zero and zilch, she attended a charity ball, a masquerade sponsored by the C.S.P.D. Her brother Pete and his girlfriend Cathy had come as cop and robber. In fact, ninety-nine percent of the cops came as cops. One, however, came dressed in briefs.

Halfway through the party she discovered that he was a lawyer—*briefs, ha-ha*—and he wore underpants because he'd lost a bet and there was a prize for the best costume. Which, she assumed, he'd win.

She had come as Pandora's box, clothed in black tights and leotard, with fish hooks, rubber worms and colorful lures pinned to her breasts and crotch. She won first prize . . . and the lawyer.

He donned slacks over his briefs when it became obvious that her costume had lured him in more ways than one. He escorted her home, changed his mind, and escorted her to his apartment. She didn't protest. The next day she moved in with him. Four months later, pregnant and already showing, she accepted his marriage proposal. He called her "Pandora." She called him Jonah.

Was she on the rebound? Had she been impressed by his sumptuous apartment? Did his body look yummy in under-pants?

Yup.

And if she didn't love him madly, passionately, she sure loved the way he doted on her, especially after Jonina's birth. Jonina Phoebe Feldman was an ugly baby. Bald except for a wispy, colorless Mohawk down the center of her skull, her eyes were lost in puffed cheeks. And yet, from day one, Jonah believed his daughter the most enchanting creature who ever crawled the earth. He delighted in changing her muddy diapers and he carried around a pocket-sized photo album that he'd whip out at a moment's notice. Rather than discuss his criminal-defense cases, a subject Beth had always found fascinating, he talked nonstop about buying a pony for Jonina, what college she'd attend—he was leaning toward Harvard, but if she preferred Yale he wouldn't fuss—and what kind of party they'd throw for her first birthday.

Beth didn't want any more kids; one was enough, thank

you very much. But Jonah *obsessed* over Jonina, and it only grew worse as she grew older, so Beth gave him a son, a beautiful child, with dark hair and blue eyes and—

Mike returned to Colorado. For the first time ever, Beth forgot her wedding anniversary. Jonah gave her diamond earrings. She gave him a blank stare.

She said she was suffering from postpartum depression and needed a vacation. He said he had a big court case coming up. She said she wouldn't mind traveling alone. He said she did look kind of wan, how about Hawaii? She said Hawaii sounded wonderful. He drove her to the airport but she never made the plane.

In truth, she wasn't thinking straight. People who vacationed in Hawaii came home with a tan, a lei, and kid-shirts that said MY MOM WENT TO HAWAII BUT ALL SHE BOUGHT ME WAS THIS STUPID SHIRT.

She told Mike their affair would be short-lived, then forgot the definition of short-lived. Hopelessly ensnared, craving him with a passion that seemed as eternal as the federal government's budget deficit, she called Jonah, confessed everything, and asked for a divorce.

When she informed Mike over a wine and venison-bisque dinner, she decided the nothingness in his eyes was her imagination. Didn't he pick her up in his arms and take her to bed? Would he have done that if her divorce declaration had bothered him?

The next day she found him in bed with a rodeo groupie.

As she stood there, her boots glued to the floor, he patted the bed and said, "Hi, Beth-be-nimble, why don't you join us?"

The groupie giggled and said, "Oooh, Mikey, you're baaaad."

*Mikey?*

He had cheated on purpose. He didn't want to be "branded." He didn't want—

A loud knock interrupted her ruminations, and a voice at the open window said, "Beth, it's me. I saw your light. Sorry I'm late."

As she opened the door, she slanted a quick glance toward the other two bedrooms. "Keep your voice down," she said, "or you'll wake the kids." She pointed to the cuckoo clock. "I thought you weren't coming." A sleepy warmth coursed through her body. The pills had finally kicked in—talk about bad timing! "It'll soon be sunrise," she said with a yawn, "and we have a lot to discuss."

# Sixteen

Filtered through a meringue cloud, the sun rose. A portion of Peter's anatomy rose, too, and Ellie was both satiated and ravenous. She licked her chops—as Duke might say—when she pictured breakfast. This morning she didn't care if the food was hearty ranch fare, illegal and fattening. Anyway, she thought, glancing at Peter, she had probably worked off excess calories.

And later, on top of a horse, she'd work off more.

Entering the dining room, she sat at the adult's table. Although her cottage clock had cuckooed nine times, Beth and the kids were conspicuously absent. Maybe they'd already eaten and were—what? Riding? Swimming?

Last night's plump cook slammed a dinner plate down on the table, almost but not quite missing Ellie's placemat.

If the cook had been a dog, she would have growled, and Ellie wondered what she might have done to incite such hostility. Mystified, she watched the cook stomp toward the sideboard, her resentment tangible. Neither old nor young, she wore pigtails that appeared to be spray-painted brown and wolf-gray. The braids drooped against a red T-shirt, tucked into blue jeans that had no fly and zipped up the side. Between her chunky waist and knees, a white apron rode her hips.

Famished, Ellie shifted her gaze to her plate. In the middle of the white china, one sunny-side up egg looked like a jaundiced eye. A side plate held four triangular slices of unbuttered multi-grain toast. A miniature box of bran cereal leaned against a blue plastic bowl. Next to the bowl, a cow-shaped milk pitcher stood sentinel. Maybe the cook's antipathy had something to do with the specially ordered breakfast that Ellie hadn't ordered.

She glanced toward the sideboard, where the smell of global bacon, American and Canadian, invaded her sensitive nostrils and traveled non-stop toward her pituitary gland.

Duke's black beard, spattered with biscuit gravy, looked like a Jackson Pollock-inspired Brillo pad. "I ordered a special breakfast for you, Miss Norrie," he said, his upper lip curling in a bad imitation of an Elvis sneer. "We keep bran handy for our *mature* guests, although I'll never understand how anyone can eat that multi-grain shit."

Ellie loathed multi-grain bread, not to mention bran cereal. She preferred scrambled eggs to runny sunny-side up, and what the heck had happened to Duke's aw-shucks demeanor?

Peter stood by the buffet, avidly filling his plate with flapjacks, home fries, ham and bacon. By the time he returned to the table, Duke was all smiles.

"I ordered a special breakfast for Miss Norrie, Pete, her bein' a veggie-tarian and all," he said, his voice as gooey as the maple syrup that drowned Peter's pancakes. "It's the same breakfast we serve our book writer. Shoot, I forgot to tell ya. We got us a guest. She writes dirty books and she mostly sticks to her cabin. I woke to use the can before sunup and seen a light in her window. Maybe she forgot to turn it off, or else she was burnin' the midnight oil. I should charge her extra for the damn electric bill, 'scuse the cussin' Miss Nor—"

"I think you misunderstood last night at dinner." Peter transferred a slice of Canadian bacon to Ellie's plate. "Norrie eats red meat."

Duke laughed so hard he choked. Peter's fault. After all, they had bonded with innuendoes.

Searching her mind for a suitable quote, Ellie decided to paraphrase Erma Bombeck. "I've heard that the dude ranch was discovered quite by accident one day in the early 1940s by a Welcome-Wagon lady who was lost," she said—Erma had been talking about the suburbs, but it fit. "I want to thank you for making me feel so welcome, Mr. Dombroski. Victor Borge said, 'Laughter is the shortest distance between two people.' And Peter's right. I do eat red meat. But I like it fresh. And tender. Not fried."

Open mouth, insert boot. She'd been at the ranch less than twenty-four hours and had already made one enemy. Her own fault. She should have ignored Duke's insinuations and blatant chauvinism. What difference did it make if Duke-ersatz-Wayne thought she and Peter were married?

Momentarily, Ellie considered "hightailing" it back to Colorado Springs, where she could love her detective in her own fashion and eat scrambled eggs.

She heard Peter's niece and nephews before she saw them. Had her son Mick ever been that loud? No. Siblings made a difference.

"I'm in charge." Jonina walked into the dining room with her brothers. "Mom said I'm in charge."

Ten-year-old Ryan black-flipped. Had he been wearing ice skates, he'd have looked like a bewigged Scott Hamilton. "Hi Uncle Pete," he said. "Hi Norrie."

"Ms. Bernstein," Jonina rebuked.

"She said we could call her Norrie."

"No, Ryan. She said *I* could call her Norrie."

"Hi Nor-eee." Eight-year-old Stevie grinned.

"Stevie, shut up." Jonina's hands splayed across her hips, encased in black stretch-pants. On top she wore a white Angora-rabbit-hair sweater. A red cowboy hat completed her ensemble. She looked like an ice-cream soda.

Underneath one short sleeve she had painted a nail-polish tattoo: the letters JF & KR within a heart.

*Jonina has a boyfriend,* Ellie thought. *Well, no wonder she didn't want to spend her summer vacation at Lonesome—*

"Whoa. Wait." Peter walked toward the three kids. "Suppose we start by saying good morning? With smiles, please."

"Good morning," they chorused. Jonina didn't smile.

"Excellent. Thank you. Now . . . Jonina, where's your mother?"

"She didn't feel well, Uncle Pete. She told me to take the boys for breakfast. She said I was in charge."

"Mommy's throwing up in the bathroom," Stevie said. "Can I have Froot Loops, Uncle Pete?"

"Stevie! Mom made us *promise* not to tell."

"Mom's pregnant, Uncle Pete," Ryan said, "but it's a secret."

Turning his back on the kids, Peter walked over to a silver-plated coffee urn. With a shaky hand, he held a mug under the urn's spigot. Craving caffeine but unwilling to intrude until Peter had regained his composure, Ellie brought her attention back to Jonina.

Who glared at her brothers. "It had better be a girl this time," she said. "If it's another shitty boy, I'm gonna hitch-hike to Florida and join the circus."

"You cursed," said Stevie. Turning toward the buffet table, he shouted, "Can I have some Froot Loops, Uncle Pete?"

Ryan said, "Circus, good idea, you can be a sideshow freak," and stretched his hands as far as they'd go, as if bragging about a fish he'd caught.

"Oooh . . . oooh . . ." Jonina panted like a woman giving birth. "At least I don't tattle," she said, lifting her chin. "And for your information, tampon head, Daddy says I ride better than Mom. He says I could be an equestrian if I wanted to."

"What's a tampon?" Stevie's freckles merged.

"A plug," said Jonina.

"What's a 'questrian?"

"A bareback rider who does tricks."

"Equestrians wear tutus." Ryan gave his sister a cruel smile. "When Mom wanted you to take ballet you said—"

"Annie Oakley didn't wear a damn tu-tu."

Ellie felt as if she watched a play that featured a Greek kid-chorus.

From the corner of her eye, she saw Peter walk back to the table. In hands that looked a tad steadier, he balanced two mugs of coffee.

"You cursed," Stevie said.

"So what?" Jonina thrust out her lower lip. "Keanu Reeves curses."

Ryan looked at Ellie. "Fatso here thinks Keanu Reeves'll fall in love with her and they'll get married. She wrote it in her diary."

"You . . . you read my diary?" Jonina's mouth opened, closed, opened again. "Wait till I tell Mom! You'll be roadkill!"

Ellie loosened one of the coffee mugs from Peter's fingers, then took a grateful gulp and burned the roof of her mouth.

"Can I have Froot Loops, Uncle Pete?" Stevie had put

132

his T-shirt and shorts on backwards. He looked like a Munchkin from *The Exorcist*.

Tears filled Jonina's eyes. "I can't believe you read my diary, Ryan."

"I can't believe you read my diary, Ryan," he said, responding with the oldest, meanest kid-trick in the history of the world.

"Stop it, Ryan."

"Stop it, Ryan."

"I'm not fooling, Ryan."

"I'm not fooling, Ryan."

"Uncle Pete!"

"Uncle Pete!"

"Ryan, hush," Peter said, almost but not quite banging his coffee mug as he placed it on the table. "Jonina, fill two plates at the buffet, one for your mom, then go outside and wait for me. Rosa, please give Stevie some Froot Loops."

"We don't got no Froot Loops," the cook said, splaying her hands across her ample hips and giving Ellie another hostile glare.

"I'll eat Tony Tiger, Uncle Pete."

"We don't got no Tony—"

"Cereal. Pour some milk over cereal, Rosa, and give it to Stevie."

Finding her voice, Ellie said, "I'll take care of the boys."

Peter shot her a grateful glance, just before the most drop-dead gorgeous woman Ellie had ever seen opened the dining room door and stepped inside.

"We don't need taking care of," Ryan said. "Marion's gonna show me and Stevie how to rope a fence."

"I've been waiting for you, Pete," the drop-dead gorgeous woman said, her voice a caress. "Down by the corral. You told Duke you wanted to ride."

133

"I do, Kit, but something's just come up. Maybe you can show my friend, Norrie, around the ranch. Or, even better, give her a riding lesson. I'll meet you at the corral as soon as I can."

*Friend?* Ellie winced. But to be fair, what else could Peter have called her? My girlfriend? My significant other? My significant lover? The little woman? The wife?

Kit walked toward Ellie, and if looks could kill, Ellie would be dead.

Evidently, Peter's "bait-fed and hooked" status had undergone a radical change. Had Duke let the cat out of the bag? Would he rather have Peter tie the knot with a carnivore than one of them veggie-tarians?

At least Ellie now knew why Kit had been so distressed yesterday. She couldn't have been much older than Jonina the last time *Pete* had paid the ranch a visit.

Peter Miller was Kit Halliday's Keanu Reeves.

# Seventeen

A horse is a horse, of course, but Ellie had never imagined that, up close, a horse could look so . . . big.

Her mesmerized gaze traveled down to the animal's hooves. *They* looked like keratin teapots (without spouts) and were badly in need of a manicure.

Thank God the horse stood inside the corral. Thank God she stood outside the corral. Fresh-cut grass and newly watered soil scented the air. Distant peaks boasted snow. Closer, ornamental magpies clung to spruce trees. Had stars topped the trees, Hallmark would have optioned them for Christmas cards.

Flicking its tail like a medieval scourge, the horse nickered.

"This isn't Lucy, is it?" Ellie asked Kit, who leaned against a corral post.

"No," the young woman replied, spitting a gob of gum toward a steaming pile of manure. "Duke said you were a novice—actually, he said 'tenderfoot'—so I saddled up Buttermilk. It's easy to tell them apart, once you get to know them," she added, her voice dripping with sarcasm. "Lucy's black. Buttermilk's white."

"To be perfectly honest, Kit, I've never been on top of a horse in my life," Ellie said, ignoring the sarcasm.

"You've straddled a man, haven't you? It's the same thing."

Surprised at Kit's candor, Ellie blurted, "A man doesn't usually rear up. Or buck you off. At least, none of the men I've straddled."

Her cheeks baked as she saw that someone with a catlike tread had approached the corral, unseen, and that he stood within earshot. Marion Dombroski. Who gazed hungrily at Ellie's riding instructor.

Clothed in faded jeans and denim shirt, Kit's first five buttons were open. Her young, unfettered breasts played peek-a-boo, I see you. Her luxurious auburn hair flirted with her shoulder blades, and she made a pair of dilapidated cowboy boots look sexy.

She had to have a flaw. She didn't have any flaws. Well, maybe one flaw. Her hips were too angular for childbearing, Ellie thought critically.

But then, who gave a hoot about that these days?

Certainly not Marion. His lips were one spit away from a drool.

Discounting dark eyes, eyebrows, and hair, Marion looked as if he wanted to look like James Dean in *Rebel Without a Cause*. Or *Giant*. Or a combination *Rebel* and *Giant*. The brim of his sweat-stained Stetson shadowed his face. Underneath a red jacket, he wore a white T-shirt. A bandana drifted from his jeans pocket and his down-at-the-heels boots needed the expertise of a shoemaker. Or a blacksmith.

"Ryan and Stevie are with Lelia, so I came to see if I could help," he told Kit, almost stuttering in his eagerness to get the words out.

"Of course you can help," she said, her voice not quite the caress she'd used for Peter, but close. "And I'm sorry about last night, Marion. Adrianna had a migraine so I had to wait at the drugstore for her medicine."

"Why couldn't the drugstore deliver?"

"You know Adrianna. She was doing the Camille bit, complete with hanky. At one point she ran for the bathroom and pretended to throw up, but she's not very good at it. She sounded like a cat with a fur ball caught in its throat. Dad and Garrett were at the gallery, so naturally I had to get her medicine."

"And that took all night?"

"Could we discuss this later?" Kit jerked her head toward Ellie.

"You're right. I'm sorry. Can I help?"

"Not unless you really want to," she purred.

Talk about pulling strings, Ellie thought. And if that story about Adrianna's migraine was true, she'd eat Marion Dombroski's fawn-colored cowboy hat.

"I do want to help," he said, "I swear."

"Okay. Ms. Bernstein—"

"Ellie," Ellie said. "Or Norrie. Please."

"Yes, ma'am." Kit pointed at the white horse, then Ellie. "*She'll* be riding Buttermilk. Pete said he'd join us, so would you saddle up Satan?"

The young man's face paled. "No one can saddle Satan, Kit. I mean, like, you know, I could try, but—"

"Silly me. Did I say Satan? I meant Brownie. First, help *her* mount." Once again, Kit pointed at Ellie.

Teeth gritted, Ellie stepped into the corral and bellied up to the white horse, tied by its reins to a horizontal fence post.

"Hello, horse," she whispered. "You're a girl horse, right? We girls have to stick together, and I mean that literally. Aldous Huxley once said, 'Facts do not cease to exist because they are ignored.' The fact is, I've never been on top of a horse before. So I promise not to pull hard on that nasty piece of steel in your mouth if you promise not to run away."

Kit yelled, "What are you waiting for, ma'am?" and Buttermilk sidestepped.

"Don't be scared of her," Marion said.

Ellie wasn't sure whether he meant the horse or Kit. "I'm not scared," she fibbed, giving Buttermilk's sweaty neck a tentative pat.

She didn't fear Kit, who was nothing more than a spoiled brat, a horsefly, bothersome but harmless. Brats were ineffectual, if disregarded, and horseflies could be swatted.

Reaching into her pocket, Ellie pulled out a rubber band. Then she gathered her hair into a ponytail. "Okay, Marion, I'm all set."

He wove his fingers together. "Put your left boot in my hands and I'll hoist you up."

"Nonsense. I'm too heavy."

"No, you're not. But you can help by grabbing the saddle horn and swinging your right leg over Buttermilk's back. C'mon, Miss Norrie, put your left leg in my hands and bend your knees a little. That'll give you more spring."

She placed her boot in his hands and bent her knees. He gave one quick thrust and, somehow, she remembered to swing her leg.

"Ellie Bernstein, human Slinky," she muttered, glad her diet club members couldn't see her. In front of her dieters she felt at ease, self-assured. Here, she was a fish out of water. Except fish didn't have legs, a vagina, and buttocks.

Every muscle in her lower body tensed.

*Kit's wrong,* she thought. *Straddling a horse isn't anything like straddling a man, unless the man is shaped like a barrel and smells like a horse.*

"Relax," said Marion.

"I can't. I feel as if I'm being tortured, stretched on a rack, examined by a Roman Catholic tribunal. In another moment they'll ask me if I'm a heretic."

"Are you?"

She laughed. "It depends on your definition of heretic. If it was the Spanish Inquisition I'd be branded a heretic, even though I was brought up Catholic. I guess I like to think I'm a nonconformist, open to new ideas, but when push comes to shove, I'm just a square peg in a square hole. How about you?"

"Me? Square peg, square hole."

"No." She shook her head and the ragged, wispy ends of her ponytail slapped her cheeks like a whisk broom. "You're too smart. Most people wouldn't have understood one word I just said."

"You said you're a conformist, except when you rebel."

"Perfect." She laughed again. "I'll have to introduce you to my son, Mick. He's around your age and he's a rebel, except when he conforms."

"You've got a son my age? You're joking."

"Knock it off," she said with a smile. "I'm not a guest. You don't have to snow me."

"*Now* you're showing your age." He smiled back at her. " 'Snow me' went out when the Beatles split up. If you're not a guest, what are you?"

"I'm not sure. An appendage, I suppose."

"To Pete?"

She nodded. "In a city, even a small city, Peter . . . Pete and I are equals. Here I feel, I don't know, subservient. Not toadyish subservient. More like dependent."

"Once you learn how to ride a horse and lasso a steer,

139

that feeling will go away."

"Lasso a steer?"

"We'll start with fence posts."

"What are you waiting for?" Kit yelled.

Marion flinched, but merely said, loud enough for Kit to hear, "You're still too tense, Miss Norrie."

"I know." She tried to figure out what to do with her legs. They dangled, useless, as surreal as the inflexible leather that pressed against her crotch. Then she caught the smug expression on Kit's face and, with an effort, untensed.

"That's better," Marion said. "I'm going to adjust your stirrups. As soon as you put your feet in the stirrups you'll feel fine, in control."

"I feel fine, even without stirrups," she said, and this time she didn't fib. Because—rather quickly, she thought with pride—she had adjusted to her spread-eagle position.

Of course, the horse hadn't moved yet.

Dear God, Marion was untying the reins.

She stroked her fox amulet, hanging between breasts that were restrained, practically shackled by her sports bra. Over the bra she wore a new plaid shirt, tucked into new blue jeans, tucked into her new cowboy boots. She felt like Tarzan's Jane—before Jane went native.

"Are you right-handed or left-handed?" Marion asked.

"Ambidextrous. I was born left-handed but my mother tied my left hand behind my back until I learned to use my right hand."

"Why would she do that?"

"Because her mother did it to her. Let's just say I'm right-handed, okay?"

"Sure. Put the reins between the first and third finger of your right hand."

"I'm giving someone the bird backwards," Ellie said. "Upside-down."

He grinned. "That's a good way to put it. If you feel unsteady, you can use your left hand to grasp the saddle horn. Here, I'll help you find the stirrups."

How did Marion suddenly become her riding instructor? Ellie didn't mind. He was a good kid. And Kit had disappeared. No. There she was. Strolling toward the barn. No. The house. Maybe she had to go to the bathroom. Maybe she didn't want to give "ma'am" a riding lesson. Maybe, like a bloodhound, she planned to follow Peter's scent.

"Are you ready?" Marion asked.

"Yes. But aren't I keeping you from something? Breakfast? Chores?"

"You're not keeping me from one damn thing," he said, darting a quick glance toward Kit, now skirting the main house.

Heading, Ellie surmised, for the guest cottages.

Marion glowered. His face wore an ugly, churlish scowl, and she thought: *He's a good kid, but I wouldn't want to rub him the wrong way.*

"Who's Lelia?" she asked. "You said Stevie and Ryan were with Lelia."

"Rosa Hamilton's daughter," he replied. "Rosa's the cook," he clarified.

*Ah, the cook who hates my guts. I hope she's never seen* Sweeney Todd.

"Lelia cleans the cottages," Marion continued, "and, in her spare time, she carves wood."

"Did she carve that lovely headboard in my bedroom?"

He shrugged. "I'm not allowed inside the cottages."

Ellie wanted to ask him why, but lost her nerve. Because

141

his James Dean persona had evaporated and he looked a little like Norman Bates in *Psycho*. Like Anthony Perkins, smiling his psychotic smile while the movie's voice-over said he wouldn't hurt a fly.

# Eighteen

Marion put Buttermilk through her paces. First, a long walk. Then a trot. Then a brief canter.

The walk was effortless, the canter fun, like riding a carousel horse. The trot was a different story and Ellie blessed her sports bra.

She tried to focus on the lesson but her mind kept straying.

Peter, she assumed, was talking to Beth.

But what if Kit had found him, afterward? What if she had lured him to a distant pasture? For the first time since her divorce, Ellie felt a jealous jolt. She envied Kit her youth. And her angular hips.

Kit wore—what? A size five? Three? Thanks to diet pills, Ellie had once whittled herself down to a nine. And met drop-dead gorgeous Tony. And married him. And gave birth to Mick. And never went below a plus size again.

Until Weight Winners.

*Don't equate everything with weight,* she told herself. But she couldn't help it. She had too much baggage, too many demons. Her biggest demon was a mother who thought she was being helpful when she said, "No man will ever want you if you don't lose weight. I suppose you can always be a nun." Or, "It's easy to lose ten (twenty, thirty, forty) pounds. Just stop eating so much." Or, "I hate to say I told you so. No use crying over spilt milk. I've made all the arrangements. Your cousin will take you to the prom. We'll hit the stores tomorrow, Ellie. I just hope we can find you a decent dress that fits."

By the time prom night rolled around, her dress was bursting at the seams. Shopping with her mother had led to the biggest eating binge of her life. Every piece of food she could lay her hands on went down her throat. Except, of course, during meals. "You eat like a bird," her mother said. "It must be glands. From your father's side of the family. Your brother has *my* genes, thank God."

Cruel mother who didn't know she was being cruel. Nasty playmates who knew they were being nasty but didn't care. Walker Seidman, her first and only high school boyfriend, who didn't care how much she weighed because she had "hair the color of blood." Walker moved to Boca Raton, prior to the prom, and Ellie never heard from him again. Maybe he'd found another, more accessible redhead. Or maybe he'd found a woman with hair that matched the Florida sand.

Speaking of sand-colored hair, Adrianna Halliday was sure to be at tonight's dinner party. Ellie didn't relish bumping into the provocative skater again, but figured she had no choice. John Halliday had willed his house to his sons, Garrett and Gideon. Shortly before his death, John's speculative stock portfolio had gone belly-up, so he'd borrowed on his life insurance policy. To put it bluntly, and Garrett had, Adrianna didn't have a pot to piss in or a window to throw it out of.

Naturally, the Halliday brothers had given her a house to live in. "Until she gets her act together," Garrett had said on the phone, his voice peevish.

Ellie hadn't asked, but she wondered how Heather and Kit felt. Did Adrianna sheath her claws when Garrett's wife and niece were in close proximity? Kit looked as if she could give as good as she got, but Heather was a gentle soul, unwilling to step on a spider, not even a deadly black wid—

Holy cow, black widow! Ellie pictured Adrianna at the gallery. Ms. Merry Widow. If she had sported a red, hourglass-shaped tattoo, along with abdominal spinnerets—

How had John Halliday died? Heart attack. Had Adrianna, unaware of her husband's stock losses, "induced" the attack?

Ellie grimaced. *Here I go again,* she thought, *reading ulterior motives into every fluke. First, Serafina Lassiter. Now, Adrianna Halliday.*

But what about the skater with scrambled eggs for brains? To be fair, no one could actually *prove* Adrianna had bopped her rival over the head. And, as far as Ellie knew, no suspicions had been aroused when it came to John Halliday's demise. Sudden heart attack. Gone. Cremated. Ashes to ashes, dust to—

"Miss Norrie?"

"Sorry, Marion, daydreaming." She tossed her ponytail. "If I do that on the trail, I'll probably wake up and find myself in New Mexico."

He grinned. "I don't think so. Buttermilk ain't what she used to be. Only one thing can make her take off like a bat out of hell."

Before Ellie could ask what that one thing might be, she saw Peter and Kit, arm in arm, heading toward the barn.

With her free hand, Kit brushed tangled hair away from her face. She walked with a suggestive swagger. Three of her five buttons had been buttoned and the shirt that had once been tucked into jeans now hung loose, undulating along with her angular hips. She broke stride to cuddle in closer and lean her head against Peter's shoulder. As they entered the barn, her saucy behind seemed to wriggle triumphantly.

Jealousy was a familiar garment, a plus-size cloak that Ellie had worn while married to Tony. Earlier, she had compared Kit to a pesky horsefly. Somewhere, probably the library, she had read that horseflies were bloodsuckers.

# Nineteen

Ellie watched Kit and Peter emerge from the barn. Apparently, they'd done nothing more than saddle their horses. And what, exactly, had she expected them to do? Engage in a hayloft-quickie while she bounced around the corral?

Mentally, she chastised herself. Lonesome Pines wasn't some reality TV show called Temptation Ranch and Kit was—what? Twenty-one? Twenty-two? After she and *Pete* talked about horses (and country music) what else did they have in common? Presumably, Kit had never heard of Joplin. Okay, maybe Janice, and The Doors because Hollywood had made a movie with Val Kilmer and Meg Ryan, but not Perry Como. Or The Drifters. Or Percy Sledge. Heck, Kit probably thought The Orlons were a sweater, The Chiffons a scarf.

On the other hand, Ellie's father had left his family for a waitress barely old enough to drink the liquor she served, and Tony had become smitten by a Dallas Cowboys cheerleader, had even married the young, skinny, big-breasted show-off.

Ellie scrutinized Peter, at ease in sneakers, well-worn jeans, and a somewhat faded black-and-silver Oakland Raiders T-shirt. He led a brown horse by its reins, the same horse his sister had ridden yesterday. What was its name again? Brownie. Kit led a smaller, coal-black horse, and Ellie heard the echo of Duke's effusive description: *A pint-*

*sized filly, smart and dainty-gaited, but don't let that fool ya.*

Duke had been fleshing out both Lucy and Kit.

Marion adjusted his Stetson until his eyes were wholly shadowed. "Looks like Kit and Pete plan to hit the trail," he said, his voice sour. "No, wait. Pete's waving you over, so I guess you'll ride with them. Don't be nervous, Miss Norrie, and don't forget what I told you. Hug Buttermilk with your knees and kick her barrel . . . her belly with your boot heels if you want to go faster."

"Oh, God. Do you think I'm ready to leave the corral?"

"Absolutely. You'll ride single file. Pete and Kit will put you between them so Buttermilk can't stop to graze. They're predicting rain this evening. But right now it's beautiful, not a cloud in the sky, and except for Angel's Ravine, the trail's easy to navigate."

"Why don't you come with us, Marion? I'd feel so much better if you did."

"I haven't been invited," he said brusquely. "Would you do me a big favor, Miss Norrie?"

"Sure. As long as it's not illegal or fattening and you drop the Miss in front of Norrie."

"Okay, deal." He took a deep breath. "Would you call me Dom? Jonina's the only one who calls me that, and I kind of like it."

"I like it, too . . . Dom."

He smiled. Gently grasping Buttermilk's reins, he led Ellie out of the corral and over to Peter, now on top of Brownie. Buttermilk and Brownie were the same size, Lucy smaller, and it gave Ellie a perverse pleasure to sit higher than Kit.

Leaning sideways, Peter ran his finger along the curve of her cheek, and she had a feeling that, if alone, he would have kissed her. *All's right with the world,* she thought, and if thoughts could purr, she'd have purred. She was dying to ask him about Beth, but Kit sat within earshot. Kit hadn't been at the supper table last night when Beth hinted—more than hinted—that she'd left her husband, and Kit hadn't been present this morning when Ryan and Stevie let the pregnant cat out of the bag.

In other words, it was none of Kit's business.

"Are you all set to enter the Kentucky Derby, sweetheart?" Peter asked.

"A few more lessons and I'll be ready. I've done everything but gallop," she replied, and heard the pride in her voice. "Correct me if I'm wrong, but I believe you've got to gallop if you want to win the Kentucky Derby. Last night, when Roy and Dale galloped, it looked easy, so I'm fairly certain I'll get the hang of it. And Dom's a great teacher. Smart and patient and . . . well, patient."

"Dom?"

She sensed rather than saw Marion's discomfort. "Some people call Marion Dom," she said. "He doesn't care, one way or the other, but I think he looks like a Dom." Staring into Peter's eyes, she hoped her own eyes conveyed a message: *Give the kid a break.* "Don't you think he looks like a Dom?"

"Yes, definitely," Peter said, as if he'd given her question serious, albeit brief, consideration. "Dammit, Norrie, we forgot to buy you a hat."

"I never wear hats. When have you ever seen me in a hat?"

"I've seen you in bunny ears," he said with a grin.

"The Weight Winners Halloween party." She sighed. "Was it only seven months ago? Seems like forever. I trashed the costume, but I still have my ears."

"Maybe we could get started," Kit said, a pouty declaration rather than a question. "I haven't got all day and Lucy's skittish as a grasshopper."

"Norrie can borrow my hat," Marion said.

"Next, she'll want a parasol," Kit muttered.

"Norrie doesn't want anything," Peter said. "The hat's my idea. The sun's fierce and redheads tend to burn easily."

"Okay, you're right, I'm sorry. Lucy's straining at the bit."

Apparently, only Ellie heard her murmur, "As if red's her natural color."

*It is and I can prove it,* Ellie thought. But she left the thought unsaid, more concerned with the look on her new friend's face. Without his hat, she could see Marion's eyes. They were angry slits. The hollows beneath his cheekbones were more pronounced and his sensuous mouth had thinned into a straight line. Damn! She should have asked Peter if Marion could join them, ride with them. Too late now. Kit was way ahead, leaning from her saddle to open a pasture gate. Peter had already seized Buttermilk's halter and was leading Ellie away from the barn.

Although her big white horse plodded docilely alongside Peter's big brown horse, Ellie had a feeling Buttermilk had never read the Weight Winners introductory pamphlet. The pages included "legal" foods, sample menus, recipes, motivational advice, and an exercise program.

On the surface, it appeared that Buttermilk wasn't into exercise.

Not even power-walking.

# Twenty

Tall, seemingly endless treetops served as leafy parasols, shielding Ellie from the aggressive sun. But when she rode into a defoliated clearing, Marion's hat was a godsend. Hat or no hat, the panoramic view left her emotionally defenseless—awestruck and breathless.

*Garrett should paint this,* she mused, gazing out over a vista profusely dotted with green pines, reddish boulders, and narrow blue streamlets. She didn't know all that much about art, but she knew enough to know that portraitists deviated every now and then with still lifes and landscapes. And while Garrett was primarily recognized—and duly acclaimed—for his eroticism, it wasn't what you *saw* when you looked at a painting but how you *felt.*

At least that was the way Heather had once described it to Ellie, and she had to agree. She liked Garrett's earlier works better than his new paintings. He had refined his technique, but he'd lost something in the translation. A feeling of naïveté, innocence, and, strange as it might sound, virtue. Even *Christmas Carol,* the painting purchased by Owen Lassiter—if one hadn't seen Garrett's recent canvasses, one would never think Santa was copping a feel.

Did cop-a-feel date her? Age her?

Probably. And speaking of cops, where was Peter?

They had navigated the pasture together, side-by-side, but then he had led the way, Kit bringing up the rear. Obviously, he'd ridden into the grove that lay ahead. If she hadn't been contemplating Garrett's complex, chameleon-like paintings, she would have seen Brownie disappear. After all, she had been fixated on the horse's swaying rump for half an hour, maybe longer.

Okay, where was Kit?

Nowhere, that's where. Kit had vanished into the woods, too.

Unless she'd plummeted down a nearby incline.

Ellie shuddered. No way would she nudge her horse to the top of the incline.

*If Kit plummeted, she'd scream. But what if I was so self-absorbed I didn't hear her scream?*

No one could be that self-absorbed.

"Listen, horse, we're going to walk very slowly over to the edge of that incline."

What had Marion said? Kick the horse's belly if she wanted to go faster.

"I don't want to go fast, Buttermilk, I want to go slow, s-l-o-w, understand? So please, please remember that when I kick your belly."

Ellie kicked. Nothing happened. She kicked a little harder. Buttermilk lowered her head to graze, practically tugging the reins out of Ellie's hands.

"Well, there goes that idea." She didn't know whether to feel relieved, angry, or frustrated. "If you stop eating grass," she said, "I'll give you a carrot when we get back to the ranch. Two carrots. If the cook . . . what's her name? Oh, yeah. Rosa. If *Rosa* doesn't have carrots, I'll buy a whole bunch tonight on my way to Aspen."

This ridiculous situation reminded Ellie of her first driving lesson. Rather than a woodland field, she and Tony had found a deserted parking lot. Instead of reins, her sweaty hands had gripped a steering wheel. She had toed the clutch with her left foot and stepped on the accelerator with her right foot while Tony sat in the passenger seat, a smug expression on his face. He didn't think she could learn to drive a stick shift and she was determined to show him she could.

The car radio and tape deck had been stolen, and Tony's portable radio had blared "Dueling Banjos." Loud. Very loud. Loud enough to cover the sound of an engine. Her feet kept pressing down on the clutch and accelerator, but she couldn't feel any power surge, so she had shifted her gaze to the stick shift, which was in neutral, then the emergency brake, which she knew darn-well she'd released.

The banjos finished dueling and Tony said, "It helps if you turn the car *on.*" While she just stared at him, tears blurring her vision, sweat pouring down her face, he added, "You forgot to turn the ignition key. It's on the steering column."

So . . . where the heck was Buttermilk's steering column? *Not her belly, that's for sure.*

Ellie could hear Buttermilk chewing her cud. Did horses have cuds? Did horses have ignition keys?

As if she had asked her question out loud, she heard a voice say, "Here, try this."

"Kit! You startled me. Where were you?"

"Behind that tree." She pointed toward the grove. "I had to pee. If you have to pee, you'd better go now. Once we ride into the woods, the trees are so thick you can hardly squeeze between them." Critically, she examined Ellie's size twelve curves.

"I'm okay, thanks, except for Buttermilk. No matter how hard I kick, she won't move."

"That's because you let her graze," Kit said, her voice

accusatory. "Here, try this."

"A tree branch?"

"A switch. You could use the ends of your reins, but I don't think you have much control over them anymore."

"Look, Kit, I think we got off on the wrong foot. If I said or did something wrong, I'm sorry. I need you to help me and I wish you wouldn't be so condescending."

"Pete's way ahead of us. Soon he'll discover we're not behind him. I plan to catch up. Do you want the switch or not?"

"Not." Reaching a shaky hand into her shirt pocket, Ellie pulled out a pack of sugarless gum. Unwrapping a stick, she shoved the tin foil back into her pocket and extended the pack toward Kit.

The young girl shook her head. "I'll never understand how anyone can chew that sugarless shit," she said, sounding as if she were Duke Dombroski's protégé.

Ellie pocketed her pack, then stared at the leafy branch. "I don't want to hurt the horse."

"Just wave the leaves in her face and tap her gently on her haunch," Kit said. "I'll collect your reins for you and you can follow me and Lucy. If Buttermilk lags behind, show her the switch. You probably won't even have to hit her with it. When we catch up to Pete, we'll put you in the middle again and you can throw the damn thing away."

"Can't you lead Buttermilk by her halter?"

"No, Norrie. We wouldn't be able to ride side-by-side, the trail's too narrow. If I snap a lead to Buttermilk's halter and she gets too close to Lucy, Lucy'll kick. Then Buttermilk could *really* get hurt. Or she'll rear up and you'll fall off and Pete would *kill* me if anything happened to you."

At least Kit had called her Norrie rather than ma'am. Ellie stifled a sigh of relief. "Okay," she said, reaching for the slender tree branch. "As long as you're sure I won't hurt her."

In one fluid motion, Kit dismounted, gathered up Buttermilk's reins, and handed them to Ellie. "Marion showed you how to hold these, right?"

"Yes. But I was daydreaming and let them slip through my fingers."

"Hold them tight, but not too tight, and for goodness sake, don't daydream. You're doin' great, Norrie, especially for a beginner."

"Thanks. Maybe by tomorrow I won't be a 'tenderfoot' anymore."

"Oh, don't let Duke bother you." Kit swung herself up into the saddle. "Duke's harmless, even though, a long time ago, he killed a woman."

Kit's boot heels nudged Lucy's belly. The "dainty-gaited" filly took off like a bat out of hell and Ellie could only watch the trees swallow up girl and horse.

"Well, that friendship was certainly short-lived," she told Buttermilk. "Do you want to follow Lucy's dust cloud or should I 'tap' you with the branch?"

Buttermilk's ears flickered, as if she contemplated her options. Then she plodded toward the grove. As they continued along the narrow trail, Ellie felt breathless again. This time the scenery was straight out of an illustrated fairy tale. Any moment now, a Gingerbread House would appear. If it did, would she break her diet?

Much as she disliked Duke Dombroski, she couldn't believe he'd murdered anyone. If true, why wasn't he rotting away in prison? Wait a sec. Kit had said, "killed," not murdered. Drunk drivers killed. It could be as simple as that.

Buttermilk stumbled.

"Good horse, good girl," Ellie crooned. "Take your

time, there's no hurry. I'm sure Peter's waiting for me, or backtracking. No, no, leave that clump of grass alone. I can see it looks juicy, as grass goes, or grows, but you've had enough to eat, more than enough. God, you're stubborn, just like Charlene Johnson, one of my Weight Winners members. She not only cheats, but she tries to get everyone else to cheat. They say she cheats on her husband, too, but that's another story. I don't think Charlene is hopeless, no one's hopeless, but she's so damn stubborn. And to tell the God's honest truth, Buttermilk, I don't like her very much."

Apparently, the horse had only grasped two words of her lengthy diatribe—stubborn and grass.

As Buttermilk strained toward the juicy clump of weeds, Ellie waved the leafy branch in front of the horse's eyes, then tapped her gently, very gently, ever so gently, on the rump.

Buttermilk bolted.

Dropping the switch and reins, Ellie clutched the saddle horn with both hands. *Hug with your knees,* she thought. *Marion said to hug with your knees.*

Marion didn't know what the heck he was talking about.

No way could she hug with her knees when she bounced like a rubber ball.

Too bad her tush wasn't made of rubber.

She didn't want to fall off. She wanted to fall off. But she wanted Buttermilk to slow down, first.

Not that she had a choice. A horse is a horse, of course, and this one ran like the bus in the movie *Speed*.

What would happen when Buttermilk slowed to under fifty miles an hour?

Ellie lost her stirrups. Then, of course, she lost the horse.

She wasn't sure where she landed. Oh, she knew, for sure, she landed on hard-packed dirt, but she didn't know, for sure, if she landed on her head or her back or—probably her head, since she saw two Peters looming above her. As he sank to his knees, he merged into one Peter and his face looked anxious. Worse than anxious. Alarmed. As though he thought this was all his fault. Which, of course, it was. He never should have left her alone with Kit.

Alone with Kit. That didn't sound right. If she was alone, she wouldn't be with Kit. Confusion must have showed in her eyes because Peter said, "Norrie, say something."

*Nothing to breathe but air,* she thought. *Quick as a flash 'tis gone. Nothing to fall but off. Nowhere to stand but on. Ben King, born 1857, died—*

"Norrie, please *say* something," Peter repeated, panic in every syllable.

"I lost my gum."

"What do you mean, you lost your gum? Is your mouth bleeding?"

"No, *hic,* I lost my chewing gum. I'm glad I wasn't riding, *hic,* across Independence Pass, *hic.* Why am I hic-cupping?"

"Because you've had a bad scare. Look at me."

"I am looking at, *hic,* you."

"No, you're not. You're looking at the sky. Look at my hand. How many fingers am I holding up?"

"Holding down, *hic.* Four."

"Five!"

"I didn't, *hic,* count your thumb. If I count your, *hic,* thumb, it's five."

"Focus on my hand, please. How many fingers now?"

"Em."

"What?"

157

"You're making the letter 'M.' "

"I told you to count, not spell."

"Three fingers, Peter. Where's Kit?"

"Riding back to the ranch."

"To 'round up' Buttermilk?"

"No. Buttermilk will head straight for the barn."

"Did Kit catch up to you? Of course she caught up to you. Stupid question."

"Kit said she told you to follow her and thought you were right behind her. She was distraught, useless. She said it's her responsibility if a guest gets hurt—"

"Technically, I'm not a guest."

"—so I sent her back to the ranch to call 9-1-1."

"You're kidding. You're not kidding. I don't need paramedics or a stupid ambulance. I'm not even hiccupping anymore. I feel fine." She grabbed his M-fingered hand, then his arm, and hauled herself to her feet. "See? Ohheck! Ohheckdarn! Ouch!"

"Jesus, Norrie, define ouch."

"My ankle. Not broken. Sprained. Maybe." Still hanging onto his arm, she said, "I don't think I can walk. How on earth will I get back to the ranch?"

"Simple. You'll ride in front of me. We'll take it very slow—"

"No way! I'm never getting on top of a horse again. And if you say the best thing to do when you fall off is to get back on, I'll strangle you. A car won't make it down this narrow trail, so you'll have to rent a motorcycle. I'll wait here."

"Norrie, sweetheart—"

"I'm serious. Don't you dare put me on a horse!" She took a couple of steps backwards. "Ohheck. Ouch! Ohheckdarn, I think I'm going to throw up. No. Never mind. I'll faint, instead. Is that okay with you?"

She felt Peter's arms around her, felt herself lifted up, felt leather against her crotch, felt Peter's chest against her back. His forearm pinioned her waist.

"Please don't put me on top of a horse," she managed, just before the earth and trees and Peter and Brownie turned as black as caviar, as black as licorice, as black as an Oreo, as black as—

*There aren't many foods that are black,* she thought—her last thought.

# Twenty-One

Marion watched Kit unsaddle Buttermilk. Standing inside the white horse's stall, she hummed a tuneless tune, off-tune, something that sounded like "Happy Trails To You."

She left the stall, walked into the tack room, then out again, and he scuttled down the loft ladder. He timed it so that he landed directly in front of her.

"Okay," he said, "why didn't you show last night?"

"Get out of my way."

"First, tell me why you didn't show."

"I already told you. Adrianna had a migraine and—"

"Bull! Please give me credit for a modicum of intelligence. You could strain spaghetti through your story."

"What's a modicum?" she asked, her brow creasing. "And what do you mean, strain spaghetti?"

"Sorry, I forgot you quit school halfway through the tenth grade."

"I didn't quit. Gramps sent me to a convent school in—"

"Yes, I know." He smiled at the anger that sparked her eyes. "Shall I dumb it down for you, Kit? The truth is, you leave too many holes in your lies."

Now he couldn't decipher her expression. She looked pained, thoughtful, maybe even a little chagrined.

"If you don't believe me," she said, "you can go straight to hell!"

Abruptly, she made an about-face and ran back into the

tack room. He followed but she shut the door in his face.

"Leave me alone!" she screamed.

She sounded scared. "What is it, Kit? What's wrong?" When she didn't respond, he said, "I'm opening the door. I won't hurt you. Just tell me what's wrong."

He inched open the door. She threw her weight against it. Off balance, he took a clown's pratfall, landing on his butt. He sprang to his feet. And caught her in front of Buttermilk's stall. Her face was chalk-white, except for her cheeks, which blazed like twin poppies.

"Did it ever occur to you," she said, "that I didn't tell the truth because I can't?"

"Why can't you?"

"I'll get in trouble."

"How will you get in trouble?"

"He'll tell my father, only he'll make it sound like it's the other way 'round."

"Kit, I don't know what the hell you're talking about."

"Garrett will tell my dad."

"Tell him what?"

"That I tried to sleep with him."

"What? You seduced Garrett?"

"No, you idiot. He . . . Garrett . . . he . . . ."

"Garrett seduced you?"

She nodded, then covered her face with her hands.

He pried her fingers free and held her hands tightly in his. "Was last night the first time?"

"Yes. I'm so ashamed."

"That bastard!"

"Heather won't, and he said he needed someone to inspire him. He said that without sex, an artist, a really great artist . . . I said no, but he said all he wanted to do was touch me, so I let him, and then he kissed me, and that was okay, and then he . . . well, you know." She and Buttermilk heaved syncopated sighs. "I tried to get away," Kit continued, "but he put something in my drink . . . that date-rape stuff they always talk about on TV. I found some Roofies and XTC in one of the cottages, after the guests had left. Stupidly, I took the stuff home. Marion, I swear to God I couldn't move. Garrett raped me twice, and that's why I didn't meet you or call you."

"That bastard! That son of a bitch! I'm gonna beat him to a pulp."

"Don't be stupid, Marion. He's twice as big—"

"I'll slip something into *his* drink. Then, when he's unconscious, I'll cut off his—"

"No! I don't want you to get in trouble. I'm sure it won't happen again."

"If you don't call the cops, I will, I swear I will. Dammit, Kit, he raped you!"

"Oh, he used a condom so I wouldn't get pregnant."

Turning away from him, she leaned her arm against the stall and hid her face against her arm. He saw her shoulders shake.

"Kit, are you crying? Kit, are you laughing?"

"Marion, you're so funny. You should have seen your face. I couldn't tell if you were horrified or jealous."

"Your uncle didn't drug you, or rape you. You made up that whole story. You little bitch. Why would you do that?"

"To see if I could. And because you said you could strain spaghetti through my lies. But you bought that one, didn't you? Hook, line, and sinker. I realized I'd gone too far when you swore you'd call the cops."

On tiptoe, she performed one and a half pirouettes, then stared at him and bit her lip. To keep from breaking into new gales of laughter, he supposed.

"I'm curious," he said. "Why, all of a sudden, did you decide to cut my strings?"

"Huh?"

"Up until now you've strung me along. I've panted after you like a damn dog. Sometimes you even let me sniff your butt."

"How rude, *Dom*. Marion would never say something like that."

"Why did you cut my strings, Kit?"

"I never wanted you, Marion. I was just passing the time till I saw Pete again. Now I've got Pete bait-fed. We met outside Beth's cabin. He was upset. We hiked to Angel's Ravine and sat under the oak. He kept saying he wanted to be alone, but he didn't really mean it. When I moved in for the kill, he got antsy over leaving his city mouse alone. So, like it or not, I had to change my game plan."

"You're lying again. God, I hate liars."

"No, I'm not. And his hoity-toity, city mouse girlfriend will hightail it out of here so fast it'll make your head spin. Even if she doesn't, Pete loves to ride more than anything and *she* won't ride, won't even try. Buttermilk ran away with her and she fell off and all I need is some *quality* time alone with Pete."

"Buttermilk never runs away unless someone hits her with a switch. What did you do?"

"A *leafy* switch, and I didn't do anything. Miss Tenderfoot did it all by herself."

"You know what, Kit? I used to think I loved you, but now I don't even like you."

"You know what, Marion? Tell someone who cares."

# Twenty-Two

Ellie's ankle wasn't broken, just badly sprained, but pain pills knocked her out for the rest of the day. When she woke, she was ravenous. And very, very sore.

"I feel like I've been tossed into a cement mixer," she told Peter. "By the way, did you find Marion's hat?"

"What?"

"His hat fell off during one of my more volatile bounces."

"Norrie, the kid's hat was the last thing on my mind."

Peter adjusted the two plump pillows behind her back. He checked the bedroom closet, then walked into the living room. When he returned, he was carrying a couch cushion. Tenderly, he placed her bandaged foot and ankle on top.

"I'll ask Duke for more pillows," he said.

"Ask Lelia Hamilton. She's the one who cleans the cottages."

"I remember Lelia. Tiny, barely five feet tall. Long, dark hair. She has a daughter, a beautiful child . . . Angel."

"I'm fairly certain Lelia carved the angel in our headboard." Ellie glanced over her shoulder and winced at the sudden, sharp crick in her sore neck. "Peter . . . ?"

"Yes?" He sat on the edge of the bed.

"Marion said there was only one thing that would make Buttermilk run away. He didn't say what it was, and I didn't ask, but I think he meant leaves. A branch with

164

leaves. I flicked Buttermilk's rump with a leafy branch."

"Sweetheart, you couldn't possibly know—"

"Wait, I'm not finished. Kit gave me the branch. Kit said to show Buttermilk the leafy end. Kit said if Buttermilk still didn't move, to hit her on the—"

"Norrie, you misunderstood."

"I misunderstood a leafy branch? Which part did I misunderstand, Peter? The leaves or the stem?"

"Calm down."

"I am calm," she said, groping for Jackie Robinson. Fingers spread, she trawled him from the middle of the mattress. He resisted, at first, then let her deposit him in the crook of her arm. With her free hand she caressed the cat's fluffy ruff, a hypnotic motion that effectuated human tranquility and feline purrs.

"Maybe," said Peter, "Kit didn't know about Buttermilk's fetish."

"She's the riding instructor. How could she not know? Marion knew."

"Whoa. You just said that Marion didn't tell you—"

"Listen to me, Peter. Buttermilk wanted to graze. Kit gave me a leafy switch and told me to wave it in front of Buttermilk's face. Then Kit took off like a bat out of hell."

"She thought you were right behind her."

"Did she? Then why didn't she wait until I turned Buttermilk's ignition key?"

"Ignition key? What do you mean?"

Before Ellie could explain, the phone rang and Peter left the bedroom.

When he returned, a crease crinkled the bridge of his nose.

"What?" she asked, alarmed. "Mick? Sandra?"

"No, sweetheart. Will McCoy." Peter ran his hands

slowly, very slowly, through his hair. "Precinct update," he finally said.

"And the update is?"

"It's after five. Don't you have to get dressed for Halliday's dinner party? Or should we call and ask for a raincheck?"

As if on cue, lightning flashed and thunder drummed. "No," she said. "I want to see Heather. I'll get dressed soon, but first the update."

"Norrie, it's not my case."

"Aha! Rudolph Kessler. Obviously, they didn't catch his killer. What's the latest bulletin? And if you say it's not my case again, I'll strangle you."

"You've been threatening to strangle me a lot lately. Jonina and baby fat. Getting back on top of a horse."

"Stop procrastinating. Don't you know that running your fingers through your hair like that will make you bald?"

"Says who?"

"My mother."

"I thought it was reading by flashlight will ruin your eyes."

"According to my mother, reading by flashlight will wear out the batteries and starving to death will make you live longer. Forget my mother. Tell me what's new."

"Kessler placed a classified ad in the paper, so anyone could have read it. The paper is one of those giveaways and it's delivered everywhere. Duke even has a stack in his office, along with real estate and cars-for-sale and—"

"We already thought of an ad. Come on, Lieutenant, what's the real scoop?"

Raindrops pelted the windowpanes like a lover tossing too many pebbles as he said, "Serafina Lassiter was murdered."

"Oh my God! How?"

"Strangled. Pantyhose. Odds are, the perp's a woman."

"You're kidding, right? You can buy pantyhose at any supermarket. When was she killed?"

"This morning, around six, give or take an hour. She was supposed to meet friends for brunch but never showed. Her friends didn't panic, just figured she'd overslept. Several Bloody Marys later, they decided to pay her a surprise visit."

"And got the surprise of their lives. Serafina's husband killed her, right?"

"Wrong. He, himself, was wounded."

"I'll bet his wound was self-inflicted."

"No, Norrie. Owen Lassiter was hit on the back of the head. If someone wants to self-inflict, he'll stab himself, maybe shoot an arm or foot. I'm not saying it can't be done, but smashing your own head hard enough to lose consciousness is like trying to drown yourself in a shallow pond. Sooner or later you'll rise to the surface, gasping for air, and—"

"Did Lassiter recognize the perp? No. Of course he didn't. Stupid question. If he did, you'd know the perp's identity. Lassiter was hit from behind and never saw it coming, right? Okay, suppose he hired someone to kill his wife? And he told the killer to tie him up and/or wound him so he wouldn't be suspect. But the perp, enthused, whacked too hard and—why are you looking at me like that?"

"I love the way you ask and answer your own questions, and what's Lassiter's motive?"

"That's easy. A bazillion-dollar insurance policy. Or how about a hefty inheritance? Serafina's perfume cost a pretty penny and she bought a very expensive paint . . . holy cow!"

"Yes," said Peter. "Holy cow."

"*Christmas Carol.* Whomever killed Serafina stole *Christmas Carol.*"

"Correct. 'Whomever' didn't even try and make it look like a run-of-the-mill robbery, didn't touch expensive jewelry or electronic equipment or—"

"Why wasn't *Christmas Carol* at the gallery? When someone buys a painting it usually stays on the wall until the end of the exhibit. With a sold sticker."

"Lassiter talked the gallery into letting him take it home. He wanted to show it off at a party, brag about its exorbitant price tag. Saturday night he threw a big soirée for his clients and business associates. The C.S.P.D. is trying to track down everybody who attended the party, virtually impossible. It was *not* invitation only. Lassiter wanted to woo new clients."

"So the perp could have been a guest. But how would the perp know about the party? He, or she would have to be a client or a business associate."

"Or the client of a business associate. Or the friend of a client. And . . ." This time Peter wove his hand through his hair quickly. "It was on the news."

"The news," she parroted.

"Yup. Every damn TV station. One of the guests was rock star Yogi Demon. He left the party early, drunk as a skunk. He was only a couple of blocks from Lassiter's house, driving the wrong way on a one-way street, when he ran into a squad car. The squad car had been called to the scene because the party was, by that time, earsplitting."

She almost smiled at his "earsplitting," thinking most people would have simply said "loud." One of the things she loved best about her lieutenant was his quirky terminology.

"Yogi Demon hit a cop car?" she asked, as she watched

Jackie Robinson jump down from the bed and leap up onto the rocker. "Peter?

"Sorry, I was waiting for you to answer your own question."

His quirky sense of humor, however, left a lot to be desired. "Very funny," she said.

"Demon was *stopped* by a cop. Unfortunately, the fracas that followed took place in a posh neighborhood, where every other resident owns a state-of-the-art videocam."

"Define fracas."

"The rock star's drunk companion, a Vegas dancer named Rose something, decided on the spur of the moment to audition for *Charlie's Angels*. Then she fled. McCoy says she might have gotten clean away since she managed to kick the cop in his . . . uh . . ."

"Balls, Peter."

"Halfway down the block she stepped in dog crap and stopped to scrape her shoe against the curb. The videocam people caught the whole thing, from soup to nuts, and in less time than it takes to sing 'American Pie,' Yogi Demon was on every local TV channel. An hour or so later, an enterprising reporter crashed Lassiter's party, which was still in full throttle. The station interrupted their 'regularly scheduled program' for a 'live update.' The reporter interviewed Lassiter—"

"Who was more than happy to provide Yogi Demon details. Did the station show the painting?"

"Yes. Lassiter stood right in front of it. So did his wife. A few guests waved or made obscene gestures, but one young female tried to get out of camera range. That's not unusual, some people don't like to be caught on camera, but so far no one seems to know who she is. McCoy says they're looking for 'a nondescript woman with either brown or blue eyes, who wore a dark gray, hooded sweatshirt.' The hood was, of course, up. So much for hair color." Peter shrugged. "I'm glad I'm not involved. *We're* not involved," he amended.

"The party was only a couple of blocks away," Ellie said thoughtfully, "which explains how the 'enterprising reporter' found it. But did the station televise or mention the address in their 'live update'?"

"No. And Lassiter's phone is unlisted."

"But he gave out business cards at the gallery. I saw him."

"Thanks, sweetheart. I'm going to call McCoy back. He can check and see if Lassiter's cards have an address on them. Or a home phone number. A slick thief can ferret out an address from a phone number." Peter shook his head. "There were as many people at the gallery as there were at Lassiter's party, but maybe somebody showed an excessive interest in *Christmas Carol*. At least it's a start."

*And at least, for the moment, it's taken your mind off your sister,* Ellie thought.

All she'd gathered from Peter's abridged summary was that Beth was three months pregnant, Jonah wasn't the father, and Beth hadn't decided what to do about the baby. Beth wouldn't reveal the father's identity, Peter said, but he had a sneaking suspicion it was Mike Urvant.

Now, as Peter left the bedroom, Ellie gazed at the painting on the opposite wall.

*What's the deal, Heather? Why are people stealing, or trying to steal your husband's paintings?*

*Why would they commit murder just to get their hands on you? Or me?*

*Maybe Garrett has an explanation.*

Ellie suddenly realized that the bridge of her nose had

morphed into Peter's crinkle. Because it was storming outside. Because Garrett's directions included a hill—not as high as a mountain, but her acrophobia didn't tote a tape measure. Because she ached from head to foot, especially foot. Because any sane person would stay home, home on the range, curled up in front of a fire, with Roy and Dale and Shirley Temple. Because any sane person would call Garrett and cancel dinner and pig out on Colorado Fried Chicken.

But then, any sane person wouldn't shun sleep so she could finish Sunday's *New York Times* crossword puzzle by the time Monday's sun came up.

As if to mock her mental sun image, incessant rain began to spank the windowpanes and heavy raindrops scuttled across the roof like a field of Kentucky Derby contenders.

"Curiosity killed the cat," she told Jackie Robinson, "but my mother would say that satisfaction brought it back. For once in my life, I agree with my mother."

# Twenty-Three

Beth Feldman hated rain. It reminded her of the day she found Mike Urvant in bed with his rodeo groupie. It had been raining that day too, marble-size drops, and her breasts had been clearly visible through the thin material of her blouse.

In those days she didn't wear a bra. Or carry an umbrella.

Striding through the hotel's luxurious lobby, heading for the elevators, she had fielded two come-ons with uncharacteristic haste, anxious to reach Mike's suite and give him his present—tickets to the opera. He needed some "culturing" (his word) and she had chosen *Porgy and Bess* because it was in English and she loved the music.

Mike, naked and unashamed, had made his Beth-be-nimble comment, and her profanities had been punctuated by lightning.

His laughter overrode the thunder.

Hair dripping rain, face dripping tears, she had fled Mike's suite, then searched the hotel's sports bar, a Broncos game blaring in the background, until she found one of the nameless lobby men. Forty minutes and three slushy, impotent margaritas later, he escorted her to his room and peeled her damp clothes from her body. The top of his head scarcely reached the bottom of her chin, but he kept calling her his "itty-bitty sugah."

He stopped momentarily to ogle her breasts, whereupon she became his "itty-bitty sugah wid chehwies on top." He sounded like Elmer Fudd, assuming Fudd had developed a deep Southern accent. Then he'd shoved her onto the queen-size mattress so that she lay on her back, helpless as a turtle. Eyes feral, hair Einstein-ish, giggling with maniacal glee, he had dried her with a portable hair dryer.

Staring at the framed scenic watercolor on the wall opposite the bed, she had pretended to be drunk. She warbled "Summertime" from *Porgy and Bess.* She moaned, "I'm so dizzy the room's spinning." She writhed convincingly from the hair dryer's hot air wafting between her legs, even gave Nameless a Meg Ryan *oooh-oh-god-oooh,* which obviously pleased him because she heard him whisper, "Am ah good or what?"

She wasn't sure why she pretended to be drunk, maybe to dissuade him, maybe to dissuade herself, but Nameless was oblivious to her inner turmoil.

While he donned a condom and continued his ministrations—without the hair dryer; she was dry enough, thank you very much—she considered several get-back schemes against Mike. Nameless came with a rebel yell, then assumed a fetal position and snored like Adam West on Sominex—she could practically see the capital Zs above his head. Suppressing the desire to chortle, swallowing a crucial throat-chirrup, she furtively left the bed and stole his wallet. She felt bad about that—he had been very nice about paying her inflated bar bill—but she needed money, preferably cash. Her credit cards were maxed, her checking account overdrawn, and she was willing to bet that Jonah had terminated their joint savings account. She had seen him all too often in plea-bargain mode.

She stole the portable hair dryer, too.

It rained every day for a week. Streets flooded and tires plumed dirty water and even the talented Gene Kelly couldn't have tap-danced his way down sidewalks, much less gutters.

But the gray skies and unmerciful raindrops provided cover as she slipped into a shapeless yellow slicker and a floppy rain hat and, dry-eyed, spied on Mike.

Every hotel sported a sports bar. She shouted "Go Broncos!" as she cruised one where you'd have to mortgage your house to pay your bar tab. Finally she hit a bonanza— a nerdy-looking man who was smart enough to work for Microsoft but stupid enough to carry around a thousand dollars in his wallet, sandwiched between a photo of his wife and three kids and a photo of his Golden Retriever.

When at long last the rain stopped, she allowed her tears to fall. Then she made a phone call, her voice raspy from her wild weeping spree.

"Jonah," she croaked, "I want you to take me back, no questions asked, and I swear you'll never regret it. If you say no, I'll understand, but—"

"Are you sick?" His voice sounded alarmed.

"I'm sick as a dog," she fibbed, picturing the Golden Retriever.

"If I take you back, you'll be kept on a short leash," he said, unaware that he'd punned.

"Agreed."

"And I want another child."

She paused no longer than a nanosecond before she said, "Okay."

"And you have to promise you'll never break your marriage vows again."

"I promise."

"I've never known you to break a promise, Beth."

"I lied, Jonah. That's the same thing."

"I lie all the time, especially to myself. I lie to my clients and I lie to the jury and breaking a promise is not the same thing."

"I probably shouldn't ask," she said, "but why are you taking me back?"

"You haven't asked about the kids," he countered.

"How are the kids?"

"Ryan's fine. Jonina wants her mother."

Up until three months ago, Beth had kept her promise.

Damn Garrett Halliday!

God, she hated rain.

# Twenty-Four

Martina Brustein loved rain.

She couldn't explain why. All she knew was that she wrote better, with more urgency, more panache, when a sudden cloudburst steamed the pavement or bolts of lightning cleaved a slate-gray sky.

Even as a child she had never chanted "Rain, rain, go away." She didn't give a rat's spit if April showers brought May flowers. Rainy days and Mondays didn't get *her* down—she couldn't have cared less if it rained on Mondays, Tuesdays, or the Fourth of July. Lightning inspired uninhibited passion and thunder reminded her of Wagner's *Parsifal*—which she sometimes listened to when she wrote steamy sex scenes. *Parsifal*'s 1904 Metropolitan Opera debut had included a forty-five second kiss—a major shock to one's 1904 psyche. Critics had panned the opera, which tickled Martina's funny bone. Critics, she told herself, could be outrageously provincial.

Her favorite song was "Raindrops Keep Fallin' On My Head." Oh, what she wouldn't give to look like Katherine Ross in *Butch Cassidy and the Sundance Kid*.

Staring up at the ceiling, she barked a laugh, then stared down at the floor. "Are you listening, Lucifer? I'm ready to deal. My soul for eternal skinniness," she said, and practically jumped out of her skin when the windowpanes rattled.

So did Becky. Out of her fur, that is.

"It's okay," Martina said, soothing the cat. "That was thunder, not the devil. But if it was the devil, I'd probably sign the damn contract."

Lowering herself onto a couch cushion, Martina thought about her book contract. She now knew that she'd never finish writing *Sweet Bestial Love*.

She had needed Halliday to start it and she needed him to finish it.

Why, oh why, had she asked him about a wife?

Maybe she should retrieve one of her unsold "emergency manuscripts" from the bank vault. She'd done it before, submitting a romantic suspense, circa 1993. But she was too big (*ha-ha*) to be edited. The book had gone through production as-is and she'd been crucified by the critics. "Marty Blue seems to have lost her touch—and her mind," said *Publishers Weekly*. The kindest review had come from *Romantic Times* magazine, which gave it a measly three stars. The *RT* reviewer had written "vastly disappointed" twice. Despite the nasty reviews, Martina won a Romance Writers of America award. Cheeks flaming, she practically whispered her gracious, Marty Blue acceptance speech. Then she hid the award in an upstairs linen closet.

There had been one silver lining. Her next book, an erotica, was so much better, the critics raved. Again, she cringed. Because she knew that *Pussy in the Wellington* was a half-hearted effort, at best.

Last night she had asked Halliday if he had a wife and he had said no, he didn't have a wife. Then he had zipped his fly and, without another word, he'd left her flat. Literally.

What, exactly, had she done wrong? It was a fair question.

So it was only fair that he explain his abrupt departure.

This morning, after a ghastly breakfast of bran cereal,

dry toast, and an egg that looked like phlegm, she had pe-
rused the Aspen telephone directory, conveniently—and
ironically—placed next to the bedroom's Bible. But she'd
found no listing for his name. Undeterred, she had called
his art gallery, closed on Sundays, leave-a-message-please.

So she'd left a message, praying he'd check his messages.

If he had a wife and his wife listened to the answering
machine, yawn.

*No,* she thought. *I take that back. If he has a wife and his
wife checks his messages, I'm screwed. Not!*

Leaving a message had led to a major dilemma. Should
she assume he'd heard the message?

Angry and "vastly disappointed," she hadn't bothered to
vet the weather channel, a daily ritual. She had simply told
him to meet her at Angel's Ravine, under their favorite tree,
at twilight. "Bring wine and thou," she had said, "and I'll
bring bread and cheese, and we'll have a picnic. It's my
birthday," she had added, trying to sound wistful rather
than despondent. She never commemorated her birthday,
never circled the date on a calendar, never anticipated pres-
ents, always threw away, unopened, the annual cards from
her agent and dentist. She had once said she didn't have
birthdays. A friend had replied, "You have them, Martina.
You just don't celebrate them."

Twilight had sounded so romantic. Of course, as a best-
selling author, she could have said dusk. Or gloaming. Or
shank of the evening. Or moonrise. Or cockshut. All those
words sounded romantic, nostalgic, and she had used
"cockshut" in three of her RWA-award-winning Regency
romances.

Rising from the couch, Martina walked over to the window. Outside, rain fell by the bucketful. An umbrella would
be useless. She pictured herself as a wet waif, but knew, re-

alistically, that her carefully applied makeup would melt—
like wax dripping from a candle. Her complexion, greased
by too many pans of homemade fudge, wasn't exactly porcelain, and the lines around her eyes looked as if leprechaun
junkies, high on crack, had decided to hold a tic-tac-toe
tournament.

If she didn't show up at Angel's Ravine, would her
Prince Charming wend his way through the woods and
knock on her cottage door? They could picnic in front of
the fireplace, and she'd read him her latest, *very* erotic
chapter, and they could play Snow White and—no!

They could play anything he wanted to play.

Tonight she wouldn't be picky.

Scooping up Becky, Martina held the cat against her
breasts. "Oh, God, what if my hero decides he doesn't want
to come knocking?"

She had an even bigger concern.

What if he believed her threats?

She had made a couple of suggestive threats this morning, over the phone; had, in fact, used the word "cockshut"
in a different connotation—an implication that had nothing
to do with twilight.

"Words unexpressed sometimes fall back dead, but God
himself can't kill them once they are said," she told Becky.

*Meow.*

The cat, who usually sounded like a viola, sounded like
gargled mouthwash. An omen? A warning?

Martina wasn't superstitious, except when it came to her
writing. At home she kept a stuffed vulture on top of her
computer—a "deadline vulture" whom she had named Michael, after her first editor. Her office was filled with lucky
angels, her bulletin board thumb-tacked with printed mot-
toes. Her favorite motto was "Writing requires a loner's

temperament, a high tolerance for silence, and an unhealthy preference for the company of people who are imaginary or dead."

On her office wall were framed Marty Blue book covers, along with framed movie posters. Daniel Day Lewis in *The Last of the Mohicans*, Mel Gibson in *Braveheart*, Brad Pitt and Aidan Quinn in—

"I'd better stop procrastinating and get dressed," she told Becky. "I wonder what Marty Blue would wear to a picnic in the rain."

She could almost swear she saw her cat's mouth move, could almost swear she heard: *How about a birthday suit?*

# Twenty-Five

The newly christened "Dom" Dombroski thanked God for the rain.

Or he would have, had he not been an agnostic.

If there really was a God, he—or she—had a comedic sense of humor when it came to Marion-Dom. God liked to tempt Marion-Dom. But before Marion-Dom could bite the juicy apple, God snatched it away. And if God didn't snatch away the apple, ten times out of ten it would be sour and wormy.

Or maybe God was a tricky magician. Maybe, instead of long white robes, he wore an old-fashioned tuxedo and top hat. Tucked into his sleeves were colorful scarves. And at least one American-flag scarf. These days, everybody put an American flag in their act. It reminded Marion of vaudevillians saying "Brooklyn" to get a rise out of their audiences.

Except, today's applause sounded vastly different. Enthusiastic but serious. Patriotic but angry. Sad, even.

Sad applause—did that make any sense? Was sad applause the same as a sad smile?

He'd ask Jonina. Or Lelia. They were both so smart. Or, even better, he'd ask Martina. He had read one of her books and she used "sad smile" a lot.

Cupping his hands around his mouth, he formed a microphone. "Pre-senting God in the guise of Houdini, David Copperfield, Teller and Penn, transported to Lonesome

Pines by P.T. Barnum, direct from Las Vegas."

Hold the phone. Barnum and Houdini would have been transported from somewhere else. From somewhere over the rainbow. Or from somewhere underneath California's fault line.

California's fault line—good line, considering how drunk he was. Much too drunk to finish his chores, thank God for the rain.

The hayloft had become his haven, rain or shine, but he really should stop drinking so much. Like a food addict who eats when he's on top of the world or down in the dumps, Marion used any excuse to drink, and therein lay his problem.

He had begun to experience blackouts.

Driving to Colorado Springs last Thursday, he had planned to spend the night with Kit. First, she said, they'd attend her uncle's gallery reception. Why not take advantage of the free food and champagne, she said, especially the champagne?

Her invitation had been flirtatious, seductive, irresistible.

Ecstatic, moonstruck, and dead sober, he had walked around, window-shopping, until it was time to pick her up.

Except, "God's juicy apple" wasn't home.

Her roommate, Moony, had answered his knock. She said Kit wasn't there but would be back soon. When he became antsy, Moony, a pale blonde who blended into the room's decor, pacified him with pale Scotch. He remembered, or thought he remembered, messing around with Moony, who was compliant but unresponsive, limp as a dead fish, as if she'd been told to keep him occupied. He remembered, or thought he remembered, background music. Shania Twain.

*But he didn't remember leaving the loft!*

He vaguely remembered waking up with a splitting headache and a missing watch. He vaguely remembered rising from a park bench and stumbling through the darkness to find Kit's loft. Kit still wasn't home, but this time Moony told him to go away. He looked and smelled like a drunken bum, she said. And no, he couldn't wait for Kit, because she, Moony, was leaving. In the words of the immortal Ann Margaret, Moony had places to go and people to see. So . . . bye-bye, birdbrain.

"Party hearty," he had said to the door she'd slammed in his face. Then, somehow, he'd managed to find his car, parked in front of the loft's entrance.

His next coherent thought—he had missed Garrett's "gallery gala."

Or had he?

If he had, where the hell had the empty bottle of champagne come from? And why did he vaguely remember a bunch of redheaded women hanging onto his every word? Pinned to the wall like dead butterflies, they really had no choice. One lay in the bathtub, stalked by a lion. One sat on Santa's lap. One held a black cat. The majority of the painted women were dead ringers for Heather Halliday, a few looked like his new friend Norrie, and, in all probability, each and every one could have doubled for his absentee mother. He vaguely remembered driving home, fury welling up inside him. Obviously, he had turned around and driven back to—where?

Downtown Colorado Springs.

He emerged from his car into sunshine that spiked his aching head, and found a note on his windshield. With an effort, he focused on the note.

*Dear Marion, its 6 am. I won't be at the ranch today*

*so take care of the horses. You past out in your car. I tried to wake you but couldn't. Anyway Moony's pissed and don't want you in the loft. Sorry I wasn't home last nite. I forgot. But I will make it up to you. Meet me at Angels Ravine Sat nite at 11. Rosa hid me a 6 pack of bear. I get <u>hot</u> thinking of you and I at the ravine. Kit.*

Her spelling and punctuation left a lot to be desired. However, underlining "hot" made up for that, and he had to laugh when he visualized a six-pack of "bear."

Stumbling into a nearby café, he asked to use their bathroom. Told it was okay if he bought something to eat or drink, he discovered that it was noon, and whomever had stolen his watch hadn't stolen his wallet. So he ordered a Bloody Mary, then God-knows-how-many shots of tequila. He vaguely remembered the bartender kicking him out, even though he had tipped the S.O.B. twenty bucks.

And then—nothing.

He had driven back across Independence Pass, but he couldn't remember making the drive. Or exactly *when* he'd made the drive. As darkness covered the ranch like a cheap tourist blanket, he had somehow managed to feed his cat, navigate the loft ladder, and drain a bottle of cheap vodka.

Upon awakening Saturday morning, hungry and hung over, he'd sworn he'd never drink again. And he'd kept that vow until eleven o'clock Saturday night—or, in Kit-speak, "Sat nite at 11."

"Dom, are you up there?"

*Jonina! Shit!*

"Dom, I can hear you breathing."

"You can not," he blurted, just before her smug face crested the ladder.

184

"Works every time," she said, hoisting herself up like a gymnast. "If Ryan or Stevie hide, I always say I hear them breathing and—"

"Are you comparing me to your little brothers?"

"Boys will be boys." She sat on her heels. "You look awful. Have you been drinking?"

"That, little girl, is none of your business."

"If I'm a little girl and you're a little boy, it evens the playing field."

"Meaning what?"

"My, my, aren't we grumpy? Is it the rain?"

"I like the rain and you're all wet."

"Touché, Dom. I love double entendres."

"When you're not around your brothers, you sound smarter."

"I know." She sighed. "Ryan always makes me revert to childhood."

"What do you want?"

"Poor Dom. Gruff ole Pooh bear."

"Knock it off!"

Pursing her lips, she made a *tsk-tsk* sound. "Did you get out on the wrong side of the bed this morning?"

"I never made it to bed. So I decided to come up here and take a cat-nap."

"Bull," she said sweetly.

"Excuse me?"

"You came up here to drink." She glanced at the vodka bottle. "Can I have a sip?"

"Sure," he said. "Why not?"

"Ugh." She wrinkled her nose. "That tastes awful."

"Vodka has no taste."

"Coulda fooled me. Why do you drink so much?"

"I don't know."

185

"You don't know? Or you won't tell?"

"Do you want to ride, Jonina? Should I saddle a horse for you?"

"I can saddle my own horse, thank you very much, and right now you couldn't tie your shoelaces." She eyed his boots. "Anyway, I have a much better idea."

Before he could respond, he saw Stanley Hastings circle Jonina like an Indian circling a wagon. Then, as if walking on eggs, the "feral housecat" walked across her lap. Wisely, she kept her arms still and her hands motionless.

"Listen, kid," Marion said, "I didn't invite you up here and I'd really appreciate some privacy." He heard the roughness that imbued his voice. He resented the cat's betrayal, even though Stanley Hastings had retreated into the shadows again. Damn cat never walked across *his* lap.

"Shut up, Dom." Jonina yawned, or maybe she mock-yawned; hard to tell. "I didn't get any sleep last night, either, so I thought we'd take a nap together. Not here. In my cottage."

"You can't be serious," he said. "Your mother—"

"Left the cottage this morning and won't be back until suppertime. Lelia and Rosa are watching Ryan and Stevie. Lelia's teaching them how to whittle while Rosa bakes cookies." Holding her breath, Jonina gulped down the rest of the vodka, practically a whole damn bottle. "There! Unless you've got more stashed, you have no excuse."

He smiled what he hoped was a cruel smile rather than a sad smile. "You're going to get awfully sick, little girl."

"So what? My friends drink and throw up all the time. They *brag* about it."

"Oh, I doubt—"

"Last night I got wasted," she said in a high-pitched voice, undoubtedly mimicking one of her classmates.

"And I *puked* my guts out."

"Jonina . . ."

"I got so drunk," she continued, lowering her voice an octave to impersonate another classmate, "I woke up this morning with my face in a pool of puke. Is that cool or what?"

He stared at her, fascinated. He'd never heard stuff like that in high school, but then he always had his face in a book. A few kids even called him "Marion the Librarian." He had once asked a popular red-haired girl to the movies. She told him she'd be busy that night, washing her hair and watching *The Music Man* on TV. Upon rejoining her friends, she had whispered and pointed at him. They had all giggled like freaking hyenas, and if there'd been a machete inside his locker, the redhead's yearbook photo would have shown her headless.

He could have invited Lelia Hamilton out. She was ostracized, too. Mainly because she was so frightfully smart, not to mention poor as the proverbial church mouse. But pretty Lelia supposedly had a boyfriend, an older man, identity unknown, and then she became pregnant and—

"If you think *that's* cool," Jonina said, upping her voice several octaves, "I puked all over Matthew's sheepskin seat covers. The car radio was playing Sandy's 'Unglued,' or maybe it was Madonna. Then I drank some more and we did it on the back seat and I threw up all over Matthew."

"Who the hell is Matthew?"

"The most popular boy in my school. He could double for Brad Pitt."

"Aren't you exaggerating just a little?"

"About Matthew doubling for Brad Pitt?"

"No! About puking then bragging."

"Maybe boys don't brag like girls do, or they brag about

other things." She burped, then gave him a sheepish grin. "Please come to my cottage, Dom? Pretty please? With sugar on top? We'll cuddle. I'll pretend you're Matthew and you can pretend I'm Kit Halliday."

"I'd rather pretend you're Jonina Feldman."

"Really?" She blushed, or maybe her cheeks were flushed from the vodka.

"Why can't we cuddle here?" he asked.

"Because I'm all wet," she said with a grin.

While her retort was clever, it was also true. Her sweater smelled like damp dog and if she stayed up here much longer she'd come down with something—at the very least, a bad cold.

He helped her descend the ladder, then led her outside the barn. Without even a smidgen of sunshine, the weather had cooled considerably and the cold rainy air slapped her face like a wet washcloth.

By the time they reached her cottage, she was mumbling incoherently, still trying to mimic classmates. He hesitated on the threshold, then entered and half-carried her to her bedroom.

Sweat beaded her brow, mingling with drops of rain.

She sank onto the bed. In less than a minute she was snoring lightly through parted lips. He took off her sneakers, stripped her wet clothes, and covered her with a quilt. He propped two pillows against her back and shoulders, making sure she slept on her side. Then he left the cottage.

No one stood there to denounce him. Or, even worse, rat on him.

Oh, wait. Damn! In the distance he saw the shadowy shape of a man. Or a woman.

He sprinted for the barn. To hell with the rain.

No time for a saddle.

Stumbling into the tack room, he snatched up a bridle, then a bottle of wine from his hidden stash. His hands were all thumbs. Swearing a blue streak, he bridled Scout.

As he swung his leg up over the pinto's back, he heard the echo of Jonina's voice: *Why do you drink so much?*

# Twenty-Six

"Are you all right?"

"Please, Peter, that's the third time you've asked me that."

Ellie stared through the windshield, but couldn't see much. Rain lashed the car and beat like a snare drum against the convertible's ragtop.

The defroster and windshield wipers were both on HIGH.

Maybe she should have called Garrett and canceled. Or, at the very least, confirmed their dinner plans.

*Nonsense,* she thought. *What's a little rain to an Aspen resident who has to contend with snow?*

Except it wasn't a little rain.

"And I'll keep asking," Peter said, as he maneuvered around some fallen tree branches.

"Come on, honey," she said. "What's a little rain to a cop?"

"I'm not worried about me. I'm worried about you."

"Me? I'm dry as a bone."

"That's not what I mean and you know it. How's your ankle? Your neck? Your back?"

"My neck and back feel okay," she fibbed. "My ankle's throbbing, but I'll ask Heather for some aspirin when we get there."

"If we get there," he grumbled. "I'm reasonably familiar

with Aspen, and I memorized the directions your friend Halliday gave you, but . . ."

"But what?"

"Visibility has gone from bad to worse."

"Do you want to turn back?"

"Yes." He peered through the windshield. "Never mind. There's Halliday's hill. Close your eyes."

"Not this time, Peter. I can't see a blessed thing, even though I feel like I'm riding a ski lift."

"How do you know what a ski lift feels like?"

"I've got an active imagination."

"Truer words were never spoken," he said with a wry grin. "I'll bet, in nice weather, the view from here would knock your socks off."

Ellie couldn't see her socks, hidden beneath a pair of black rubber boots. She had insisted on wearing her white dress because the last time she'd worn it, three nights ago, a stunned Garrett had asked about the loss of her Rubenesque curves. At the gallery she'd prevailed over Adrianna's cleavage and abbreviated panties, but this time she'd have to compete against Kit's perky breasts and angular hips. Thank goodness Heather's beauty wasn't intimidating. Her naiveté might attract a man, but her devout spirituality would stop him in his tracks. Whereupon, he'd bob his head and call her ma'am.

*And,* thought Ellie, *Heather would die a thousand deaths before she'd wear black rubber boots with a white dress.*

"If Cinderella had sprained her ankle, she wouldn't have married her foot-fetish prince," Ellie had groused, inside the cottage, after putting on her dress.

"Did it ever occur to you that Cinderella's prince was turned on by amorphous, inorganic, transparent substances?" Peter had asked in his Groucho voice, trying to cheer her up. "Prince Charming didn't have a foot fetish, Norrie. He had a glass slipper fetish."

"I can't slide my foot into sandals, Peter, much less slippers. And," she had added mournfully, "I never thought to pack a raincoat. Or even a winter jacket."

Peter had scavenged inside the main house, coming back with what he called "buried treasure"—size 9 boots that accommodated her swollen foot and a fleecy red poncho that matched but concealed the poppies on the front of her dress. The black rubber boots and white silk dress didn't exactly compliment each other, but she hadn't had the heart to tell him that.

"The only 'view' I want right now is Heather's face," she said, as she reached behind her seat for the boxed gift she'd bought at Lilly's Apothecary, the same shop where she'd purchased her fox amulet. She had found *the* perfect crystal; a superior piece of glass, tinged blue. Sydney St. Charles, the shop's proprietor, had told Ellie that blue crystals possessed "healing, protection, and strength." For fun, Ellie had also bought a fluffy stuffed rabbit, left over from Easter. Sydney said her great-aunt Lillian stitched all the shop's animals by hand, and that she put a "happy spell" inside with the stuffing. The card, attached to the box's shiny orange wrapping paper, said, simply: FOR HEATHER.

"Stay right where you are," Peter ordered, as he parked beneath an enormous evergreen oak. "I'll carry you inside."

"Nonsense. I can walk."

"You can barely limp. I'll carry you."

"Yes sir, lord and master," she said, secretly pleased.

Pleasure turned to apprehension when no one answered the bell, so loud its ring seemed to bounce off the walls of the vestibule.

192

She could see the vestibule, thanks to the bowed glass that crested the front door. Decked with movie posters, a red velvet divan, an old-fashioned popcorn machine, and an upright piano, the entrance hall looked like a small theater lobby; the ideal backdrop for a Judy Garland-Mickey Rooney movie. Judy would say, "I know how we'll save the ranch (farm, school, town) . . . let's put on a show!" Then she and Mickey would sit at the piano and he'd play "Let's All Sing Like the Birdies Sing," and from nowhere an orchestra would join in and they'd sing.

"I don't get it," Peter huffed into Ellie's ear. "We're a few minutes late, but in this weather they should have been waiting for us with open arms. And dry towels."

"I don't get it either, honey. I'm positive Garrett said seven o'clock, and I'm equally positive he said tonight. And it's not like the house was dark or anything."

As if someone had heard her, the light from an outdoor strobe cut through the rain and a voice shouted, "Who's there?"

# Twenty-Seven

Beth Feldman hit the top of the dresser so hard, a small bottle toppled over, opened, and spilled nail polish that looked more like blood than blood.

Shaking the pain from her hand, she glared at her daughter. "You're grounded, Jonina, and this time your father's not around to un-ground you."

"Grounded from what, Mother? Video games? Shirley Temple movies?"

"Don't get snippy with me, kiddo. Your father might tolerate a certain amount of disobedience, but—"

"Lucky for you he does." Jonina struggled to a sitting position. Goose-bumpy from the cold as well as her mother's wrath, she tried to find her quilt.

*There it is.* Leaning over the side of the bed, she grasped a corner and fished it from the floor.

The quilt, a patchwork quilt, looked as if it belonged in a country store staffed by the man and woman in that famous painting, *American Gothic*. The woman who had posed for the painting was the artist's sister, the man with the pitchfork the artist's dentist, and wasn't it funny what one remembered during moments of crisis? *Trivia, thy name is Jonina Phoebe Feldman!*

Mom's eyes narrowed as she said, "Lucky for me? What's that supposed to mean?"

"Mike Urvant." Who wasn't trivia, Jonina thought. Or trivial.

Mom breathed in and out. "What do you know about Mike?"

"Exactly how did I disobey you, Mother?" Jonina wrapped the quilt around her like a shroud. "You never said I couldn't drink."

"I didn't think I'd have to say it. You're only fifteen—"

"Almost sixteen."

"—and what do you know about Mike?"

"I know you whored around with him."

"How dare you!"

"If you want to slap my face, Mother, go ahead. I couldn't feel any worse."

"Oh, wouldn't you just love that? Then you could stand up in court and swear under oath that I abused you."

"Court?" Rising from the bed, Jonina walked toward the window, the quilt trailing behind her. "Does Daddy plan to fight for custody?"

"He's willing to accept visitation when it comes to the boys but he wants you to live with him. I said it was out of the question."

Jonina never made it to the window. Instead, she turned and stared, dumbfounded, at her mother. "Why would Daddy fight for me?"

"That's a stupid question. He thinks the sun rises and sets—"

"He thinks I'm Mike Urvant's daughter."

Silence. Then, "I've told your father over and over that our bedroom walls are too thin." A deep sigh. Then, "You're not Mike's daughter, Jonina, I swear."

"And why should I believe you, Mother?" Slanting a glance at the alarm clock on the bedside table, Jonina saw its numbers solidify into "7:23" p.m. She'd missed supper, served promptly at six-thirty, no leniency for latecomers.

Good. Maybe she'd lose a couple of ounces.

"If you don't believe me," Mom was saying, "go through our family albums when we get home. You look exactly like Nana. And stop calling me 'Mother' in that nasty tone of voice."

"Nana's fat!"

"She wasn't at your age. Look at her bas mitzvah pictures."

Jonina shook her head, confused rather than skeptical. "Then why did Daddy say what he did?"

"Because he was angry. He lost his temper. Lost control. When people lose control, they lash out mindlessly, recklessly. And it's worse if you keep your emotions under wraps."

"Like you do," Jonina snapped. "Not always," she hastened to add. She was beginning to discover small cracks in her mother's perfection camouflage, but now wasn't the time—or place—to mention them.

"Too much self-discipline," Mom continued, ignoring the interruption, "is like blowing up a balloon until it stretches beyond its capacity. Sooner or later it'll burst." She heaved another deep sigh, deep enough to make her cough. "Look at the old snapshots of Nana, Jonina, especially the bas mitzvah pictures, then tell me you're someone else's daughter."

Jonina felt as if a hundred-pound weight had been lifted from her shoulders. She'd seen the family albums and she did look like Daddy's mother. Her relief, however, evaporated when she considered her present predicament. She had to lie and lie well. Make up some convoluted, believable story, good enough to fool her mom, who had the instincts of a freaking cat on the prowl. What she wouldn't give for an invisible Martina Brustein whispering in her ear.

Twenty or so minutes ago, Mom had entered the cottage and walked straight into Jonina's bedroom. Ferris Bueller might be able to successfully perpetrate an elaborate scam, but Jonina, half awake, didn't even have time to think.

Not that *that* mattered. She wasn't, nor had she ever been, good at pretense.

One startled glance and Mom knew the whole story.

Since the age of twelve, Jonina had refused to sleep in anything other than pajamas. Because she hated her naked body.

Today's bra and panties were a dead giveaway. And she had napped with her mouth open, breathing out alcoholic fumes. Even if she didn't reek of vodka, her bedroom did. Add to the mix her miserable, guilty face.

Mom had said one word. "Who?"

Jonina had tried to brazen it out. "Who, what?"

"Really, Jonina," Mom had said, "should I call a doctor to examine your hymen?"

"Really, Mother," she had replied, "you sound like Sandra Dee's mother in that old movie, *A Summer Place.*"

"There's only one person it could be," Mom had said, just before the boys burst into the cottage.

"We made cookies," Stevie bellowed from the living room, "and when no one came for supper, Rosa cooked peanut butter and jelly and bug juice, 'cept I couldn't find no bugs in it."

"Lelia made me a whistle," Ryan yelled, then demonstrated with shrill blasts that effectively ended all conversation.

Mom left the bedroom to deal with the boys and, despite her angst, Jonina whispered, "You don't look like a whistle."

By the time Mom returned, Jonina had taken the fastest

hot/cold shower in the history of the world, a sobering experience. Then she'd aired out her bedroom. She didn't know, nor did she care, what Mom had done with her brothers. Mom could have left them in a vat of boiling oil, for all Jonina cared.

While Mom was busy boiling her brothers, Jonina had silently sworn to J. K. Rowling, Keanu Reeves, Frodo, and God that she wouldn't get Dom in trouble, not even if she was grilled, tortured, and grounded for life. How many times had she heard Daddy say that the best defense was a good offense? In this case, her best defense was to accuse her mother of something, and Mike Urvant would do nicely.

If Mike didn't pan out, Jonina would ask Mom why she'd been shaking like a leaf when she entered the bedroom, and why she'd been soaking wet, so wet she'd left puddles all over the floor.

Had Mom gone riding? Had she fallen off her horse?

Jonina tried to remember if any of the horses had been missing from their stalls, but she hadn't focused on the horses. Or the stalls. Totally focused on Dom, determined to seduce him until he seduced her—chase him until he caught her—she had ruined everything by stupidly chugging from a bottle of vodka. She had wanted to look and act like a grownup, but all she'd really proved was that everybody was right when they said she was "just a kid."

Dom, however, had been wrong when he said she'd get sick. Anyhow, sick was okay. He'd have held her head. Then, with any luck, something else. Her breasts, for instance. How many times had she visualized Keanu caressing her body? But now the dark-haired, dark-eyed Dom *dominated* the intimate image. And while other girls might think Marion Dombroski too short, too thin, maybe even too brainy, he reminded Jonina of Heathcliff in *Wuthering Heights*.

Mom could call a doctor, big deal. She could call a hundred doctors and let them examine her "snippy" daughter's hymen. Jonina Phoebe Feldman was, and had a feeling she always would be, a virgin.

While she had been thinking about the photos in the family album, Mom had been staring out the window, counting raindrops or something. Making an about-face, she said, "What's the name of the boy who plied you with liquor, Jonina? If you don't tell me, I'll lodge a complaint with Mr. Dombroski."

Jonina prayed to the pretense-gods, just before she said, "Matthew. His name's Matthew and he could double for Brad Pitt. He's a friend of Dom . . . uh, Kit's, and he wants to board his motorcycle . . . I mean his horse . . . he wants to board his horse here at Lonesome Pines."

She paused to picture the high school jock who'd seduced ninety percent of her classmates. Every time he "deflowered" a girl, he got a new tattoo, keeping score, the more the merrier, and he would have deflowered Jonina Phoebe Feldman too, had he known she was alive.

"Matthew rides a Harley," she continued, warming to the subject, "and he plays tennis and soccer and football and—what's the matter? Do you have to throw up?"

Mom hugged her belly. "I want you to stop seeing that boy," she said, her voice strangled. "Now leave me alone. Go to the kitchen and ask Rosa if she'll break the rules, serve you some leftovers, even if it's only peanut butter and bug ju . . . bug ju . . . oh, God!"

Sinking onto the edge of the mattress, Mom bent her head between her legs and threw up. As if she, not Jonina, had chugged Dom's vodka.

★ ★ ★ ★ ★

Most people believed a maid's worst task was cleaning the bathrooms. Even though Lelia wished men would take better aim, the task she hated the most was cleaning up vomit, and it happened more often than one would think.

Duke Dombroski might stock G-rated videos in his office, but he stocked the bar with potent, X-rated booze. Mean-spirited guests might leave Lelia a dollar tip (or less; she had once found fifty cents and a thank-you note on a pillow), but budgetary considerations went out the window when it came to bingeing. It was as if dude ranches—far away from the Starbucks-on-every-corner-cities—gave consenting adults a license to eat too much and drink too much.

Lelia could and should write a book. Older men, she would write, seemed to know that too much alcohol would severely limit their genital competence, while twenty-something men didn't seem to care. During the height of the season, once the sun had set, you'd find twenty-somethings sprawled all over the ranch. They'd puke into the corral, heave into the swimming pool, even hang onto each other and barf in a weird sort of line-dance. Some never got much beyond the bar's exit and some made it all the way to a pasture gate. Some hunkered, some crawled, and some stood very still, like one of those Italian *Three Coins in a Fountain* statues, their mouths spouting vomit rather than water. If you set their barfs to music and scored it with retch-laden lyrics—"Oooh, I'm gonna die"—and choreographed it like an *Oklahoma!* dance number and performed it at an avant-garde theatre, you'd have a major hit.

Then there were the Shirley Jones clones. No! Shirley Jones—in *Oklahoma!*, *Carousel*, *The Music Man*, *Elmer Gantry*, and *The Partridge Family*—had a lovely figure, not too fat, not too thin. Women today dieted until they looked like Bic pens, only they didn't call it a diet, they called it a lifestyle, and if their tiny tummies couldn't hold more than one glassful of zinfandel, it went right to their tiny heads. Then, of course, it gushed from their tiny, Betty Boop, collagen-injected mouths.

Unlike older men and women, most of whom had the smarts to find a bathroom if they drank too much, unlike twenty-something men, even, lifestyle ladies looked grotesque when they barfed—as if their hinges had come loose.

And they had an attitude. "Hey, you! I barfed! Clean it up!"

Although younger than most of the lifestyle ladies, Lelia had been brought up to hide her messes. She thought that Beth Feldman had been raised the same way, so she was surprised when the button on her phone flashed and Beth said, "Hey, Lelia, I puked. Get your butt over here and clean it up."

She was not only surprised but dismayed. Dog-tired, leg muscles cramping, she wanted nothing more than to sink into the bathtub and let the hot, lilac-scented water soak the pine needles and mud from her dripping wet, not too thin, not too fat body.

So she said something she had always wanted to say, but never dared to say. She said, "Clean it up yourself."

Marion Dombroski found it difficult to tiptoe when he couldn't even walk a straight line.

Then there was the screen door, which wailed like a requiem. Someday he'd rip the damn door from its hinges and—

And what? You couldn't burn a screen door, you

couldn't chop it up for firewood, and it was too hefty to stuff into a trash bag.

Come to think of it, how did one get rid of a screen door? The same way one got rid of a dead body, he supposed. Leave it somewhere to decompose.

Or rust.

Damn, his Stetson felt too tight, more like a bike helmet.

Cowboy boots in hand, Marion visualized the hayloft—his haven, his sanctuary. Briefly, he thought about backtracking through the living room, then the front office. But if he did that, he'd have to challenge the dirge-singing door again. In any case, his clothes were filthy, his boots were drenched, his red wool socks looked and smelled like overripe tomatoes, his feet were as frostbitten as they could get without necessitating amputation, and for the second night in a row he battled the urge to puke.

Starting tomorrow, no more booze!

But it was still tonight, so while one of his hands clutched a pair of wet leather boots, his other hand strangled the neck of a bottle of red wine.

Which presented a problem. His bedroom was upstairs and he needed a third hand to hang on to the banister. No way could he climb those stairs without hanging on to the banister. In fact, he had a feeling he'd have to scale the staircase, then, eventually, rappel down—

Oh, God, once he reached his room he could lock the door and drink himself senseless (*for the last time, because starting tomorrow, no more booze*). There was even a small attached bath with sink, tub, and toilet, where he could take a leak if nature called, or take a puke if Bacchus beckoned.

Good old Bacchus. Mythic god of wine. Originator of the drunken feast, otherwise known as the bacchanalia. Didn't Bacchus have Bacchae—women who participated in his drunken feasts and orgies? Sure he did. So where were Bacchae when you really needed them?

Wait a sec. Grammatically-speaking, was it Bacchae or *the* Bacchae? Was Bacchae plural? Like moose and moose?

He'd have to ask Jonina. Or Lelia. They were both so smart.

Hey, wouldn't it be cool to have the women who participated in orgies named after you?

Bacchus's mother must have been so proud.

Domae sounded better than Marionae (*or even Bacchae*). So as soon as he inherited the ranch, he'd have a monthly domanalia. With at least a dozen Domae (*plural, like moose*).

He heard his father snoring. If Duke starred in a Disney cartoon, his snores would chainsaw wood. And if he heard about Marion's sojourn inside Jonina's cottage, Marion Dombroski would be listed in the credits as the voice of the animated kindling.

Or the *voices* of the animated kindling.

Kindling was another moose-moose.

While he had been contemplating the plural of moose and kindling, he'd managed to stagger upstairs. Without a climber's rope, even . . . hallelujah brothers and sisters and Bacchus, his new mentor.

Last year, sober as a judge, he had messed around with one of the guests. It had been such a cliché. She was the bored young wife of a retired judge who drank gin and tonic and played gin rummy night and day. One night, suffering from indigestion, the judge had retired early, only to find his wife, naked as a jaybird, writhing on the cottage davenport. Had Marion been on the bottom, the judge's wife would have accepted a generous divorce settlement and that would have been the end of it. Instead, she'd yelled rape.

Incensed beyond reason, the elderly judge threatened to

sue Lonesome Pines and press charges against Marion. The judge, it seemed, had a bit of an ego problem. Marion's first clue should have been the prescription bottle of penile dysfunction meds.

Rosa Hamilton had come to Marion's rescue. Rosa said she'd swear in a court of law that the judge's wife had *invited* Marion to her cottage. Rosa, serving dinner in the dining room, had heard every word. As a good Christian, she didn't want to repeat those dirty words, including the F-word and the C-word, but she would under oath. Because Marion Dombroski "weren't no prevert!"

The apoplectic judge had swallowed his threats, but there'd been repercussions just the same. Duke told Marion that he had two choices—leave the ranch for good or stay out of the guest cottages. Should he mess around with a guest again, or be found inside one of the cottages, his butt would be kicked all the way to Denver.

Marion had chosen to remain at the ranch for one reason and one reason only.

If he "left for good," how would his mother ever find him?

# Twenty-Eight

At first Ellie thought the man who opened the door was Garrett.

Then her sensitive nostrils told her it couldn't be Garrett.

The man who opened the door wore men's cologne and Garrett hated cologne. He said it was a "dishonest smell to hide an honest smell."

Peter felt the same way, only he wasn't quite so poetic. "One stink to cover another stink," he had stated, while watching a *Jeopardy!* commercial. "Manufactured by noxious skunks in three-piece suits."

The man who responded to the doorbell's strident ring, the man who looked like Garrett, said, "I'm Gideon Halliday. Welcome to Hamlin."

After carefully lowering Ellie to the red velvet divan, Peter arched an eyebrow. "Hamlin?"

"The Pied Piper of," Ellie said. Summoning up the lightest, most carefree voice in her repertoire, she added, "Are you being insulting or caustic or alliterative, Mr. Halliday?"

She knew from experience that first impressions were often wrong, dead-wrong, but for some reason she couldn't fathom, she didn't particularly care for Gideon Halliday. He spoke with a British accent that sounded forced, rehearsed, perhaps even a tad prissy, but he'd done nothing

205

improper. On the contrary, once she and Peter had identified themselves, he had ushered them inside with little clucking sounds of distress, like a mother hen fussing over two vagrant chicks. He didn't look like a mother hen, not even close. He looked like his brother—tall, handsome, and physically fit—except Gideon Halliday's short hair wasn't dreadlocked.

Ellie tried but failed to picture Gideon in tight jeans. Or any jeans. Tonight he wore black silk, Hugh Hefner lounging pajamas. With, of all things, a white cravat. On his head was a whimsical French beret, as if he planned to attend a poetry reading at a Beatnik café. Or a limerick reading at the Playboy Mansion. In his left hand he clutched an unlit meerschaum pipe, either for effect or because he had to clutch something. From her low vantage point on the divan, Ellie could see that his other hand was always in motion, clenching and unclenching, fingers snapping silently.

"I would never insult a guest, nor was I being sarcastic," he replied, having given her question earnest consideration. "As you may have noticed, we live on a hill. What you may not have noticed is that we don't exactly live on top of the hill. Our house is cut into the hill and when it rains the cellar smells musty. When we have a downpour, like tonight, the cellar floods. I've been telling my brother we should shore up the floors and walls, putty the cracks . . ." He shrugged his broad shoulders. "I hope you're not afraid of mice, my dear."

"I've never actually seen a mouse in person, unless you count Disneyland." Ellie's swallowed. "How many mice are we talking about?"

"When you rang the doorbell I was looking up Pied Piper in the telephone directory. Does the name 'Willard' mean anything to you?"

She had decided she liked Gideon's wit, despite his bogus accent, when Peter, as always, cut to the chase. "Is that why Garrett and his wife aren't here to greet us?" he asked, and Ellie could *feel* his cop vibes winging through the entrance hall.

"I beg your pardon?" Gideon looked genuinely puzzled.

"The dinner party," Ellie said, rising. Arms extended like Frankenstein, she began to lurch over to Peter. But, embarrassingly, her balance was impeded by the orange gift box. Halting briefly to place it on top of the piano, she saw that the instrument was a player piano, and her Judy Garland-Mickey Rooney scenario died away.

"What dinner party?" Gideon brought the pipe to his mouth, sucked on its stem, and coughed. "It helps if you light it," he said, staring at the bowl.

"We're staying at Lonesome Pines," Ellie began.

"Yes, Kit mentioned that."

"Last night your brother called the ranch and invited us to dinner," Peter said, cutting to the chase again.

"That's inexcusable." Gideon clucked twice. "Garrett didn't say one word about a dinner party. I can't believe he'd do that. My goodness, you two are saturated." Fingers snapping silently, he turned his face toward Ellie. "Come into the living room, my dear. There's a nice fire in the fireplace and—"

"What about the mice?"

"They prefer the kitchen."

Peter said, "Where's Garrett?"

Gideon shrugged. "He's not here."

"Do you know where he is?"

"He usually doesn't tell me where he's going."

Ellie sensed animosity. "Heather," she said, striving to

keep her desperation at bay. "Heather has to be here. Surely she wouldn't go out in this storm."

"Come into the living room, won't you? Heather's here, my dear, upstairs."

Heading for the living room, Ellie spied a staircase. "Heather!" she yelled.

"Hush, my dear." Gideon looked distraught. "Please keep your voice down. Heather's sleeping. The mice, don't you know? Not Heather's cup of tea."

"She won't mind if I wake her, Mr. Halliday. She'll want to see me."

"I'm sorry, but that's not a good idea. When the bloody mice began stampeding, she screamed something awful. Scared them half to death." He gave Ellie a tentative grin. "Seriously, my dear, I thought we'd have to call 9-1-1. For Heather, not the mice. But she finally calmed down, took some tranquilizers, then locked herself inside her bedroom. Obviously, she didn't know about the dinner party."

Now Ellie understood why Gideon Halliday bothered her. He was much too pseudo British for words, and she despised men who called women "my dear." Gideon reminded her of Richard Burton at his worst. Did Richard Burton have a best? She had always thought him highly overrated as an actor, no more artistically gifted than Eddie Fisher. Except Burton had a hairstyle that was conventional rather than curly, a complexion that was pitted rather than apple-cheeked, and a pretentious voice. Ellie had seen him on Broadway in *Hamlet*. She had believed then, and still believed, that Eddie Fisher would have given a more credible performance. Maybe because Burton, clothed in black slacks and a black turtleneck, had articulated like an overwrought Danish émigré with a fake passport, as he postured in front of a black backdrop. Maybe because she and her grandmother had both fallen asleep before the second act, even though they were seated one row behind Elizabeth Taylor.

D.H. Lawrence, in his poem *When I Read Shakespeare,* wrote: "And Hamlet how boring, how boring to live with. So mean and self-conscious, blowing and snoring. His wonderful speeches, full of other folks' whoring."

Boy, if that didn't seem, at least on the surface, to define Gideon Halliday.

And yet he seemed to possess a hidden core of sensuality, as if he belonged in an Anne Rice novel. He wasn't obvious or crude, like Owen Lassiter, but Gideon looked as if he could be—*explosive.* Explosive with a petulant oh-gosh-I'm-sorry afterwards. She wondered if John Halliday's first wife had favored Garrett over Gideon, the same way Ellie's mother had given all her love and affection to Ellie's brother, Tab. Except Ellie had been a docile sibling. She would never explode, and Tab, no dummy, had taken advantage of that.

Peter said, "Where's Kit?"

"Out," Gideon replied. "She doesn't tell me where she's going, either. There's no one here except Heather and me and—"

"The rats," Peter interrupted.

"I was going to say mice. All the rats left for Denver. And Washington D.C."

If you could package Peter's demeanor, Ellie thought, you'd never need an air conditioner. She remembered her reaction to the now-widowed Owen Lassiter. Multiply that by, oh, say one hundred, and you'd have Peter's reaction to Gideon Halliday. Or maybe Peter was just pissed off because of their fruitless "rain date."

"Mr. Halliday," Ellie began.

"Gideon."

"Right. Gideon. We're sorry to have bothered you, Gideon, but we need to head back now. I'll call Heather tomorrow. Or if she wakes up, tell her to call me at the ranch, no matter how late. I'm fairly certain she has my cell phone number, but I'll write it down, along with my cottage exten—"

"That won't be necessary, my dear. I have an excellent memory, especially for numbers. House numbers, fax and telephone numbers, license plate numbers, you name it. My sweet mum used to call it a gift from God. Of course, Garrett's gift from God is much more fertile."

*Is it my imagination or does Gideon sounds a tad petulant?* Ellie recited the numbers, then gestured toward the vestibule. "The orange package on top of the player piano is for Heather. A small gift. Please give it to her."

"Of course I will. But come into the living room and dry yourselves in front of the fire before you leave my humble abode to slog through the boggy moors and crags of Aspen. It's the least I can offer, aside from my profound regrets. I do apologize, profusely, for my brother's absence. And for his abysmal lack of communication. How about a nip of brandy? Surely that wouldn't be amiss."

"Peter," Ellie said, "why don't you nip while I use the bathroom?"

"The loo is down the hall, second door on the left," Gideon said, pointing his pipe toward a narrow, dimly lit, wood-paneled corridor.

Ellie watched him turn right and stroll through an archway. Peter followed.

"Rats," she said softly. She smiled at her apropos expletive, then quickly glanced around to see if she'd accidentally summoned Gideon's mice. She smiled again, this time at her foolishness. Aside from the fact that one couldn't summon mice by saying the word "rats," she was fairly certain (*but not one hundred percent certain*) that Gideon's squeaky rodents didn't exist. She trusted her gut feelings, and she had a gut feeling Gideon had lied. But why? Why would he invent a story like that? His idea of a joke?

Mice notwithstanding, she had hoped the bathroom would be upstairs rather than downstairs. A hopeless hope, considering how large the house was, considering how many people lived here. Gideon and Kit, Garrett and Heather, Adrianna and, once upon a time, her husband John. Was Gideon widowed? Divorced? Obviously, he didn't have a wife. If he did, he would have mentioned her during his at-home-tonight cast list. Or maybe she was "out," too. Or maybe he sequestered her in the attic. Like Jane Eyre. No, wait. Jane hadn't been sequestered. The *mad wife* had been locked away. With a chambermaid and a chamber pot.

Ellie's childhood home, erected in the fifties, had been moderately large, but the builder, probably a leftover Munchkin from Oz, had constructed very low ceilings. Even as a kid, Ellie had been tempted to duck her head every time she walked inside. Except for the kitchen, all rooms were covered, practically overgrown with shag carpeting. The ranch house, or "rancher," cheapest model in the development—the most expensive looked like David O. Selznick's Tara—sported three bedrooms, a guest room, a living room, a dining room, an eat-in kitchen, a basement "rumpus room," a laundry room, and *one* bathroom.

So her second hope, apparently another hopeless hope, had been that this old house, older than her childhood home, would have one bathroom—situated on the second floor.

Maybe she could traipse upstairs anyway, pretend she'd

misunderstood Gideon's directions, sneak a peek inside Heather's bedroom. Or, if the bedroom door was locked, knock. Even better, she'd sing or whistle Heather's favorite song, from *Brigadoon,* and—

No. That wouldn't work. Gideon had distinctly said, "down the hall, second door on the left."

And he'd used his pipe as a compass.

Anyway, with her injured foot it would take her forever to "traipse," or climb, or even crawl. By the time she reached the top landing, Peter's nip would have been nipped.

As she longed for the days of yesteryear, before she'd sprained her damn fool ankle, she sniffed and smelled—turpentine.

Directly across from the bathroom—in Gideon-speak, "loo"—a door stood ajar.

*Define ajar, Ellie.*

*Olive Oyl might be able to slither inside, but not Popeye. Or, for that matter, Christiffer Columbia Daniel Boom, also known as Swee'Pea.*

She had no right to explore. Gideon hadn't given her permission to explore.

But then, she hadn't asked.

# Twenty-Nine

Inching the door open, Ellie flicked the light switch and stepped into an amusement park.

The Fun House at an amusement park.

A variegated kaleidoscope of shifting colors.

Paint-spattered walls were dotted with mismatched mirrors. They reflected canvasses, or parts of canvasses. Four of the mirrors were cheval glass, tilted at different angles. All of the mirrors reproduced, multiplied, or in some cases mutilated painted images, and everything looked overly bright, as if Garrett had borrowed the sun from Mother Nature and forgotten to give it back.

No wonder Aspen was suffering from a torrential downpour.

Awed by Garrett's genius, undoubtedly "a gift from God," Ellie nevertheless managed to catalog the differences between Garrett's early works and recent works, more evident here in close quarters. At the Colorado Springs gallery, Melody had tastefully hung one or two, at the most three paintings on the maze-like walls, which gave prominence to each individual canvas. There, the paintings danced without partners. Here, Ellie felt as if she wore 3-D glasses while scrutinizing a dissected movie screen.

In other words, she stood *inside* the kaleidoscope.

Near her left elbow, on a sturdy easel, a recent painting depicted a woman seated sidesaddle, atop a black horse. A man with dark hair held the woman's stocking-clad foot in one hand, her small leather riding boot in his other hand. The woman wore a long blue skirt, a yellow blouse, and a head kerchief from which tendrils of fire-engine-red hair had escaped. The red, corkscrew curls framed her face and brought out the green in her blue-green eyes. A light dusting of freckles enhanced her prominent cheekbones, and if Ellie hadn't discussed Prince Charming's foot fetish with Peter less than two hours ago, she probably wouldn't have thought: *Cinderella.*

Heather as Cinderella? Yes. No. Maybe. A definite maybe.

Except for the freckles, the face looked like Heather's, but the body appeared thinner, more angular. Of course, Heather could have lost weight. Hospital food was a genuine, if unbidden weight loss program and, according to Melody, Heather had undergone several skin grafts.

Holy cow! The painted woman looked like Kit, too. *She* could have been Garrett's model. For the first time, Ellie noted the resemblance between Kit and Heather. Strange, because Heather was Kit's aunt by marriage, not blood. But Ellie and Heather weren't related by blood and they generated double takes. Most people thought they were sisters. A few—undoubtedly nearsighted—thought she and Heather were twins.

Even Adrianna, at the gallery, had asked Ellie if she and Heather were related.

Bottom line: Heather Halliday possessed red hair and blue-green eyes. Kit Halliday, no blood relation to Heather Halliday, possessed red hair and blue-green eyes. Ellie Bernstein, no blood relation to Kit or Heather, possessed red hair and blue-green eyes. Period. End of story. Unless you counted, as an epilogue, three complexions without freckles. She didn't have them. Neither did Kit and Heather.

*And your in-depth analysis of this freckle conundrum, Ellie?*

*Well, Mr. Wallace, or may I call you Mike, I don't have a clue.*

In any case, what was wrong with Garrett using Kit as his model? Nothing. The woman on the horse was clothed, not nude. And while the eroticism wasn't exactly understated, Ellie had seen book covers that were more provocative. Her mother, a voracious reader, bought romance novels by the truckload, raiding bookstores and supermarket shelves as soon as a new shipment came in, which generally meant any day that had a "y" in it. As a kid, Ellie had watched her mom rev up the car, preparing to drive through dense fog, solid sheets of rain, even blizzards that grounded planes, in order to get her Harlequin fix. On more than one occasion, Ellie had clung for dear life to the passenger seat as her mom's snow tires skidded into a Barnes & Noble parking lot.

Shaking off the past, stepping closer to the "Cinderella" painting, Ellie saw the barest outline of cacti in the foreground, mountains in the background. So this was a work in progress. She had to admit that, up close, Garrett's trademark eroticism was more palpable, and not just because the charming "Prince Cowboy" was slyly fondling "Cinderella's" foot. It was the expression on the young horsewoman's face. Orgasmic, but in a good way, not lewd or vulgar.

*There's a big difference between eroticism and porn,* Ellie thought. *Garrett's painting is seductive, maybe even titillating, but it isn't pornographic.*

A sketchpad leaned against one leg of the easel. Curious, Ellie bent down, picked up the pad, and opened it. She saw several detailed sketches, mostly hands, feet, and eyes, then a colored-pencil draft of the "Cinderella" painting as a whole, then the painting's title, written in efficient, ruler-straight letters: THERE'S NO BUSINESS LIKE SHOE BUSINESS.

On the top of the page, in letters that slanted to the right, Garrett had written: "Angel's Ravine 5 o'clock." This time his handwriting looked as slapdash as a doctor's prescription. And the memo was scrawled inside a heavily penciled box, which probably meant that it had been inscribed during a phone conversation.

Ellie felt her face flush. How would she like it if someone invaded her study and read her private memos? Carefully, she placed the sketchpad in its former position, propped against the easel. Then she stepped back a few paces and studied the painting again. *There's No Business Like Shoe Business* now looked vaguely familiar, even though she knew for a fact she'd never seen it before. Except for Garrett's gallery show, she hadn't seen any of his paintings in five years. And she could tell that this painting was up to date because Garrett's current compositions were stunningly accentuated by a lusty, van Gogh-like intensity. Primary colors, palette-knife-thick, dominated, but that only served to strengthen his subtle flesh tones and sparse, intricate brush strokes. Garrett gave new meaning to "less is more," and his paintings reminded Ellie of writers who use the F-word so many times it becomes meaningless. Cuss once—like Rhett's "frankly my dear, I don't give a damn"—and it smacks you across the face. And yet, rather than smacking people across the face with his vivid, almost garish reds and blues and yellows, Garrett consciously controlled an observer's gaze by leading it where *he* wanted it to go.

Speaking of controlling one's gaze, another easel stood facing the corner wall, where there were no mirrors.

Mounted on that easel, the back of a fairly large painting stuck out like the proverbial sore thumb; a single monochrome blotch adrift in a sea of riotous color.

Stretched onto a wooden frame, the unraveled threads of the painting's coarse canvas seemed to undulate, blown by a nonexistent breeze, almost as though they waved Ellie closer.

Which was as good a reason as any for satisfying her curiosity.

As she slid her body between the canvas and the wall, facing the canvas, she thought: *I couldn't have done this before I lost fifty-five pounds at Weight Winners.*

Her second thought was: *Mary, Mother of God!*

Which seemed apt, since the painting depicted the Annunciation . . .

Mary and the angel Gabriel . . .

And flowers.

Ellie's brow scrunched. She recognized the flowers. Periwinkle, also known as "The Virgin Flower." And lungwort, often called "Mary's Tears" because the white spots on the leaves were supposedly Mary's tear stains. The white, yellow, and purple flowers had to be the "Herb Trinity." There were also roses—representing the Virgin Mary herself—and lilies.

" 'The white petals of the lily symbolize physical purity, the gold anthers the radiant light of her soul,' " Ellie said softly, probing her rusty Catholic-school memory.

Thinking she'd rather quote Lewis Carroll than nuns, she whispered, " 'Curiouser and curiouser!' cried Alice."

*Because the woman in the painting wasn't Heather.*

*Nor was she Kit.*

*She wasn't even a redhead*

*And,* thought Ellie, stepping backwards and wincing as

her rapidly-stiffening neck and shoulders encountered the wall, *the colors of the flowers are subdued, a whisper rather than a shout, as if Garrett suddenly and illogically decided to resurrect his old style.*

Last but not least, the painting wasn't very good. Even her inexperienced eye could see that the composition was out of sync, the brush strokes tentative, the proportions askew.

Maybe it was a very old painting. No. It couldn't be. Heather had once said that Garrett quickly primed then painted over what he called his "practice pieces."

Extending her index finger, Ellie traced a rose petal.

Holy cow, the paint was wet! Another work in progress? If yes, how come this painting was poles apart from the "Shoe Business" painting? Did her friend Garrett have a Jekyll and Hyde personality? A Rembrandt and Jackson Pollack persona?

Rubbing her red-stained finger against her red poncho, she squinted at the Annunciation canvas. Its one saving grace was Garrett's depiction of "Mary." Young and beautiful and very, very sad, the girl's hair was cappuccino brown, her eyes periwinkle blue. Above her head was a halo.

Ellie grimaced. Although hyped by religious fanatics and evangelistic politicians, haloes were highly overrated. She wouldn't want one. And, for the record, Mary didn't look all that happy in the Annunciation paintings Ellie had seen during her pious childhood. After all, Mary, a virgin, had pledged herself to Joseph, so it was a bit of a shock when the robed and winged (*and haloed*) Gabriel enunciated God's game plan.

But Garrett Halliday's painted woman was beyond grief, inconsolable, and Ellie felt an empathetic angst; a sorrow so pure, so uncontaminated by cynicism—

Whoa. Wait. The "Virgin Mary" in Garrett's painting looked familiar.

An actress? Definitely.

Gene Tierney? Loretta Young? No. But someone of that era.

It would come to her, Ellie concluded, if she didn't *try* to remember.

Meanwhile, she needed to leave Garrett's studio immediately if not sooner. She had a feeling Peter had asked for coffee or hot tea, rather than a nip of brandy, which would account for her uninterrupted, whirlwind art tour.

But if she knew Peter, and she did, by now he would have looked at his waterproof watch and determined that she'd trapped herself inside the loo. Or fainted.

Or, as Owen Lassiter had so delicately put it, "fell in."

# Thirty

Trees still dripped like arboreal shower curtains, but at least the rain had stopped. Streets, however, were as slippery as butter and, in places, as marshy as a Louisiana swamp, so Ellie didn't dare relax her stressed neck and shoulders. Instead, she surreptitiously watched Peter navigate the "boggy moors and crags of Aspen," his left foot hovering above the clutch and brake pedals.

"I've a gut feeling something's wrong," she finally said, warming her cold hands against the dashboard heater.

"No kidding." Peter gripped the steering wheel tighter. "Do the words 'wild goose chase' mean anything to you? And your gut feeling is probably hunger."

"That's true. I'm so hungry I could eat a goose." As if to prove it, her stomach growled. "For the record, Peter, I'd bet the farm that Adrianna wasn't there with Heather and Gideon. The house was too quiet. No music, no TV, and she's not the sort to sit and read a book. Or write her autobiography."

"Maybe," he said, "she was in bed, fast asleep."

"At seven o'clock in the evening?"

"Maybe she passed out, like she did at the gallery."

Ellie shook her head. "I'm not saying she couldn't have passed out, but the house didn't smell of liquor. Or even liqueur. Just the faintest whiff of her perfume. Plus, oil paint, turpentine, and mildew."

"Well then, she could have been sitting, quiet as a *mouse*—"

"Very funny!"

"—in front of her computer. E-mailing her skating buds and/or her Playmate buds. Maybe she was setting up an X-rated website where she could be the star attraction."

"You really didn't like her, did you?"

"I didn't dislike her."

"But you detested Gideon. I felt your vibes. The vestibule was ten degrees colder than the porch, and if you were King Midas you'd have turned Gideon into a twenty-four-carat, gold-bullion statue."

"Your mythology is a bit off-kilter, sweetheart. In point of fact, Gideon *is* Midas."

"He's a king who turns *you* into gold?" she asked, arching an eyebrow.

"That's just one legend. I prefer the one where Midas, having umpired a musical contest against Apollo in favor of Pan, had his ears changed by Apollo into those of an ass. Midas hid his long, furry ears under a cap, and he swore his barber to secrecy. But the barber was so tormented by the secret he dared not let slip, he dug a hole in the ground and whispered the secret into it. A reed sprang up, which, in the wind, murmured, 'Midas hath ass's ears.' Why are you laughing?"

"Because your story is funny, because you used the word 'umpired,' rather than 'judged' or even 'refereed,' because I didn't know you knew so much about classical myths, and because I pictured Gideon hiding his ass-ears underneath his silly French beret. So tell me, Lieutenant, why didn't you like him?"

"Elementary, my dear Norrie," said Peter in a pseudo-British accent. "I hate affectations, like . . . oh, say, an unlit

Sherlock Holmes pipe and whatever the heck he was wearing round his neck. And he's veddy, veddy pretentious, *my dear.* Do you have any idea what we discussed while you were trespassing inside Garrett's studio?"

Ellie felt her cheeks bake. Gideon was much too urbane, much too Cary-Grant-ish, to question her lengthy stay in the bathroom. However, knowing Peter would grill her mercilessly, she had told him about her "art tour" on the way to the car. Without fibbing, exactly, she'd made it sound as if she had—*oops*—turned right rather than left while searching for the loo. But she now realized, and should have realized before she even opened her mouth, that she hadn't fooled him one little bit.

"What did you and Gideon discuss, honey? Classical myths? Ass's ears?"

"Not even close," Peter said, abandoning his Brit accent. "We talked about cop stuff. He said he didn't think all those *CSI* programs—that's the word he used, programs rather than TV shows—were on the up and up, what did I think? Then he gave me a couple of 'hypothetical murders' and asked me how I'd solve them."

"What's wrong with that? My mother always said I should never talk about myself on a date, that I should bat my eyelashes and talk about my date's hobbies, *his* interests, *his* well being. That way, she said, I'd be 'popular.' Maybe Gideon felt your vibes, like I did. Maybe he wanted to make a good impression. So," she added, somewhat lamely, "he asked you about cop stuff."

"Right." Removing one hand from the steering wheel, Peter lightly smacked the side of his head. "Of course. That's why he did it. So he could be 'popular.' He must have sensed I'd already classified him as a pompous, ostentatious, supercilious smartass, and he wanted to change my mind by bombarding me with asinine questions. Why didn't I think of that?"

"Sarcasm has never been your strong suit, Lieutenant."

"Sorry, sweetheart. I'm tired and hungry and cranky, but I shouldn't take it out on you."

"Apology accepted." She watched him grip the steering wheel again. "Getting back to my gut feeling . . ."

"Yes?"

"Just for grins, could *we* do a 'hypothetical'?"

"Sure." He gave her a tired but sincere grin. "I'll play Groucho and you can play Hypo."

"Harpo! You may be well versed in classical myths, Peter, but you're sorely lacking in classical Marx. Okay, hypothetically speaking, let's say the sketchpad memo I saw was written earlier today."

"Or three days ago. Or last week. Or last month."

"This is *my* hypothetical!"

"Sorry."

"This morning Marion said something about Angel's Ravine." Ellie probed her memory. "I was about to join you and Kit, and I was a tad nervous about riding outside the corral, and Marion said that, except for Angel's Ravine, the trail was easy to navigate. So Angel's Ravine must be a part of the ranch. Am I right, or am I right?"

"I think you're right, Hypo. Toot your horn like a good little Marxist."

"Toot, toot. What do you mean you *think* I'm right?"

"When I visited the ranch four years ago, there was a Mike's Ravine. But, to my knowledge, Lonesome Pines only has one arduous trail, so let's assume Mike's Ravine had a name change."

"That really does makes sense, Peter. Maybe a tree looks like an angel. Or a mountain looks like an angel. Or Lelia

Hamilton sculpted an angel out of a tree stump. Or some-body simply decided Angel's Ravine sounded prettier than Mike's Ravine."

She didn't want to think about a fourth reason—that a rider had fallen into the ravine and died.

"Getting back to my 'hypothetical,' " she said, "if the appointment at Angel's Ravine was for today, that puts Garrett at the ranch around five p.m. Can one drive a car along that 'arduous' trail?"

Peter shook his head. "Your friend Garrett would have to walk or ride. My guess is, he'd ride. He boards a horse at the ranch. A beautiful Appaloosa mare. Kit pointed her out this morning, while we were saddling our horses. And be-fore you ask, her name is Merrylegs."

Ellie smiled. "That had to be Heather's brainchild. If I remember correctly, Merrylegs was the name of one of the horses, or ponies, in Anna Sewell's *Black Beauty*. Heather adored that book. She said Garrett loved the illustrations, especially the color illustrations. I forgot to mention Mick's copy when we discussed horses at the Dew Drop Inn, but I must have read it to him a hundred times. Holy cow! No wonder *There's No Business Like Shoe Business* looked so fa-miliar. The black horse in Garrett's painting looks a lot like the color frontispiece of Beauty . . . long, bushy mane and tail . . . gosh, what a relief!" She smiled again, then sighed. "Now, if I could only figure out who the Virgin Mary looks like."

"I may be wrong," Peter said, "but my guess is that she looks like the Virgin Mary."

"I'm talking about Garrett's second painting, the one that wasn't very good. Oh, well, it's not important. What's important is Garrett." She closed her eyes, formatting a script inside her head. Then, opening her eyes, she said,

"Let's suppose Garrett rode to Angel's Ravine, fell off his horse, and clunked his head. Or he fell into the ravine and broke his arm, or his leg, or something. And that's why he wasn't home," she concluded, giving herself an A for effort, a D for scriptwriting. Because she'd left out a few minor details. Like a cell phone. Or suppose he had screamed for help? Did ravines echo?

"If Garrett met someone at the ravine," Peter said, "he or she would have sounded an alarm when Garrett hurt himself."

"True. Unless it happened after the . . . meeting."

Ellie bit her lip. She'd almost said *rendezvous*, because, in her own mind, she was fairly certain she knew the name of the woman Garrett had planned to tryst with. Peter might believe Mike Urvant responsible for his sister's pregnancy, but Peter hadn't caught the nuances, the almost tangible signals Beth had given off during their first conversation, the one where she'd quoted Andy Warhol, the one where she'd said that Garrett's big mouth was going to get him in big trouble some day.

From the corner of her eye, Ellie saw Peter shake his head. "What?"

"Garrett's a superb horseman. I'm talking Zorro. The mare belongs to the whole Halliday clan, but Kit said Heather hasn't ridden in months while Garrett rides all the time. He broke and trained Merrylegs and—"

"The rain."

"What?"

"It began raining shortly after five," Ellie said. "Storming, actually. I remember listening to the rain hit the roof and comparing it to a field of Kentucky Derby contenders— the rain, not the roof. Hoof beats."

"I get the image." He grinned. "And the sound bite."

"So let's say Garrett finished his meeting, or tryst, or whatever it was, and was heading home, or getting ready to head home, when his horse stumbled or slipped and went down. Maybe Garrett was trapped beneath the horse." She shivered, thinking her mother would say a goose walked across her grave.

"If his mare was all right," Peter said, "she'd have returned to the barn."

"Are you playing devil's advocate with *my* hypothetical?" When he nodded, she said, "Okay, fair enough. So let's suppose the mare slipped and Garrett fell and broke his leg, or his head, or whatever. By now there was thunder and lightning, as well as rain. I know more about cats than I do about horses, but wouldn't Merrylegs act skittish? Sure, she would. So let's say Garrett tied her reins to something, maybe a tree, so she couldn't move. But before he could climb into the saddle, he passed out. Like I did when I fell off Buttermilk."

"This is just a wild guess," Peter said, "but you'd like me to ride to the ravine and check out your supposition."

"Will you?"

"Yes."

"You will? I really hate to ask, but—"

"Norrie, I said yes. Please don't try to talk me out of it when you're dying to talk me into it. I'm not sure your 'hypothetical' has much substance, but I agree that *something* happened to your friend Garrett. I only met him briefly, but he didn't strike me as the kind of man who'd forget a dinner engagement. Or shrug it off. Especially since you'd be there."

"Meaning what?"

"Meaning you're a juicy little lamb chop, a tasty morsel—"

"And Garrett gives good flirt."

"Exactly." Peter peered through the windshield. "There's a gas station up ahead, and it looks open."

"We need gas?"

"No, Hypo, but we need food, and that station looks like it sells food. I'll grab a bag of chips, two cans of soda, and a couple of sandwiches. I'll eat mine in the car. When we get to the ranch, I'll change my clothes and head out as quickly as possible." He shook his finger like the needle on an old-fashioned applause meter. "But only if you promise to eat your sandwich, change into your pajamas, take a pain pill, and go to sleep like a good little lamb chop."

"Please make my drink a diet Coke or Pepsi," she said. "Or if they don't have any diet soft drinks, I'll take bottled water."

"I'm not spending my hard-earned money on bottled water," he grumbled. "If you want bottled water, drink Coors Light. Wait in the car, please. Hum a few bars of 'One Hundred Bottles of Beer on the Wall.' I should be back before you hit ninety, eighty-five max."

"Yes, sir. Whatever you say, Groucho."

Despite Garrett's desertion, and her anxiety, Ellie took a moment to admire Peter's taut, sculpted backside as he stepped out of the car. Then, rather than counting beer bottles, she started humming "Heather on the Hill" from *Brigadoon*—the song she and Heather had always used to signal each other.

In retrospect, she should have sung it at the top of her lungs while she was inside the Halliday house. Because she had another gut feeling.

Earlier, she had imagined a mad wife, Gideon's mad wife, locked away in the attic, just like the mad wife in *Jane Eyre*. At the time it had seemed like a nonsensical supposition, but what if *Heather* had been locked away?

*Based on what, Ellie?*

Well, for one thing, Gideon's distraught look when she'd stood at the bottom of the staircase and shouted Heather's name. For another, the fact that nobody had seen Heather for months.

*Except, of course, the Hallidays.*

But why would they . . . why would *anyone* lock Heather in her bedroom? If she had truly gone mad, from her disfigurement, from an addiction to drugs, from a myriad of other reasons, why not send her to a top-notch country club sanitarium? Garrett could afford it.

*Oh, God, suppose Heather was dead!*

Ellie shook her head. That made no sense. Why keep it a secret? For that matter, *could* it be kept under wraps? Was it possible to hide a fatality in a closet, along with other skeletons? Like Garrett's affairs?

Assuming, of course, he was having affairs.

*Let's assume he is.*

Melody had said that Garrett's phenomenal success was attributable to Heather. So what if Heather had discovered Garrett's covert activities? What if she wanted a divorce?

Yes, okay, but would the Hallidays lock her up, permanently, just to keep her from getting one?

Talk about an off-the-wall theory! A private sanitarium sounded much more logical. And the Halliday family wouldn't want the public to get wind of *that* because . . .

Because the public was fickle and Garrett's "love affair of the century" status would take a nosedive.

Which would drastically alter the income from his paintings, his print reproductions, his coffee table books, and, especially, the postcards that, according to Melody, women purchased in droves.

The family needed Heather, alive, producible, and sane, because Garrett's income kept them in croissants and Perrier, rather than bread and water, steak and lobster, rather than hamburger and fish sticks, Godiva Passion Truffles, rather than—

*Scrub "producible." Beth said it's been ages since anyone's seen Heather.*

What else had Beth said? "Except for Garrett's paintings, she doesn't exist."

The death supposition niggled at Ellie's brain again.

Wait a sec. Melody had said that Heather helped plan Garrett's gallery show.

How? In person? By phone? Fax? E-mail?

A call to Melody would solve that ambiguity. First thing tomorrow morn—no. Tomorrow was Monday, which meant Melody would be subbing for Ellie at her nine a.m. Weight Winners meeting.

First thing tomorrow afternoon!

# Thirty-One

The Lonesome Pines sign was missing more letters, but Peter made no comment. He seemed to be fully focused on his Angel's Ravine expedition. Ellie couldn't tell if his attitude was one of placation or trepidation, and although she wanted reassurance, she was afraid to ask. As soon as they entered the cottage, he changed into a pair of practical jeans and a warm, fleece, hooded, NFL-sanctioned, Oakland Raiders pullover.

"It'll take me fifteen or twenty minutes to ride to the ravine," he said, knotting the laces on his sneakers. "Longer if the trail is rain-slick. Then ten or so minutes to look around. When I get back to the ranch, I have to rub down my horse. So let's say an hour and a half, two at the most."

"Oh, God, Peter, this is stupid," she wailed. "Another wild goose chase."

"No, Norrie. I'm beginning to share your gut feeling. Something's wrong. I'll saddle up a second horse and take it with me, just in case your friend Garrett really has suffered an injury . . ."

He paused, but Ellie filled in the rest. *And Merrylegs has suffered an injury, too.* She knew darn well that horses with broken legs were shot, just as Peter knew darn well she turned off the TV before the end of *Old Yell*— "Horse!" she exclaimed. "Why don't you check the barn, Peter? The stalls, I mean. If Merrylegs is still there—"

230

"It wouldn't prove a thing. If you're right and the five o'clock appointment was for today, your friend Garrett might very well have walked to the ravine. He'd have started out before the weather turned foul, before the rain hit."

"You said it takes fifteen or twenty minutes to ride to Angel's Ravine. How long does it take to walk? Wait a sec! Garrett's car!" In her excitement she clutched Peter's arm so hard, she almost breached his fleecy sleeve with her fingernails. "All we have to do is look for his car. That'll tell us if he was here, at the ranch."

"*We* aren't looking for anything," he said, gently unclasping her fingers, "and I don't want to take the time to search for a car. I'll check the area around the barn and corral before I ride out, but your friend Garrett could have parked anywhere. The ranch has recessed alcoves all over the place. Mike Urvant has always mollycoddled his guests—god-forbid they should step out of their Mustangs and hike an eighth of a mile—but he didn't want any vehicles to blight the scenery. So while the parking spaces are well crafted, with hitching posts and other doodads, they're also well hidden. Duke gives out 'ranch maps' when guests check in. To answer your question, Norrie, in good weather it takes less time to walk to the ravine than it does to ride. There are shortcuts a person on foot can circumvent—routes that are virtually impossible for a horse, or even a mule."

Had it been any other occasion, Ellie would have smiled at "mollycoddled" and "doodad." Instead, she wished Peter Godspeed, emphasis on the speed.

Opening the cottage door, he said, "Don't take this as a John Wayne-ish remark, sweetheart, but when I return I'll expect to find you in bed, sound asleep. Remember, you promised."

She gave him a wave of her hand and a kiss, not necessarily in that order, and watched him walk toward the main house and dining hall, which hid the barn and corral from sight. Only then did she shut the door. Restless, she added a can of wet cat food to Jackie Robinson's kibble. She changed the litter in Jackie Robinson's litter box. Then she realized she hadn't changed *her* damp, soggy clothes.

Discarding the red poncho, white dress, black rubber boots, and all underwear except panties, she threw on an oversized Denver Broncos jersey that masqueraded most nights as a nightshirt. Exhausted, she plumped her pillows with her fists, over and over again, trying to alleviate her pent-up emotions. However, her efforts to plump feathers, rather than pump iron, scared the living daylights out of Jackie Robinson. So, naturally, she had to scoop him up, plunk her sore body in the rocking chair, and calm her frenzied feline.

*Maybe the sway of the rocker will lull* me *to sleep,* she thought.

Except rockers rocked, and she kept thumping her sore foot against the floor.

"Sorry, J.R.," she said, rising from the chair.

Still holding the cat, she limped into the bathroom and stared into the mirror above the sink. Oh, God, she looked awful. Her face was pale, haggard, practically *pinched,* and to add insult to injury, her favorite actress had perjured herself on TV. No way was her waterproof mascara waterproof. Unless, of course, it had been manufactured for raccoons.

"You lied through your perfect teeth, you cow," Ellie muttered, limping back into the bedroom and placing Jackie Robinson on the rocker's cushion. "Good thing I didn't buy the lipstick you hyped."

With a Garfield smirk, Jackie Robinson jumped down

from the rocker and inaugurated his fresh, clean-smelling, baking-powder-sprinkled kitty litter.

Ellie felt a new wave of anger wash over her. Almost immediately, she realized she was behaving irrationally, as if she'd replaced an empty toilet paper roll with a full roll and someone had dared to use it.

"Why am I so crabby, J.R.? Never mind. I know why. I'm hungry."

Hungry was an understatement. How about starved? Famished? Ravenous?

Even the cat's canned tuna looked tasty, assuming one could tolerate the color. And the smell.

She stared with distaste at the sandwich Peter had bought for her. Ham and Swiss on a roll that felt as hard as Woody Guthrie's hard rock candy mountain. If the roll *had* been rock candy, she would have sucked it, chewed it, crunched it, swallowed it, and diet be damned. But while she loved the taste and texture of Swiss cheese melted over corned beef and sauerkraut, she didn't care for Swiss cheese cold and clammy. And for some reason she couldn't fathom, in the back of her mind she heard her ex mother-in-law, Florence Bernstein, saying over and over that she'd brought Tony up kosher, so Ellie shouldn't mix meat and dairy. Ham was okay. After all, nowadays they *processed* pork. But Ellie shouldn't let the ham rub against butter, margarine, or cheese.

Oh, God, if she only had a stove handy, and some pots and pans, and the ingredients for honey lasagna. Carrots and celery and onions, sautéed. Canned tomato sauce, mushrooms, and two tablespoons of honey, added to the sautéed veggies. Layers of noodles, cottage cheese, cheddar cheese, and, of course, the sautéed sauce. On top, a little more sauce and mozzarella. Bake for fifty minutes, cool for ten.

On second thought, honey lasagna was too heavy for a late night nosh. And the emergency food she'd stashed in her suitcase—Weight Winners snack bars, popcorn, toaster pastries, and yogurt bars—didn't sound all that appetizing.

What she really wanted was a fresh salad. Crisp lettuce, tart radishes, chopped raw carrots, sliced green peppers and tomatoes, grated hard-boiled eggs, and maybe a wee bit of avocado—fattening, but right now she didn't give a hang. How about a handful of bacon bits, and fresh-ground pepper, and ranch dressing? If there was no ranch dressing, she'd settle for a few squeezes from a lemon, but there *should* be ranch dressing because, after all, Lonesome Pines was a ranch.

Come to think of it, Lonesome Pines had a kitchen. And before she'd joined Weight Winners, Ellie Bernstein had been the best damn raider in the universe.

*No, Peter, not a football-playing Raider of the Oakland variety. A raid-the-kitchen raider. An ice-cream-by-the-light-of-the-refrigerator raider. Don't you know that calories don't count when you stand inside a dark kitchen and chow down ice cream straight from the container? Or when you eat strawberry short-cake with your fingers, guided by the light of the fridge—or by the moon shining through the kitchen window?*

And tonight's moon was as round and fat as her aunt Janice's cheeky left buttock.

Food problem solved, Ellie scrubbed her face. Next, she donned a pair of knee socks and, with a grimace, slid her feet into the black rubber boots. Then she put Peter's sheepskin-lined, blue denim jacket over her nightshirt. The jacket encircled her hips and thighs like an un-elasticized girdle, and she knew she looked ridiculous, but who would she run into during a late-night kitchen raid? Anyway, she wasn't sure she could "wrangle" her heavily bandaged foot into a pair of straight-legged jeans. Best of all, the only parts of her body that would feel the cold were the couple of inches between the ribbed tops of her socks and the bottom of her number seven, orange and blue, Denver Broncos jersey.

"I didn't actually *promise* Peter I'd go straight to sleep," she told Jackie Robinson, whose tail was waving like a sinuous, albeit hirsute, snake as he fastidiously nosed his foul-smelling tuna. "Oh, before I forget, Peter said Martina Brustein has a cat, so tomorrow I'll take you on an introductory visit and you can work off some of that furry pudge. Meanwhile, be a good little Persian and, with any luck, I'll be back before you can say 'Jackie Robinson.' "

As she stepped outside, the rain started up again, and she chastised herself anew for sending Peter on what was almost certainly a fool's errand. By now Garrett was most likely in his own bed, under the blankets with Heather, surrounded by a gaggle of sightless, tailless rodents singing "Three Blind Mice."

It never occurred to Ellie that the dining hall might be locked until she stood in front of it. She was so sure it would be locked, she almost turned around and limped back down the path to her cottage.

*My God,* she thought, *I haven't been this negative since before I joined Weight Winners.*

Grasping the door handle, she tugged it open and, with a sigh of relief, stepped inside.

She had been here twice—at last night's supper and this morning's breakfast—but she hadn't realized how truly cavernous the room felt when it was dark. And empty. Any moment now, dozens of vampire bats would swoop down from the ceiling and land in her dripping-wet hair. Any moment now, the Phantom of Lonesome Pines would make an appearance, rip off his mask, and sing Andrew Lloyd Webber. With a shudder, she made a beeline for the kitchen. Which, providentially, was illuminated by bright florescent lighting that shined like a beacon.

She had been in restaurant kitchens before, and this one was no different. Maybe a little larger. Maybe a lot larger. It had the requisite chopping-block counters. And two enormous stoves, with one, two, three . . . *eight* ovens. Wooden shelves shelved clean dinner plates, salad and dessert plates, soup bowls, plus family-size bowls and platters. She spied a long stainless steel counter, directly underneath multiple heat lamps, where waiters picked up their orders. Looking like something out of a Piers Anthony novel, or a Steven Spielberg movie, dishwasher apparatus slumped menacingly against a far wall.

Ellie zeroed in on two large silver doors: Door Number One and Door Number Two. One of the doors led to a refrigerator, one to a freezer, but which door led to which chamber?

An unbidden recollection invaded what little remained of her caffeine-free, food-craving mind. Melody's surprise birthday party—a M*A*S*H theme, complete with costumes: Hawkeye and Hot Lips and Radar. The Dew Drop Inn's walk-in freezer, its shelves filled with brown-paper-wrapped slabs of beef and—*surprise!*—a plastic bag that contained a dead, un-skinned rabbit, with furry bunny ears and dead marble eyes. On the freezer's floor, a dead body.

So there was no way, repeat *no way* she'd ever cross the threshold of a walk-in freezer again, nor would she open the stainless steel doors and sneak a peek inside. Not even if the entire U.S. Winter Olympics team cheered her on, not even if Michelle Kwan *and* Sasha Cohen offered their support.

And, dammit, if she couldn't determine which was the freezer door and which was the refrigerator door, that meant no fresh salad.

She ventured a fleeting look into a non-refrigerated room. Even though it didn't have a door, it was, technically, Door Number Three. It was also dry storage, with floor-to-ceiling shelves.

Entering, Ellie scrutinized the shelves. For the most part, they held paper goods and condiments, including bottles filled with white, malt, and cider vinegar, and cute plastic bears filled with honey. There were tubs of creamy and chunky peanut butter, unopened jars of jellies, jams, and pickles, sacks of potatoes and onions, and—her mouth watered—cookies.

One shelf boasted boxes of instant soup and uncooked pasta. Plus, cans of spaghetti sauce, tomato paste, baked beans (*with molasses, oh yum*), and tuna fish—real tuna, not cat tuna.

Tuna fish, fresh or canned, was "legal" on every Weight-Winners-recommended menu, from the beginners' handbook to the lifetime members' maintenance guide, so she'd make a tuna salad, rather than a lettuce and tomato salad. She preferred mayonnaise with her tuna, but could live with mustard. All she had to do was mince an onion, add a few drops of cider vinegar, find a can opener, and—

She heard footsteps.

# Thirty-Two

Two people entered the kitchen. One wore shoes, or boots, that tap-tapped across the kitchen floor. One shuffled in something that sounded like bedroom slippers. Even though she couldn't see the prowlers, Ellie's sensitive nostrils detected three smells: soap, probably Ivory, and shampoo, definitely Herbal Essence, and wet dog, no definitive breed.

If she guesstimated the distance correctly, they had just halted somewhere in between the freezer and refrigerator doors.

"All I want is a couple of peanut butter and honey sandwiches," said a young voice.

*Jonina?*

"The kitchen's closed, Lelia, and you know the rules," said an older voice.

*Ah, Lelia Hamilton. With her mother, the ranch's cook . . . Rosa.*

"That dumb rule is your rule, Mama," the young voice said. "Which means you can break it. I didn't have any dinner and I'm hungry."

"That rule is Mr. Duke's rule. He don't allow no midnight snacks."

*Midnight? It couldn't be midnight. Of course it wasn't midnight. Midnight snack was just an expression. Like afternoon delight.*

"If Mr. Cheapskate doesn't like it, he can find someone else to clean his toilets." One pair of footsteps tap-tapped closer to the dry storage room, then stopped. "And if Kit Halliday said she was hungry, you'd whip up a steak dinner so fast it would make your head spin."

No response. Then the shuffle of slippers. Then, "Why weren't you here for dinner, Lelia?"

"I was otherwise occupied."

"Doing what?"

"That, Mama, is none of your business." A long pause. Then, "If you must know, I was out riding. I saddled up Merrylegs. She needed some exercise."

Ellie swallowed a sigh of relief. If Lelia rode Merrylegs, that meant Garrett had walked to the ravine. Or, most likely, the assignation had been for another, different evening.

Relief immediately became dismay, along with a full measuring cup of guilt and a tablespoon of consternation. Thanks to her, Peter was spending his whole vacation chasing wild geese. First the dinner party that wasn't, now Angel's Ravine. And just for grins, where did the expression "wild goose chase" come from? Shakespeare had used it in *Romeo and Juliet*, but long before that—

"Where did you go?" Rosa asked, after another pause.

Her voice sounded frightened, and Ellie wondered why.

"Here and there," Lelia replied. "Riding helps clear my head, and I needed to think. I ran into Marion and we had a nice chat. Don't worry, Mama," she added, her voice wry. "We didn't mess around."

*Was that why Rosa had sounded frightened? Was Lelia . . . promiscuous? Holy cow! Could Lelia Hamilton be Garrett's tryst partner?*

"I never said you messed around with Marion, Lelia.

239

Never thought it, neither. I saw him go into Beth's cottage with Jonina, but I told him I wouldn't tattle. He didn't stay there long and he's a nice boy."

"Yes, he is. Except he has a drinking problem, not that I blame him."

"Your father had the same problem and I blamed him good and plenty."

"Which is probably why he killed himself."

A sharp intake of breath that, fortunately, hid Ellie's gasp.

"I'm sorry, Mama, I didn't mean that."

"Yes, you did. Make yourself some sandwiches, Lelia, but be quick about it."

*In another moment she'll be inside the dry storage room,* thought Ellie. *And there's no place to hide. So I'd better say hello.*

"Hello," she said, stepping into the kitchen. She gestured toward the storage room. "I'm so very sorry. I should have made my presence known before now, but . . . well, to tell the God's honest truth, I didn't want to get caught raiding the pantry. You see, I missed supper too."

"You're the diet club lady," Lelia said with a musical laugh.

"You're trespassing," Rosa said at the same time.

"For goodness sake, Mama, the kitchen is part of the ranch," Lelia said. "She might be breaking Duke's stupid rule, but she's not trespassing."

Ellie scrutinized the two ranch employees. Rosa was either just over, or under, forty. Her full-length chenille bathrobe tried, unsuccessfully, to hide her plump curves, while mules effectively hid her toes. If one was unkind, or untactful, one might call her "dumpy" or even "doughy." Her reddish cheeks looked towel-chafed and her dark hair, combed straight back from her forehead, had merged into one tightly woven, shiny-wet braid that smelled of Herbal Essence shampoo.

Lelia was wet, too, but rain-wet rather than bath-wet. She wore cowboy boots, blue jeans, and a denim jacket, not unlike the jacket Ellie wore, except Lelia's had a fake fur collar that smelled like wet dog. Her cappuccino-brown hair, French-braided in two wrist-thick plaits, dripped rainwater from their ends as they flirted with her breasts.

Taking a few steps toward the beautiful young woman, Ellie thrust out her hand. "I'm Ellie Bernstein, but here on the ranch everybody calls me Norrie. I've been wanting to meet . . ." With an effort, she kept her arm and hand steady, her legs from pedaling backwards. "You," she finished.

*The Virgin Mary,* she thought. *Lelia's the Virgin Mary in Garrett's Annunciation painting. And now I know the name of the actress I couldn't remember. Jennifer Jones.*

Unlike the Black Beauty revelation, Ellie didn't feel any sense of relief, just bewilderment.

Lelia was Garrett's Mary, there was no doubt in her mind, but in person, face-to-face, she saw differences. For one thing, Lelia's eyes were brown, not blue. Her eyebrows were more winged and her chin had a slight indentation, as if God had begun to mold a cleft but changed his mind in midstream.

Garrett could have painted Lelia from memory, Ellie mused. Which would account for any inconsistencies. But why would he do that? Why not simply *invite* her to pose?

To camouflage her confusion, she said, "I've been dying to ask you if you carved the angel in my bed's headboard. It's exquisite. And Peter . . . Pete remembers your little girl. Her name is Angel, right?"

Lelia opened her mouth, closed it. Her bottom lip quivered. Abruptly, she turned away from Ellie. For a moment she just stood there, shaking from head to toe. Then, boots tap-tapping, she fled.

"She don't like to talk about Angel," Rosa said, seemingly unaffected by her daughter's hasty retreat. "Everybody knows that." Her last three words sounded accusatory.

"I . . . I don't understand," Ellie stammered.

"She ain't never gotten over it. Like the cancer, if you get my drift. You can stop it with them treatments where your hair falls out, but the cancer don't go away for good, and then it starts growing all over again. Sometimes," she added, "worse."

"Are you saying that Lelia's daughter . . . your granddaughter . . . is dead?"

"Of course she's dead," Rosa snapped. "What do you think I've been talking about? She died three years ago, and, if you ask me, it's time for Lelia to put it behind her."

Ellie shook her head. "I don't think you can ever put something like that behind you."

"Not that she listens to me," Rosa said, ignoring Ellie. "Just like her father, two peas in a pod. His folks came over on the Mayflower, or some such boat, and he had so many numbers after his name he coulda been a zip code. But when he knocked me up, he married me, which is more than I can say for . . ." Clamping her mouth shut, she tightened the belt on her robe. "I suppose you want me to make you something to eat."

She glared at Ellie, then shifted her gaze to a knife rack, as if to suggest that, should Ellie say yes, her days were numbered.

"That's not necessary," Ellie said. "I'm perfectly capable of making my own—"

"What do you want?"

"To eat? I was thinking a green salad might be nice, but—"

"I got salad, and it's already made. It's for the lady that writes dirty books. Miss La-di-da, just like you. Always giving orders, always on her high horse, always—"

"I'm not giving you an order, Rosa, and the last time I sat on a high horse I fell off."

"That's what I heard," she said with a nasty snicker. Flinging open a stainless steel door, she stepped into the refrigerated chamber.

*Door number two,* thought Ellie. *Good thing I didn't try to guess. I would have picked door number one.*

Within moments Rosa was back, a plump apple tucked beneath her chin, a salad bowl balanced precariously on her right palm, a clump of floppy, lifeless carrots in her other hand.

Ellie stared at the carrots. If they had been stamped with an expiration date, it would have predated the turn of the century. The *twentieth* century.

She rescued the salad bowl, which had no wrap on top, and, at first, thought she was gazing down at croutons. Then she realized that the "croutons" she saw were brown curlicues of sick lettuce. Make that *dying* lettuce. Had there been any croutons, they would have stood-in for gravestones, and R.I.P. would have been etched onto their crusty surfaces. A cut-up tomato smelled pungently overripe, and a stream of poppy seed dressing looked like it was full of drowned ants.

Oh, God, she was too tired to deal with this. Let Martina Brustein dicker over smelly tomatoes and formerly succulent, now defunct, inorganic leaves.

"You can save this for the writer." Ellie thrust the bowl at Rosa. "I'm sure *she'll* appreciate your thoughtfulness, cutting up the salad ahead of time then leaving the bowl uncovered. I'll take that apple, please. And the carrots," Ellie said, as a thought occurred. "And I do apologize for disturbing your rest, or whatever the heck it was I disturbed. Oh, before I forget, tomorrow morning I plan to fill my breakfast plate from the buffet, so don't squander an egg, dry toast, and bran cereal on me."

Rosa's towel-chafed cheeks turned as red as twin stoplights. "Don't you be giving me orders!"

"That's not an order. It's a request. No. A fact. Because I'm sure Mr. Duke . . . what did Lelia call him? Oh, yes, Mr. Cheapskate. I'm sure he wouldn't appreciate the wasted egg and toast, just like he wouldn't appreciate the rotting lettuce in that bowl. Not that I'd ever tell him, if you get *my* drift."

"Yes, ma'am." Rosa tossed Ellie the apple. "I get your drift."

"Good." Thrusting the fruit inside her jacket pocket, Ellie limped toward the exit. "Goodnight."

Head high, she entered the dining room, then sped as fast as her injured ankle allowed, until she stood, panting like a dog, outside the building. If this morning she had thought that *looks* could kill, tonight she had the distinct feeling *cooks* could kill. Funny. She could count on one hand the number of enemies she'd made over the years—if she didn't count the killers she'd exposed—while here, in less than two days, at a "practically deserted" dude ranch, she could count on one hand the number of enemies she'd made. Duke. Kit. Rosa. Buttermilk?

What about Lelia? Leaving the girl a hefty tip for cleaning the cottage was a given, but tomorrow Ellie would seek her out and apologize. For what? For opening mouth, inserting rubber boot. In any case, she was curious. Rosa had said that Angel died three years ago, and Ellie's gut feeling told her the child's death had something to do with Garrett's studio fire. She didn't know why, exactly, but Melody had said the fire occurred three years ago and gut feelings were . . . well, gut feelings.

Meanwhile, her *empty* gut was sending an S.O.S. to her brain. Exhausted and so hungry she could eat a horse, a reluctance to return to the cottage overruled her more crucial needs. Peter wouldn't be there, and despite Jackie Robinson's presence, the cottage would feel as hollow as her belly. She hurt all over, from head to toe, and her self-confidence had been badly bruised by a cook who loathed her for no good reason, a riding instructor who wore size three jeans, and a fat white horse. She wanted Peter to comfort her, to caress any body parts that didn't ache, to tell her he loved her. She should have asked him to call when he arrived at the ravine—after all, he had a cell phone—but if she knew Peter, and she did, he believed her fast asleep. It would never cross his mind that she had disobeyed his "John Wayne-ish" order, or that she hadn't promised him one damn thing. Even if Chicken Little screamed "The sky is falling, the sky is falling," Peter wouldn't wake her. Later he'd say, "I'm sorry, sweetheart, but I felt your rest was more important than a falling sky."

She looked down at the carrots she clutched. While they weren't fit for human consumption, they'd be fit for horse consumption.

And she owed Buttermilk an apology.

Did one apologize to a horse? One did to a cat. How many times had she said, "I'm sorry" to Jackie Robinson? For feeding him late. For leaving his litter box full and his water bowl empty. For giving him a tasteless rubber mouse when she knew he preferred catnip.

Apology aside, Peter loved horses, loved riding, loved riding horses. And while she truly doubted she'd ever climb on top of a horse again, she hated dreading what he loved.

One phobia was enough. She'd never lose her irrational fear of heights, a fact she'd have to live with, but tonight she could start working on her fear of horses.

Besides, the horses would be inside their stalls and stalls had doors. Right?

Of course, right.

*Toot your horn like a good little Marxist.*

"Toot, toot," she whispered as she bravely limped toward the barn.

# Thirty-Three

Ellie didn't expect the barn to be locked, and it wasn't.

Unlike the kitchen, she'd never been inside a stable before. She was, however, familiar with how a stable *should* look. Tony adored John Wayne—big surprise!—so she had watched quite a few John Wayne movies in her time. Seated next to Tony on the family room couch, stuffing her face with potato chips and avocado dip, low-fat pretzels, and Pepperidge Farm Chocolate Chunk cookies, she had waited impatiently for *The Searchers* or *She Wore a Yellow Ribbon* or *True Grit* to end. As soon as John Wayne rode off into the sunset, or wherever the heck he opted to ride off into, Tony would avidly paw at her breasts. For reasons she couldn't fathom then, but thought she understood now, the butt-kicking actor turned Tony on. In fact, John Wayne turned Tony into Don Juan. Thus, John Wayne became a significant if transitory hero in Ellie's eyes, too. Because, until she met Peter, she had always equated sex with love.

Softly lit by night-lights, the Lonesome Pines stable smelled like horses and dry Cheerios and polished-leather shoes. She also detected the odor of alcohol. Not rubbing alcohol or liniment, which she'd expect, but alcohol-alcohol. As in liquor. The scent seemed to originate above her head. The loft?

"Hello? Is anybody up there?"

No response. And she didn't hear any breathing or shuffling of body parts. She did, however, hear various noises from the horses' boxy stalls. Snuffles that sounded nosy, and hoof stomps that, she told herself, sounded curious rather than angry.

The stalls sported half-doors, not unlike the bottom half of a Dutch door. Nailed to the doors were brass name plaques.

As she approached Buttermilk's stall, the white horse didn't seem quite as large as she'd looked this morning. A good omen?

Next to Buttermilk's stall was Satan's stall.

"Be back in a minute," Ellie told Buttermilk. Then she limped toward Satan's stall until she was close enough to polish his name plaque with her jacket's cuff. All she wanted to do was take a quick peek at the horse that everybody *else* seemed to fear.

The stallion walked out of the shadows, toward Ellie. What a beauty, she thought. Black from head to hoof, his coat looked as silky as the silk on an ear of Indian corn. Long, thick mane and tail and—

"Black Beauty has a star," she blurted. "On his forehead."

She pictured the illustration that adorned Anna Sewell's frontispiece.

Yes. Definitely. A white star.

Scrutinizing Satan, she said, "I wonder if *you're* the horse in Garrett's painting."

She didn't realize she was thinking out loud until the stallion tossed his head.

"Is that a yes?" Enthralled, Ellie limped closer, until she felt her belly press against the stall's door. As she did, she saw that Satan's gaze was locked on her hand.

*The carrots!*

"Would you like a carrot?"

This time the black stallion whinnied—a word Ellie had only seen in books. But, to tell the God's honest truth, "whinny" sounded just like it . . . well, sounded. A low, gentle, nasal neigh.

She placed one of the carrots on her palm, stiffened her fingers, and extended her hand.

It never occurred to her, until afterwards, that Satan could have bitten her hand off. For one thing, she wasn't afraid of his teeth. She feared his hooves. Or, to be more precise, what his hooves could do. Kick her. Run away with her. Neither of which would happen because his feet were safely ensconced inside the stall and she didn't plan to climb on top of him. Ever. She might be foolish but she wasn't stupid.

Oh, God, what was he doing now? He had stretched his head and neck over the half-door in order to nuzzle her jacket. Or, to be more precise, her jacket pocket. Holy cow, he wanted her apple!

"Oh, no you don't," she said, taking a step backward. "You can't imagine what I went through to get that apple. All *you* have to do is stand here and look fierce. I had to stand up for myself against a pissed-off cook who guards a kitchen filled with sharp cutlery, a cook who looked as if she wanted to bop me over the head with a skillet. A *cast-iron* skillet."

The horse's ears flattened against his head.

"Okay, okay, I'll *share* my apple with you. I'll cut it in half. You can even have the biggest half, the half with the core and seeds."

If there was a knife lying around, thought Ellie, it would probably be with the saddles and bridles. She placed the clump of corroding carrots on the floor, near Buttermilk's stall. Then, following her nose, she entered a room that smelled like the inside of a mint condition car. Almost immediately, she saw a large green wheelbarrow. Next to the wheelbarrow was a long wooden table topped with a plethora of horse products and horse medicines. Plus, a hypodermic needle as big as her ex-husband's penis, an unraveling rope, and . . . two knives.

Good. Not so good. While the knives weren't as filthy as knives that gutted fish or—she shuddered—rabbits, they didn't look all that clean, either.

"Oh, to hell with it." Limping back to Satan's stall, she palmed the apple.

Satan chomped it down like a *Survivor* contestant who'd just won a food challenge.

"Now that you've eaten *my* dinner," Ellie said, "I'll feed the rest of the carrots to your fellow inmates. It's getting late and—oh, please, don't flatten your ears again. This time it won't work."

The stallion stomped one hoof.

"Stop that, you devil! I know for a fact they feed you here, and your hay smells fresh, so I don't understand why you're so bad-tempered. I've been told your sister Lucy is temperamental, but I've met her, and although she's a wee bit unruly, she's not mean-spirited. Therefore, *you* must be the black sheep of the family."

Another hoof-stomp.

"Oh, so you don't care for the designation 'sheep,' huh? Put your gums back down over your teeth; you look like Eddie Murphy in *Shrek*. I'm warning you, Satan. If you insist on behaving like a brat, I'll scratch out Satan on your nameplate and change it to Patty McCormack."

She realized he couldn't understand one word she said, except maybe "Satan," but he tossed his beautiful head and let loose with a whinny that sounded like a laugh.

"Tell you what," Ellie continued. "When my son Mick was out of sorts, I'd sing to him. Suppose I sing to you? Is that a yes? Okay, what would you like to hear? I know. A horse is a horse, of course, of course . . ." She finished the silly ditty, repeated it, then tried to think of another song with a horse in it. The only thing that came to mind was, "Ride a cock horse to Banbury Cross, to see a fine lady upon a white horse. With rings on her fingers and bells on her toes, she shall have music wherever she goes."

Satan's ears flicked forward. If he had been a cat, thought Ellie, he'd have purred.

*She had found his ignition key!*

"What's a cock horse?" asked a young voice.

Startled, Ellie would have whirled about, had her injured foot allowed it. Instead, she carefully navigated an about-face. And saw Jonina.

"Hi, kiddo."

"Please don't call me kiddo, Norrie. That's what my mom calls me, and I hate it."

"Okay, Jonina, but I hope you don't mind my asking what you're doing here. It's very late."

The girl darted a glance toward the loft. "When I can't sleep," she said, "I visit the stable. Pet the horses." She ran her hand across her forehead, pushing back her bangs. "What's a cock horse?"

"A horse that prances and preens like a rooster. And the lady who rode the white horse to Banbury Cross, the lady with all the fancy jewelry, was Queen Elizabeth the First."

"Henry the Eighth's daughter." Jonina smiled. "I saw it on PBS."

"I did, too. Glenda Jackson." Ellie felt Satan's nose nudge her back.

251

"He likes you," Jonina said, "and, as a rule, he doesn't like *anyone*. Not even Kit."

"Oh, I bribed him with food. A carrot and an apple."

"Everybody tries to bribe him with food, Norrie. I even tried sugar cubes. No go."

"Well, that shows good horse sense," Ellie said with a grin. "Sugar isn't good for you." She felt Satan nudge her back again. "Along with the food bribes, I sang to him. He seemed to like that, but to be perfectly honest, he's the only one who does. I can't carry a tune in a bucket. Even your uncle needs earplugs when—"

"Are you going to marry Uncle Pete?"

"I don't know, sweetie. Probably. Some day." Moving away from Satan's stall, Ellie scooped up the carrots. "These are for Buttermilk," she said, hoping to change the subject.

"Lelia calls you the diet club lady," Jonina said, changing the subject on her own, "and Mom says you work for Weight Winners. So I was wondering if you could give me the diet, Norrie. Write it down for me, you know, the foods I'm supposed to eat and the foods I'm not supposed to eat?"

"I'd be glad to, Jonina. But first you have to understand that you'll lose weight slowly and it won't be easy." Extending her hand, Ellie offered Buttermilk one of the carrots.

As the whiskery white muzzle tickled Ellie's palm, she made a mental note to bring more carrots on her next visit—enough for all the horses—and she almost fell over backwards at the thought that she not only planned a second visit, but looked forward to it.

"Mom says I have big bones." Edging up to Ellie, Jonina scratched Buttermilk underneath her throat. "But Daddy says if I set my mind to something I can do it, and I *want* to lose ten or fifteen pounds, no matter how long it takes. I don't want to be skeleton-skinny, like all those supposedly perfect movie stars and TV celebs. I think Queen Latifah is the most beautiful actress in the whole world, don't you? Her eyes and, especially, her smile. She's not fat but she's not skinny." With a sigh, Jonina finger-combed her bangs away from her forehead. "Skinny isn't pretty, even if the kids at my school think it is." She heaved another, deeper sigh. "I'd just like to wear pretty clothes."

Ellie gave Buttermilk the last two carrots. "Why don't you come to my cottage tomorrow, Jonina? We can go over the Weight Winners program together."

"Thanks. I will, if Mom lets me." A look of panic transformed her face. "Oh, God, Mom. I'd better go back now. Mom sort of grounded me."

"Where is she?" Ellie led the way out of the barn. "Your mom, I mean."

"I'm not sure. Earlier, she didn't feel well. Then she said she craved anchovies. So she ordered a couple of large pizzas, one with anchovies, one with mushrooms and sausage. They deliver here, at the ranch. Is pizza allowed on Weight Winners?"

Ellie tried not to laugh at the wistfulness that tinted Jonina's last six words. "Yes, honey, as long as you carefully blot the grease on paper towels. We'll talk about that when we go over the food program. I have a friend, Hannah Taylor. She's not 'skeleton-skinny,' but she reached her goal weight and moved from Colorado Springs to Denver. She's a group leader for Weight Winners, and she has a special class for teens, and she'll take you under her wing. She also manages a boutique with the most adorable clothes . . ." Ellie paused, then said, "Do you think there's any left-

253

over pizza inside your cottage?" and almost laughed at the wistfulness she heard in *her* voice.

"Oh, I'm sure there is," Jonina said. "Unless Kit ate it."

"Kit Halliday?"

Jonina nodded. "Kit came to our cottage . . . around eight, I guess. Her hair was so wet she looked like a drowned rat, but her clothes were dry, so she probably came straight from her cottage. Kit and Mom whispered and giggled. Mom kept telling Kit to hush or she'd wake me and my brothers. Which would set the two of them off again. You could almost swear they were at a slumber party . . . or a sleepover."

Wrinkling her nose, Jonina continued to walk at a fast clip. "It really grossed me out. Mom looks young and all, but she's almost twice Kit's age. Then Mom said she had a craving for a banana split with extra whipped cream, nuts, and cherries. Kit said she was hungry too, so they decided to raid the kitchen."

*There's a lot of that going around,* Ellie thought, as Jonina came to an abrupt halt, then furtively opened her cottage door and slithered inside.

In less than no time she was back.

As she handed Ellie the pizza box, she said, "Mom and Kit aren't here, but I'd better not push my luck. And . . ." She pushed back her bangs with her knuckles as she studied her sneakers, then the moon. "I didn't go to the barn to pet the horses, Norrie. That was a lie. I thought . . . hoped Dom . . . Marion would be there."

"Is Dom the reason why you're grounded?"

"No. Yes. It's a long story. Boring." She smiled. "Uncle Pete would say 'humdrum.' If I told you, I'd probably put you to sleep. See you tomorrow."

Ellie hefted the pizza box, which felt half full or half

empty, depending, she supposed, on one's point of view. "Thanks, kiddo," she said. Then, "Oh, I'm sorry."

"That's okay. I don't mind 'kiddo' when you say it." Jonina smiled again and shut the door.

By the time Ellie had finished scarfing down the microwave-heated, mushroom and sausage pizza leftovers, she didn't need Jonina's "long story" to put her to sleep.

Her problem was staying awake.

Belly full to bursting, foot throbbing mercilessly, she stared at her bottle of pain pills. Finally, she swallowed one pill, cutting the doctor's prescribed dosage in half.

She wanted the pain to go away, but she didn't want to fall asleep. It was taking Peter well over the two hours max he'd calculated. *Why?* Was Angel's Ravine a terra firma version of the Bermuda Triangle? Should she organize a search party for Peter, as well as Garrett?

Good idea, but first she'd stretch out on the bed and shut her eyes . . .

For five, maybe ten minutes . . .

She had no idea what time it was when she heard Peter in the shower. Usually he sang in the shower, but not tonight.

Feeling headachy, she managed to sit up, focus on the window, note that it was still dark outside, then find the floor with her good foot then swollen foot.

Peter's muddy sneakers were just inside the front door.

She darted frantic glances around the living room, hoping and praying she'd see a sound asleep Garrett, a bandaged Garrett, even a blood-soaked Garrett, but all she saw was John Wayne, positioned against his black velvet background, and a cuckoo clock whose accusatory hands practically shouted two-fifteen.

Still wearing her Denver Broncos jersey, she eased the

shower curtain aside and, with her good foot, stepped into the bathtub.

Peter gently grasped her shoulders. "I found your friend Garrett at the ravine," he said as water soaked her hair. "He was propped against a tree."

She shook the drops from her head like an Irish Setter. "Was he hurt?"

"No." Peter cradled her chin with his hands.

"Dead?"

"Yes."

"Murdered?"

"Yes."

"I knew it."

"Another gut feeling?" Peter asked softly.

"Yes and no." Although the bathroom was hot and steamy, Ellie shivered. She had a hunch she'd never experience warmth again, never feel safe again.

"It suddenly occurred to me that 'wild goose chase' was coined before firearms," she said, "when killing a wild goose would be difficult and *chasing* a wild goose would be futile. But nowadays you don't have to chase a wild goose, Peter. You hardly have to track it. All you have to do is shoot it."

"Norrie . . ."

"Garrett was shot, right?"

"No, sweetheart. Stabbed."

# Thirty-Four

"Uncle Pete! Uncle Pete!"

*Jonina! On the other side of the cottage door.* Somehow, Ellie managed to raise her lashes, which felt as though they'd been pasted to the tops of her cheeks by a kindergarten class.

Despite her puffy eyelids, she saw Peter reach for a pair of jeans.

She shifted her gaze to the bedroom window. Streaks of pink and lavender stained a faded denim sky. Which meant that, after crying her eyes out in Peter's arms, she'd slept for approximately three hours.

"Last night I invited Jonina to visit," she mumbled, "but I didn't mean the crack of dawn."

"Uncle Pete! Come quickly!"

"I'll be right there," Peter yelled. "Dammit," he said to Ellie, "where the hell are my shoes?"

"By the front door where you always leave them," she replied. "What's going on?"

"Don't know. Be right back." Barefoot, shirtless, he raced toward the living room.

Right back wasn't an exaggeration. Before she could do more than sit up, he reentered the bedroom. "Socks," he said.

"Top drawer." She pointed toward the bureau.

"Boots."

"In the closet, next to mine."

"Shirt."

"Your shirts are in the same drawer as your socks." She watched him cross to the bureau. "Peter, what the hell is going on?"

"Beth," he said. Carrying his boots, socks, and T-shirt, he sped toward the living room, and once again she heard the front door slam.

Still somewhat groggy, she maneuvered her butt to the edge of the mattress, swung her legs over the side, and looked down at her foot.

After her impulsive shower, Peter had swathed her ankle with dry bandages. The dressing didn't feel too tight, but her foot looked even more bloated than yesterday. And it throbbed from the inside out, as if it were a flesh-covered robotic foot that kept short-circuiting.

In fact, her whole body ached.

Naked, she limped to the bathroom, where a white terrycloth robe with an embroidered Lonesome Pines pocket-logo hung from a wall hook. She had ignored the garment, priced at ninety-nine ninety-five, but now she tugged it from its wooden hanger and put it on. The cottage cabinets didn't stock any knives or scissors, and her manicure scissors wouldn't cut it, but later, even if it meant she'd have to use her teeth, she'd sever the seam on the leg of her jeans. She found her knee socks from yesterday, then the black rubber boots. Knotting the sash on her shapeless, one-size-fits-all robe, she hobbled outside.

Last Thursday night, at the Dew Drop Inn, she had compared herself to Scarlett O'Hara. Now, for the second time, she felt as if she'd been cast in a *Gone with the Wind* scene; the one where Bonnie Butler, Rhett and Scarlett's daughter, urges her pony over a jump while

Scarlett says, "Stop her, Rhett."

Beth rode a black horse. Even from a distance, Ellie could see that the horse had no saddle. She could also see that Beth was speeding toward a pasture fence.

As if she'd read Ellie's mind, Jonina said, "Stop her, Uncle Pete!"

"I'm too far away, honey," he replied, shading his eyes with a shaky hand.

"Your mom's an excellent rider." Ellie tried to soothe Jonina, clothed in her Pooh jeans and a plaid flannel shirt, buttoned wrongly.

"The ground's too mushy from last night's rain," Jonina wailed, "and Lucy hasn't been trained to take jumps."

Peter didn't respond, but Ellie saw all the color drain from his face.

"Mom had the TV on for Ryan and Stevie," Jonina continued. "A special bulletin broke in and some reporter said that Garrett Halliday was dead. Mom ran to the barn. I ran after her. She didn't even take the time to saddle up Lucy. Dom was there. He tried to stop her. So did I. But she wouldn't listen."

With horrific clarity, Ellie saw Lucy approach the pasture fence. Beth clutched the reins in one hand. Bent at the waist like a jockey, she urged the horse on.

"Slow down!" Peter shouted.

"Mommy, no!" Jonina shouted at the same time.

Lucy skidded to a halt. If the dirt hadn't been sopping wet, she would have raised dust whorls.

Beth sailed over the mare's head and landed, in a heap, on the other side of the fence.

*Thank God she didn't land* on *the fence,* Ellie thought, her wobbly mind trying to grasp one piece of irrefutable logic. *The rain-soaked, spongy ground may have saved her life.*

Peter began to sprint forward when a voice shouted, "Pete, wait up!"

Marion rode a white horse with brown patches. In his hands he held the reins of the horse Peter had ridden yesterday. Lashed to the horses' saddles were rolled-up blankets, canteens, and a first-aid kit.

"Thanks," Peter said. In one fluid motion he was on top of the brown horse. Ignoring stirrups, he galloped toward his sister.

Marion followed.

Ellie grabbed Jonina by the hand and dragged her inside the cottage.

"Sit!" Ellie ordered.

The stunned girl sank onto the couch.

Jackie Robinson jumped up into Jonina's lap while Ellie hobbled to the phone and dialed 9-1-1.

Beth was badly hurt, but alive.

The paramedics had arrived, then driven her to the nearest hospital.

Jonina was dispatched to find Ellie a pair of scissors.

Changing from his tee into a clean button-down-collar shirt, Peter said he'd drive to the hospital and phone Ellie as soon as he knew more details.

No mention was made of Beth's pregnancy.

Neither Peter nor Ellie discussed the reason for Beth's recklessness.

Fifteen or twenty minutes ago, summoned by the noise of the ambulance, Lelia had offered to round up Ryan and Stevie. "They can stay with me," she said. "I've got dozens of old movies. And if the boys get bored watching movies, I'll teach them how to vacuum floors and clean windows. Beth will appreciate that."

Lelia hadn't seemed all that upset over Garrett's death, but maybe she hadn't been told about it. Peter had said that another trail led to the ravine from the Lonesome Pines entrance. So although Angel's Ravine was now a crime scene, with cops sniffing around and collecting evidence and tying yellow crime-scene tape to the old oak tree, there was no urgent need to disturb the ranch's occupants. Until such time as they'd all be microscopically grilled, Ellie mused.

*And yes, Peter, I know. Cops grill cheese sandwiches, not suspects.*

She had barely finished the thought when Peter made what he called "an executive decision."

While he was at the hospital, waiting for word on Beth, Jonina would "stick like glue" to Ellie.

"But I have to go to Heather," Ellie objected, very close to fresh tears.

"Later, when I get back, we'll go together," Peter said. "Right now I have to call Jonah."

"And I have to brush my teeth," she said, thinking it didn't pay to argue with Peter, not as long as the convertible's ignition key was in his possession.

When she emerged from the bathroom, into the living room, he was hanging up the phone.

"Jonah's leaving right away. To his credit, he didn't waste time on idle chit-chat, just said he'd be here in an hour and a half."

She looked at the phone, then raised her gaze to Peter's face. "Even if you break every speed limit and there's no traffic, it takes roughly four hours to drive from Denver to Snowmass."

"Not if you fly. Aspen has an airport and Jonah owns his own Cessna. Just a run of the mill perk for a . . . successful defense attorney."

She caught his brief hesitation before "successful."

"You left out 'sleazy,' " she said.

"Jonah isn't really sleazy, Norrie. He has his job to do and I have mine."

"And never the twain shall meet. Does *your* job include finding Garrett's killer?"

"Hush." Peter stood by the open door. "Here comes Jonina . . . with a pair of wicked looking scissors. We'll talk later."

*We'll visit Heather later. We'll talk about Garrett's murder investigation later. Dammit,* Ellie thought, *later is too late.*

She glanced toward the phone. No. Too impersonal. She hadn't spoken to Heather in five years. She needed to *touch* her. And she had no desire to talk to Gideon, Adrianna, or Kit, even though she knew that, eventually, she'd have to express her condolences to all of them.

Ellie felt a sob inch its way up her throat. At the same time, a dirge kept running through her head—cop-speak from the bazillion police dramas she'd watched on TV.

*Sorry for your loss ma'am, sorry for your loss sir . . .*

# Thirty-Five

With a few fiendish snips of Jonina's "wicked scissors," Ellie severed the seam on her brand new jeans.

*Like the casing on a sausage,* she thought.

The provocative slit made her feel like an eighteenth century demimondaine. Or she would have felt that way, had her legs been longer, her waist smaller, her breasts bigger.

Maybe it was time to bring back the corset. And bustle.

Her black rubber boots would have looked okay with jeans, certainly better than they'd looked with a white dress and a Denver Broncos nightshirt, but Ellie had another option. Despite her slenderness, Beth's feet were larger than Ellie's and, along with her mom's scissors, Jonina had scrounged up a pair of "designer flip-flops."

Looking down at her sneakers, Jonina said, "I have small feet. My dad is short and my mom is tall. I used to pray my feet would grow big, like my mom's, so I'd be tall."

"That's puppies," Ellie said with a smile, the first time she'd smiled since last night's visit to the barn. "And it's not always true. My ex mother-in-law, Florence, decided she'd adopt a puppy from the pound. She wanted a medium size dog, no bigger than a cocker spaniel, a short-haired dog so it wouldn't shed, and a female dog so it wouldn't 'lift its leg against the furniture.' Florence came home with a brindle-colored pup that she named Brindle. We all grinned and nudged each other. We were positive Florence had been taken to the cleaners . . ." Ellie paused. "Do you know what that means?"

"Taken to the cleaners? Sure. Scammed."

"Right. Brindle was around eight weeks old, female, and shorthaired, but she could hardly walk without tripping over her own feet. She had the biggest paws I've ever seen."

"And when she grew up she looked like Marmaduke," Jonina said with an impish grin.

Ellie was glad to see the grin. "Nope. Florence couldn't stop Brindle from piddling when people came to call. The poor dog would get all excited and dribble. But she never shed a single hair, and when she grew up she was a medium size dog."

"With big paws?"

"Yup. The biggest paws I've ever seen. In fact, had Brindle possessed rabbit ears and soft gray fur, she could have doubled for Thumper in a *Bambi* sequel."

Jonina actually giggled.

Encouraged, Ellie said, "Let's grab us some breakfast, pardner," and opened the door.

The sun shone brightly, as if to apologize for last night's stormy outburst.

Arm in arm, Ellie and Jonina walked/limped toward the dining hall.

All Ellie really wanted was a cup of strong black coffee. However, she forced herself to swallow several bites of scrambled eggs and two flaky biscuits. She had to give Rosa credit. The plump cook's made-from-scratch biscuits were to die for, especially when one added a few squirts of honey from the cute plastic bear that squatted above Ellie's napkin-shrouded silverware.

Hunched over an empty bowl that smelled like brown sugar and oatmeal, Duke's eyebrows were drawn together above the bridge of his nose. His scowling mouth might have looked fearsome, had his beard not been thoroughly infiltrated by toast crumbs and orange marmalade.

Ellie had no desire to ask him what was wrong but Jonina was less reticent.

"I had to call off the barbeque," he replied. "First time in eight years."

"Well, I can certainly understand why," Ellie said. "And I'm sure everybody else will, too. You can't be expected to throw a party when a man was murdered right here on the ran—"

"Ain't got nothin' to do with no murder, leastwise not straight-out. Gid Halliday, dang his hide, plans to hold a shindig at his gallery the very same day."

"A wake?"

"I should hope so. Wouldn't make no sense if he was asleep."

"No, I meant . . . never mind. Is he really called Gid?"

"Yep. He don't like it none, neither. His brother used to call him 'El Gid.' "

"Norrie, can I have another biscuit?" Jonina asked.

"Yes. But this time use honey rather than butter."

"Damn . . . darn! I should have thought of that."

"Don't worry, kiddo. We'll start with baby steps. Then, when you go back to Denver, you'll be ready to slide right into the Weight Winners program."

As Jonina pushed herself away from the table and headed toward the buffet, Ellie turned to Duke. "More letters are missing from your sign," she said.

"*All* the dang letters are gone. Cops think it's kids."

"You don't?"

265

He shook his head and toast crumbs flew in all directions. "Kids'll change letters around and leave something stupid, like 'eel nose' or 'piss on me.' Or they steal all the letters in one hit. I could swear it ain't kids, but I can't think why anybody else would take them, unless Garrett wanted them for a what'cha'macallit . . . moan-something. Gluing stuff to a picture."

From the corner of her eye, Ellie saw Jonina heading back to the table. "Where'd you hear about Gideon's shindig, Duke? Did he phone you?"

"Naw. I seen him on TV. There he was, lookin' sad as one of them basset hounds, the lyin' bastard."

"You don't think he was sincere?"

Jonina, who had almost reached the table, abruptly changed direction and walked toward Marion, who'd just entered the dining hall. Feeling free to probe a little deeper, Ellie said, "Didn't Gideon get along with his brother?"

"Kit told me more than once that her dad was grudgeful." Duke fingered a couple of toothpicks, as if choosing the best cigar. "Gid studied art in Paris, France, but it was Garrett that got famous. Gid even met Heather first, in France. They came back to Aspen together and Heather saw Garrett and that was it. In Kit's words, 'love at first sight.' Heather and Garrett moved to the Springs and right away Gid married some mouse . . . shoot, she was so mousy I can't even remember her name. Her car went off a cliff, just like Grace Kelly. I think she did it on purpose."

"Who? Grace Kelly?"

"No. Gid's wife." Duke chewed his toothpick like a beaver that'd just given up smoking. "Anyways," he continued, "early this morning Gid found a roomful of new paintings. Seems he broke down the door to a room Garrett always kept locked—Gid was thinkin' maybe there was something inside the killer wanted real bad—and there they were. Dozens of paintings, from the way Gid was talkin'. He said he'd hang three or four in his gallery, for the shindig, but after that they'd be boxed and shipped to Paris, France, and New York City."

Although Ellie still stared at Duke's beard, her vision was filled with a red flag. Hadn't Melody said that Garrett absolutely refused to display his work in worldwide galleries? And with Garrett's sudden demise, the demand for his work would increase radically while the prices would go sky-high.

She heard the echo of Owen Lassiter's voice, inside the Dew Drop Inn. *I thought that only happens when the artist goes belly-up.*

So on the one hand, the death of his brother wouldn't necessarily eradicate Gideon's meal ticket, not if there were "dozens of paintings" available. On the other hand, why kill the golden goose?

Unless . . .

She pictured the crude rendering of the Annunciation painting. Unless Garrett's "gift from God" had soured. Did painters get writer's block?

A thought nagged at the back of her mind. Something to do with the stylistic differences between Garrett's early works, recent works, and the Annunciation painting. But before she could mentally fit the pieces of the puzzle together, Duke mopped his face with a napkin and the white cloth eclipsed her imaginary red flag.

"Guess I'd better trot down to the ravine and check up on them cops," he said, shoving his chair back with his butt. "Ain't gonna give 'em no free food, but they might welcome a thermos of hot coffee, and it don't hurt none to be nice to cops."

*Especially when you once killed a woman and the nice cops know that,* Ellie thought, remembering Kit's words in the clearing.

"Where were you last night when Garrett Halliday was killed?" she asked, hoping she sounded curious rather than suspicious. She'd never been able to master Peter's laidback interrogation technique. Not that Duke was a suspect. Why on earth would he kill Garrett? What did he have to gain?

However, she'd been wrong before. You could almost say dead wrong. The perp in the M*A*S*H murders had been a big surprise; had, in fact, nearly cost her the life she'd so carefully reconstructed after her divorce.

"Ain't sure what time Halliday was kilt," Duke replied, "but I spent the whole damn night writin' down the food I'd need for the barbeque. Planned to call the order in to my supplier this a.m. Now it don't matter a damn."

Duke looked like he might cry, a spectacle Ellie had no desire to witness, so she quickly said, "Didn't Beth organize your barbeques?"

"Yep." Duke looked surprised, as if he'd just been handed a writ—a summons to Alice's tea party, hosted by the dormouse and the Mad Hatter. "Her and Rosa took charge."

Ellie winced at the bad grammar, but merely said, "With Beth out of commission, I would think you'd have to cancel the party anyway."

This time Duke didn't say anything, just tipped the brim of his hat as his bowlegged tibias and fibulas creaked toward the exit.

Tim Burton should film Duke's walk, Ellie mused, and use it for a *Beetlejuice* sequel.

As soon as Duke had shut the door, Marion approached the table, a starry-eyed Jonina by his side. Ellie had the feeling he'd waited until his father left. No love lost between those two, she thought, wondering why.

Marion looked freshly showered, his hair tousled and spiked like an American Idol.

"Would you like some more coffee, Norrie?" Jonina pointed at Ellie's empty mug.

"You bet. Thanks."

While Jonina headed for the coffee urn, Marion hunkered down near Ellie's chair. "I want to apologize," he said.

"For what?"

"Yesterday I started to tell you what would make Buttermilk bolt, then got sidetracked. If you had known about her fear of leafy switches—"

"It probably wouldn't have made any difference. Kit wanted to sabotage my ride."

"Yes, I know."

"It's hard to believe I've made three enemies in such a short time."

"Three?"

"Kit, Rosa, and your father."

"Duke isn't an enemy. He's just . . . Duke."

"Do you know why Rosa seems to hate me?"

"No, but I can venture a guess. She adores Kit, always has. It's almost an obsession. If Kit said the ground was too muddy, Rosa would fall to the ground and play 'plank.' So if Kit doesn't like someone, Rosa doesn't either. Lelia could probably tell you more about that."

"If you don't mind my asking, Dom, where were you last night around five o'clock?"

"Riding. I talked to Rosa, then rode around the ranch. I was hoping to spot the kids who've been stealing our letters—letters from the sign, not the mailbox. I ran into Lelia and we rode together. It was raining, getting worse and worse, so I went back to the barn and rubbed down Scout. My horse. Well, the ranch's horse, but I ride him ninety-nine percent of the time. Then I sort of mellowed out. With . . . a book . . . a mystery . . . a Stanley Hastings mystery . . . called *Detective*. Not 'the' detective. One word."

Ellie didn't want to be rude or confrontational, but until the last part of his recitation the boy had sounded sincere. Then he'd stumbled over the book part. Why? Before she could probe further, Jonina sidled up to the table.

She handed Ellie the mug. "I want to hear what's happening with my mom as soon as Uncle Pete calls," she said, "but do you mind if I go to the barn with Dom? Kit isn't here, and won't be coming, and he could use some help with the horses."

Ellie caught Marion's wink. He didn't need any help. He just wanted to keep Jonina's mind and body occupied so she wouldn't dwell on her mom's near-fatal accident.

"I think that's a great idea." Sipping from her mug, Ellie nearly burned the roof of her mouth.

As she ineffectually fanned her mouth with her fingers, she saw Rosa smirk. Then, catching Ellie's gaze, the cook stuck out her tongue.

# Thirty-Six

Ellie had barely entered her cabin when she heard the phone ring.

Voice emotionless, definitely in cop mode, Peter said that Beth had lost the baby and undergone an emergency D & C. Other than that, she had "come off lucky."

Beth could have seriously scrambled her brains, Peter said, but she hadn't. She could have broken her back, but she hadn't. The spongy ground had not only saved her life, it had saved her bones. She'd sprained her ribs and, rather badly, one of her wrists. Her face was a mess. She'd need a neck brace for a while. The doctors were waiting for the X-ray results before they'd know if her right leg needed a cast. She was in a great deal of pain and still groggy from the anesthetic. If it was okay with Ellie, he'd wait around until Beth was at least partially coherent, then *gently* interrogate her—find out what the hell had contributed to her wild, senseless ride. Garrett Halliday's death, of course. But even before this morning, Peter had deduced that something was terribly wrong—something other than her split with Jonah and her pregnancy. After talking to Beth, he might hit the cop shop.

Almost as an afterthought, he asked how *she* was holding up?

"I'm fine, Peter, as long as I don't think too much about Garrett, but would you do me a huge favor? Drive to the

Halliday house on your way back to the ranch and personally give my condolences to Heather?"

"No, sweetheart. The Halliday family has enough to cope with. The last thing they need is some stranger knocking at their door."

"You're not a stranger. You know Kit and you've met Gideon. And Adrianna."

"If you're worried about your friend Heather, she's okay. 'As well as can be expected' was the precise terminology."

"Used by whom?"

"The police."

"When did you talk to the police?"

"I called the precinct."

"To offer your help?"

"Not really. I called to tell them about Rudolph Kessler and Serafina Lassiter. There has to be a correlation between Kessler, Lassiter, and Garrett Halliday. My guess is that the murderer decided to kill the artist, rather than steal and/or destroy any more of his paintings."

"That makes no sense, Peter. If true, why didn't the murderer kill Garrett in the first place?"

"Killers seldom make sense, Norrie, and a murder is rarely the kind of solvable crime you see on TV. We hardly ever go from A to B to C, with theme music introducing each new locale. On TV, you *know* that A and B are false leads, and that C or D is the bad guy."

"I'm not saying our killer has brains, Peter, or even good judgment. All I'm saying is that he or she has been stealing and/or slashing Garrett's old canvasses, not his new ones, so killing Garrett doesn't make sense. In fact, Garrett dead or Garrett alive makes little, if any, difference."

As she paused to catch her breath, she decided that Peter's presumptions weren't worth disputing. Why waste her breath? "When did the cops talk to Heather?" she asked, instead.

"This morning. At the morgue. She and Gideon identified Garrett's body. A formality, but it had to be done."

"Oh my God, poor Heather!" A thought occurred. "How did the cop know it was Heather?"

"Excuse me?"

"Melody said Heather always wears a heavy veil," Ellie said, "so how did the cop know it was Heather?"

"I'm sure she introduced herself."

"Right. But did the cop check her ID?"

"Why would I even think to ask him that? What are you getting at?"

"I'm not sure. A hunch that could grow into a *big* gut feeling. Can I talk to him?"

"Who? Joe? No!"

"Listen, Lieutenant," she said, glad that anger had temporarily supplanted grief. "If you don't give me *Joe's* phone number, or badge number, I'll track him down. And I'll use *your* name to cut through whatever red tape they throw at me."

She jotted down the phone number, even though Peter called her Ellie, and he cussed a lot, and his voice sounded colder than a Weight Winners frozen dinner.

Ellie asked for "Joe" but didn't catch his last name, so she decided she'd call him "Sir."

After she had identified herself as Lieutenant Miller's friend and ascertained that "Sir" had been one of the cops at the morgue, she said, "Could you please tell me what Mrs. Halliday looked like?"

"Excuse me?" he said, sounding like Peter.

She felt like a lawyer who'd just been told by the judge

that she should rephrase her question. "I need to know what Mrs. Halliday looked like, if you don't mind."

"A nun," Sir said.

This time it was Ellie's turn. "Excuse me?"

"She looked like a nun. Black dress, black stockings, black shoes."

"Was she wearing a wimple?" Ellie asked, hoping she didn't sound as sarcastic as she thought she sounded.

Sir said, "A wimple?"

"A covering over her head, around her neck and chin."

"No, ma'am. She wore a hat that covered her hair. And a veil. A long veil."

"So you never really got a good look at her."

"No, ma'am, I didn't. Will that be all, ma'am?"

"What did she sound like?"

"Ma'am?"

"Did she sound literate? Educated? Did she have an accent? Perhaps a French accent?"

"Well, ma'am, she never really spoke. Gideon Halliday did all the talking. Mrs. Halliday just looked at the body, then nodded, then cried. Why all the questions?"

Ellie took a deep breath. "Sir, I don't think the woman you saw at the morgue was Heather Halliday."

"Based on what?"

*Now that's an interesting question,* Ellie thought. She had a hunch Sir wouldn't be impressed by gut feelings.

"It's based on the fact that no one will let me see her," Ellie said. "I've tried and tried and all I get are excuses. She's asleep, she's sedated, she isn't taking phone calls."

"Well then, what do *you* think happened to her?"

Ellie took another deep breath. "I think she's a prisoner in her own house. Or maybe she's dead. I think the woman at the morgue wasn't Heather. I think she was Heather's

274

niece, Kit, or Adrianna Bouchet Halliday, Garrett's step-mother. Since you didn't hear Heather speak, it's difficult to—"

"She had a scarred face, if that helps."

"I . . . I thought you didn't see her face."

"I didn't, ma'am, not straight on. But when she lifted her veil to look at her husband's body, I saw the scars on her face."

"Are you absolutely certain you saw scars?"

"Yes, ma'am. They were half-hidden by the veil, but they were unquestionably scars."

"Which side of the face was scarred?"

"The right side."

"But you know . . . *everybody* knows . . . that Heather Halliday scarred the right side of her face. During the studio fire. Her husband's studio fire. Three years ago. Correct?"

"Yes, ma'am."

"So maybe you *thought* you saw scars. Because . . . well, because you *expected* to see scars."

"No, ma'am."

Since *she* couldn't see Sir's face, she couldn't decipher his expression, but she thought that maybe, just maybe, he was grinning.

"Was there anything else you wanted to ask me, Ms. Bernstein?"

She told him no, and thanked him, and it wasn't until after she'd hung up the phone that she realized she'd never given him her name.

Damn Peter! While she had been cutting through red tape, he had dialed straight through to Joe. In his man-to-man, cop-to-cop voice, Peter would have said, "My girl-friend thinks she's a detective. She'll most likely ask you some really dumb questions. Humor her."

# Thirty-Seven

Ellie opened a window, basked for a few minutes in the rays from the sun, then retrieved her laptop from the bedroom. Perhaps she could get some work done on her long neglected, practically abandoned mystery novel.

Stretching out on the couch, she began humming the Neil Sedaka song she'd often sung during her separation and divorce from Tony. Breaking up was hard to do, but waiting for Peter to return from the hospital was, in a sense, even harder.

Ever since Weight Winners she'd been active; Peter would say "full of zip." She jogged every morning, rain or shine, her ears plugged with Golden Oldies—Simon and Garfunkel and The Byrds, Aretha Franklin and Otis Redding. She had, briefly, taken up square dancing. She'd joined a Pilates class. She swam at the Y and was center fielder for a woman's softball team. The only sports she hadn't tried were skiing, mountain climbing, parachute jumping . . . and horseback riding.

Immobility drove her crazy, and, as her son Mick would say, it wasn't a very long drive.

She scowled at her foot. If she had crutches—or even better, a motorized chair—she could find one of Duke's ranch maps and wend her way to Angel's Ravine. Watch the cops in action. Probe for information. And probably incur Peter's wrath, but what the heck, it was better than just sitting here . . . waiting!

If she could only see Heather, touch Heather, she'd be content. Maybe she could call a taxi. No, damn it, she didn't have any money. Peter had said she wouldn't need any. Her mother, without fail, had always insisted that Ellie carry "mad money," but this time Ellie hadn't listened to the prerecorded voice inside her head: *Never leave the house without mad money, Ellie. Tuck a ten or twenty dollar bill inside your panty girdle.*

The ranch had a van that Peter had said was "in the shop, on hiatus too," but surely someone owned a car. Who?

Lelia, maybe, except she was taking care of Ryan and Stevie.

Duke was doodling around at Angel's Ravine.

Rosa was a lost cause.

Marion had chores to attend to, and at any rate, he was keeping a watchful eye on Jonina.

How about Martina Brustein? She couldn't be writing her book amidst all this . . . chaos. Or maybe, hibernating inside her cottage, she wasn't aware of Garrett's—

A polite knock shattered Ellie's concentration.

"Come in, the door's not locked!" she shouted, without thinking.

"You really shouldn't invite somebody inside unless you first ascertain who's there," a man said, entering the cottage.

The chastisement was uttered in a voice that was both authoritative and compassionate. *Jonah Feldman*, thought Ellie. *Holy cow!* With a mere dozen words he inspired confidence, and even though Garrett was dead and Peter was absent, she felt as if a Paul Robeson-size cotton bale had been lifted from her shoulders.

Jonah looked like Al Pacino. If they made another *God-father* sequel, Jonah could easily play the aging Michael Corleone. Shorter than Beth, he had black, silver-streaked hair and dark, soulful, Al Pacino eyes. Jonah's lashes could sweep crumbs from a tablecloth. His jeans and white shirt were well-worn, but appeared brand new, and Ellie had the feeling that, in court, his demeanor was more Johnny Cochran than Clarence Darrow.

"There's a killer on the loose," the man who had to be Jonah chided.

"You're right, I wasn't thinking," Ellie said, thinking she'd agree even if she disagreed. This attractive man would indisputably have the same effect on juries. Had he ever lost a case? Doubtful. "I'm Ellie Bernstein," she added, "but here at the ranch people seem to prefer Norrie, Peter's nickname for me."

"I'm pleased to finally meet you, Norrie. Pete sings your praises every time he visits us in Denver. Oh . . . sorry . . . I'm Jonah, Jonina's dad."

Ellie noted the designation "Jonina's dad" rather than "Beth's husband."

She offered him a cup of coffee, which he refused with thanks, then told him where he'd find his kids.

"I'll say hello to the boys and shanghai Jonina," he said. "She can accompany me to the hospital." He ran his hand across his forehead, as if pushing back bangs, and Ellie now knew where Jonina had picked up the habitual gesture.

"A hospital is no place for two rambunctious boys," Jonah continued, "so they'll stay with Lelia, if she's amenable."

"I've no doubt she will be."

"Yes, Lelia loves kids and she's very good with them,"

Jonah said in a somber voice. "It's a shame about her daughter."

"I heard about Angel. Do you know how she died?"

Jonah nodded. "In Garrett Halliday's studio fire."

"Oh my God!" Ellie shuddered from head to toe, then quickly capped the camera lens that was her mind's eye. "What was she doing at the studio?"

He shrugged. "No one talks about it, least of all Lelia. The subject seems to be taboo."

"How did the fire start?"

"I think it was some sort of electrical snafu, but I don't know for sure." He stared at Ellie's bandaged foot and ankle. "What happened?" he asked. "Another serendipitous mishap?"

"Yes . . ." She almost added *sir*. "I fell off a horse, too." *But it wasn't serendipitous.*

"The best thing to do is get back on again," Jonah said, and this time his voice sounded both authoritative and poignant. "That's what I always do."

Beth was nuts, dangling this lovely man on the end of her hook, Ellie thought, as she watched him head toward the barn. Peter's natural impulse was to protect his sister, justify her every action, satisfy her every whim, but . . . holy cow! What if *Beth* had something to do with Garrett's murder? What if she had found him with another woman and, in a jealous rage, killed him?

That made no sense. Would Beth carry around a knife, like her brother carried a gun, so that, on the spur of the moment, she could stab somebody to death? And if she *was* the perp, why take this morning's grief-stricken ride?

Ellie glanced toward her bedroom. Inside was the wickedly sharp scissors Jonina had retrieved from her cottage. Peter had said that Garrett had been "stabbed," not "stabbed with a knife." Could Beth's scissors be the murder weapon? The smoking gun?

Oh, sure, her mind mocked. Beth wouldn't carry a knife everywhere, but she'd pocket her scissors, just in case she needed to cut the price tag off a new piece of clothing, sever a pair of jeans, or stab somebody. And then she'd wash the blood from the scissors and leave it in her cottage, rather than getting rid of any evidence that might lead to a murder conviction. Ellie could almost believe Kit and Adrianna were dumb enough to do something like that, but not Beth.

Maybe Peter would have some relevant information when he returned from the hospital.

Without Jonah's comforting presence, the cottage seemed emptier than before, and Ellie felt the imaginary but heavy cotton bale lower itself onto her shoulders again. With a sigh, she began to brew a pot of coffee. She was limping back to the couch when she heard a tentative knock on the door, as if the person who stood outside had opted to play the Cowardly Lion in a *Wizard of Oz* remake.

Changing direction, Ellie hobbled to the door. Her ears still resonated with Jonah's warning, so this time she said, "Who's there?"

Despite the open window, she couldn't hear the muffled reply.

Oh, hell, what the heck! Would a killer knock timidly? No. He'd fling open the door, which, foolishly, she hadn't bothered to lock after Jonah's departure.

Ellie flung open the door and stared at the most ravaged face she'd ever seen.

The owner of the face was a heavyset woman. She wore a colorful muumuu that transformed the aforementioned Cowardly Lion into a Hawaiian tourist. Her face was pretty. Or would have been pretty, had it not been bruised by incessant weeping. She possessed short, dark, almost-black hair. And, in a startling contrast, beautiful doe-eyes that were more green than hazel.

Except right now they were more red than green.

The woman's complexion needed a makeover, not necessarily extreme; perhaps a thin layer of non-allergenic base and a soft brush of blush.

Makeup notwithstanding, Ellie recognized the face that had embellished—and still enhanced—countless book covers. Her mom bought every Marty Blue romance as soon as it came out, and had done so for years. Marty Blue was the only author Mom collected who wasn't alphabetized. Marty Blue had a special shelf, all to herself. Now Marty Blue, in person, stared back at Ellie. Except, in her present condition, she looked at least twenty years older than the glitzy author's photo that graced bookstore posters, ads in *Publishers Weekly* and *The New York Times*, and airport kiosks.

"I killed Garrett Halliday," she said.

Then, with an anguished cry, she collapsed on Ellie's doorstep.

# Thirty-Eight

Ellie now understood what the expression "on the horns of a dilemma" meant. Even if she hadn't been nursing an injured ankle, she doubted she could have helped the dough that was Martina Brustein rise.

There was only one way. Swallowing any semblance of sympathy, Ellie snapped, "Stand up, Ms. Brustein! If you don't, I'll shut the door in your face."

Startled, doe eyes brimming with tears, Martina maneuvered to her knees, then her feet. Still shaky, her body swayed to and fro. She looked a little like a transvestite Humpty Dumpty, assuming Humpty had opted to wear a red and yellow, flower-patterned muumuu.

"Inside," Ellie continued in the same brusque tone. "Sit in that chair." She heard a strangled burble from the coffee machine. "How about some coffee?"

"Do you have anything stronger?"

"Stronger than caffeine? No." Ellie filled two mugs. "Cream? Sugar?"

"Both, please. It was on the radio. Sometimes I play the radio when I write. For the music. Today they broke in with a news announce—"

"When you said you killed Garrett Halliday, were you talking literally or figuratively?"

"I didn't kill him off in a book, if that's what you're getting at."

"You wielded a knife and stabbed him?"

"Of course not. But I sent him to his death," she wailed.

Ellie handed the distraught woman a coffee mug, then retrieved her own mug. "Let's start at the beginning, shall we? Where did you meet Garrett?"

"I didn't meet him."

"What?"

"Oh, you mean the first time. I visited his Aspen art gallery and bought a painting." She hesitated then said, "We went out the next night, for dinner, and afterwards we . . . you know."

"You had sex."

Martina nodded. "For hours and hours. All night long. After that, he visited me here at the ranch, three or four, sometimes five nights a week. We also met at Angel's Ravine."

Disappointment sliced through Ellie. So much for fidelity. Devotion. Trust.

"Okay, let's cut to the chase," she said. "How, exactly, did you send Garrett to his death?"

"I left a message on his answering machine, telling him to meet me under the oak tree at Angel's Ravine. Yesterday was my birthday."

"Happy birthday. So what happened? Didn't he show up?"

"*I* didn't show up. I started walking toward the ravine, but it was raining so hard I turned back. If I hadn't, he might still be alive. Oh, look, you've got a cat."

"Yes. Jackie Robinson." Ellie darted a glance at the bookshelf, where Jackie Robinson had curled up with a good book.

"I've got a cat, too," Martina said. "Becky. I named her for Tom Sawyer's girlfriend. I almost called her Jody Foster, but—"

"Did you see anybody on your way to the ravine?"

"What? Oh. No. To be perfectly honest, I didn't get very far. I thought maybe Garrett would come to my cottage, instead. We could celebrate my birthday and I'd read him the latest chapter from my book-in-progress. The story's a bit of a cliché, but it's the most evocative writing I've ever done. You could almost call it erotica, and erotica's *hot* right now. My new book's about a stuffy but drop-dead gorgeous Englishman who visits the heroine's ranch. He wants to be a cowboy and race Thoroughbreds and he's the hero. Garret was my role model. I even named my hero 'Garth,' using the first three letters of Garrett's name. I was kind of hoping I could talk Garrett into doing the cover. You know, the cover art? He did it for one of my other books, *Ashes to Ashes, Lust to Lust*. It was the best cover I ever had. *Ashes* became a bestseller, number one on the *Times* best—"

"Martina, please. Focus!"

"Yes. Sorry. Garrett never came to my cottage. Well, how could he? Some . . . somebody kill . . . killed him."

Her sobs sounded like the burbling coffee machine. "What time was your rendezvous?" Ellie asked, trying to get the woman back on track.

"Five o'clock. But I was run . . . running late. Because of the rain." She swallowed another sob then sniffled noisily. "And because I couldn't decide what to wear. I've lost weight since I met Garrett, and I bought a couple of nice outfits on sale in Aspen. Very flattering, if I do say so myself. Garrett even said I looked like a model. You won't believe this, but I found a two-hundred-dollar sweater for thirty-nine-ninety-five. Oh, that reminds me. I want to talk to you about Weight Winners. Did I tell you that Garrett was my only love, my one true love?"

Ellie was getting dizzy from the woman's constant rambling and abrupt change of subject. But she'd answered all of Ellie's questions . . . except one. "Martina, you write books. That means you're good at thinking up plots. As a connoisseur of well-written scenarios, what do *you* think happened at the ravine?"

She preened at the compliment, then said, "I think the sign kids killed Garrett."

"The sign kids," Ellie echoed.

"When Rosa brought me my breakfast she said the police said kids are stealing letters from the Lonesome Pines sign. I think last night a gang of kids stole all the letters and partied near the ravine. I think they were high on drugs, maybe alcohol too, when Garrett discovered them. I think they stabbed him. With a shiv or something."

"I suppose that sounds plausible," Ellie mused out loud.

"He was my one true love."

"Yes, you said that."

"I even thought we'd get married someday."

"He has a wife."

"He said he didn't have a wife. You've got a different picture." Martina stared at John Wayne. "Mine's a horse, a black horse. Come to think of it, he looks a little like the horse on the cover I told you about, the one Garrett painted, *Ashes to Ashes, Lust to Lust*. Except the stallion on my wall doesn't have a rider and he's rearing up. Tell me about Weight Winners."

"Your coffee must be cold," Ellie said, adjusting somewhat to Martina's perpetual change of subject. "Would you like a fresh cup?"

She grimaced. "To be perfectly honest," she said, "I hate the stuff. Never developed a taste for it. Cokes, yes. Coffee, no."

"You'll have to switch to diet soda if you follow the

Weight Winners program. Or iced tea without sugar."

"I'll never get used to hearing soda called soda. I was born in Green Bay, Wisconsin, and we called it pop. Oh, wait, I want to pay you."

"For what?"

"Weight Winners. You know, giving me the diet and all."

"Nonsense. I'll be doing it on my own time. And it's a program, not a diet," she said automatically.

"No, no, I want to pay you. How much? Fifty? A hundred?"

Ellie opened her mouth to protest again, then clamped it shut. She desperately needed money for a cab. She desperately wanted to see Heather. And if Martina was willing to pay a hundred dollars, she could afford it. How much would a cab cost? Surely no more than twenty dollars. "How about thirty dollars, Martina? Do you have that much cash?"

"I've got cash all over my cottage. Sometimes I order pizza. Or Chinese. And I tip the girl who cleans every day. I like her. She's sweet and friendly and . . . well, nice. I planned to tip the cook, but she's a bitch. I'll get the money for you, then we can start. Although, to be perfectly honest, I don't know why I want to lose weight. Or who I want to lose it for . . ." She paused to place her coffee mug on the coffee table. "I've lost my one true love, the only man who didn't give a damn if I was fat or thin."

*That sounds like Garrett,* Ellie thought, watching Martina haul herself up from the couch, head for the door, fling it open, and step outside. *But the hero in Martina's new book doesn't. No one, not even a bestselling author, would choose Garrett as the role model for a stuffy Brit who races Thoroughbred horses.*

Had Garrett impersonated his brother? It wouldn't be difficult. If he imbued his voice with Gideon's pseudo-British accent—

But why on earth would he do that?

Because he wanted to hide his identity?

She shook her head. If Garrett wanted anonymity, he'd simply tell Martina he was Gideon. He wouldn't pretend to be Gideon and then ruin everything by telling Martina he was Garrett.

Before she could ponder any further, she heard a series of strident squeals.

Somehow, she was able to make out eight words.

"Now the sign kids want to kill me!" Martina shrieked.

Ellie swore at her injured ankle, using words Peter—and especially Tony—had never heard her use before, as she hobbled outside and trailed the terrified author.

Who kept glancing over her shoulder and shouting, "Hurry up!"

"Give me a new leg and I'll pull ahead of you," Ellie muttered under her breath.

Out of breath, she entered Martina's cottage. The living room décor was similar to Ellie's, except, as Martina had stated, the picture on the wall depicted a black stallion, its front hooves flailing at the sky. Next to the microwave and coffee pot table, Martina had added what looked like a 1.8 cubic foot mini-fridge, doubtless to store and chill her "pop."

"Bedroom," Martina said, also out of breath. "Excuse the mess. My clothes . . . all over the place. For the last two days . . . sorting laundry," she panted. "Haven't even hung up the clean stuff yet."

Ellie limped into the bedroom. Again, it was similar in décor to Ellie's bedroom, except it didn't have a sculpted angel headboard or a Garrett Halliday painting. What it did have was a huge, walk-in closet, its door ajar.

"Inside," Martina said, nodding like a bobblehead doll. "I was looking for one of my new outfits."

A light shone. On the floor of the closet, brown paper had been ripped to shreds.

"Worms." Martina shuddered. "I hate worms."

"Those aren't worms," Ellie said. "It's string. Thick brown string. My guess is that it goes with the brown wrapping paper. What was inside the paper?"

"Over there." Martina pointed toward the back of the closet. "It's called *Polly Wants a Quaker.*"

Ellie shifted her gaze to the back of the closet, then limped closer.

Propped against the wall was a painting. Heather dressed as a Quaker. Standing next to Heather was a goofy goose, straight out of the movie *Friendly Persuasion.*

All the painting needed was Gary Cooper and Dorothy Maguire, waving from a window.

And, of course, a new face for Polly.

Glued to the canvas, underneath Polly's slashed face, were letters from the Lonesome Pines sign. A lower case "d" that had once been a capital "P" and an "I" and an "E." The message was very clear.

d I E

"See?" Martina screeched. "The sign kids want to kill me."

"Nonsense," Ellie said, her heart pounding in her ears. "Somebody wants to kill Heather Halliday."

# Thirty-Nine

Martina drove like a maniac. As if she'd been brought up in California or New York City, rather than Green Bay, Wisconsin.

Despite Martina's tendency to take a crack at wheelies when she turned corners, her inclination to challenge yellow stoplights, and her penchant for running stop signs, Ellie was beginning to develop a soft spot for the pretty author. Her eyes still looked bruised, but she'd applied a thin layer of makeup, hiding her somewhat pitted complexion. With lipstick, a sultry mouth had emerged. With blush, high cheekbones.

None of which would have mattered to Garrett. He had worshipped women from the inside out, and Ellie knew, without a single doubt, that Martina's insides had been repeatedly abused—especially her heart. She must have heard "You'd be so pretty if you'd only lose some weight" a bazillion times.

Ellie had read a couple of Marty Blue books, where the heroines were models of perfection, the heroes a fantasy come to life. Sometimes Marty Blue's men had physical flaws, especially strategically-placed scars and wounds, but her women always possessed long, lush hair, big eyes, porcelain complexions, swan-like necks, rounded breasts, teensy waists, and slender hips. Barbie in a bustle. Colette in a camisole. Scarlett in a nineteenth-century euphemism.

"Did we lock the door?" Martina asked for the third time.

"Yes," Ellie replied. As if speaking to a child, she added, "And we left a 'Do Not Disturb' sign on the doorknob so Lelia won't clean the cottage."

"I suppose that's best, but she never goes into the closet. *I* haven't even gone into the closet for a couple of days." Martina heaved a deep sigh. "I still think we should have called the police."

"You're probably right," Ellie said, "but they would have insisted we stay put and I need to see Heather."

Fortunately, thought Ellie, Martina hadn't touched the painting. Mistaking the brown string for worms, she'd turned tail and raced down the path, toward Ellie's cottage. Even more lucky, for Ellie, Martina didn't want to be alone. She still half-believed the "sign kids" wanted her dead, even after Ellie had made it clear that, logically, if Martina had been their target, the letters would have been glued to something more conspicuous, something in plain sight. For instance, the mini-fridge.

Ellie had asked Martina if she'd drive to the Halliday house.

Martina had said she'd be more than happy to get away—far away—from the ranch, and she didn't need Ellie's directions because she knew where the house was. She'd followed Garrett home once and watched him walk inside. Then she'd lost her nerve.

Ellie had promised she wouldn't stay very long.

Martina had said she'd wait in the car. Leaving the contents of the closet undisturbed—"just in case the cops need to dust for prints or something"—she hadn't changed into one of her new outfits. So she still wore her shapeless muumuu and she didn't want to "be seen in public wearing schlock."

The *public* would be Gideon, Kit, Adrianna, and, hopefully, Heather. But if Heather was missing, thought Ellie, she'd bluff her way to the second floor. And/or the basement.

She was so anxious to see her friend that she merely formed a prayer wedge with her fingers and stared straight ahead as Martina downshifted into first gear and recklessly sped up the Halliday hill.

Once they'd reached the top, Ellie noticed the cars. A sleek white Cadillac and a nondescript Ford with rental plates.

In the distance, set several feet back from the house, was a detached, two-car garage.

Granted, last night's rain had eclipsed vision. But the bright strobe lights hadn't revealed any parked cars. Which meant what? Which meant that two cars could have been parked inside the garage. Gideon's car and—

"Have you changed your mind? I wouldn't blame you one bit if you had."

Ellie shook her head. "At the very least," she said, "I've got to tell Heather about the slashed painting. She could be in grave danger."

"But we don't *know* when the painting was slashed, so maybe the danger has passed. I didn't leave the cottage this morning, but I took breaks yesterday and the day before. I don't like to be there when the maid cleans. I feel guilty about the mess, like I should have kept the rooms neater, so that's when I ride. Riding gets the kinks out and clears my mind and I have my own saddle. Tooled leather. It cost a bloody fortune. Good thing it's insured."

"What's insured? Your saddle?"

"No. The painting. *Polly Wants a Quaker.*"

"You've already insured the painting?"

"Of course. I called my insurance agent on my cell as soon as I left the gallery, while I was putting Polly in the trunk of my car. To be perfectly honest, I don't care about the painting. It's the letters that scare the bejesus out of me."

"Well, that's my point," Ellie said. "Heather should hear about the letters."

"So should the police."

"And they will, I promise. Peter will take care of everything."

"Who's Peter?"

"My boyfriend. He's a cop."

"I didn't know that." Her face brightened. "I feel much safer now."

*I wish I did,* Ellie thought glumly, stepping out of the car. *But in a few minutes I'll see Heather, and then I'll clean the chalkboard like I used to do in school, only it'll be a mental chalkboard. I always volunteered to stay after school and my teachers were infinitely grateful, although I'm fairly certain they were unnerved by my desperate need to be acknowledged. And thanked. In a few minutes I'll see my good friend Heather, and then I'll erase the ominous, chalky shadows my overwrought imagination has conjured up.*

Clasping her handbag tightly in an effort to anchor her shaky fingers, Ellie limped down the path and rang the doorbell.

# Forty

Just like last night, Gideon Halliday answered the door.

"If you're from the media," he said in his pseudo-British accent, "I'll be making a formal statement later this aft . . ."

He paused when he recognized Ellie, but recovered quickly. "How nice of you to come calling, my dear," he said with a smile that didn't quite reach his eyes. "Won't you come in?"

*You bet I will,* she thought, clutching her handbag even tighter.

Lurching through the vestibule, which reeked of Adrianna's perfume, Ellie saw that the orange-wrapped package from Lilly's Apothecary—Heather's gift—still perched on top of the player piano.

Why was she not surprised?

Across from the stairwell, a suitcase leaned against the wall. A Canadian-flag scarf had been tied around its handle, the red maple leaf writhing in a granny knot. As Ellie considered her next move, three people emerged from the living room. Kit, dressed in air-conditioned-at-the-knees jeans and a rumpled denim shirt. A tall, pencil-thin man in a three-piece suit, most likely the driver of the rental car. And Adrianna, clothed in shorts and a white T-shirt. Stretched by her breasts, red block letters spelled out EH?

On Kit's feet was a pair of shiny black shoes, at odds with her faded jeans. Dollars to doughnuts Kit had impersonated Heather at the morgue. What about the scarred face Joe had seen? Probably one of those rubber Halloween masks, Ellie thought with disgust.

"You've already met Kit and Adrianna," Gideon said. He nodded toward the man, whose churned white hair looked as if it had come from an aerosol can of whipped cream. Or a cow with aerosol udders. "May I present Richard Braverman, our attorney? Richard, this is Ellie Bernstein. She was a close friend of Garrett's."

"I'm Heather's close friend, too," Ellie said, "and that's who I came to see. Once you lead me to Heather, you can go back to your family summit." *Where you are doubtless dividing the spoils from Garrett's estate, you pompous vulture!*

"I'm afraid that's impossible." Gideon silently snapped his fingers. "Heather's tranquilized, and other than the house going up in flames, I won't disturb her rest."

Ellie winced. "That's an awful thing to say, knowing that Heather burned her face while saving your brother's paintings."

"I didn't mean anything by . . . I could just as easily said an earthquake or an invasion from outer space." Gideon's eyes blazed. "And now, Ms. Bernstein, I'd like you to leave."

"It's about time," Kit mumbled. "I wouldn't have let her in."

"I'm not leaving," Ellie said, "until I see Heather."

"Dad," Kit said, "tell her to go to hell."

"No, Kit. We are never rude to our guests, even when they are rude to us." Fingers snapping incessantly, Gideon turned his face toward his daughter.

Ellie took advantage of the momentary diversion. Ignoring the pain in her ankle, she made a dash for the stairs.

She didn't get very far, maybe three and a half steps.

Gideon yanked her, backwards, down to the landing. His fingers dug into her shoulders as he said, "That'll be enough of that, my dear. If you don't leave immediately, I'll call the police."

"Good." She looked longingly up the staircase, then shook off Gideon's grasp and, somewhat awkwardly, made an about-face. Her foot throbbed like crazy. "Because if you don't call them, I will."

"What's going on here?" Richard Braverman walked toward Gideon and Ellie.

"Heather is being kept a prisoner in her own house," Ellie told the lawyer.

"Oh, please." Making her way toward the banister, Kit rolled her eyes. "That's the stupidest thing I've ever heard."

"My guess is that she's been drugged and locked in her bedroom," Ellie continued, ignoring Kit.

"You can't be serious." Gideon scowled.

"All I want to do is see her." As Ellie stared into the lawyer's face, she felt tears trickle down her own face. "If she's asleep I won't wake her up, and that's a promise. Maybe I could just leave the gift I bought for her, the gift that's in the vestibule, so she'll know I was here. Please?"

"Why are you asking him?" Gideon practically screeched. "He has nothing to do with this."

"I see nothing wrong with that," Richard Braverman said, at the same time.

Richard's "nothing" and Gideon's "nothing" sounded like a Sondheim duet.

Adrianna's voice, flavored with a French accent, cut into the silence that followed Richard and Gideon's duet. "You cannot see Madame Halliday. She is not here."

"Shut up!" Gideon snarled.

"Where is she?" Richard asked, taking the words out of Ellie's mouth.

Cowed by the attorney's authoritative voice, or perhaps by the simple fact that he *was* an attorney, Adrianna said, "She is *morte* . . . dead."

All eyes stared at Adrianna, standing next to the Canadian-flag-handled suitcase. Then everybody began talking at once.

"She's not dead, she's in Paris," Gideon said, his cheeks flashing like twin stoplights.

"She can't be dead," Kit moaned, clutching the banister for support.

"When did she die?" Richard asked.

"What do you mean, she's dead?" Ellie managed, glancing at a wall clock. She wished she could turn the hands back an hour—before this dreadful nightmare had begun.

Adrianna said, "Which word did you not understand, Madame Bernstein?"

"If she's dead, how did she die?" Ellie shifted her gaze from the clock to Adrianna's face.

"Under the knife, Madame."

Ellie heard four gasps, including her own. "Are you saying that Heather was stabbed? Like Garrett? Murdered?"

"No, no, a doctor's knife. During the operation on her face. Is that not how you say it? Under the knife?"

"How do you know this?" Richard asked.

"The clinic called Tuesday. No. Wednesday." Adrianna looked at Kit, who was still clutching the banister. "Mademoiselle Kit answered the phone, but they spoke French, so she gave it to me. I told them to sit stiff—"

"Tight," Gideon muttered.

"*Oui,* tight. I told them Garrett would fly there, after his art exhibit."

"What were you thinking?" Gideon's face was a mask of fury. "And why didn't you say anything to the family?"

"Don't you get on your tall horse with me," Adrianna said angrily. "I did not say anything because Garrett would have left for the clinic and I wanted to make love in a hotel."

"She can't be dead," Kit said again. All the color had drained from her face. Letting go of the banister, she slumped to the floor.

Richard Braverman picked her up and, with Kit in his arms, walked toward the living room. "I'll give her some brandy," he called over his shoulder.

Ellie felt as if she'd been placed in a cryogenics chamber. She knew, without a single doubt, that if she burst into tears, her eyes would yield icicles. "You wanted to make love in a hotel," she repeated, and heard the incredulity in her voice.

"*Oui,* Madame, after the exhibit. I wanted to drink champagne and get . . . how you say? Titsy?"

"Do you mean tipsy?"

"*Oui,* tipsy. Garrett liked me tipsy and . . ." She shrugged.

*Uninhibited,* Ellie finished. No wonder Garrett had looked so rapacious at the gallery. She saw Gideon lick his lips, as though the thought of a tipsy, uninhibited Adrianna turned him on too.

"But I drank too much," she said, "and fell out."

"Passed out," Gideon said.

"No, she definitely fell." Ellie wrapped her fingers around her handbag's strap. She wanted to bop the busty Canadian over her empty head, but to tell the God's honest truth, she felt much too weightless to lift the damn handbag. Even though last night, outside the convenience store, she had surmised that Heather was dead, she hadn't really believed it.

"Why didn't you tell us about Heather *after* the exhibit?" Gideon asked Adrianna.

"Tell you what?"

"That she had died, you idiot."

"I knew you'd be mad, so I didn't say anything."

The girl was too stupid to live, thought Ellie, gritting her teeth. Later she'd allow herself to react appropriately, mourn Heather, but right now she had to keep her emotions in check, hear the rest of this unbelievable story. She looked at Gideon. "You said Heather was in Paris. What was she doing there?"

"She found a doctor on the Internet. He runs a clinic. Heather speaks French. That's where I met her, in Paris. They e-mailed back and forth, Heather and the doctor, and he said he could reconstruct her face, get rid of every single scar. He said she'd be prettier than she was before the fire."

"Oh, God, and she believed him?"

"Absolutely. She *wanted* to believe. Garrett said the doctor was a quack. Garrett said he loved Heather just the way she was and her scarred face didn't make any difference. She seemed to accept that, but she wouldn't . . . share his bed. They occupied separate bedrooms, had ever since the fire. It wasn't just her face. She felt incredibly guilty about . . . something. She went to church every day, sometimes twice a day. She refused to receive the sacrament until—"

"What was she guilty about?"

"That's not important now, my dear. What's important is that Garrett had an affair five years ago."

298

His voice was barely audible, and Ellie was reminded of the expression "Little pitchers have big ears." It was an expression her mother used a lot, an expression Ellie had never really understood.

"Heather knew about it," Gideon continued, still speaking very low. "She insisted Garrett confess to a priest, which he did, and she forgave him. But then, three months ago, she found him with another woman."

"Beth Feldman."

Gideon looked startled. "How'd you know that?"

"A lucky guess." *Gideon doesn't know about Beth's pregnancy, and now, with the miscarriage, he'll never know. Thank God Heather didn't know. If she had, it only would have added to her angst.*

"Beth had flown to the ranch to supervise Duke's Valentine's Day bash," Gideon said. "It's an annual event. Heather left for Paris on February sixteenth. Garrett begged her to stay. She said she didn't care if she died on the operating table. She said she had confessed her sins and received absolution. Then she closeted herself inside a room with Kit, to say goodbye. Kit was devastated. I thought she'd go out of her mind. Heather has been a surrogate mother to Kit, ever since my wife died."

Ellie didn't want to talk about Kit. Her foot throbbed horribly, a souvenir of the girl's duplicity. "Why did you keep Heather's vanishing act a secret?"

"Garrett's success was, in part, predicated on his everlasting love for Heather, and hers for him. We were afraid of public backlash."

*Another lucky guess,* thought Ellie. She hadn't guessed Paris, how could she? But she'd guessed the reason why the Hallidays had feigned Heather's accessibility.

"Heather can't, or won't lie," Gideon continued. "As far

as I know, she's only told one lie in her whole life. So if we'd made it known that she was in Paris, or, even worse, that she'd checked herself into some quack's clinic, an enterprising reporter would have tracked her down, interviewed her, and Garrett's affairs would have become a matter of public record. He's always been fodder for the press, just like our father. But, in Garrett's case, it's always been positive fodder."

Adrianna still stood near the suitcase. She hadn't reacted to anything Gideon had said since her "I knew you'd be mad" comment. In fact, she looked as though she was thinking in French.

"Why don't you go into the living room, my dear," Gideon said to her. "Perhaps you'd like to sample the brandy."

She giggled, and the sound made Ellie's teeth hurt. "Gid, you naughty boy," she said, "you know what happens when I drink brandy." With a sensual wiggle, she walked toward the living room.

Gideon had the grace to look embarrassed. "Adrianna just got back from Toronto," he said, as if that explained her lack of sensibility—her giggles in the wake of Garrett's murder and the horrific disclosure regarding Heather's fatal surgery.

"When did she get back?" Ellie asked.

"This morning. She was visiting friends, and I've a feeling she'll soon be moving to Canada."

*I've a feeling you'll pay her way,* Ellie thought. *At least you will when you've finished with her. Sample the brandy, indeed. Sample the brandy and get "titsy" would be more to the point.*

As he ushered her to the door, Gideon said, "And now, my dear, I must ask you once again to leave my humble abode. I do hope you'll keep what I've told you under your hat."

"I don't wear hats," she said, "but you needn't worry. I won't say a word to anyone but Peter, and I'm sure it'll stop there. I'm not a gossip, Mr. Halliday, and I have no intention of besmirching the reputation of people who were once my friends. Who, even in death, remain my friends."

"Thank you. And please call me Gideon. 'Mr. Halliday' was my late father."

"Hold it." Ellie limped over to the piano and snatched up the bright orange package. She wasn't sure what she'd do with the blue crystal, but Jonina would probably love the magic rabbit.

Stumbling toward Martina's car, her eyes blinded by tears, Ellie heard the echo of Gideon's voice: *Heather has only told one lie in her whole life.*

She wondered what that lie was. A little white lie to make somebody feel better? Or one hell of a whopper?

*Oh, Heather, why didn't you call me? I'd have talked you out of Paris. Or flown there with you.*

She swallowed a sob. Now there'd be two commemorations at Gideon's "shindig," and Gideon would add another zero to the price tags that embellished Garrett's paintings.

Gideon's reaction to Adrianna's announcement had seemed genuine, but was it an act for Ellie's benefit? For Richard Braverman's benefit? Had Gideon learned about Heather's death "under the knife," then knifed his brother to preserve the legend and up the ante?

# Forty-One

Back at the ranch, inside her cottage, Ellie was so angry she wanted to smash something. Or, even better, smack someone—preferably Peter.

Martina had entered her own cottage, very briefly, to retrieve her cat. Now she was snoozing inside Ellie's bedroom. Becky and Jackie Robinson eyed each other suspiciously from across the room, Jackie on the bookshelf, Becky stretched out on the floor, in front of the fireplace.

The police had been called. They arrived just as Peter pulled up. Ellie barely had time to tell him about Heather, and no time to vent or cry, before he'd joined his fellow cops. The slashed Polly painting was reminiscent of the slashed Kessler painting, which Peter had seen first hand, and the cops were grateful for his assistance.

But, oh God, she needed him to hold her.

Peter had brought Jonina back with him. The girl was once again in the barn, "helping" Marion.

Beth was out of immediate danger, but Jonah would stay at the hospital a while longer, just in case.

*He wants to get back on the horse,* Ellie thought. *I wonder if Beth knows how lucky she is.*

Ellie ached for lost opportunities. Now she'd never get a chance to apologize. Heather had left her with an albatross as heavy as a gorbellied ox. If she believed in guilt, and she did, she'd have to atone for years of Heather-neglect.

Friendships were like grains of sand, sifting through one's fingers. After she returned to Colorado Springs, she'd contact every friend she'd ever made. By letter. By phone. By carrier pigeon, if that was her only means of communication.

*And I'll solve Garrett's murder, Heather. It might not be atonement, but it's the least I can do. I owe you that much.*

She had learned very little at the Halliday house. Or, depending on how you looked at it, she'd learned a lot.

For one thing, Adrianna had been in Toronto during Garrett's murder. Ellie had never considered the petite figure skater a viable suspect . . .

*But even if I had, I don't now.*

What about Kit? According to Jonina, Kit had been at the ranch last night. Or at least she'd been in Beth's cottage around eight o'clock. What was Kit's motive? She had no motive. She might have one for slashing the faces on the paintings—resentment at what her mind could have construed as Heather's desertion; hadn't Gideon said that Kit was devastated? But why would she want *Garrett* dead?

If the two Colorado Springs murders were linked to Garrett's murder, and Ellie wasn't at all certain they were, had Kit been anywhere near the Springs when Rudolph Kessler was killed? Duke had said Kit owned a loft, which she shared with another woman . . . someone named Moony. So Kit could have attended her uncle's art exhibit, stayed overnight at the loft, and killed Kessler the next day. Even if that were true, which Ellie strongly doubted, Serafina Lassiter had been murdered Sunday morning when Kit had been here at the ranch. Flirting with Marion. Aborting Ellie's riding lesson. "Stalking" Peter. Handing over the leafy switch that would turn Buttermilk's ignition key.

Kit couldn't have killed Serafina, driven back to Aspen, then driven to the ranch. The timeline was too iffy. No, not iffy. Impossible.

Unless Kit had a pilot's license and owned a plane, like Jonah did.

Oh, God, what if Jonah had found out about Garrett and Beth's affair? What if he had flown his Cessna into Aspen, killed Garrett, then flown back to Denver?

*That has to be the most off-the-wall supposition I've brainwaved so far. Even if Jonah knows the ranch like the back of his hand, how could he possibly know that Garrett would be at Angel's Ravine, seated under the oak, at five o'clock?*

Was it *feasible* that Jonah, himself, had arranged the tête-à-tête?

Ellie shook her head. For one thing, Garrett wasn't confrontational. Why would he agree to meet the husband of his pregnant paramour? For another, Jonah Feldman was no killer, and as a lawyer he'd have to realize that it would be easy as pie to check the Aspen airport and find out exactly who had landed there. And when.

Jonah wasn't a viable suspect.

So unless a stranger had appeared out of nowhere and killed Garrett for the hell of it, that left Gideon Halliday.

Or somebody who lived at the ranch.

Or the "sign kids."

First, the sign kids. If they had been stoned and/or drunk, they would have left evidence strewn about. Candy wrappers. An empty cigarette pack. A marijuana butt. Shoe prints. No, not shoe prints. The rain would have washed away shoe prints. Tire prints, too. Still, the sign kids wouldn't have had the smarts to clean up after themselves. Just like Hansel and Gretel, they'd have "breadcrumbed" a path, straight to their doorsteps. If the sign kids—assuming they existed—had killed Garrett, they'd be under lock and key by now.

Second, Beth Feldman. Didn't Peter say his sister had a temper? Yes. As a kid, she'd broken his ukulele because he wouldn't let her play his guitar. And after Mike Urvant had given her the old heave-ho, he'd suffered a back injury. Could Beth have hired someone to sabotage Mike Urvant's rodeo ride?

*That sounds plausible.*

Beth had slept with Garrett in February, three months ago. She had told Peter that she was three months pregnant and that Jonah wasn't the father. If Garrett was responsible, and if Beth had confronted him, he might have insisted on an abortion, unwilling to jeopardize his efforts to reunite with his "one true love"—his Heather, his model, his wife, his life.

Jilted again, Beth might have lured Garrett to the ravine and stabbed him to death. With a knife. Or her scissors. Except, Ellie didn't want the killer to be Beth . . . Peter's sister . . . Jonina's mom.

Third, Lelia. Her daughter Angel had died in Garrett's studio fire. Gideon had mentioned an affair five years ago. Could Angel have been Garrett's daughter? If yes, why would her death have anything to do with his murder?

*The thing is, I just don't know Lelia well enough to "dissect" her.*

How about Marion? His running into Lelia had sounded fine, but his reading-a-book excuse hadn't. What was he hiding?

She recalled the smell of liquor that seemed to drift down from the loft when she'd entered the barn. She also remembered her father drinking beer in the garage, hiding his excessive intake from her mom. Until he decided to avoid his wife's frequent tongue-lashings by frequenting a neighborhood bar. There, he'd met the young cocktail waitress who would become his second, more tolerant wife.

*Was Marion a secret drinker?*

So what if he was? That didn't mean he'd killed Garrett. Anyway, Marion had no motive that Ellie could discern. He was a question mark.

So were Duke and Rosa. Again, no motives. Garrett might have pissed Beth off, but he hadn't pissed off Duke and Rosa.

*And how do you know that?* Peter would say. *I'll bet it's your incredible facility for assembling criminal profiles. What's really beyond belief is that you've only been here two nights and two days.*

"Sarcasm has never been your strong suit, Lieutenant," she muttered.

"Are you talking about me behind my back again?" Peter removed his boots at the door, and left them facing the wall like reprimanded students. "Or are you grousing aloud to Jackie Robinson and . . . whoa, have we adopted another cat?" He stared at the black calico.

"Jackie Robinson adopted me," Ellie said, "and that pretty little feline is Becky, Martina Brustein's cat."

"Who?"

"Martina Brustein. Marty Blue. The romance author. You just came from her cottage, Peter."

"Right. Sorry, I'm brain-dead. So, obviously, we're cat-sitting. Where's the author?"

"Asleep in our bedroom. She conked out, after driving me to the Halliday house . . ." Ellie paused, then continued. "She said she was responsible for Garrett's murder and she saw worms on the floor of her closet, which scared the bejesus out of her. I think they were *Tremor* worms, you know, that movie with Kevin Bacon?"

Around a yawn Peter said, "The author is asleep in *our* bedroom?"

"I knew you weren't listening. You didn't hear a word I said after 'asleep in our bedroom.' "

"Yes, I did. You said something about a movie with Kevin Bacon, but he's in every movie, or linked to somebody in every movie, so—"

"Peter, sit down before you fall down."

"Sweetheart, do you mind if I use another cabin and crash? All I need is a couple hours sleep, then we'll go out for dinner."

Ellie couldn't believe her ears. She wanted to talk about Heather and he wanted to take a catnap. But then, she reasoned, he'd never met Heather. Moreover, she had died in Paris, of legitimate causes, if one could consider an Internet quack legit. Peter's whole focus was on his sister, and rightly so.

"I don't mind," she said. "You look like a zombie. Can you stay awake long enough to tell me about Beth?"

"She'll heal. But she's in bad shape, both physically and emotionally. Jonah plans to fly her to Denver's St. Luke's, where he can keep an eye on her. He's leaving in his plane, early tomorrow morning. I'll go with him."

"You? Why?"

"They want . . ." He yawned twice. "They want me to deliver the Polly painting to the C.S.P.D. Compare it to Kessler's painting, check for DNA, and my squad needs help. Everyone, it seems, has some sort of flu. McCoy says it's a Stephen King virus, whatever that means. In any case, the precinct ran out of puke-pails and sent half the squad home."

Ellie hid her disappointment, although, in his present,

heavy-eyed state, Peter probably wouldn't have noticed. "Did you talk to Beth?"

"Yes. Briefly. She said she and Kit drugged Garrett, then transported him to the ravine. But she swore he was conscious, mumbling incoherently, when they left him under the oak."

For one of the few times in her adult life, Ellie had no words at her disposal. She opened her mouth, closed it, then stared at Peter as he sank onto the couch.

Elbows on knees, he used his palms to prop up his face. "It was a prank, Norrie. A prank that backfired."

"A prank? She called it a prank?"

"No, *I* called it a prank. She called it a joke. What would *you* call it?"

"Reckless endangerment. Why would she and Kit *do* something like that?"

"I don't have a clue. Beth was groggy. She kept drifting in and out. Getting information was like pulling teeth, and then the nurse told me to leave. All I know is that Beth and Kit cooked up the scheme in Beth's cottage, two night ago. Kit told Beth she'd seen an old Burt Reynolds TV show where one of the characters walked around naked, his private parts hidden by rocks, trees, and bushes. Kit said she laughed so hard she peed her pants, so last night she and Beth drugged Garrett with Valium. They drove him to the ranch, tossed his body into a wheelbarrow, and . . ." Peter yawned again.

"I still don't understand why they'd *do* that," Ellie said, picturing the green wheelbarrow in the tack room, not far from a couple of filthy knives. "Were they drunk? Stoned?"

"My sister doesn't do drugs!"

*Maybe you don't know your sister as well as you think you do. When it comes to Beth, you wear blinders.* With an effort,

Ellie kept her temper in check. "Are you telling me they stripped Garrett naked before they left him under the tree?"

"Yes." Rising, Peter swayed on his feet. "Norrie, could we please discuss this later? If I don't get some sleep, we'll fight, and I don't want to fight. All I need is a couple of hours, and I promise I'll take you out for dinner."

"You'd better," she snapped. "If I eat here, Rosa might poison my food. As a *prank.*"

"What do you mean?"

"She doesn't like me."

"Rosa doesn't like anybody who fiddles with her menu, especially vegans. And dieters."

*It's more than that,* Ellie thought, but right now Rosa was the least of her concerns. "Will the police arrest Kit?"

"No. She'll be given a severe reprimand, and so will Beth when she's fully recovered, but they didn't know their little stunt would lead to murder."

"It wasn't a 'little stunt.' "

"You're right, sweetheart, but it wasn't murder."

"So they'll get a slap on the wrist."

"Yes. What would *you* like the police to do?"

Ellie almost said "a mere slap on the wrists will set a bad example for others," but stopped herself when she realized she'd sound like a woman who had fervently volunteered to rate censorable movies. When it came right down to it, Ellie Bernstein, middle-aged girl detective, had broken the law on more than one occasion. Minor stuff like, oh, say, trespassing, but wasn't there a well-known phrase about casting the first stone?

"Go crash, honey," she said, instead. "We'll talk later."

As Peter left the cottage, she thought: *What if Kit doubled back and stabbed Garrett with a knife from the tack room? But why would she do that? What had Garrett ever done to incur her wrath?*

Nothing, that's what. While Kit looked like she might have a lot of wrath to incur, it had been directed at Ellie, not her uncle. And although Peter had interrupted Ellie's analyses before she'd thoroughly dissected Gideon Halliday, he had a much stronger motive. Money. And jealous—holy cow.

*Holy cow!*

Limping took too long. Ellie hopped on her good foot, over to the phone. Then she called her mother. The Dragon Lady.

# Forty-Two

Her brother Tab answered the phone.

"Sissy," he said, even though she'd asked him a million times not to call her that.

"Tabby," she said, knowing he hated the nickname with a passion. "Is Mom there, by any chance?"

"You know she is. It's Monday. Oprah, the news, *Wheel of Fortune, Jeopardy!* And later there's an A&E bio about my namesake."

"*You* were named for Tab Hunter," she said. "You're *his* namesake, not the other way around. Would you get Mom for me?"

"I didn't hear the magic word, Sissy."

"Tab, you're thirty-eight years old and living at home. If you need a magic word, I'll give you one. In fact, I'll give you two. 'Grow up.' "

"You used to be nice," he muttered, then screamed "Ma" so loud, Ellie thought she'd hemorrhage.

She glanced at the cuckoo clock. She'd give Mom ten minutes before she'd call a bookstore.

In the background she heard her mom say, "Who is it?" and Tab reply, "It's Sissy." Mom said, "What does she want?" Tab said, "How the hell should I know?" Mom said, "Don't use that tone of voice with me, young man." Which was funny, in a way, since Tab was pushing forty.

Then, closer to Ellie's ear, Mom said, "Hello. What can

I do for you?" as if Ellie was someone who'd called for a charity donation.

"You can do me a huge favor," Ellie said, cutting to the chase. "Please," she added—the magic word.

"How is Paul?"

It took Ellie a minute. "You mean Peter. He's fine."

"Peter, Paul, I knew he shared a name with one of Christ's disciples."

"Apostles, Mom. Paul wasn't a disciple. He was an apostle."

"Whatever. I always use the Bible to remember names."

*What if the name is Bob or Zelda?* Ellie thought. Aloud, she said, "Do you still have that shelf full of Marty Blue books?"

"Of course I do. While I have you on the phone, Ellie, Tab has been trying to get in touch with your boyfriend. Tab wants to talk to him about this marvelous investment opportunity. Is he there?"

"No, but I'll tell him Tab wants to talk to him." She looked at the clock, halfway to the ten-minute mark. "Please don't tell me you invested in another one of Tab's crazy schemes."

"Well, I certainly did. Tab says my five thousand dollars will soon be fifty thousand."

"And last time he said your ten thousand—"

"That wasn't Tab's fault! His partner was a scam artist. I hope you've kept the weight off, Ellie. You looked more like a seal than a whale the last time I saw you. I even wrote letters to Larry King and Regis. Diets are big news right now, and I thought your little group could use the publicity."

"It's not a little group, Mom. It's a national org . . ." She looked at the clock. "Would you check your Marty Blue collection, please, and see if you have a book called *Ashes to Ashes, Dust to Dust?*"

"*Ashes to Ashes, Lust to Lust,* Ellie, and I don't need to check. I have it."

"Would you pull it off the shelf? If I remember correctly, there's a black horse on the cover."

"Yes, that's right. The girl on the horse is barefoot, or maybe she wears stockings, and the hero is holding her shoe, or maybe it's her boot. The book is based on the Cinderella fairy tale, only Marty Blue calls her heroine Cynthia. Or maybe it was Ellen. I can't remember. I'm getting old . . ." She paused, waiting for Ellie's response.

Ellie gave it to her. "You're not getting old, Mom. The last time I saw you, you didn't look a day over fifty."

"That's what everyone tells me. Why do you want my Marty Blue book? Have you decided to write a romance?"

"No. All I need is the name of the cover artist. That book's a hardback, right?"

"Yes."

"Then I'm fairly certain the artist's name will be on the dust jacket."

"Okay. Hang on."

In the background, Ellie heard Tab say, "Is Paul there?" Her mom said, "His name is Peter, not Paul. Paul was an apostle, not a disciple, which you'd know if you ever bothered to read your Bible." Then Ellie heard Mom pick up the receiver, drop it, pick it up again.

"And the artist's name is . . ." Mom sounded like the come-on-down man on *The Price Is Right,* one of her favorite quiz shows. "G. Holliday."

"Holliday or Halliday?"

"Halliday."

"And there's just an initial? No first name?"

"Just an initial. If there was a first name, I'd have given it to you."

"Thanks, Mom."

"You're welcome. Do you want me to send you the book?"

"That's very nice of you," Ellie said, taken aback. "I know how much you treasure your Marty Blue books."

"Oh, I have two copies. One in hardback, one in paperback. I planned to donate the hardback to the library. Oprah's about to start, Ellie. I'll phone you if Mr. King wants you for his show. Or, even better, Regis. Don't get fat again and please ask Paul to call Tab."

Ellie heard a click in her ear.

*Well, that wasn't much help,* she thought, disconnecting on her end. She had been so convinced, in her own mind, that the cover artist was Gideon Halliday.

She still was.

*Okay, let's take this step by step.*

Once upon a time Gideon Halliday, living in Paris, had studied art.

There, he met Heather.

With Heather in tow, he returned to Colorado.

Whereupon, Heather and Garrett fell in love, wed, and moved to Colorado Springs.

Gideon scratched out a living as a book-cover artist while Heather, with a full-time job, supported Garrett; believed in Garrett.

So, apparently, did Garrett's father. Or else John Halliday knew he didn't have many years left and wanted both his sons near him. Especially his favorite son, the son with the "gift from God."

So John built, bought, or rented Garrett an Aspen studio. Which burned down—*holy cow!*

Had Gideon, blinded by jealousy, lit the match?

If he had, his plan backfired, pun intended, because Heather ran inside to save her husband's paintings and a reporter, who knew a good human interest story when he tripped over it, exploited the brave deed. Which led to national exposure and Garrett's humongous success.

Garrett hired Gideon to run his Aspen art gallery, the final humiliation. Since Garrett refused to exhibit outside of Colorado, Gideon couldn't even wheel and deal, internationally, and play his brother's manager. How he must have seethed.

*Now it gets dicey,* Ellie thought.

Suppose Gideon had begun to paint again? Or he'd never really stopped? But he couldn't exhibit under his own name because, while his style was bolder, it was too much like his brother's. People would say he'd copied Garrett. Also, he didn't have Heather as his gimmick. He'd be stuck in a kind of limbo, like a mid-list author.

*Okay, here's where it gets really dicey.*

Suppose Garrett couldn't paint? What if Heather's incredible sacrifice and resultant disfigurement had led to "artist's block"?

Whereupon, Gideon said he'd paint the canvasses. They'd tell everybody Garrett had changed his style a bit and they'd exhibit under Garrett's name.

Why would Garrett agree to that?

Only one person could convince him to go along with Gideon's plan. Heather.

Gideon knew something about Heather that Garrett didn't, and Gideon had held it over her head like a guillotine's blade.

That made sense, didn't it? All that stuff about Heather confessing to a priest and receiving absolution before she took off for Paris. Not to mention the one lie she'd told. Which, Ellie now decided, had been one heck of a whopper.

Garrett tried to paint again, his first attempt the Annunciation canvas. Even if the background was somewhat "sketchy," the rendering of Mary wasn't, and Gideon wouldn't have liked that. Because it meant that Garrett was unblocking, on the verge of a full recovery.

By now Gideon had amassed "dozens of paintings"—his own—so he could afford to kill the golden goose. He'd still have to exhibit under Garrett's name, but he'd reap the rewards he'd never reaped before. The finest food and drink. Affairs with beautiful women. Expensive clothes. He could pick up a phone, make a reservation, and travel anyplace in the world.

The world was, in fact, his oyster.

But only if his brother was dead.

He must have been at the house, maybe even painting merrily away, when Beth and Kit played their "prank." They had drugged Garrett, and Gideon had trailed them to Angel's Ravine. In his jacket pocket, a knife. He'd have been ecstatic. The studio fire hadn't worked—had, in fact, boomeranged—but fortuitously, and serendipitously, the perfect opportunity to rid himself of his brother had presented itself. *And* he could pin the murder on somebody else. For instance, the "sign kids."

Returning home in time to greet Ellie and Peter, he had stored his wet car in the garage, hidden his wet, bloody clothes . . . somewhere . . . and changed into a dressing gown. He'd worn a beret to hide his wet hair. Then he pretended to know nothing about the dinner party. Or Garrett's whereabouts. Worse, he had fabricated a tale about a tranquillized Heather and a mouse invasion—what a nefarious rat!

*There's only one teensy problem with my lengthy supposition,*
Ellie thought, retrieving a granola bar from her stash,
wishing with all her heart that it was a glazed doughnut.
*How the hell can I prove it?*

# Forty-Three

Peter overslept. Then he broke his promise. He didn't take her *out* for dinner. With an "I'll be right back," he hopped into the car.

"Right back" seemed like forever, but the sacks he toted smelled scrumptious.

To her surprise, Ellie scarfed down every bite of her Greek salad and every crumb of her chicken parmesan sub. She had honestly thought she wouldn't be able to swallow one morsel.

Peter turned on the TV and they watched the ten o'clock news. Gideon's press conference, taped a few hours earlier, superceded a three-car smashup and a missing C.U. college student. Gideon looked appropriately somber. His attorney, Richard Braverman, stood next to him. Kit and Adrianna stood behind him. Kit looked tearful. Adrianna looked "titsy."

A reporter asked about Heather. Gideon said she was "mourning in private and didn't wish to be disturbed." Obviously, he hadn't decided how he'd break the news of her demise. Or Richard Braverman had told him to keep it under his beret.

Although sorely tempted to share her Gideon theory with Peter, Ellie had decided to keep it to herself. She needed more information, which meant a trip to the library. She wanted to read up on the studio fire—at the very least, find out how it started. She also planned to have a chat with Lelia.

For the second night in a row, Peter held her in his arms as he urged her to weep for Heather, weep for lost opportunities, weep for the senseless deprivation of two people whom she had cherished. Then slowly, tenderly, he made love to her. Stomach full to bursting, heart full of Peter, Ellie fell into a dreamless sleep.

When she awoke the next morning, Peter was gone. He'd left her a note, printed neatly on a Lonesome Pines scratch pad: DECIDED TO DRIVE RATHER THAN FLY. JONAH WILL FLY THE BOYS BACK TO DENVER. JONINA WANTED TO STAY, SO SHE'LL BUNK WITH YOU. HOPE THAT'S OKAY. I LOVE YOU. DON'T SNOOP.

*Don't eat on the sly,* Ellie thought, although she knew that wasn't what Peter meant.

Late yesterday afternoon. Marion had helped Martina move her things into a two-bedroom cottage next door to Ellie's. Martina said she wanted to be closer to the main house, just in case the sign kids—or anyone else—decided to pay her another call. When she heard that Jonina would be sharing Ellie's one-bedroom, she confronted Duke at the breakfast table. "Jonina will stay with me," she said, an assertion rather than a request. "I'd appreciate the company."

*So would I,* Ellie wanted to say, until she saw the awestruck expression on the girl's face.

"Wait till I tell the kids at school," Jonina whispered. "And if they don't believe me—"

"I'll visit your class on Career Day," Martina said with a wink. "As your guest."

After a "legal" breakfast of eggs, orange juice, and toast, Ellie corralled Lelia outside Martina's old cottage. The pretty housekeeper was smoking a cigarette and looking guilty about it.

Fishing a crumpled pack from her jeans pocket, she said, "I stole this from Beth's cottage."

"I'm sure she wouldn't mind," Ellie said. "She won't be smoking anything for a while."

"You'd be surprised at what the guests leave behind, Norrie." Lelia crushed the cigarette butt beneath the heel of her sneaker. "Duke's Lost and Found is a treasure trove of miscellany. Expensive clothes. Shoes. Jewelry. Monogrammed underwear. Condoms and birth control pills. One jerk forgot his pet iguana. How can you forget an iguana? Guests will steal towels and rolls of toilet paper, but leave their prescription meds. Kit likes to raid the bathrooms, after the guests depart. She has a huge stash, everything from Midol to Roofies."

"Roofies?"

"Rohypnol. 'Roofies' is a street name. It's a benzodiazepine sedative, a member of the Valium family. I guess you could say the children's version is Noctec, which is legal. Roofies aren't. But they're easy to find. On the street they go for five dollars a tablet." She shook her head in disbelief. "I'm always finding bottles of prescription Noctec. I think it's awful to sedate a child, don't you?"

"I've never really thought about it. When my son was hyper, *I* wanted to be sedated." Ellie auditioned a smile. Lelia didn't smile back. "How do you know so much about drugs?"

"Every time someone leaves behind a new med, I look it up on the Internet. I guess you could say I'm nosy."

"I prefer 'curious.' Nosy sounds sneaky, curious sounds smart."

"Okay, curious." She shrugged. "I'm supposed to turn

in all prescription meds, and I do, assuming I get my hands on them before Kit does. She could open a pharmacy."

"Yes, I know all about Kit's 'stash,' " Ellie said, trying to keep the raw bitterness out of her voice. "She used Valium to drug Garrett Halliday. So she could haul him to the ravine."

"Did she? I didn't hear about that. What an awful thing to do."

Lelia's voice sounded dispassionate and Ellie couldn't decipher the expression on the girl's face.

"I shouldn't have told you," Ellie said. "The police are probably keeping it a secret."

"I can keep a secret."

This time the girl's tone betrayed the bitterness Ellie had tried to hide, and her gut feeling told her that Lelia's last remark had something to do with Angel. *Now or never,* she thought.

"I want to ask you about Angel," she said. "If you don't want to talk about her, that's okay, but I'm a good listener and you have my promise that I won't repeat one word."

Lelia's bottom lip quivered. With shaky fingers she lit another cigarette. "What do you want to know?"

"My guess is that Angel was Garrett's daughter," Ellie began. "If I'm wrong, you have my permission to slap me across the face. But not too hard."

The girl finally smiled. Then she said, "Angel was more mine than Garrett's. He called her the Immaculate Deception."

Ellie quirked an eyebrow.

"I was seventeen and stupid," Lelia continued. "I knew my father had married my mother because he 'got her pregnant.' I told Garrett I was on the pill. I thought if I became pregnant, he'd divorce Heather and marry me. Stupid," she repeated.

"Young," Ellie amended.

"Garrett said he'd pay for an abortion. I cried and carried on, but finally agreed. Then I changed my mind at the last minute. I wanted the baby. I told myself he'd have Garrett's genes, which meant that someday he'd be a great artist. Have you ever seen the movie *Portrait of Jennie?*"

"No."

"It stars Joseph Cotton and Jennifer Jones, and it's about an artist. Five minutes after I found out I was pregnant, I decided to name my baby Joseph. For Joseph Cotton and—" she blushed "—Mary's Joseph. And once the baby had a name, I couldn't abort it."

"I can understand that." With an effort, Ellie kept her opinion of Garrett to herself. She wanted to spew her rage, damn him for cheating on Heather, damn him even more for his cavalier reaction to Lelia's pregnancy. "So when you had a girl," Ellis said, "rather than naming her Mary, you named her Angel."

"No. I named her Jennifer. Angel was her nickname. She was a perfect little angel. I loved her so much. My housekeeping job at Lonesome Pines was perfect, too. Duke pays peanuts, but the position comes with room and board. After Angel died, Duke said he'd pay me more if I moved in with my mother. So I did."

As Lelia stomped out her cigarette, Ellie said, "Did Heather know? About Angel, I mean?"

"I don't think so. I'm part Hispanic, so Angel's coloring wasn't a big surprise. Nobody suspected Garrett, and his father offered me ten thousand dollars to keep her birth and death a secret. Mama spent the money on a big-screen TV, new furniture, stuff like that. I didn't care. I was mentally anesthetized."

"Tell me about the fire."

"I don't know if I can. I've never talked about it."

"Okay."

Lelia stared into Ellie's eyes. Then she sighed and said, "Garrett was painting me and Angel, in his studio. Heather always left us alone. She didn't like kids. She couldn't or wouldn't have a baby, and she insisted Garrett have a vasectomy. He didn't want one, but he could never refuse Heather anything. After the vasectomy, he paid more attention to Angel. After all, she was his only child, his blood."

Looking down at the ground, Lelia toed a cigarette butt. "He paid more attention to me, too. He knew I wouldn't get pregnant again, at least not by him, so he . . ."

"Started sleeping with you again."

She nodded. "I couldn't say no. I wanted to, but Garrett was my Heather. I couldn't refuse him anything." She took a deep breath. "On the day of the fire we put Angel down for a nap. She was thirteen months old. It was a beautiful day, but very cold. The house had a propane heater. The studio was attached to the house. Garrett said let's pick apples and wrap them up in goofy paper . . . for Heather, who liked to bake apple pies. We were in the orchard when we heard the propane tank explode. I . . . we . . ."

"That's okay. You don't have to say anymore."

"No. I want to tell you. Heather had come back. From shopping. For groceries. The studio was on fire. She ran in. Three times. She saved eight paintings. They were barely singed. I like to think she never saw Angel . . ."

Tears streamed down Lelia's face. Except for the trail of tears, she looked exactly like the woman in Garrett's Annunciation painting.

Ellie's heart ached. "Are you all right? You'd better sit down. I'm so sorry."

Lelia swallowed a sob. "Everybody made a big deal out of Heather saving Garrett's paintings and burning her face. They . . . the papers, *People* magazine . . . they never even mentioned Jennifer Jones Hamilton. It was as if my Angel didn't exist. I waited for Garrett to say something, anything, but he was totally focused on Heather. The end," she added in the most sardonic voice Ellie had ever heard.

"I'm so sorry," Ellie repeated, thinking how inadequate that sounded. She wondered if Angel's death was Heather's guilty secret—the secret Gideon had mentioned.

Lelia seemed to shake herself from head to toe, like a dog coming in from the rain. She retrieved her cigarette pack from her jeans pocket, then put it back. "Let's visit the kitchen," she said. "I know where Mama hid a chocolate cheesecake."

"Sure. Good idea. I'll have a small sliver."

"Bad idea. I forgot. You're the diet club lady."

"That doesn't mean I can't join you." Ellie linked her arm with Lelia's and began walking toward the dining hall. "Speaking of the kitchen and your mother, do you know why she hates me?"

Lelia didn't try to deny it. "It probably has something to do with Kit."

"That's what Marion said. He said your mom is obsessed with Kit."

"Oh, it's more than that. She thinks Kit's her daughter." Lelia stopped walking, lifted her finger to her head, and twirled a circle. "Mama hasn't been all there since my dad killed himself. You overheard that bit Sunday night, right?"

Without waiting for an answer, she continued. "When Mama's in her right mind, she knows I'm her kid. For one thing, I look like my dad. Same eyes. Same nose and chin. But when Mama's in lalaland, she insists Kit and I were switched at birth."

"Were you born on the same day, in the same hospital?" Ellie asked, trying to hide her stupefaction. Lelia sounded so matter of fact.

"We were born on the same day, but Kit was born at home. Her mom had a difficult pregnancy and took to her bed for the last few months. Gideon used a midwife. The busybodies went bananas, citing all kinds of risks, you know, like the baby might be breach or something, but he insisted and his father concurred. Gideon shopped, cooked, even built a projection room so his wife could see the latest movies." Lelia heaved a deep sigh, her first show of emotion. "Wasn't that nice of him?"

Ellie nodded. She now understood the vestibule's eccentric décor.

"Heather and Garrett hadn't been married three months when she left him," Lelia continued.

"What? Heather left Garrett?"

"Oh, not for good. She came to Aspen, to help out. Garrett stayed in Colorado Springs. He and his dad weren't getting along . . . and that's an understatement. It must have been torture for Heather, not seeing Garrett, but I think she felt she owed Gideon. Everyone knows she was engaged to him, first. At any rate, Kit's mom had been trained as a nurse. When she went into labor, she coached Heather, who delivered the baby. Maybe that's why she never wanted kids. The trauma and all. By the time Gideon returned with the midwife, it was over. But rumor has it that Heather looked worse than Kit's mom. Supposedly, Heather made it through the delivery, even cut the cord, before she fainted dead away."

Lelia shrugged. "Kit's mom never checked into the hospital, so I don't know where Mama got the idea that Kit and I were switched at birth. Marion says it has to do with 'smart genes.' Mama can barely read and write. Kit's not very bright, but she's smart enough to pander to Mama. By the way, Gideon never paid much attention to Kit, so she must be in hog heaven, helping him plan Garrett's wake."

*She's in hog heaven, masquerading as Heather,* Ellie thought. *And her father might not have paid much attention to his daughter, but dollars to doughnuts she's the model for his paintings.*

Ellie had just about reached the dining hall when she had another thought. Lelia hadn't reacted to Kit's drugging of Garrett, and she'd sounded so embittered when she talked about his duplicity after the fire. Could she carry a grudge?

Of course she carried a grudge. She hated Garrett's guts.

She had been riding around the ranch Sunday night, right?

Right.

So suppose she had galloped to the ravine, where she'd found Garrett totally defenseless; semi-conscious and incoher—

Oh, sure, and she just happened to have a sharp knife in her pocket, lest she encounter a mountain lion or grizzly bear.

*Get real,* Ellie thought wryly, *and stop answering your own questions.*

That afternoon the police set up temporary headquarters in the Lonesome Pines front office. There, they interviewed the ranch's occupants—even, briefly, Jonina.

Ellie couldn't wait to expound her Gideon theory, but

she wasn't questioned. Apparently, Peter had vouched for her whereabouts.

Standing outside the main house, frustrated beyond belief, she watched the exit of those who were interviewed. Jonina. Duke. Marion. Rosa. Lelia. Martina. All looked as if they'd just taken a Civil Service exam and failed.

Only one person showed any hint of hostility. Duke Dombroski, who wore his patented scowl. Ellie heard him mutter, "I shoulda said I done it. Then they'd know for sure I didn't do it."

Peter called, just as Ellie—feeling lonely and depressed—was trying to decide whether to watch TV or go to bed. He sounded tired. She asked him about Rudolph Kessler and Serafina Lassiter. He said that McCoy had a new lead on the mysterious woman in the gray hooded sweatshirt. Also, a phone call to Kessler, on the day before the murder, had been made from a pay phone outside a convenience store. But there were way too many fingerprints on the phone equipment, since kids tended to hang out there and smoke pot. Peter still felt the Colorado Springs murders were connected to Garrett's murder, but he was damned if he could figure out how.

Ellie asked if the C.S.P.D. had checked the Hallidays' alibis, and Peter said yes. Kit had attended her uncle's Colorado Springs exhibit, but returned to Aspen the same night. The next day, while Kessler was getting himself killed, Kit had been at the movies with Rosa—an Alfred Hitchcock retrospective. Yes, Rosa had vouched for her. No, Peter didn't remember the name of the film, what difference did it make? Something with James Stewart.

Adrianna had been in Toronto.

Gideon had been at home, whipping up a New Orleansinspired feast for Antonio Banderas. With his wife Melanie, Banderas had arrived at the Hallidays' house around six p.m.—for hors d'oeuvres.

It wasn't an ironclad alibi, Peter admitted, but close enough.

Ellie then told him *her* Gideon theory. Peter said it had "merit," but he was sure the Aspen P.D. would have checked out Gideon's alibi during Garrett's murder, and since Gideon wasn't under arrest, he'd been cleared. "Let the Aspen cops do their thing," Peter said.

So she would, Ellie thought, just before she said, "I love you, too," and hung up the phone. Upon her return to the Springs, she'd "snoop" like crazy, solve Rudolph Kessler's murder and Serafina Lassiter's murder, and—if Peter was right—Garrett's murder.

Fidgety but feeling less depressed, she raided the kitchen, left half her stash in the cottage, then visited the barn. After feeding the horses carrots and apples, she crooned her horse-is-a-horse song to Satan. Then she sang "Goodnight Irene," only she changed the words to "Goodnight Satan."

The other horses listened, of course, but Ellie had the feeling that, if they could, they would have covered their ears with their hooves.

# Forty-Four

Ellie sprawled on a cushioned chaise, one leg bent at the knee. She wore khaki shorts and a T-shirt that stated: THE ONLY THING ACHIEVED WITHOUT EFFORT IS FAILURE. In her lap was a book, on her head Dom's Stetson, shading her face from the sun. Everyone called Marion Dom now, even Duke.

Not far from her chaise lounge, Jackie Robinson and his new bud Becky stalked something—an insect, a squirrel, or maybe one of Gideon Halliday's imaginary mice.

The last two days had passed slowly but steadily, like the downward soar of a hang glider. Not that Ellie had ever been tempted to strap herself into a harness and ride the kitelike thingamabob. To hang glide, one started from the top of a steep cliff or hill. Her analogy came from watching three magpies circle her chaise like black and white feathered kites. Idly, she wondered if "her" birds would return to Colorado Springs when she did, like Capistrano sparrows.

If yes, they were *tourist* magpies.

She no longer felt like a tourist. Or a tenderfoot. Or even a square peg in a square hole. Dom had taught her how to rope a fence post. He had tried to teach her how to dance inside a whirling lasso. But since she'd never been very good at dancing *outside* a lasso, her attempts were laughable.

Wednesday morning she had given Martina and Jonina

their first Weight Winners lesson. Jonina absorbed like a sponge, but, like so many of Ellie's members, Martina had been recalcitrant. And petulant. Until Ellie said Martina couldn't eat the skin of a turkey or chicken.

"Why can't I?" she had protested. "The skin is the best part. I like the skin."

"So do I," Ellie had said. "That's why I'm overweight."

"You? I'd give anything to look like you."

"Ah, but I was once fifty-five pounds heavier."

"You were? Really?"

"I swear. Everybody who works for Weight Winners has lost weight on the program."

After that, Martina stopped complaining.

Following the Weight Winners lecture, the doctor paid Ellie a visit and pronounced her "as good as new." However, he said, she should take it easy for the next few days. So Wednesday afternoon she tested her "good as new" ankle by walking around the ranch, Martina in her wake.

"My heart's broken," Martina huffed, "but at least it'll be a healthy heart. As long as I don't keel over from exhaustion, first."

Exhaustion forgotten, she saddled Pegasus, her favorite horse, and took a long ride. Jonina rode by her side. The two had tried to coax Ellie into joining them, but—unlike childbirth—memories of her fall from Buttermilk hadn't faded. "The doctor said to take it easy for a while," Ellie told them, pasting a mournful, "I'd-rather-ride-horses-than-eat-chocolate" expression on her face.

Fortified with the other half of her stolen food bribes, she visited the barn Wednesday night and Thursday morning. Jonina insisted on coming with her, to keep her company. Yeah, right, and Ellie had a bridge in Brooklyn for sale. Jonina's arm now sported a "J & D" nail polish tattoo—a dead giveaway.

The child didn't know how to play hard to get, Ellie thought with a smile. But then hard to get didn't always work and it was, in a sense, deceitful. She hadn't played hard to get with Peter. Au contraire.

Satan whinnied and tossed his head at Ellie and Jonina's approach, but he didn't flatten his ears or bare his teeth. And although he ate a carrot and nuzzled Ellie's pocket for "his" apple, he seemed to prefer her silly horse-is-a-horse and ride-a-cock-horse songs. She added *Love and Marriage* (go together like a *horse* and carriage) to her repertoire. She had always loved the musical adaptation of *Our Town*, starring Frank Sinatra. Her ex-husband despised *Our Town*. He felt it was a "cheap play" since there weren't any elaborate sets or costumes. Tony didn't "get it," had never really gotten it, but Ellie didn't regret her marriage. Without Tony, there'd be no Mick.

Once she had figured out that Buttermilk liked to be scratched underneath her whiskery chin, the white mare became Ellie's best bud. In fact, the only horse she couldn't make friends with was the haughty, regal Merrylegs. "If Queen Elizabeth's carriage had broken down and Merrylegs had been there," Ellie told Jonina, "Merrylegs would have ridden Queen Elizabeth to Banbury Cross."

Jonina, who worshiped the beautiful Appaloosa, had suggested with a giggle that they string bells around Merrylegs' fetlocks and hooves. Jonina had also introduced Ellie to Dom's cat, Stanley Hastings. "He won't let anyone pet him," Jonina said, "but you've charmed Satan, so maybe you can tame Stanley."

"The only cat song I know is 'The Ballad of Cat Ballou,' " Ellie had replied, "and I don't think that'll cut it."

"What about a song from *Cats*, Norrie? Daddy took me to see *Cats* when it came to Denver, and then he bought me the sheet music so I could play it on my guitar."

"You sing *Cats* to the cat," Ellie had suggested. "I don't remember the words."

So Ellie sang "a horse is a horse" and Jonina sang about Macavity the mystery cat, while Satan looked ecstatic and Stanley Hastings looked skeptical.

Jonina soon gave up singing, but she still wanted to talk about *Cats*, which she said was the best musical ever. "Did you know that the license plate on the car at the back of the stage says 'TSE 1' for T.S. Eliot?" she asked Ellie.

"I never saw the show, kiddo, but I've listened to the soundtrack."

"I know every song by heart, Norrie, and I've studied up on T.S. Eliot's *Old Possum's Book of Practical Cats*. The words 'Jellicle cat' came from when Eliot's niece tried to say 'dear little cat' and the words 'Pollicle dog' came from when she tried to say 'poor little dog.' Isn't that fascinating?"

Ellie agreed it was fascinating. "You are I are kindred spirits," she told Jonina. "Trivia nuts. If you want to try out for the teen tournament on *Jeopardy!*, I'll go with you."

"Would you, Norrie? Wow, thanks. If I made the show, that would show them."

Ellie didn't need to ask who.

Kit had taken a leave of absence from the ranch. Rather than shovel manure, she helped her dad with the "Garrett Halliday Memorial Exhibit."

*Which begins tonight at the gallery*, Ellie thought, sitting up and swatting a fly with her book.

Another, more flamboyant service would be held tomorrow afternoon, at a church renowned for its stained glass, and Kit had been put in charge of that, too.

Aspen flower shops had been duly notified.

A choir was being flown in from Utah (along with, some said, Robert Redford).

There were pews reserved for celebrity guests.

Sandwiches and cold drinks had been prepped for the TV crews.

Following the church service, people would once again congregate at the art exhibit, where, Ellie presumed, Garrett Halliday paintings would sell like hotcakes. Or, if her supposition was correct, *Gideon* Halliday paintings would sell like hotcakes.

She didn't miss Kit one bit. Every time she thought about the girl, Ellie felt renewed anger at the deadly "prank"—the so-called "joke" that Kit and Beth had concocted. Beth had paid the price for her foolishness, but Kit had managed to get away scot-free.

*Garrett's killer seems to have gotten away scot-free, too,* Ellie thought, as she slathered more sunscreen on her arms and legs.

Yesterday, she and Martina had taken Jonina shopping, having decided the pretty teen needed "something special" for the memorial service. Dom had invited her as his date— her first date, she confided shyly.

Combing the boutiques, they found a pair of black jeans, not too loose, not too tight. Rather than a pocketful of Pooh, silver beads adorned the sides of the legs, forming stars, moons, and galaxies. Jonina wanted a glitzy top to wear with the jeans, preferably a red-sequined, stretchy number that left her midriff bare, but Ellie and Martina talked her into going with a charcoal-gray turtleneck shirt.

"Don't you think it's too . . . well, plain?" Jonina had asked.

"Not with this," Ellie had said, handing over her fox amulet.

"Oh my gosh, I love it," Jonina had squealed, sounding like the fifteen-year-old she was.

Martina wanted to visit the boutique where she'd found her discount sweater. As soon as they entered the store, a heavy red cardigan with appliquéd horses called Ellie's name, loud and clear. But even with fifty percent off, it cost too much. Grinning like a Cheshire Cat, Martina bought the silk-lined sweater for Ellie. When she protested, Martina said, "It's a loan. After I lose enough weight, I'll take it back."

Since Martina had paid for the clothes, Ellie insisted on taking them all out for dinner. Peter had once mentioned a satirical cabaret theatre that included gourmet dining, and she was dying to try it.

She and Jonina ordered Tai Spice Wild Salmon with sesame ginger sauce. Martina played it safe with Slow-Roasted Prime Rib. And they all shared an appetizer of Quail and Shitake Mushroom Wontons.

After the plates had been cleared away, they were entertained by the wait staff, who staged an elaborate show of songs, dances, and skits, centered on current events, famous people, and politics.

Ellie asked for the check, and was told it had already been taken care of.

Martina beamed. "They add the gratuity," she whispered, "but our waiter was so cute, I added a wee bit more."

*No wonder Our Waiter sang his ballad to Martina,* Ellie thought. By Martina's standards, "a wee bit more" could have been anything from ten dollars to a hundred dollars.

When Ellie protested again, Martina said, "You sound

like a broken record. Don't be a party pooper. I haven't had so much fun in years."

Jonina giggled at "party pooper," an expression she'd never heard before. "I'll have to remember that for Ryan," she said, a wicked gleam in her eye. She hugged Martina. "Thank you so much. This was absolutely, positively the best day and night of my whole life." Then, as if she didn't want to be disloyal to her father, she said, "Not counting *Cats*."

Jackie Robinson leapt into Ellie's lap, effectively ending her reverie.

Reaching beneath the cat's belly, she rescued her book, a mystery novel by Parnell Hall. Dom had loaned it to her, so she could "see where Stanley Hastings got his name," whereupon Ellie decided that Dom's reading-a-book-alibi had sounded valid, after all. Dom had also suggested another riding lesson, but Ellie told him she "wasn't up to it," a small fib. Her ankle felt better than new and she didn't fear horses any more. On the contrary, she adored every horse in the Lonesome Pines stable, especially Satan. She just didn't want to push her luck.

Peter had called an hour ago, to tell her he was on his way. Traffic, however, was fierce. So if he didn't arrive at the ranch in time, he'd meet her at the gallery. Poor Peter. Tomorrow they'd drive back to Colorado Springs. So much for his stress-free vacation. So much for any vacation at all. She vowed to finish writing her mystery novel. Then she'd sell it to a publisher, become rich and famous, and treat Peter to a cruise. Once he was aboard ship, it wouldn't be so easy to lure him back to his precinct.

After Peter's phone call, Ellie had asked if she could hitch a ride with Martina. But Martina said she wanted to ride in the ranch van to "save money on gas." Ellie couldn't believe it. Yesterday the generous author had spent a fortune on clothes and dinner without even blinking. But then, every person seemed to have his or her own personal glitch.

Gideon Halliday wanted to be Richard Burton.

Kit Halliday wanted to be smart.

Adrianna wanted to make love in a hotel.

Lelia wanted—

"Norrie, are you asleep?"

Ellie took off her hat and looked up at Jonina. "No, sweetie, I'm daydreaming."

"It's almost time to get ready."

"Define 'almost,' " Ellie said with a smile.

"Less than an hour." Jonina sat on the ground, Indian-style, and Becky immediately curled up in her lap. "Daddy just called. I told him Martina will drive me home on Monday. She wants to attend the church service tomorrow while I start packing our stuff, and she wants to avoid 'Sunday drivers.'

"Mom's better," Jonina continued. "Ryan and Stevie are with Grandma Feldman. They'll stay there for the summer and go to day camp. Daddy wants me to go to camp, too. He suggested an equestrian camp or music camp, but I said I wanted to go to a Weight Winners camp." She grinned impishly. "I've already checked it out on Martina's computer. The lady I e-mailed said if I lose weight and keep it off, next year I can come back as a counselor. I'd like to do that, you know, help kids."

"You're still a kid, kiddo," Ellie teased. "But you're a beautiful, grownup kid, and it's time to get ready for your first 'real date.' "

Spilling Becky out of her lap, Jonina jumped to her feet. "Meet you at the van," she called over her shoulder, as she headed for her cottage.

"You bet," Ellie said, "unless your Uncle Pete makes it in time."

She dawdled in the shower. She shaved her legs, even though they were as smooth as glass. She towel-dried her hair, then glanced at the cuckoo clock.

The van would leave in less than fifteen minutes—and still no Peter.

Through her open window, Ellie heard the crunch of gravel and the sound of a car's engine.

Dressed in her Lonesome Pines robe, she opened the cottage door and peeked outside.

Martina stood there, smiling her Cheshire Cat smile. Next to her stood Jonina and Dom. In front of her was a white stretch limousine. "It's yours for the night, kids," she said. She stared at Dom. "You'll behave like a gentleman, agreed?"

"Yes, ma'am."

"There's no liquor, just juice and pop." She hugged Jonina, who was speechless. "Now, off with you. Have fun, but not too much fun. Get the picture?"

Ellie took a few steps backwards, until she was hidden from view. This was Martina's moment and she didn't want to spoil it.

Quickly, she clothed herself in black slacks, a black turtleneck shirt, and her new sweater.

The ranch van—mechanically sound and cleansed within an inch of its life—was waiting when Ellie—mentally sound and cleansed within an inch of her life—stepped outside her cottage.

Duke drove, and even though it wasn't Saturday, he had bathed too.

# Forty-Five

The sky was cloudy, hiding the moon, and inside the van, nobody spoke.

Martina and Ellie shared the seat behind Duke. Martina's joy at her surprise gift for Jonina had faded, and she now looked subdued and somber.

Seated behind Martina, Lelia fiddled with the buttons on her blouse. She wouldn't meet Ellie's gaze. Maybe she regretted Tuesday's confession.

If Rosa's eyes had been laser beams, she would have burned the back of Ellie's neck, and Ellie remembered her reaction, following their kitchen encounter. *If cooks could kill.*

After running a stop sign, challenging a yellow stoplight, and narrowly missing two elderly bike riders, Duke gave the steering wheel a vicious twist, turned the corner, and pulled up in front of a two-story brick building.

Ellie had expected to see a flashing neon sign, not unlike Vegas. But all she saw was a discreet brass plaque, engraved with the words PHOENIX GALLERY. For a moment she was at a loss. *Phoenix* Gallery? Then she understood. The phoenix, a legendary bird, had burned itself to ashes. Whereupon, it had risen, alive, from the ashes. Had Heather named the gallery? Or Garrett? And, as Peter would say, what difference did it make?

Duke "dismounted" from the van and slid its side door open.

338

Lelia, very pale, said, "I've changed my mind. I'll wait here."

"Don't be silly," Rosa said. "Nobody knows, or cares, who you are."

"Mama, if I go inside I'll throw up."

"No, you won't."

With a moan, Lelia hugged her belly.

Ellie stepped out of the van. "Lelia, come with me. Now!"

The gallery's plate-glass display window was nearly obscured by people milling about. Ellie led the whimpering girl around the corner of the building, into a narrow alley. Spying a trashcan, she encircled Lelia's waist and practically dragged the girl over to it.

"There you go, sweetie."

"I can't," Lelia said. "I thought I could but I can't."

"You can't throw up, or you can't attend the memorial?"

"Throw up." She shook her head, her long, loose hair flying every which way. "I can't attend the memorial, either. I thought I'd play it cool, pretend I was Jennifer Jones in *Madame Bovary*, but I'll lose it, I know I will, especially when I hear them glorifying Garrett."

As Ellie relaxed her hold on Lelia's waist, something in the trashcan caught her eye. A small painting, maybe six by eight inches. A G.H. portrait of a red-haired woman. Although the right side of the woman's face had been lacerated, the painting looked familiar. But, for the life of her, Ellie couldn't remember where she'd seen it before.

*What a find*, she thought. If she extracted the canvas very carefully, there might be fingerprints. Oh, God, what she wouldn't give for a paper bag. Or a pair of rubber gloves, the thin ones, the ones that CSI cops always seemed to have on hand.

"May I be of some assistance?" As Gideon Halliday stepped out of the shadows, the moon stepped out from behind the clouds.

"Where . . . where did you come from?" Ellie stammered.

"The gallery has a side door." He retrieved his pipe from a side pocket. "I'm playing truant."

Lelia groaned.

Gideon walked closer to the trashcan. "Lelia, my dear, is that you? Are you ill?"

"She's about to throw up," Ellie said, trying to keep her gaze away from the can, "so you'd better step back. I'd hate to see your tux ruined."

"You forgot your lighter, Dad." The side door opened, revealing a slash of brightness. And Kit. "What's going on?" Kit shut the door and walked forward. She wore skin-tight, black leather pants that hugged her hips, and a stretchy, red-sequined top, very much like the top Ellie and Martina had talked Jonina out of. In between red sequins and black leather, a diamond winked from Kit's bellybutton.

"Lelia's sick to her stomach," Gideon said.

"Oh, the poor thing," Kit said, but her tone of voice implied that Lelia's illness was on a par with the third loss of Paris Hilton's virginity.

Ellie looked at Gideon. "Perhaps you could find someone to drive Lelia back to the ranch."

"Don't be silly," Kit said. "Our house is five minutes away and we have meds for nausea."

*I'll bet you do,* Ellie thought, stepping farther away from the trashcan. *And I'll bet they're right next to your Valium stash.*

"Kit, fetch Richard," said Gideon. As his daughter re-entered the gallery, he placed his arm around Lelia's shoulder and began guiding her toward a parking lot at the rear of the building. "Richard is my friend, Lelia. He's also my lawyer and a jolly good fellow. He'll take excellent care of you."

"Lelia," Ellie said, "do you want to lie down at Gideon's house? Or would you prefer to go back to the ranch?"

"I don't want . . . to be . . . any trouble."

"You're no trouble. I'll go back to the ranch with you and—"

"The house . . . fine." Still hugging her belly, she turned her face toward Gideon. "Thanks."

"You're welcome, my dear. Here comes Richard."

Like Gideon, the attorney wore a tuxedo. Unlike Gideon, he didn't wear a French beret. Shedding his tux jacket, he put it around Lelia's shoulders.

"Thanks," she said again. She hung her head. "Ashamed."

"There's nothing to be ashamed of," Richard said. "Let's find my car, shall we?"

"Gideon, you forgot to tell Lelia to stay downstairs," Ellie almost hissed, as soon as the lawyer and the sick girl were out of earshot. "Aren't you afraid she'll go exploring and find Heather's vacant bedroom?"

"Delving into things that are none of one's business is *your* cup of tea," Gideon retorted. "Your métier, so to speak. Did you honestly believe I knew nothing of your little venture inside my studio?"

"Garrett's studio."

"Do you think I'm that naïve? Or stupid?"

"Garrett's studio," she repeated stubbornly.

"Yes, of course, *Garrett's* studio," he said with a scowl.

"You look like you looked last Monday," Ellie said, "when you ordered me out of your house. Are you going to ask me to leave your gallery?"

"Garrett's gallery."

"No, Gideon, it's your gallery. That much I'm sure of. Do you want me to leave?"

"Not at all, my dear. I will, however, request that you enter through the front door. The side door is an emergency exit. I use it when I want to escape unseen." He held up his pipe. "Aspenites have an avid aversion to smokers." He tamped the pipe's bowl with his finger. "Kit smokes out here, too. Cigarettes. She picked up the dreadful habit from her Colorado Springs roommate, a girl with an incongruous name."

*Moony,* thought Ellie, watching him pat down his pockets. She stifled an impatient grimace. Kit had walked away with his lighter. Hopefully, he didn't have another one. If he lit up his pipe and stuck around to suck its stem, she couldn't raid the trash can and retrieve the telltale canvas.

Suddenly, she recalled where she'd seen the painting before. On the dashboard of Garrett's car. "Everybody else carries around Saint Christopher," Garrett liked to say. "I prefer Saint Heather."

But that was five, six, maybe even seven years ago. Which meant it was an old painting, not a new painting. Which meant somebody was slashing *old* paintings, just like she'd told Peter.

*Very good, Ellie, go to the head of the class.*

*And now, my dear, how, exactly, does that brilliant revelation solve Garrett's murder?*

"I don't have a clue," she muttered, heading back to street. "All I know is that somebody 'salvaged' the painting from Garrett's car, then slashed St. Heather's face."

But who?

Somebody who had access to the car, of course.

Unless Garrett, himself, had taken the painting from the dashboard, following Heather's flight.

Even if he had, somebody who lived in Aspen—*and had access to the ranch*—was slashing Garrett's old paintings.

An Ellie Bernstein "motivational suspect list" would include Kit, Gideon, Adrianna, and Lelia.

Except, Adrianna was in Toronto when Polly perished.

Delete Adrianna.

Lelia had access to *Polly Wants a Quaker*, but she couldn't have trashed the dashboard painting.

Delete Lelia.

That left Gideon or Kit.

And one big, unanswered question. *Why?*

# Forty-Six

"What took you so long?" Martina leaned against the van, illegally parked in front of a fire hydrant. She was dressed in one of her new outfits, black slacks and a white silk blouse. Around her neck was an elaborate necklace of beads and feathers. Arms crossed, she tapped her toes.

"Sorry," Ellie whispered.

"Why are you whispering? How's Lelia?"

"She's okay. Gideon Halliday told his tame attorney to drive her to the Halliday house. She'll lie down a while. Then she should feel as good as new. Why is your forehead all crinkled?"

"Who the hell is Gideon Halliday?"

"Garrett's brother. Oh my God, don't tell me you didn't know he had a brother."

"He never said anything about a brother, or anybody else in the family. I mean, I knew Kit was his niece, but—"

"Martina, don't you watch the news?"

"Never. It's too depressing. Especially when I'm writing. Especially when I'm writing a book set in the nineteenth century. I check the Weather channel every morning. Sometimes I watch the History channel. And I'm addicted to *South Park*. But if I watch the news, I lose my focus. Why do you ask?"

"For five days every newscast has highlighted Gideon . . . never mind that now. I have to figure out some way to find a pair of rubber gloves. Or a paper bag."

"I have a paper bag."

"You do? Where?"

"In the van. Under the seat. Don't look at me like that. I bought another gift for you, but then I thought it was too . . . presumptuous. I thought you'd think I was too . . . conceited."

"Martina, please show me what the heck you're talking about."

"Good thing this isn't locked," she grumbled, sliding open the van's side door, bending forward and running her hand underneath the seat.

"Of course it isn't locked," Ellie said. "It just got back from the mechanic and it's clean as a whistle. What on earth could somebody possibly steal?"

"The van. They could steal the van." Martina slid the door shut. Then she handed the bag to Ellie.

Ellie reached in and pulled out a framed, professionally rendered photo. Marty Blue's chin rested upon her knuckles. She wore a straw hat festooned with fake flowers. Around her neck was a pink boa. Ellie handed the photo back, but kept the bag.

"You don't like it," Martina said. "It's the boa, right? Pink is such a bad color for me. It makes me look fat. Like Miss Piggy. I told the photographer—"

"I love the boa. I love the hat. I love the frame. I'll hang you on my wall as soon as I get home. But right now I have to dig a painting out of the trash, so please put the photo back in the van."

After Martina had complied, Ellie sneaked a peek around the corner of the building. "Okay," she whispered, "he's gone."

"Who's gone, and why are you whispering?"

"Gideon Halliday, and I'm whispering because I don't want anyone to hear me."

"Cool. Where are we going?"

"To the trash can." Ellie stepped into the alley. "That one over there."

"Why didn't you say so in the first place?" Martina scurried past Ellie and stopped in front of the can. "Now what?" she whispered.

"Don't touch anything."

"Are you crazy? Why would I touch trash?"

"Keep your voice down. I meant the painting. Don't touch the painting."

"What painting?"

Ellie peered into the can. "It's not there. Shit!"

"I've never heard you cuss before." Martina quirked an eyebrow.

" 'Damn' doesn't cut it." Envisioning the lighter Kit had brought outside and Gideon's subsequent search of his pockets, Ellie sniffed. "Nobody set it on fire."

"Set what on fire? The trash?"

"No. The painting. So it's probably hidden inside the gallery."

"Oh, goody, a mystery to solve. Marty Blue loves to solve mysteries."

"Not on your life, Marty Blue." Crumpling the paper bag, Ellie chucked it into the trash. "We'll wait for Peter. He'll handle it."

"Did the painting have any letters glued to it?"

Ellie shook her head. "Not this time. And that's another thing. All the letters on the Lonesome Pines sign are missing, but so far the perp has only used three. Where are the other letters?"

"I've an idea. We'll walk inside the gallery together, nod-

ding graciously to all and sundry. Then you'll keep everybody entertained while Marty Blue searches for the
missing—"

"And how, exactly, am I supposed to keep everybody entertained?"

"Sing."

"You've *got* to be kidding."

"The horses like your voice. Jonina said—"

"The horses do not like my voice. The only horse who
likes my voice is Satan, and he has a tin ear."

"Then plunk yourself down in front of the most erotic
painting you can find and tell diet club anecdotes. I, for
one, find them fascinating. While you talk, Marty Blue
will—"

"Stop referring to yourself as two different people!" Ellie
linked her arm with Martina's. "Leave Marty Blue in the
alley, please. We'll pick her up after the eulogy."

They turned the corner and began plowing through the
outsiders. Martina fanned her face with her fingers. "Mobs
make me sweat," she groused.

"Don't you give talks to mobs? About your books, I
mean."

"Sure, but I'm always behind a podium."

"Oh, look," Ellie said. "There's Kate Hudson. Peter said
if I saw movie stars, I should act cool, not make a big deal
out of it. Celebs put their panties on one leg at a time, he
said. I said they wear thongs, not panties, and he said . . .
oh my God, over there! Look, Martina, it's Kevin Costner."

As she crossed the gallery's threshold, Ellie saw Gideon
holding court. His tuxedo hugged his faultless body, but his
silly beret ruined the effect somewhat.

"I must be dreaming," Ellie said, placing her hand over
her heart like a soldier who watches a parade flag go by.

"There's Hillary Swank. And Clint Eastwood. Don't you think he's drop-dead gorgeous? His face shows so much character. And look at his eyes. You could drown—"

Martina screamed.

Ellie thought the scream sounded very loud, but only a few people glanced their way. Maybe the residents of Aspen were accustomed to tourists shrieking at the sight of celebs. Certainly the celebs were accustomed to tourists shriek—

"He's alive!" Martina screeched. "But he can't be alive." Then she turned and fled.

Ellie followed her outside.

"Sit down," Ellie said. "No, dammit, there's no place to sit. Yes, there is. Sit on the fire hydrant."

"Are you crazy? It's dripping with dog urine."

"Then lean against the van," Ellie said, before she realized her friend was no longer hysterical.

"That rat bastard," Martina said, her voice angry but composed. "That rat bastard is *Gideon* Halliday, right?"

Ellie nodded.

"He let me think he was Garrett." Martina waved her hands in the air, as if orchestrating the music for Ingrid Beaumont's cult concerto, *Speedballs*. "No, he didn't. Not really. I never actually called him Garrett. But he let me *assume* he was Garrett. Oh, God, he didn't even do that. Wait a minute. He said he was the artist for one of my book covers, *Ashes to Ash*—"

"That's true, Martina. He used the initial 'G' . . . but it was for Gideon, not Garrett."

"So when he said he didn't have a wife—"

"He was telling the truth. His wife died a long time ago. Her car went off a cliff." Ellie shuddered at the thought. "Hey, look on the bright side. Your only love isn't dead."

"Goody-goody for my only love. I don't need him anymore, and I don't want him." She looked smug. "I had a phone call this afternoon, from my cute waiter."

"The waiter at the cabaret?" When she nodded, Ellie said, "How did he get your number?"

"I gave it to him when I signed the credit card slip."

"You plan to sleep with him?"

"No. Of course not. I plan to party with him. And the rest of the wait staff. They get a night off, you know. I spoke to Duke. He'll have his barbeque. I'll host it, pay for everything."

"When?"

"Sunday."

"Oh, I wish I could be there."

"Ask your cop if he'll stay an extra day."

Ellie sighed. "Even if Peter didn't have to work, I have a diet club meeting Monday morning, and I can't miss two Mondays in a row. Speaking of Peter, where the heck is he? He said traffic was bad, but it can't be *that* bad."

"Maybe he drove to the ranch and crashed. Why don't we look at some paintings, schmooze a few celebs, and happy-trails it back to the Pines? If Duke wants to stay, I'll call a cab. My treat."

"No, my treat, except I hope the cab driver doesn't charge extra for three passengers."

"Three?"

"We can't leave Marty Blue in the alley."

"I never leave Marty Blue anywhere," Martina said. "I couldn't even if I wanted to. She's the one who writes my books."

As Ellie reentered the gallery, she said, "Maybe *Martina Brustein* should try writing a book."

"Martina Brustein can't write."

"Oh, I doubt . . ." Ellie paused to squint at the opposite

wall. "Martina, see that painting over there? The one with the lion? I want to look at it up close."

"Go ahead. I need to find the restroom."

As Ellie walked toward the canvas that had hung on the wall at the Colorado Springs exhibit, she wondered why Gideon had chosen to display *Dessert Song,* so different from the bold expressionism of Garrett's more recent works, assuming they *were* Garrett's works.

Advancing closer, she saw why. The tag that had read NFS last week now read a hundred and fifty thousand dollars. And if the painting hadn't sold by the time Gideon announced Heather's death, the price would probably go up another fifty, maybe even seventy-five, thousand. Ellie was willing to bet the farm he'd say Heather had died of a broken heart, which would make Garrett's early works practically priceless.

Ellie's mind raced. *I own an early Garrett Halliday painting. Oh my God, I could sell* Pussy Willow *for a quarter of a million dollars, maybe more.*

*Or I could die at an early age, killed by whomever wants Heather Halliday's face destroyed.*

*Good thing Melody used my maiden name in the brochure, rather than Bernstein.*

She wondered if her maiden name would protect her.

Not if she wanted to sell her painting.

*Which is undoubtedly how Rudolph Kessler met his end. Peter said Kessler put an ad in the paper.*

So it was really quite simple. When she returned to the Springs, she'd put ads in all the papers, offering to sell *Pussy Willow.* Then she'd just wait and see who showed up at her door.

But first she'd ask the FBI—or even better, Clint Eastwood—to hide in her kitchen.

# Forty-Seven

Stepping closer, until she was almost on top of the painting, Ellie noticed something she hadn't noticed before, and she'd be willing to bet that her painting, *Pussy Willow*, had the same incongruity.

Or should she say modus operandi?

As she examined the bathtub-woman's red hair and the lion's tawny mane, she saw that every brush stroke slanted just a little to the right, as if the wind blew (just a little) from the left.

Except, Garrett hadn't painted wind. Not one blue-tinged frond stirred, not one tuft on the lion's tail whisked—not even a little bit.

Art critics might recognize the slight slant. After all, they analyzed and dissected an artist's technique. However, they would have shrugged it off as insignificant.

Ellie wasn't an art critic, but she *was* a leftie.

Furthermore, she was a leftie who had been trained to use her right hand.

And she didn't find the slant irrelevant. Because it re-minded her of the slanted handwriting in Garrett's sketch-book—the sketchbook she had discovered inside his studio.

Garrett was right-handed. Ellie knew that for an indis-putable fact. How many times had she seen him lift a fork to his mouth? He'd even cut his meat with his right hand, then switch the fork from his left hand to his right hand.

She remembered telling Dom that her mother had tied her left hand behind her back. Dom had asked why, and she had said that Mom's Mom had done it to Mom.

What about Gideon? Had his "mum" done the same thing to him?

Ellie didn't think so. Because every time she'd seen Gideon hold his pipe, or raise it to his mouth, he'd used his left hand.

She stepped back, almost to the center of the room. Then she looked around. A few feet beyond the hallway that led to the restrooms, a familiar painting hung on the wall. It had been ornately framed. It depicted a girl on a black horse. And it was the perfect painting to judge against *Dessert Song* because, while the girl's hair was hidden by a kerchief, the horse's mane and tail weren't.

Ellie walked over to the painting. The first thing she saw was that its title had been changed. *There's No Business Like Shoe Business* was now *Ashes to Ashes, Lust to Lust*.

She scrutinized the horse's mane and tail. She wouldn't swear on a stack of Bibles, or even a stack of *Da Vinci Codes*, that the fibrous black strands slanted to the left, but unlike the lion's mane in *Dessert Song*, the stallion's mane didn't slope to the right.

Once again she noted "Cinderella's" resemblance to Kit.

Then she saw the discreet price tag: NFS.

Surprised, she took a step backward, and came up against something that felt like a brick wall, only a tad more pliable.

"You're treading on my toes," said a familiar voice.

"Oh, I'm sorry." Ellie stepped forward, then made an about-face. She had been so absorbed by her *Ashes to Ashes* inspection, she hadn't even felt Gideon's dark presence. As she met his gaze, she blurted, "How come this painting isn't for sale?"

"It's a gift."

"For whom?"

"Martina. She more than deserves it. I've spent many a pleasurable hour in her company."

"Why didn't you tell her you were you?"

"Excuse me?"

"Oh, please. Don't pretend to misunderstand. Martina thought you were Garrett. You had to know that. She even left a message for 'Garrett' on the gallery's answering machine. It was her birthday, Gideon, and she wanted to celebrate it with *you*. And don't tell me you didn't check your messages."

"I didn't. Garrett did."

"The poor woman believed you dead," Ellie continued, her temper simmering. "The least you could have done was pick up a phone and—"

"Ruin a splendid relationship."

"What do you mean?"

"Spiteful words would have been exchanged. Feelings would have been hurt." Gideon pulled his pipe out of his tux pocket. "Martina wanted a commitment. She tried to hide it, but she was as transparent as glass. And a commitment was the last thing I wanted."

Ellie's temper boiled over. "Of course you didn't want a commitment, you rat. It would have spoiled your game plan."

"What game plan?"

"Wait a minute. You said Garrett checked the gallery's messages. Did he write Martina's message in his sketchbook?"

"*My* sketchbook. But you've already figured that out, haven't you?"

353

"I'm surprised *he* didn't keep the rendezvous," Ellie said bitterly. "He could have sampled Martina's wares."

"Marty Blue's wares. But Garrett was already in way over his head, my dear, what with Beth demanding his undivided attention."

"And he had a dinner to cook." Again, Ellie heard the bitterness in her voice.

"Garrett couldn't boil an egg," said Gideon, "and he was drinking vodka like it was bottled water. I presume he was worried about Heather, how he'd keep her vanishing act a secret from you. My guess is that he planned to meet you at the door and suggest an outing at a local restaurant. How he'd stop you from prying ad nauseam is anybody's guess, but if he had told me he planned to serve you and your companion dinner, I'd have cooked up a feast. I'm a gourmet chef."

"A gift from God?" she asked sarcastically.

"No. A diploma from Le Cordon Bleu."

"So you really didn't know about the dinner party. Well, that shoots my theory all to hell."

"What theory?"

She clamped her mouth shut, even though she was dying to tell him.

Gideon said, "Does my 'spoiled game plan' have anything to do with your shot-to-hell theory?"

Ellie's mind raced. If she spilled the beans, what could he do to her? He wouldn't *dare* stab her in front of Kevin Costner and Clint Eastwood, not to mention Hillary Swank, who could probably knock him flat with one punch. He might decide to get rid of Ellie later, but later she'd have Peter and the Aspen P.D. to protect her. Or he might simply laugh and say, "It's your word against mine."

Gideon was staring at her, waiting for an answer. He had

returned his pipe to his pocket and his fingers snapped silently, rhythmically, in time to a melody only he could hear. She wished she could hear it, too. She wished she could probe his mind. "As a matter of fact," she said, "the spoilage of your game plan has a *lot* to do with my theory."

"Then I wonder what it would take for you to tell me your theory. How about ten percent off one of Garrett's paintings?"

"One of *your* paintings, Gideon, and even with a ten percent discount, I'd have to sell my house."

He laughed. "I can already tell that your supposition will knock my socks off . . . or as Adrianna would say, 'Sock my knockers off.' "

"You just made that up, right? I truly admire your wit, Gideon."

"Thank you. If you ever decide to give your companion the boot, my dear, I'm at your disposal."

"If you ever decide to stop calling me 'my dear,' my dear, I might take you up on it."

Holy cow, she was playing the same game she'd always played with Garrett—a light, easy banter, imbued with innuendoes. How had Gideon evolved into his brother so quickly?

Gideon laughed again. Then, cupping her elbow, he walked her over to the only seat in the gallery; a window seat that was partially blocked by an exquisitely handsome man.

"Pardon me, Kurt," Gideon said, "but my lovely friend and I need a few moments alone."

"Sure, Gideon. By the way, Goldie and I want to talk to you about the lion painting."

*Oh my God,* thought Ellie. *Kurt Russell.*

As she watched Kurt join Goldie Hawn and Kate

Hudson, Gideon said, "Sit down, my dear."

She understood what Gideon was doing. He wanted to loom above her, intimidate her, but that was all he'd be able to accomplish. If he threatened her in any way, she'd scream her bloody head off.

Except . . . no one had responded to Martina's screams.

Suppose people ignored Ellie's screams? Or suppose Gideon pressed his hand against her mouth? Then she'd struggle. She'd bite, kick, scratch, fight him tooth and—

Gideon would never make a scene in front of his "guests."

As she sat, or rather perched on the window seat, he said, "Tell me your theory."

Before she could begin, Kit approached. "You don't have a drink, Norrie," she said. "Can I get you one?"

Gideon, Ellie saw, was silently—and impatiently—snapping his fingers. "No, thanks, Kit," Ellie replied. "I didn't have time for supper and I don't want to drink on an empty stomach."

*A blatant fib,* she thought. She'd noshed all afternoon. She had even eaten one of the apples she'd stashed for Satan. But, like Gideon, she wanted the girl to go away.

"We'll be serving food soon," Kit said. "We're just waiting for the caterers to arrive."

"Then I'll wait for the caterers."

"How about a soda?"

"Do you have Diet Coke? Or Diet Pepsi?"

"I'm pretty sure we do. I'll be right back."

"Perhaps we should go outside," Gideon muttered.

"No." Ellie tensed, then, with an effort, untensed. "I'm thirsty and Kit said she'd be right back."

"Very well." He stilled his snapping fingers. "I apologize

if I sound irascible, but I'm keen to hear this hypothesis of yours."

So she told him, every word, down to the last detail. She averted her gaze from his, afraid she might falter, but once she'd finished, she stared, defiantly, up at his face.

His eyes crinkled at the corners—not exactly the reaction she had anticipated.

*The rat-bastard was smiling!*

"Which words didn't you understand?" Seething, she rose to her feet. "The part where Garrett displayed the canvases *you* painted? The part where you killed your brother? Or perhaps it was the part where you hid your wet hair under a beret."

"My hair was quite dry," he said. "I wear a beret because I'm going bald. And if you ever repeat that to a living soul, I'll have to kill you." His smile grew even broader. "I must admit you did quite well. Obviously, you're not just a pretty face. Aside from the dinner party that I supposedly knew about, you only made two minor mistakes."

"Here you go, Norrie. The stupid waiters forgot to chill the cans, so I poured your soda into this." Kit handed Ellie a frosted beer mug. "Now you can pretend you're drinking dark beer."

"Why would I do that?"

"Don't you think it's a bit *immature* to drink soda at a party?"

"I didn't know this was a party, Kit. I thought it was a solemn occasion. A wake for your uncle."

"A wake is a party, isn't it, Dad?"

"In the sense that it's often accompanied by festivity. Technically, a wake is a watch held over the body of a dead person, prior to burial. So you and Norrie are both right."

"Well, festivity means food, Dad, and the caterers are finally here, setting up in the room where we do our framing. Norrie, would you like me to bring you something to eat?"

"No, thanks. I'll help myself later."

"Okay, but let me know if you need anything. Anything at all."

The girl seemed eager to please, thought Ellie. Too eager. She had most likely planned to sprinkle arsenic on Ellie's hors d'oeuvres. That way, she could have Peter all to herself.

Speaking of Peter, where the heck was he?

As if she'd asked her question out loud, Kit said, "Oh, I almost forgot. Pete called. There was a *huge* accident on the highway and it's been stop and go ever since. Mostly stop."

"Peter called here?" *Of course he called here,* thought Ellie, watching Kit nod her head. *If I live to be a hundred, I'll never get used to carrying a cell phone. Where the heck did I leave it this time?*

"Pete said he was about to cross the Pass," Kit said, "so he should be here soon."

"Independence Pass?" Ellie tried to keep her voice on an even keel. "In the dark?"

"Everybody drives it in the dark," said Kit. "I drove it myself, after my uncle's exhibit."

"No you didn't." Just like last Sunday morning, at the corral, Dom appeared as if by magic.

"Yes, I did." Kit voice sounded petulant. "I wanted to get back in time to catch some sleep before Rosa and I went to the movies."

"No, you didn't," Dom insisted. "Don't you remember? You left a note on my windshield at six in the morning. You told me to take care of the horses. You said you planned to stay in the Spring—"

"And *you* were so drunk you passed out behind the

wheel of your car. It's a wonder you can remember anything at all."

"I hate to contradict a *lady*, Kit, but I still have the note. It's in the glove compartment of my car."

"Okay, okay, when you're right, you're right. Rosa and I went to the movies on Saturday. I thought it was Friday, but it was Saturday. My mistake. When I make a mistake I own up to it, unlike some people I know. Isn't that true, Dad?"

"It's always good to own up to one's mistakes, Kit. Unless, of course, one's mistakes are in the past, not the present, and owning up to them causes nothing but pain and suffering."

Ellie felt her brow scrunch. Was that Gideon-speak, or did it have some underlying implication? Before she could respond, Dom turned to her and said, "Jonina sent me on an important mission. She asked me to ask you if you needed a drink, but I can see you're all set." He shook his head. "Are you really drinking beer on the rocks?"

"Nope. It's Diet Coke, at least I think it is." She took a few sips. "Or Diet Pepsi." She took a few more sips, then drained the mug. "Definitely Diet Pepsi. What are *you* drinking, Dom?"

"Diet something. I swear I feel like that guy who drinks whatever his wife drinks so she won't drink alone." He hummed a few bars of the theme music from *The Days of Wine and Roses*.

"That 'guy' was Jack Lemmon," Ellie said. "Are you telling me you're drinking diet soda because Jonina is drinking diet soda?"

"Yup. And I'd better get back to her before I lose her."

Ellie followed his gaze. Jonina, adorable in her new outfit, seemed to glow from within. She was surrounded by three waiters, distinguished by their white slacks and short red jackets. She waved at Ellie, then turned her fox amulet over so the waiters could read the words on the back.

All looked at the amulet, resting against her breasts. All pretended to read the charm.

Martina, who stood a few feet away, was thrusting dollar bills down the front pants pocket of a muscular waiter. Holding his tray above his head, the waiter swiveled, then stuck out his butt so she could feed his back pockets.

Ellie had once tossed pieces of bread to a single seagull. Within seconds, a dozen seagulls swirled above her head.

Within seconds, more waiters flocked to Martina's side.

Kit said, "I'd better order another case of diet soda, for tomorrow. Let me have your glass, Norrie. I'll fill it up again before we run out."

Ellie heard loud laughter. Two waiters were shoving money down Martina's blouse. "I gotta pee, I gotta pee," she cried. "If I don't pee, I'll wet my panties. Oh, dear, I'm not *wearing* panties."

A woman in a sedate business suit said, "That's disgusting."

The woman standing next to her said, "No, that's Marty Blue."

A third woman said, "Oh my God, I love her books. The last two weren't so hot, but I can't wait until the next one comes out."

She was looking at Martina the same way Ellie had looked at Goldie Hawn, Kate Hudson, and Hillary Swank. Awestruck.

"If I can pry a waiter loose from Ms. Brustein," Kit told Ellie, "I'll have him deliver your soda."

"Kit seems to have found her rightful place in your world," Ellie said to Gideon, as she watched the girl walk

toward the flock of waiters. "You might even say manage-
ment is her *métier*."

"Yes," he replied somewhat distractedly, also watching
his daughter. "She blackmailed me into letting her plan
Garrett's memorial, but now I'm glad she did."

"How did she blackmail you?"

"It was a figure of speech."

*You're lying*, Ellie thought. Her gut feeling told her that
Kit's blackmail was the same blackmail Gideon had used on
Heather, but she let it pass, anxious to hear his response re-
garding her theory.

"You said I made two minor mistakes," she reminded
him.

He nodded. "Yes, but let's start from the beginning. You
were right about Paris. I studied art. And cooking," he
added with a grin. "I met Heather there and brought her
home to Colorado. However, we weren't engaged. We had
an 'understanding.' "

"That's *very* minor, Gideon."

"I didn't count it as one of your mistakes. Shall I go on?"

She nodded.

"I did a little better than 'scratch out a living' as a cover
artist. I was very much in demand. I even won an award at a
romance convention. That's where I met my wife."

"She was a romance writer?"

"No. She was a nursing student, in attendance so she
could *meet* romance writers. I asked her to marry me at the
awards banquet. After I accepted my award, I fell to one
knee and proposed."

"That's romantic. Was it love at first sight?"

"Isn't 'love at first sight' a bit of a cliché, my dear?"

"Did you love her?"

"What difference does it make?" he asked, sounding like

361

Peter. "My friends said I was rebounding from Heather, but they were mistaken. I thought it out very carefully."

"Yes, I can see that. You had all of . . . what? Two days?"

"Four. Which was three more than I needed. She was smitten and I liked her hair. I'm partial to red hair, especially when it doesn't come from a bottle. I liked her nursing background, too. Nurses are sensitive, compassionate . . . Let's get back to the subject at hand, shall we? You were right about my father wanting Garrett nearby, and you were right when you said I'd never really given up painting. You were also right about Garrett being blocked, after Heather burned her face. But you were wrong about the fire. I didn't set it. I was nowhere near Aspen when the propane tank exploded. In any case, my career was healthier than Garrett's. My marriage was healthier, too. I was happy with my wife and she was happy raising my child. I wasn't the least bit jealous. And yet, to this day, people believe I set that fire." He took a deep, calming breath. "You were right about Garrett exhibiting my paintings under his name. And he *had* begun to paint again."

"Let's cut to the chase," Ellie said. "What was my second mistake?"

"I didn't kill my brother."

# Forty-Eight

"But you must have killed him," Ellie heard herself saying. "Every puzzle piece fits."

"Yes, it does," he said, "except for my iron-clad alibi."

"What iron-clad alibi?"

"At four-forty I was on the phone, talking to Adrianna. She was giving me her flight information so I could pick her up at the airport. The call came from my house, not my cell. From five-fifteen to six-thirty, a couple of burly plumbers pumped water out of my basement, which was flooded from the rainstorm."

"Did you really have mice?"

"Yes. I may have exaggerated a bit, and in case you're wondering, I didn't kill one mouse. I've never killed anything in my life. I gave them all pre-paid airline tickets to Orlando."

She wanted to smile but couldn't. "You really loved your brother, didn't you?"

"Of course I did. Why do you think I allowed him to exhibit *my* work under *his* name? That way, he could keep his pride intact."

*And earn a fortune for you and Kit,* she thought, but bit her lip. Let Gideon keep *his* pride intact.

He glanced around the room, where people were milling about in front of *his* paintings. "Once the New York exhibit opens and the reviews come in," he said, "I'll come out of

Denise Dietz

the closet, so to speak. But rest assured that I'll fly Heather's body back long before that."

A thought occurred. "It was you," Ellie said. "You were the one who helped plan Garrett's Colorado Springs gallery show. You were the one who worked with Melody."

Gideon nodded. "I 'borrowed' Heather's e-mail address. And I used the family fax machine. And now, my dear, I must circulate. Thank you for your hypothesis. It made for a delightful respite."

*No Marxist toot-toot this time,* thought Ellie. How could she have been so wrong? And if Gideon didn't kill Garrett, who did?

364

# Forty-Nine

As Ellie watched Gideon "circulate," she ran her tongue across her dry lips. She felt the same way she used to feel when she chugged White Russians. She'd need a second Russian to quench her thirst from the first Russian. By the third drink, her senses would be blunted, her head awhirl, her stomach rebellious, and where the heck was the waiter with her Diet Pepsi?

There was no bar, not even a cash bar, which meant the champagne and soft drinks were most likely in the framing room, where the flock of waiters were collecting their trays of catered food.

She glanced around, hoping to spot a server, and saw Dom talking to a woman with red hair. At least it had started out red, before a beautician—or the woman herself—had added grape-purple, tangerine, and something that looked like the rotting spots on an apricot.

Dom had a strange expression on his face. He caught Ellie's gaze, and she could almost swear he was begging her to rescue him. She scurried to his side.

"Norrie," he said, "I'd like you to meet Shirona Dombroski, my, uh, sister."

"Bronson," the woman said, extending a hand with the longest fingernails Ellie had ever seen, longer even than Barbra Streisand in *Funny Lady*. "My last name's Bronson now, but I forgot to tell Wayne."

Shirona Bronson looked as if she'd clothed herself for the opera. Or the Academy Awards. Her low-cut crimson gown fanned out at her heels and swept the floor. Her fruit-tinted hair was piled on top of her head, fenced in by a tiara. Knotted around her throat like a hangman's noose was a rope of pearls that dangled to her waist. Suspended from her lobes were long, multi-colored, beaded earrings.

"Guess I dressed wrong, huh?" She laughed nervously. "Guess I should have toned it down some. But as soon as I walked inside this artsy-fartsy place, I said to myself, 'Shirona, you ain't got nothing to be ashamed of, and if others don't like it they can lump it.' "

"That's what I always say," Ellie told the woman. "Except my name's not Shirona. Dom, could you help me find a waiter?"

"Sure," he said with obvious relief. "I'll be right back, Shirona."

"No hurry, Wayne. I've got to tinkle." She turned to Ellie. "Do you know where the little girls' room is, hon?"

Ellie pointed toward the hallway, then grabbed Dom's arm and led him over to the lion-bathtub painting. "I hate being called hon," she said, "and who the heck is Wayne?"

"My brother, who died fifteen years ago."

"I didn't know you had a brother. Shirona must be your half-sister. Duke's too young—"

"I don't have a sister, or a half-sister. Shirona's my mother. Duke thought it was time I 'met' her, so he sent her an invitation . . ." Dom paused, breathing hard. "She and Duke are divorced, she lives in Denver, and she wants me to come live with her. But if I do, I have to tell people I'm her brother because she's too young to have a grown-up son." He made a face. "God, Norrie, I'm only twenty-two!"

"She's afraid of growing old, Dom. I'm over forty, my

brother's pushing forty, and my mom thinks she's fifty. What's wrong with *that* picture? Is your mother's name really Shirona?"

"No. Shirley."

"Are you going to move in with her?"

"No way! She keeps calling me Wayne and I've barely gotten used to Dom. I think I'll help Duke with the ranch. And write books. Martina says if I finish a book and it's any good, she'll find me a publisher. Jonina says she'll edit me, chapter by chapter. We plan to e-mail each other . . ."

He paused to blush, and Ellie thought he looked adorable. "What kind of books do you want to write? Romances?"

"No. Mysteries." He shaded his eyes with his hand, as if he was facing the sun. "My dad's over by the door, Norrie. I need to thank him for Shirona, maybe even mend a couple of fences. Do you still need me to help you find a waiter?"

She shook her head. "Go talk to your father. I'll be fine."

Maybe it was time for her to mend a fence, too, she thought. Rosa stood alone, near the window seat. She balanced a plate of hors d'oeuvres on the palm of one hand and she looked as if she was about to burst into tears. Walking over to the unhappy cook, Ellie said, "Are you okay?"

"I don't know what these are," she wailed.

"Mushroom wontons," Ellie replied. "But I'll bet they're not half as good as your made-from-scratch biscuits." When Rosa didn't respond, Ellie tried again. "I hear you like Alfred Hitchcock movies. Me, too. I've even got a friend who named her dog Hitchcock."

"We went to the movies on Friday," Rosa said, "Kit and me. We saw the second show. It was an Alfred Hitch—"

"I thought you went to the movies on Saturday."

"We went to the movies on Friday, Kit and me," Rosa repeated, shifting her plate to the window seat. "We saw the second show. It was an Alfred Hitchcock ret-tro-speck-tive . . ." She paused, as if to make sure she had pronounced "retrospective" right. "After the movies we had a little snack—"

"What kind of snack?"

"Stop interrupting! The cops didn't interrupt." Breathing hard, talking faster, she said, "We went to the movies on Friday, Kit and me. We saw the second show. It was an Alfred Hitchcock ret-tro-spect-tive. After the movies we had a little snack . . ." She glared at Ellie. "Then we went home. I have the ticket stubs, if you want to see them. Two tickets. Kit and me."

"What movie did you see?"

"Alfred Hitchcock."

"Yes, I know," said Ellie. "But didn't Kit tell you what movie you saw?"

"I forget."

"I think Kit said it was *Rear Window*. Or maybe *Vertigo*."

"Yes."

"Which one?"

"The last one."

"*Vertigo*?"

"Yes, ma'am."

"That's one of my favorites," Ellie said. "I think Grace Kelly should have won an Oscar, don't you?"

Rosa nodded. "We went to the movies on Friday, Kit and—"

"Cary Grant was even better. In *Vertigo*, I mean. He was so cool, especially when Judy fell."

"Judy?"

"That's the name of the girl Grace Kelly played." Ellie made a diving motion with her hand. "When she fell off the balcony, Cary Grant said, 'Judy, Judy, Judy.' He kept saying it until she hit the ground. Don't you remember? It was the funniest part. I laughed so hard, I had a stomach ache."

"Me, too," Rosa said eagerly. "I had a stomach ache, too. Lelia has a poster of Cary Grant. I wish she'd come back. I don't want to stay here no more, but I don't think I should leave without her."

"Rosa, you didn't go to the movies with Kit."

"Yes I did, and I got the ticket stubs to prove it. Two tickets. Kit and me."

"I've seen *Vertigo* a dozen times, maybe more. It stars Kim Novak, not Grace Kelly, and James Stewart, not Cary Grant. The girl in the movie falls from a tower, not a balcony, and James Stewart feels dizzy . . ."

Suddenly, Ellie felt as dizzy as James Stewart, so she leaned her hand against the wall to steady herself. "You drove to the movies," she continued, hearing her voice slur. "You bought two tickets, then drove home." Again, her voice slurred, and she began to feel like the Leaning Tower of Pizza . . . Pisa.

"Kit told you to rip the tickets in half," Ellie slurred, "so it would look like you'd been to the movies. Right? Of course, right. Oh, God, why're you cryin'?"

"What's going on here?" Kit put her arm around Rosa.

"She knows," Rosa said with a sniffle.

"She knows nothing," said Kit. "She's drunk."

"Am not," Ellie said indignantly.

"Oh yes you are. Look at you. You can hardly stand up."

"I can't look at me. No mirror. Kessler's painting had mirror init. Why talking funny, me?"

"Because you're *drunk*, Norrie. Don't you remember? I gave you a rum and Coke. Why are you shaking your head?

The rum and Coke was in a *huge* beer mug."

"Die' Pepsi."

"Okay, so it was rum and Diet Pepsi. Then I sent the waiter with a second rum, and now you're falling-down drunk. Honestly, Rosa, it's disgusting the way some people can't hold their liquor."

"She knows you didn't go to the movies," Rosa said.

"Hell, I figured she caught that. Who'd of thought Marion would keep a stupid note?"

"Dom, his name's Dom," Ellie said, wagging her finger.

"The funny thing is, I didn't even need an alibi. No one saw me at Kessler's house and the cops sounded bored. I could have said I was on the moon and the cops would have said 'Did the man in the moon see you?' and I would have said, 'No, but the cow did,' and they would have said, 'Okay, thanks.' "

"Cow jumped *over* the moon," Ellie said.

"Jeeze, Norrie. You'd better sit down before you fall down. Tell you what. I'll take you back to the ranch so you can sleep it off."

"No."

"Don't be silly. I don't mind a bit. I'll drive you home. Then I'll drive back here."

"I'll come with you," Rosa said eagerly.

Kit shook her head. "I need you to wait for Pete so you can tell him Norrie wasn't feeling good. Tell him I drove her home but I'll be right back and he should wait here because it's *very* important I speak to him. If anyone else asks about Norrie, say 'Norrie was drunk. Kit took her outside to puke. Then Kit drove her to the ranch so she could sleep it off.' Can you remember that?"

"I can," Ellie said. "Norrie was drunk. Kit took her outside to . . . wait a sec. Don't hafta' puke."

"Sure you do. We'll go out the side door, into the alley, so no one'll see you."

"Alley has trash can," Ellie said. "Saw Heather painting."

"Yes, that was stupid. I was tired of looking at it, and it made me mad, so I chucked it."

"Why are you telling her that?" Rosa frowned. "Are you going to kill her?"

"No, of course not. I'm going to put her to bed. She's so drunk she won't remember a thing when she wakes up."

Ellie took a couple of steps forward and nearly fell on her face. She felt nauseated, but she didn't have to puke. She felt scatterbrained, giddy, but, at the same time, sleepy. She wasn't drunk, but she felt drunk. So maybe if she walked outside, the cold air would sober her up. Or at least help her stay awake.

"Take one arm, Mama," Kit said to Rosa.

*Oh, that's mean, calling her Mama,* Ellie thought. But she didn't protest when Rosa and Kit led her outside. She needed cold air. She wanted cold air . . .

She wanted Peter.

"Peter," she said, almost falling to her knees.

Kit encircled Ellie's waist and half carried her to the parking lot. "Don't worry, Norrie. Rosa will tell Pete I drove you home. There's my Mustang. Only a few more feet to go. God, you're heavy. You really should lose twenty or thirty pounds. Help Norrie into the car, Rosa, but be careful. She weighs a ton."

*Do not,* Ellie thought, as Rosa propped her against the side of the car.

Ellie pressed her hands against the car to maintain her balance.

Rosa reached for the front door handle.

Ellie stared through the car's back window. Although her legs felt watery and her vision was a tad blurry, she saw letters from the Lonesome Pines sign. Some were on the floor and some were spread out across the rear seat. The rear seat letters spelled out: SOON ME dIE.

# Fifty

The trick, Ellie thought, was to say something in your head before you said it out loud. Kind of like thinking in a foreign language, then translating the words into English before you opened your mouth.

"What did you put in my Diet Coke?" she asked, but the effort was so wearisome, she let her head fall back against the car's headrest.

"Noctec," Kit replied.

"Why tell Rosa rum?" Ellie gave up the struggle to translate. If she sounded weird, too bad.

"Because I wanted her to think you were smashed," Kit said. "As you may have noticed, Rosa's a blabbermouth. If anyone asks her about you, she'll tell them you were drunk. She'll say I drove you back to the ranch. And, hopefully, she'll remember to tell Pete to wait for me."

"Not drunk."

"I know you're not. You're drugged. But if it makes you feel better, the drug will wear off . . . in time. I just need you sedated for a little while."

"Owtotsy."

"What?"

"Owtotsy. Cut open. Find drug."

"Do you mean an autopsy?"

"Uh-huh."

"If I planned to kill you, Norrie, I'd simply wipe the

bottle clean, then press it against your hand and leave it in your bathroom."

"You don't plan to kill me?"

"Of course not. I'm no killer. I've never killed anything in my whole life."

"Kessler," Ellie slurred.

"That was an accident. I'll admit I lost my temper when he wouldn't sell me the painting of my mother, but you could almost say he killed himself."

"Ser'fina."

"Who?"

"Olive Oyl lady."

"The skinny lady who bought the Santa painting? I didn't know she died. When was she killed?"

"Early. Sunday. Morning."

"Then it couldn't have been me. I was at the ranch, giving you a riding lesson."

"Dom gave lesson, you killed Garrett," Ellie slurred.

"No, I didn't. Why on earth would I kill Garrett?"

"Who did?"

"Can you keep a secret?"

"Uh-huh. Cross heart an' hope to die."

Kit laughed.

Ellie said, "Funny?"

Kit said, "Very, especially the hope to die part."

"Promised not tell," Ellie slurred, "so who killed Garrett?"

"Rosa," Kit said. "She was cutting a piece of meat or a chicken or something in the kitchen, and she had her knife with her when she took a break outside. She saw Beth and me with the wheelbarrow. And, of course, Garrett's body *in* the wheelbarrow. She followed us to the ravine and watched Beth and me mess around with him. That was Beth's idea.

She wanted to get a rise out of him." Kit laughed. "A rise. Get it?" She sighed. "Rosa thought we were trying to kill him. When we left and the drug began to wear off, Garrett tried to crawl away from the tree, so she stabbed him with her kitchen knife."

"Why?"

"Because she thought I wanted him dead. She'd do anything for me. She thinks I'm her kid."

"Thanks, Kit. Never woulda' figged Rosa."

"I never would have *figged* her either, if she hadn't told me. I'm going to have to do something about Rosa. She talks too much."

"Kill 'er?"

"Why would I kill her? She's dumb as a stick, but she's been more a mother to me than my own mother. I'll buy her a house somewhere, far away from Aspen. Jeeze, Norrie. How many times do I have to tell you? I'm *not* a killer.

"Anyway," Kit continued, "you're very welcome. And please let me know if there's anything else I can do for you." This time she laughed like a loon. Then she said, "You know what? It's a long drive to the ranch and I always follow the speed limit—I never break the law—so it's great to have someone to talk to. Hey, are you sleeping?"

*No. Resting my eyes,* Ellie thought. *That's what Peter always says when he falls asleep in front of the TV. I'm just resting my eyes . . .*

# Fifty-One

The car stopped rocking, and Ellie opened her eyes. Her first thought was how she used to drive around when she wanted Mick to sleep. He was a bad napper. So she'd drive, going nowhere, until naptime was over. Then she'd stop and he'd wake up. She couldn't do that today. Gas cost too much.

Her second thought was that *Rosa* killed Garrett, and she'd had to tell Peter ASAP.

She realized her head had cleared somewhat when she saw that Kit had parked near the barn, in a space reserved for the riding instructor. Even without reading glasses, Ellie could make out the letters on the small wooden sign: RESERVED FOR KIT HALLIDAY.

It occurred to Ellie that she should pretend to be woozier than she actually felt. She didn't think she could free herself from Kit. After all, she'd been inactive for a week. And Kit, who pitched hay and shoveled manure, looked strong as an ox. But maybe, if the perfect opportunity came along . . .

"Why Beth drunk Garrett?" she asked Kit.

"Garrett was already drunk on vodka. She *drugged* him. If you only knew how funny you sound. Miss hoity-toity from the big city, and she can't string two sentences together, can't even string one sentence together. I wish Pete could see you now."

*Me, too,* thought Ellie. Aloud, she said, "What . . . what Garrett ever do to Beth?"

"I think it had something to do with Mike Urvant, the guy who owns this place. He told Beth to piss off, which pissed her off so bad she hired someone to what'cha'macallit his next rodeo gig."

Ellie almost said *sabotage,* but remembered in time. "Beth bad," she said.

"Not really. You just don't want to rub her the wrong way, like Mike and Garrett did. And now, *my dear,* it's time to visit the barn."

"Why?"

"You're going to say goodbye to the horses."

"Goodbye?"

"Did I say goodbye? I meant goodnight. Then I'll take you to your cottage and you can sleep off the Noctec."

"Don't like horses," Ellie fibbed.

"I know you don't. Tell you what. You can watch *me* say goodnight."

"Cottage now," Ellie said.

"Barn now. I've got to return to the gallery sweet toot."

*Toot sweet,* Ellie amended, as she wondered what the girl had in mind.

*Oh, God, what if she ties me to a horse, leads the horse to the top of an incline, and—no! She'd never do that. She couldn't be that stupid. When the cops found me roped to the saddle, they'd know my death was deliberate. First degree murder.*

She swallowed a hiccup. "Why kill me?" she asked Kit.

"For the umpteenth time, I'm not going to kill you. But if I was, it would be because of Kessler's accident. And because you heard what I said before."

"About Rosa?"

"No."

Ellie felt as if she'd been hit over the head with a mallet. "Oh my God! Before, in the car, you said you lost your temper when Kessler wouldn't sell you the painting of your *mother*."

"Very good, Norrie. I think the Noctec is starting to wear off."

"Heather was your mother?"

"Yup. When she left Paris and came to Colorado with my father, she was knocked up. No big deal, except she fell in love with Garrett. Dad wanted the baby. Heather didn't. So they concocted a game plan. Heather would have the baby, but pretend . . . I really don't have time for this."

The secret sin, thought Ellie. The hush-hush, blackmail secret that Gideon had used on Heather and Kit had used on Gideon.

Obviously, Garrett hadn't known about the baby, but how was that possible? How could Heather hide a full-term pregnancy from her husband?

What had Lelia said?

One, Heather had left Colorado Springs to live with Gideon and his wife in Aspen. Two, Garrett, feuding with his father, wouldn't set foot in Aspen. Three, Gideon's wife had "taken to her bed" the last few months. And four, she had trained as a nurse. So *she* had delivered the baby, not the other way around. That's why the baby had been born at home. No wonder Heather had looked "traumatized."

Gideon had lucked out, finding his compliant, nurse-in-training wife at the romance convention. Even better, she was a redhead. John Halliday had surely paid the midwife a sum equal to Lelia's hush money, and everybody lived happily ever—

"With you out of the picture," Kit said cheerfully, "I'll get Pete."

"You don't 'get' someone, Kit. Peter loves me. He might admire your skill with horses, but—"

"Love! Heather loved Garrett so much she couldn't love anybody else, not even her own child. I guess she thought she might die during the operation, or maybe during the flight to Paris, because she told me she was my birth mother just before she took off for the airport. 'You're *my* child, Catherine,' she said. She always called me Catherine, for St. Catherine. 'I thought you should know,' she said."

*Aha,* thought Ellie, *the missing puzzle piece. The reason why Kit slashed the paintings.*

Gideon was wrong, dead wrong. Kit hadn't been devastated because Heather had been a surrogate mother to her. Kit had been devastated because Heather *was* her mother. Moreover, Heather's "Forgive me, daughter, for I have sinned" had been nothing more than a makeshift, self-serving affirmation.

In other words, Heather wanted to end her guilt trip before she left on a new, possibly fatal, jaunt.

Despite her present predicament, Ellie's heart ached for Kit. "Maybe when Heather gave you up, it was the hardest thing she ever had to do. Maybe she was concerned about your welfare. She and Garrett lived like Gypsies. They never had enough to eat and—"

"Bull! Heather was thinking of Heather." Kit took a deep breath. "Get inside the barn."

"No."

"If you don't walk, I'll drag you by your hair. That way, I won't leave bruises."

"I thought you said you weren't going to kill me."

"I'm not, and that's a promise. Now move!"

# Fifty-Two

When she tried to run, Ellie realized that her mind might be lucid but her body was still drugged.

Kit was on top of her in a nanosecond—maybe even sooner. Dragging Ellie by the hair, she entered the barn and barred the door.

Ellie cussed all the way, using words Peter—and especially Tony—had never, *ever* heard her use. Had she been auditioning for an audio porn flick, she would have scored the starring role.

"Stand up!" Kit said in a voice that didn't encourage rebellion.

Ellie complied. Now what? Kit had sounded sincere about not killing her, so what was the game plan? Cut out her tongue, and at the same time, slice off her hands so she couldn't write or play charades? Wound her so badly she'd fall into a deep coma?

Snapping her fingers like her father, Kit said, "Stay right there and don't move, while I say goodnight to the horses."

She walked slowly down the row, stopping every once in a while to pet a velvety nose, stroke a forehead, weave her fingers through a tousled forelock. She talked to the horses, calling them by name and murmuring endearments. Ellie watched, mesmerized.

Kit reached Buttermilk's stall. "Did the mean ol' lady wave a leafy branch in your face?" she crooned. "Don't worry, baby. Soon the mean ol' lady won't wave anything at all."

*Time to skedaddle,* thought Ellie. *Happy trails to you, and all that jazz.*

But she didn't move. For one thing, she was curious to see what Kit was up to. For another, she was fairly certain the girl would catch her before she'd taken three steps outside the barn, and, to tell the God's honest truth, she didn't relish any more excruciating pain. Her butt hurt and her hair hurt and—

Kit edged up to Satan's stall.

All at once, Ellie knew, with perfect clarity, what the girl planned to do. "Kit," she said, "stop this nonsense right now. Help me to my cottage and drive back to the gallery. Your game plan is much too dangerous."

"Of course it is," Kit said, opening the gate to Satan's stall.

The black stallion stepped out from the stall. His lips were drawn back over his teeth. His ears lay flat against his head. His eyes looked wild as he spied Ellie, and his hooves barely skimmed the ground as he sped toward her.

Protected by the gate, Kit laughed.

Ellie prayed she wouldn't get the hiccups. Mouth dry, she also prayed she had enough spit.

"A horse is a horse, of course, of course," she crooned, "and no one can talk to a horse, of course. That is, of course, unless the horse, is the famous Mr. Satan."

Satan skidded to a halt. His ears flickered. With a whinny, he nudged the bodice of her turtleneck. The cotton material dampened, and Ellie could feel a breathy warmth encompass her breasts as Satan snuffled through his nostrils, searching for his apple.

"What's the matter with you, you stupid horse?" Furious, Kit came out from behind the gate. At the same time, she pulled her red-sequined top up over her head. Then, using it as a whip, she began to lash the stallion on his haunches.

"Kit, no! Satan, listen! Ride a cock horse to Bam—"

"Shut up!" Kit shrieked. "Why don't you just shut up?" She hit Satan again. And again.

The stallion was facing Ellie. Technically, he should have attacked her. Then, when Peter and the others returned, they'd find her broken body. A tearful Kit would say she'd dropped Norrie off at the cottage, and, in a drunken haze, Norrie must have wandered toward the barn. The perfect game plan. Whether or not Kit "consoled" Peter, she'd be scot-free.

Except, she couldn't possibly know that Ellie was the best kitchen raider in the universe. Rosa had never even discovered the missing carrots and app—

Satan turned, reared up, and flailed with his hooves. His front legs thrashed in a mesmerizing rhythm of continuity. Kit's shrieks of terror echoed throughout the barn. Ellie thought she heard a cat's frightened meow. It came from the loft. Stanley Hastings. Instinctively, Ellie covered her eyes with her forearm. Then, slowly, she lowered her arm.

Kit lay in a puddle of blood. Her hair was matted and straw stuck to her wounds. She looked like a crimson-painted scarecrow.

An agitated Satan danced in place. Crooning "a horse is a horse," Ellie backed him up into his stall and latched the gate. Then she dropped to her knees, next to Kit's broken body.

Extending her hand, Ellie placed two fingers on Kit's neck pulse.

She thought she felt a pulse beat, very weak, but she could be wrong.

Now what? Staying here in the barn was out of the question.

She could wait inside her cottage until someone, preferably Peter, returned to the ranch. Or . . .

Hadn't a groom leapt upon Black Beauty's back, then ridden for the doctor when his mistress . . . or was it his master? . . . became hurt . . . or was it ill?

*God, I sound like my mother,* Ellie thought.

Nevertheless, Black Beauty had galloped through a storm, or a storm's aftermath, and brought the doctor back in time. So all Ellie had to do was climb aboard one of the horses and gallop to the gallery.

Yes, that sounded like the best scheme.

*Scratch me underneath my chin and I'll follow you anywhere,* thought Ellie, as she led Buttermilk out of the barn and over to the mounting block. She clambered on top of the block, then swung her leg up over the bare back of the white horse. At the same time, she tried to draw an Aspen city map in her head. She had mentally reached the Halliday hill, supposedly five minutes from the Phoenix Gallery, when two more thoughts occurred.

*The ranch has a phone.*

*All I have to do is call the gallery. And 9-1-1.*

Kicking Buttermilk's belly, Ellie rode to the main house.

As her feet touched solid ground again and she realized what she'd done, she said, "Holy cow!"

383

# Fifty-Three

Ellie lay on her favorite chaise. Once again, Dom's Stetson shaded her face. Despite an incredible hangover, subdued by three cups of strong black coffee, she was reading Martina's manuscript.

Every once in a while she'd stop reading to laugh out loud. Martina's hero, Garth, was so Gideon. Except, of course, Garth wasn't balding on top.

Garth wore a French beret when he wasn't wearing a hat with a cocky feather. Garth had Gideon's wit and Gideon's British accent, and lord have mercy but he was good in the sack.

*Mom will cream her panty girdle,* Ellie thought irreverently.

Inside the cottage, Peter was making phone calls. He'd already contacted Melody and arranged for her to cover Ellie's Monday morning Weight Winners meeting. He had insisted Ellie stay at the ranch two more days, in order to "rest up." They'd leave Monday, at the crack of dawn, then drive home very leisurely, maybe even stop along the way to "unsnap shirts."

Ellie appreciated Peter's concern, but she was dying to get back to the Springs. Although Rudolph Kessler's murder had been solved, Serafina Lassiter's hadn't, and Ellie felt her heart race. She relished the rush that came from sleuthing. She knew she was addicted. She also knew

that if Peter wanted to marry her, he'd have to deal with her
. . . obsession. Because never again would she play the
"little woman" or The Wife. Never again would she Maytag
skivvies and defrost chops while her mate trotted off to
work. Her husband might bring home the bacon, but she
had no intention of pigging out on calories and apathy.

She saw "her" magpies circle the main house, where
Duke and Dom sat on the front porch. Even from a distance, Ellie could hear Dom whistling "My Shirona" as he
and his father composed a help wanted ad. The ranch
would open for business next week and they needed a new
cook. They also needed a new housekeeper. Lelia had decided she'd just as soon clean houses in Colorado Springs,
especially since Rosa didn't seem to care one iota that she
was charged with Garrett's murder. Instead, she wailed
non-stop about Kit—her "precious baby."

Lelia wouldn't be cleaning houses for long, Ellie
thought, not after she introduced the young sculptress to
Melody. Lelia's angel sculpture was to die for, and there
was no reason why Melody's gallery couldn't display a few
of the exquisite pieces.

Peter's birthday was coming up and he liked the angel
headboard as much as Ellie did, so she would be Lelia's
first custom-furniture customer.

Jonina and Martina stood outside the dining hall. They
were churning ice cream by hand, having decided they
wanted to serve a homemade vanilla-chocolate swirl at tomorrow's barbeque. Ellie heard bursts of loud laughter and
giggles that sounded like wind chimes. They were making
much too much noise, so Ellie would just have to tell them
to . . . let her join in the fun.

She placed Martina's manuscript atop a small table, next
to her empty coffee cup, but before she could move, Peter

walked over to the chaise. Ellie bent her legs at the knees so he could sit.

"How's my girl?" he asked.

"It isn't fair, Peter. I'm fighting a horrendous hangover and I never even sampled one glass of Gideon's imported champagne. Not only that, but Kit drugged me with a *child's* sedative."

"Good thing Kit didn't put the Noctec in an alcoholic beverage, Norrie. Then it would act like one of those old Mickey Finns. Tell you what. *I'll* buy you a bottle of champagne, the best I can afford."

"That means it'll probably taste like mouthwash."

"I was thinking we'd have one glass each tonight," he said, ignoring her mouthwash comment, "and save the rest for your return trip across Independence Pass."

She studied his face. "What's up, Lieutenant? You look . . . smug isn't the word I want, but it's close. They found Serafina Lassiter's killer, right?" She waited. "Peter?"

"I was waiting for you to answer your own question."

"You might think that's funny, but I don't. Try it one more time and I'll strangle you."

"Yes, they found Serafina's killer. McCoy tracked down dozens—he says hundreds—of Lassiter partygoers. Finally, someone remembered seeing a woman in a gray hooded sweatshirt pick up a piece of sculpture, a hideous glass object that looked like a unicorn. Or an ogre. The reason the guy remembered was because Owen Lassiter screamed at Ms. Hooded Sweatshirt to put it down. Apparently, it cost more than you and I *and* your brother Tab can earn in a year."

"Tab doesn't earn a cent."

"Okay, my brother-in-law."

"Peter, please cut to the chase."

"McCoy lifted prints from the unicorn-ogre. Since the Colorado Springs license bureau requires fingerprints when you apply for a driver's license, and since our perp drives a car, she was fairly easy to find."

"She?"

"Yup."

"Okay, we know it wasn't Kit, and it couldn't have been Rosa, so who was it?"

"Kit's roommate, a woman with the idiotic name of—"

"Moony! My God, why would *she* kill Serafina?"

"Because Kit wanted the painting. Moony saw the bit about Yogi Demon on the local newscast. You do know that Kit attended Garrett's exhibit, right? Kit kept Owen Lassiter's business card, probably because she wanted to buy *Christmas Carol* some day. The card *did* have Lassiter's address on it, so Moony went to the party. She fled when the TV reporter almost captured her on camera, but came back later to steal the painting. And that, sweetheart, is all you need to know. Let's go inside and unsnap."

"I'm wearing a T-shirt, Peter, and you don't get away that easily."

"I didn't think I would." He grinned his Clark Gable grin. "Here it is in a nutshell. McCoy secured a search warrant for Moony's loft. Inside, he found a room full of G.H. paintings. McCoy says he's never seen anything like it in his life. The women all looked like they were being tortured. The only painting that wasn't mutilated was the Lassiter painting. McCoy said Kit hadn't gotten to it yet, but I doubt she even knew Moony stole it."

"*Why* did Moony steal it?"

"Because she's in love with Kit. When she heard about last night, she said life wasn't worth living and confessed. She's now under a twenty-four hour suicide watch."

"I guess Kit was Moony's Heather," Ellie said with a sigh.

Peter quirked an eyebrow.

"Lelia said Garrett couldn't refuse Heather anything," Ellie explained. "Lelia said Garrett was *her* Heather. So I suppose Kit was Moony's Heather."

"Am I *your* Heather?"

Peter's voice teased, but Ellie heard an underlying edge of weightiness. Since she wasn't sure how to respond, she said, "Have you heard any new news about Kit?"

"Yes. I spoke to Gideon. Kit's hanging in there by a thread, but her skull was crushed and the doctors aren't very optimistic. Gideon says if she dies, he'll wait for a windy day, climb to the top of a cliff, and fling her ashes with Heather's ashes, all mixed together."

"That's poetic justice, I suppose," Ellie said thoughtfully. "Kit slashed the Heather paintings because she felt betrayed. She left her dad's canvasses alone because he used *her* as his model, not Heather. So maybe, in death, Kit and her mother can mend a few fences."

"Dom wants to teach me how to *rope* a fence," Peter said.

"Oh, I can teach you that." Ellie smiled. "Let's saddle up a couple of horses and find a deserted pasture. I'll teach you how to rope a fence and, afterwards, we'll unsnap."

# About the Author

Denise Dietz is the best-selling author of several novels, including *Eye of Newt*, a Five Star Publishing Mystery that stars a witch sleuth. She lives on Vancouver Island with her husband, novelist Gordon Aalborg, and her mostly Norwegian Elkhound, Pandora. *Chain a Lamb Chop to the Bed* is the third book in her Ellie Bernstein/Lt. Peter Miller "diet club" series. Two of the book's cats—Becky and Stanley Hastings—were pet-character donations, won by the highest bidders at charity auctions. Denise likes to hear from readers. You can e-mail her from her web site: www.denisedietz.com